I0523569

THE FIRE RUNE

THE RONAN RYAN ODYSSEY - BOOK TWO

MARK KLEINSCHMIDT

Astrebla Publishing

Text copyright © Mark Kleinschmidt 2023

The moral right of Mark Kleinschmidt to be identified as the author of this work has been asserted.

ISBN:
978-0-6454623-2-6 (paperback)
978-0-6454623-3-3 (ebook)

All rights reserved.

This book is sold subject to the condition that it shall not, by way of trade or otherwise, be lent, hired out or otherwise circulated in any form of binding or cover other than that in which it is published. No part of this publication may be reproduced, stored in a retrieval system, or transmitted in any form or by any means (electronic, mechanical, photocopying, recording or otherwise), without the prior permission of both the copyright owner and the publisher, except in the case of very brief quotations embodied in critical reviews and certain other non-commercial uses permitted by copyright law.

This is a work of fiction. Names, characters, events and dialogues are products of the author's imagination. Broad geographical settings, as well as town names are real; specific settings and place names are fictitious.

Published in 2023 by Astrebla Publishing.

To Hayden and Aaron, wellsprings of love, pride and inspiration ... forever in my heart.

And in memory of Leigh Antonia Kleinschmidt (nee Hoolihan), lover of all things Irish.

I

————————

SMASHED

It was a fine Monday morning in southwest Donegal. The light was strong, but the autumn sun had not yet kissed the fields. A faded red hatchback, trailing a feather of exhaust, pulled away from a modest cottage.

You could set your watch by Darragh Kelly's workday routine. Regardless of weather, he'd rise at six, cook breakfast for his daughter and make a packed lunch for them both while she fed the horses and cleaned their stalls. By seven sharp, he was behind the wheel of his compact Opel Corsa, trundling down the farm lane on the twenty-two-minute run from Raven's Roost to Killybegs.

It was a drive he'd made five days a week for more years than he cared to remember. Not that he was sick of work, quite the opposite: making boots was a passion. In fact, if asked, he'd struggle to name anything he'd rather be doing. But the Detencin Boot Company would certainly not win County Donegal's employer-of-the-year award.

Even as head bootmaker, Darragh hadn't received a pay rise in almost ten years; over the same period, the rent for their tiny home went up with the regularity of the seasons. So, each year, Darragh and Saoirse had less to live on, while the Egan family got higher up the rich list from the earnings of their boot-making company, and their dozens of houses dotted round the emerald hills.

By quarter past seven he had passed Drimnafinagle, crossed the grand-sounding Glenaddragh River—only a modest rivulet—and was rolling along a wider section of asphalt. Ahead, a plume of exhaust smoke rose from a side road. Another truck, another construction job, he thought. As long as the lumbering beasts made room on the narrow sections, he didn't mind.

The dirt-caked lorry slowed as it approached the stop sign, but it wasn't slowing enough. It would overshoot. "What are you playing at, you bloody eejit!" Darragh bellowed, swerving into the empty oncoming lane. Unable to make out the driver behind the grimy windscreen, he brandished a fist in the general direction as he came abreast.

The tipper leapt forward under fierce acceleration. The enormous steel bumper sledgehammered into the side of the Corsa. It spun, flipped, tumbled, and crunched, steering wheel slamming into Darragh's face. The little vehicle catapulted, steamrolling a wire fence, landing upside down in the ditch with a grinding thump. A shroud of hissing steam and fuel vapour rose past crumpled bodywork and wheels canted at impossible angles.

The truck didn't pause. It roared from sight amid gnashing gears and belching clouds of black diesel smoke.

COLD BLOOD

Four days later, Darragh Kelly's cottage was deathly quiet, musty, holding its breath. Twilight was in its final throes. Nothing moved.

With a resigned sigh, the air split open, and from the gash, a shadowy figure folded outward. It froze, melting into the background. Something was wrong, very wrong. But there was no danger to detect, only emptiness and silence where there shouldn't have been. The figure stirred, striding across the room, skirting a low couch and shin-biting coffee table, reaching out, flicking a familiar switch.

Light punctured the gloom, throwing a strapping sixteen-year-old into sharp relief. "Saoirse?" Ronan Ryan called, blinking against the sudden brightness. His voice echoed through the cramped rooms, bouncing off white walls hung with framed horses and a faded family portrait. The sight of a gap-toothed Saoirse on Darragh's lap, and the wary frown of her toddler brother in Niamh's embrace, caught Ronan's attention. "Mum left with Niall when I was eight," Saoirse had once told him with resignation. "Just walked out without saying a word."

"Saoirse?" he called again, dragging his eyes from the photo, stepping through an adjacent doorway. Saoirse's pastel bedspread was rumpled, drawers sagging open, clothes draping out. Either she'd packed in a hurry, or someone had rifled through her things—he much preferred the first possibility. And try as he might, he couldn't find a trace of her in the stale air.

Anxiety clutched Ronan; only disaster could have stopped Saoirse being there to greet him. They'd both been distraught on parting the previous Sunday when he had to return to Australia. Now he was back, as promised, on Friday evening. But there was no Saoirse, not even a note.

For a moment, he wondered if he had the wrong day. But no, he'd been meticulous in aiming for the fifth of November 2004 while emptying his head of all thoughts but the cottage living room. Still, uncertainty squirmed, and Ronan had no way to quell it—no phone, no one to call.

The rumble of an approaching vehicle penetrated his growing alarm, but it wasn't the contented purr of Darragh's little car. It was the impatient growl of pent-up power, triggering unpleasant memories.

With headlights threatening to blister the building's facade, the vehicle came to a gravel-crunching halt. The engine calmed into a fitful grumble, then died. Ronan shrank from the window. The blazing light was coming from the same gold-coloured Range Rover that smashed into him on his previous visit.

Doors slammed and heels clomped toward the front door. "I tell you, there's someone in there." It was the entitled whine of Fionn Egan. A few weeks beforehand, when Saoirse rejected Egan's command to accompany him to town as arm decoration, the youth tried to regain face by bullying Ronan, and when that didn't work, set two thugs on him. After a second failure, Egan ran Ronan down. He shuddered.

"Are you sure you did not leave the light on?" It was Egan's mother. Ronan had only met Fionella Egan once, but everything about her was unforgettable, from blood-red nails to emotionless, calculating gaze.

"Of course I'm sure, woman," was the haughty response.

"Do not speak to me like that." Her tone was pure menace, devoid of parental warmth.

"I'll speak how I damn-well want."

Ronan could almost see the cold disdain in Egan's grey eyes. And he imagined the woman flashing an icy warning to her son.

But that wasn't Ronan's concern. Saoirse had been desperate for his return, and knew when he was coming. So where was she? And what were Egan and his mother doing at the Kelly's empty cottage? Ronan's fluttering gut told him to leave, but staying close was the best way to discover more.

"Do not forget," the woman hissed, each syllable dripping with threat, "what I am doing for you."

"You mean for yoursel—" An open palm cracked across a flabby cheek. Surly silence was followed by a churlish, "What was that for?"

"To teach manners." Fionella words were brittle with arrogance and restrained rage.

The apple never falls far from the tree, Ronan thought, channelling his Irish grandfather.

"Now, do you have the key?" she hissed.

"Of course," Egan snapped, his earlier insolence returning.

"Well, open the damned door."

So, rather than retreating to safety, Ronan stayed, hoping for information. For an absurd moment, he considered asking the Egans where Saoirse and Darragh were. Instead, under cover of a lock-rattling entry, he slithered beneath Saoirse's bed.

Protesting hinges gave way to Egan's griping: "I tell you, this light wasn't on last night."

"Well, let's see, shall we?" Subtle double snicks punctuated Fionella's response. Chilling fingers of fear wrapped round Ronan's throat: there was no mistaking the sound of a shotgun's hammers being thumbed back to full cock, ready for firing.

Ronan bellied further into the bed's shadows, the stone floor like a sheet of ice. Soles scraped and clicked as two pairs of legs passed the open doorway, heading for the other end of the small building. Ronan's nostrils twitched at disturbed dust.

"Is this another prank?" Uncertainty frayed Egan's words.

Doors and cupboards clicked open and snapped closed. Egan, patience clearly spent, whined, "What's it matter if someone's been here, anyway? It's not like there's anything worth stealing."

"You will learn"—Fionella's tone left no doubt where her son got his sneer—"that when you play for high stakes, you leave nothing to chance. Now, check this last room."

Ronan's nose twitched again. Pinching his nostrils in desperation, he tried swallowing the sneeze, almost succeeding. An involuntary convulsion shook him, only a tiny one, but enough to tap his crown on the underside of the mattress slats.

In panic, Ronan tried to blank his mind, to flytja away, but before he could, booming double explosions shattered the night. Twin barrels sent screaming pellets skipping off the slate floor, filling the space beneath the bed with a swarm of deadly lead hornets. A thousand excruciating stings engulfed him.

3

———

CLEAR CUT

The air beside the Home Stone exhaled Ronan's naked body. He'd learnt to recognise the subtle change in the turbulence when the rune was about to set him down, and could now avoid being spat from the air in an untidy tangle. Even so, he was yet to master his Norse grandmother's practised elegance of stepping from a rent in the air as if moving from one room to another. He peered about. As guardian of the Home Stone, and a woman of magic, Freyja sensed when someone arrived, but Ronan was alone with the ink-black boulder.

He cursed, not because Freyja wasn't there, but because he was desperate to find Saoirse and make sure she was safe. Being naked and shivering in 891 Scandinavia wasn't helping. The waning sun struggled across treetops peppered with russets, reds and yellows to where the Home Stone sat in the middle of the forest clearing, like a gigantic half-buried dinosaur egg in a nest of well-tended pine needles.

There was no doubt the mysterious stone was special, for it was sheltered by a crafted roof supported by nine ornately carved posts. Even though the chill was seeping into his bones, Ronan was drawn to the boulder. As if compelled, he laid a palm on the mirror surface, embracing the connection, revelling in the spreading warmth. "Heim Steinn," Ronan breathed, absently speaking Norse.

Anxiety melted away and his focus gravitated upward to the criss-crossing beams. Chiselled into their underside was the poem of the runes. Ronan knew it by heart, yet his eyes followed the runic symbols as he murmured the Norse words: "The bearer of the living stone, in solitude is ne'er alone; the gods shall let no ill befall its keeper with eternal thrall. Its power burns if blood enfold the lightening rune, and wealth untold awaits the one who stands apart as true of mind and pure of heart."

Of their own accord, his fingers delved through a tangle of hair to a lump at the base of his skull. There, on a shaved patch of scalp, fresh skin edging over it, nestled a tiny flattened miniature of the Home Stone, like a backward-staring ebony eye, his blood rune.

Twice before, he should have died, but both times he'd held the mysterious rune, and both times he'd arrived terrified and confused at another place, in an earlier time. When he'd asked Freyja why he'd arrived naked, she'd chuckled, her features softening. "What you carry goes with you unless it is a thing of the future," she'd said. "The rune will not take anything back to a time where it should not be."

Despite the Home Stone's enveloping calm, Ronan was anxious to return to Saoirse's time. The deserted cottage and booming shotgun filled him with dread. What did they mean for Saoirse? And there was another urgency: as soon as the dose of motion-sickness medication swimming through his bloodstream faded, his return to 2004 would be consumed by the diabolical nausea of rune travel, rendering him helpless for the best part of a day. And he couldn't afford to waste a minute once back there.

The biting air swirled across Ronan's skin, drawing a shudder.

Knowing that Norse clothes would go forward in time with him, Ronan emptied his mind of all but his target, and floated into ró, the weightless entry to flytja. The air split with a gentle inhalation and Ronan's body folded inward through the gash; half a heartbeat later, he stepped from a similar slit in Freyja's nearby longhouse.

"Grandmother?" Ronan called, searching for a glimpse of flowing copper hair. The only answer was his own hollow echo.

The building's neat beams, braces and planks were jointed with craftsman's pride; the fire pit in the centre of the floor, cold. Anaemic light filtered through the smoke-hole in the roof, highlighting dust that Freyja would never allow. She and Sten must be travelling.

The only bedding left was an old bearskin and tattered blanket, perhaps the ones Freyja wrapped him in, mere weeks ago. Still shivering, Ronan drew them tight round his shoulders.

A search of the longhouse storage boxes turned up nothing but rags. The stew pot was missing, as was all the food, Freyja's staff, and Sten's beautiful recurve hunting bow. Yet the house wasn't tidy like he'd expect if it was being locked up for an extended time. It felt abandoned at short notice. Unease stirred in his chest, but he told himself they were okay: Freyja was too experienced and wily; besides, she had her own blood rune.

Saoirse was another matter; she didn't have Freyja's powers or skill; she needed his help. The only reason Saoirse wouldn't have been at the Raven's Roost cottage to greet him, was if something dire had happened. He had to get back.

As he cast a final glance round the longhouse, black scrawl on the door snagged his attention, sending fresh goose-bumps fizzing across his skin. Embedded in the single line of charcoal-scribed runic symbols were two non-Norse numbers: 1804 and 2004. The more he studied them, the more they melded into the handwriting in his father's notebooks. More goose-bumps erupted.

Ronan's breath stilled. His father had plunged two-hundred metres from a cliff before Ronan was born, yet when Ronan was first heimmed to the Home Stone, Freyja told him that Paidin had been there before him—he'd been holding a twin of Ronan's rune when he fell. Ever since, Ronan had been consumed by the possibility of meeting the father he never knew.

The writing on the door told him Paidin had been heimmed a second time. Was the message for Freyja, or …? No, it couldn't be; in Paidin's world, Ronan didn't exist.

Again and again, he read the line of Norse with English numbers: *Flytja Killybegs* 1804 *then Maureen* 2004. His heart ached at the sight of his mother's name written by his father's hand. Paidin must have scrawled the message after the longhouse was abandoned, but why go to 1804 instead of straight back to his own time? Ronan couldn't imagine what must have happened to prevent his father returning directly to his mother.

Ronan's jaw tightened. Once Saoirse was safe, he was going to find Paidin. That settled, he dropped the bearskin, clutched the blanket tighter, pictured Raven's Roost in 2004, and drifted into ró. His head ignited.

4

TORN

Searing torment enveloped Ronan's brain, as if it were on the verge of boiling in his skull. A wave of nausea almost beat him to the toilet where he retched and heaved until spent, and lay exhausted, wedged between pedestal and wall, head pounding.

As the misery eased, Ronan's awareness returned; he began dissecting the problem. Every thought led directly to his rune. Everything about the heim to the Home Stone was normal, except that modern medication had suppressed the nausea. However, the return flytja had been an explosion of white-hot torture. Had it been milder, he might have considered it a less-than-subtle reminder not to cross a particular line; as it was, it felt like an ominous warning. But of what? If rune power came at such a heavy price, the prospect of using it was overwhelming. And there was no Freyja to consult.

Ronan dragged himself to the bathroom, sluicing away the stench of vomit, rinsing its acid aftertaste from his mouth. Apart from midday sun streaming through the windows, the cottage was unchanged. The stale air retained the acrid remnants of the previous evening's shotgun blast, and Saoirse's bedroom, the signs of rapid departure. But worse was her absence itself. There was not the whisper of a clue where she and her father might be.

Wary of the shotgun-toting Egans, Ronan had aimed his return flytja for Saturday, the day after the previous encounter. The stark white scarring on the slate floor beneath Saoirse's bed verified he'd dreamt none of it, as did the ricochet-pocked and splintered underside of the mattress slats. No wonder the rune whipped him away.

His pellet-shredded clothes had been blasted from under the bed; they lay in a tangle with his unscathed boots in the corner, clearly overlooked by the Egans. Fionella must have figured she'd fired at an imagined sound. Ronan's lips hardened into a grim line.

The cottage chill led him to Darragh's room where he found clothes that were too short at the extremities and too wide in between, yet far more comfortable than the coarse blanket. He added a leather belt and a thick, brown cardigan that hung below his waist and extended to his wrists, hiding the shortcomings of the shirt, if not the pants.

On the bedside table was a framed photo of a youthful Darragh, arm round a graceful coffee-skinned woman with Saoirse's smile—the deserted husband had never forgotten her. A bowl beside the photograph held a collection of euros and assorted detritus from emptied pockets. Telling himself that he'd repay it all, Ronan ignored his conscience and sifted the one- and two-euro coins from Darragh's stash; there was a search to fund.

Spreading the meagre borrowings among his pockets, Ronan returned to Saoirse's room, hoping to see something he may have missed earlier. Wisps of the girl he ached for were everywhere, from riding pants over the chair and sneakers beneath, to the hairbrush and huddle of soft toys on the dresser. They all stirred his longing to be with her, touching her hand, feeling her breath on his skin, drawing it into his lungs.

As he trailed fingers along the row of textbooks on the desk, Ronan pondered his own schooling. Its remnants lay scattered in the wake of his more recent education in the workings of Norse rune magic. He might never return to school; he wasn't even sure he wanted to.

Before he could contemplate further, he noticed a stuffed satchel on the floor. Heaving it onto the desk, he worked the zipper. Wedged between books was a plastic lunch box, contents intact. Alarm shot through him like an electric current. Whatever dragged Saoirse and Darragh away was sudden, serious and before school. Even as he hoped it was Darragh, or Niamh or Niall, anyone but Saoirse, shame rose through him like a warm tide. Amid rising panic, his hands raced round the bag, checking every fold and flap. There was no blood.

With a settling breath, he pondered the situation. Whatever had happened was in the past, and that threw up obstacles. If he went back and tried to change it, the rune would heim him in an instant. "You must not meddle with the past," Freyja had warned during his lessons. "The rún will not permit it."

When Ronan had asked what, exactly, constituted meddling, she'd gazed into the depths of the Home Stone, saying, "Only the gods decide that." Then she'd added, "In essence, do not try to change the course of history." Which was why Ronan suspected the ban only applied to important things. How else could he do anything in Saoirse's time, or

Freyja's? Regardless, he knew he could observe in the past; it would be worth more flytja misery to find out what happened.

Bracing himself, Ronan visualised the cottage living room, set the time for the previous Wednesday, and blanked his mind. A fireball of agony billowed through his head, killing the flytja attempt. He collapsed on the bed with a howl, curling into a moaning ball, clutching his temples, trying to breathe the pain away.

As the torment eased, fear and hopelessness took its place. Surely Freyja would have mentioned such fiery anguish if it were normal. His throat closed at the prospect of never making another flytja. How could he find Saoirse without flytjing? The mystery of her disappearance closed in on him. Where was she? Was she okay?

Without lifting his head from the pillow, Ronan took in the sideways view of the room. Still no clues or inspiration, but his eyes kept gravitating to the photo album on the desk, and the memory of going through it with Saoirse. Once the bonfire in his skull dwindled to a bed of coals, he reached for it. They'd sat in the same spot, shoulders touching, her breath warm on his cheek whenever she'd turned to him while explaining a photo.

Ronan ached for her as he turned pages. The love of his life was everywhere: posing with a group of identical school uniforms; laughing, arm linked with a round-faced girl; then the same girl, whippet thin, crutch hanging from her forearm as she held up a set of car keys in front of an old beige Mini Minor. Ronan frowned. She was Saoirse's best friend, but what was her name?

Scattered throughout were countless photos of horses of all shapes, sizes and colours. And shots of her father: hand inside a leather boot; behind the wheel of the car; sandwiched between friends in the local pub, ruddy nosed and grinning. He kept turning pages, drinking in every shot of Saoirse—there were never enough.

Unable to still his racing mind, Ronan abandoned the album, sinking onto the bed, burying his nose in the pillow, breathing the scent of her hair. Eventually, he rolled over and stared at the ceiling. *Saoirse, where are you?*

As tired as he was, sleep eluded him. Had he made the right decision in coming to Saoirse instead of looking for his father? He told himself that Paidin had the protection of a rune; Saoirse didn't. But Saoirse was in her own time; Paidin wasn't. Paidin was lost; so was Saoirse. And how could he help either of them if flytjing was too painful? Swirling what-ifs finally spun him into slumber.

Ronan dreamed of the perpetual smile of upturned lips, their breathtaking sweetness, tossed hair swirling like a dancer's skirt, eyes glowing. But as he reached for Saoirse, her face morphed into Paidin's, contorted in terror as he plummeted to his death. Then Ronan was chasing his father through the forest near Freyja's longhouse, but whenever he drew close, the rune whisked him back to the Home Stone, his head exploding. And there was Saoirse in the stables, back to him, combing Viking's mane. His pulse quickened. She turned, but it was Fionella Egan, eyes spitting fire.

Ronan snapped awake, panting, sweat soaking the pillow. Something had sliced through his tangled dreams. Ears straining, he eased upright, padding to the living room, standing clear of the curtained window. The visible slice of yard was empty, but he dared not move closer in case it was the Egans returned. A car door clicked, and irregular footsteps approached the front door.

With no time to consider consequences, he raced back, flipped Saoirse's sweat-dampened pillow and straightened the bedspread. Satisfied it would pass a cursory glance, he snatched up his boots, cleared his mind, visualised the adjacent stables, and folded away.

5

SEALED LIPS

The twisting tumble of the flytja jump triggered Ronan's newfound fear of using the ability. He braced for the onslaught, but there was none. With a relieved sigh, he wondered if it was because he'd only jumped from the cottage to the stables, barely fifty metres. Or was the pain only linked to flytjing through time? While the answer was crucial to his and Saoirse's immediate future, it would have to wait; first he had to identify the owner of the footsteps.

As he leant against the tack room's wall to pull his boots on, Ronan's eyes fell on Saoirse's name plate above her saddle. His heart skipped as he caressed the dip in the leather seat, leaving a track through a fine film of hay dust. As the saddle's lack of use registered, Ronan's imagination and anxiety leapt into overdrive. Saoirse would never neglect to exercise Viking; she loved that horse. The other tack carried even more dust; all the horses were being ignored.

Despite renewed urgency, Ronan crept toward the stables' entrance, replaying those odd footfalls in his head. The long pause between each one suggested excessive caution, but there was nothing furtive about the emphatic crunch of gravel.

Puzzled, he peered past the corner of the doorway. Close by the front door, out of sight from the living room window, sat a beige Mini Minor, its elongated shadow telling him he'd slept for several hours. And there was Saoirse's best friend, crutching toward the door—step, pause, step, pause—her right leg hanging useless. *What the hell is her name? Cath? Kate? Caitlin! That's it: Caitlin O'Toole.*

After sweeping about for unwanted scrutiny of the Egan kind, Ronan strode from the stables, his footsteps alerting the girl. She spun, key dangling from a green lanyard.

"Sorry, didn't mean to frighten you." He threw a friendly wave. "You must be Caitlin."

The girl remained sober. "And you're Ronan Ryan." Her lips tightened.

Bemused, Ronan tried again. "Saoirse has told me all about you."

"I doubt it." Caitlin looked at Ronan as if she wished him gone.

What was he missing? The key told him she knew the cottage was empty, and Ronan was positive she could tell him where Saoirse was. Even so, he couldn't let on he'd already been inside; it would raise questions he wasn't prepared to answer. "I was to meet Saoirse here yesterday after school, but there was no one home. Do you know where she is?"

"She said you would come." Caitlin studied Ronan for a beat before turning toward the door and raising the key. The lanyard hooked on a crutch handle; the key fell to the doormat.

Ronan stooped. "I'll get it." A crutch slammed down, grazing his fingers as it pinned the lanyard to the mat. He flinched.

"I'm not a cripple," she snapped, perhaps more forcefully than she intended, for her face coloured.

Ronan glanced up into defiance, noticing for the first time that her right eye was brown, the other green. Lifting the crutch, he gathered the key and stood. "I'd do this for anyone," he said, holding the key out, ignoring her belligerence.

Caitlin snatched the lanyard with a huff.

Ronan let it slide. He needed her as an ally, and sooner rather than later.

Uninvited, he followed her into the cottage. She seemed simultaneously strong and vulnerable; Ronan wondered if it was her hostility combined with the crutches giving that impression, or something less tangible. From a distance, she'd looked taller, but she only came to his shoulder, shorter than Saoirse, and much thinner. Recalling the rounded girl in the photo album, Ronan assumed the pain etched into her face was behind the lost weight.

Saoirse had told him how Caitlin befriended a foreign girl in the village, but when Caitlin went to visit, a man threw her down the stairs and disappeared with the girl. Caitlin was left with nerve damage and a crippled leg that she considered having amputated to be rid of the torment, but then it began improving. At least, that's what Ronan recalled. While she had good reason to be gaunt, there was none for remaining silent.

"What's happened, Caitlin? Where's Saoirse?"

"Why do you think something has *happened*?"

Ronan moved past her, poking his head into Saoirse's room. "Because they've obviously left in a hurry," he said, indicating the open drawers. "Saoirse would never leave things like this ... and I say *they* because there's no sign of Darragh either." This time, he swept his arm about the kitchen.

Caitlin considered him, expression neutral. "Are you a detective or something?"

"No, but I notice things."

"Well notice this: I can't tell you where she is."

"Can't or won't," he shot back, patience evaporating.

"Both."

"Why not?"

Caitlin fixed him with a silent glare.

"Has anyone ever told you you're bloody annoying?" Ronan said. As soon as the words were out, he wanted to pull them back.

She stiffened. "Often." She spun, moving away.

"Caitlin, please." Ronan was drawn after her by a thread of hope he was terrified of breaking. "Can't you just tell me where she is, and if she's okay?" Anguish rang in his ears. "If she's told you anything about me, you know she'd want that."

Caitlin stopped, but didn't turn. "I've nothing to say to you, Ronan Ryan. Now go, or I'll call the guards."

6

SHATTERED

Ronan was immobilised, unable to process either Caitlin's words or attitude. Propped on her crutches, she remained turned away, her refusal to tell him anything stirring a ripple of alarm behind his bellybutton. If Saoirse had spoken about him, Caitlin would understand how much they meant to each other, and how worried he was. "Please, Caitlin?"

With a resigned sigh, she turned. "I can't tell you," she said, this time with a dash of compassion.

"Do you even know where she is?" Despite his best effort, there was challenge in Ronan's tone.

Caitlin's eyes flashed, then softened. "I would tell you, but Saoirse made me swear not to."

A boa constrictor coiled round Ronan's chest, squeezing, smothering his lungs, his heart. There was no deceit in her face, but he couldn't believe the words. "Why?" he croaked.

"Because I'm her best friend and she trusts me."

"No," Ronan gasped. "Why doesn't she want me to know?"

"I can't tell you that"—her voice wavered—"because I truly don't know."

The boa tightened its suffocating grip. Ronan wanted his blood rune to heim him away from what felt like certain death. How could Saoirse abandon him? The memory of her sobbing as they parted the previous Sunday told him she wouldn't. But Caitlin's words said the opposite.

He gulped for breath. "Can't you tell me anything?"

Caitlin shook her head. "Saoirse said if I told you anything, you'd track her down."

Like a floundering swimmer, Ronan clutched at the memories of their brief time together. He couldn't, wouldn't, accept that Saoirse suddenly didn't love him. But she was dead right, if he had even the faintest hint of where she might be, he would find her, or die trying. The only way he'd believe she wanted him gone was to stand before her as she said it. And even that wouldn't erase the memory of those nine dreamy days.

"Can you just tell me if she's okay?" he pleaded.

"She was yesterday," Caitlin offered grudgingly.

That answer wasn't good enough for Ronan. "Well, what about today?" His tone was less neutral than he wished. Caitlin's hands tightened on her crutches; Ronan lifted an apologetic hand. "Sorry ... I need to know ... please?"

Caitlin considered him for several seconds before surrendering. "I'll try, but I can't just call her whenever I want. She has to turn her phone off in ..." After a flash of irritation—Ronan was sure she'd almost given something away—her expression softened. "She only checks it occasionally. I text ... she calls when she can."

"Well, can you? Please?"

In resignation, she sent thumbs dancing over phone keys. "It could take a while," she said, dropping it into a pocket, "so come back later. Now"—she herded him out the door—"if you'll excuse me, I have work to do."

"Can't I help with something?" Anything would be better than standing round, waiting.

But before Caitlin finished a second dismissive wave, a hungry chick called from a deep recess of her coat. "That was quick," she said, retrieving the phone, gesturing. "Go over to the stables ... I'll let you know what she says." She waved him off. "Hi, Sersh. Can you hang on a sec?"

Ronan tramped across the courtyard, turning at the stable door. Caitlin had followed him from the cottage, propping herself against the side of the Mini, temporarily discarded crutches by her side. She watched Ronan from the corner of an eye as she spoke in a low voice that died to a murmur before it reached Ronan. He strolled into the building's gloom, and when out of sight, pictured the cottage living room, blanking his mind to all else.

Next moment he was back in the cottage, flattened against the cold wall beside the open front door, exhilarated to still be able to flytja without pain.

"Ouch! That sounds ghastly," Caitlin was saying.

Ronan longed to hear the other half of the conversation, as much for Saoirse's voice as her words.

"I'm sure he'll be okay," Caitlin soothed. "He's in the best place ... Yes, I know."

There followed a silence so long, Ronan wondered if the connection had broken.

"Listen," Caitlin said at last, voice dropping toward conspiratorial, "Ronan is here ... at your place ... really upset. No, in the stables." If he wasn't such a bundle of confusion, he might have been amused by the futility of her whispering.

"Saoirse, stop!" Caitlin scolded gently. "I just watched him."

There was a pause. Caitlin's shoe scraped as her weight shifted.

"No ... hang on."

The shoe scuffed again.

"Ronan," she called, "come out where I can see you."

Damn! Saoirse was onto him. After a lightning flytja, he walked from the stable's gloom into the square of sunlight at the wide doorway. Caitlin raised a hand. From the distance, the words blurred into her melodic Irish lilt. All Ronan could do was observe. Caitlin watched him as she spoke, free hand punctuating her words.

For the first time, Ronan noticed the lifelessness of her hair. It hung to her shoulders, blonde, washed out, brittle, as if struggling to cling to her scalp. It might have been honey coloured before torment filled her world. In between gesticulations, she hooked errant strands behind an ear, perhaps to keep better sight of him without turning her head. It was an exercise in futility; the merest puff of breeze sent the dry strands swirling.

The longer they spoke, the more Ronan's hope lifted. The boa's grip was not as suffocating as it had been. A sliver of optimism pried a coil loose; his heart dared to beat.

Eventually, Caitlin snapped the phone closed, dropping it into a pocket. By the time Ronan reached her, she was back on her crutches, facing him with an unsettled look. His heart squeezed once more.

"Saoirse said to tell you she's grand," Caitlin began, struggling to hold Ronan's eye, "and that if you really care for her, you won't try to find her."

7

CODED MESSAGE

Caitlin's words knocked the wind from Ronan. It was precisely because he loved Saoirse that he'd do anything to find her. How could he not search for her while ever he drew breath? The constrictor coiled tighter.

"Why?" was all Ronan could manage. It was barely a croak. He stared into the distance, mind filled with Saoirse's red-rimmed eyes as he'd turned to leave her. That was three days ago for him, six for her, but time was losing its meaning; the more he jumped from one year to another, the less relevant it seemed. Regardless, Saoirse's tears were real, and they remained chains round his heart.

Caitlin leant toward him, but stopped as if catching herself. "And she said to tell you she's sorry ... she never meant to hurt you ..."

A lump swelled in Ronan's throat; his legs turned rubbery.

"Then she said something really weird: 'Tell Paidin I'm sorry I forgot about his hedgehog' ... she hung up before I could ask."

Ronan's head jerked. "What did you say?"

"She said, 'Tell Paidin I'm sorry I forgot about his hedgehog'." Caitlin watched him with lie-detector eyes. "Does that mean anything to you?"

Ronan's floundering heart clutched at 'Paidin'. Caitlin's words looped in his head, and each time 'Paidin' leapt out to buoy his spirits. The boa's coils eased. As well as being his father's name, Paidin was also the affectionate form of Padraig, Ronan's middle name. Saoirse knew that. *It's a message! Maybe she hasn't lost her feelings.*

While 'Paidin' was straightforward, the hedgehog reference stumped him. Ronan couldn't recall ever talking to Saoirse about a hedgehog, apart from when she pointed out where one had been scratching for food under a bush. That was the day they rode to Sliabh Liag where his father fell from the cliff. Ronan thought of Paidin in Killybegs, not twenty kilometres away, but back two hundred years. He had to have faith his father's rune would continue to protect him—Saoirse's need was greater.

"Ronan?"

"Huh?"

"Are you even listening to me?"

"I am now."

Caitlin's lips pursed. "I said, do you know what that means?"

Rune warmth squirted into the back of Ronan's brain; caution gripped him. "No. Should I?"

"Mmm ... just wondering ... I think it's code."

"Code?"

"Yeah, but I don't know what it means."

Apprehension spidered up Ronan's spine. If Caitlin was stumped, the message could only be for him. And while that made him dare to hope, it was also troubling. There were only two reasons he could find for Saoirse creating a message that only he would understand: someone was with her, controlling her calls; or she didn't trust Caitlin. He wasn't sure which troubled him most. Either way, Saoirse might be in danger, and that prospect sharpened his mind, cutting through the clutter, leaving only the hedgehog.

From what Ronan remembered, they lived on insects, snails and frogs, and, like Australia's echidna, rolled into a spiky ball when threatened. *That's it! Clever Saoirse!* He struggled to keep his face impassive. When he first arrived in Ireland, he was clutching the rune in his hand, but lost it when he fell in the Raven's Roost shower. Darragh found it and dropped it into a coat pocket with forgotten bootmakers' tacks. The super-magnetic stone, black as night and shiny as a mirror, had come out bristling with razor-sharp spikes, looking like an echidna. Close enough to a hedgehog.

Saoirse was telling him that she'd forgotten about his rune, which was the same as reminding him of it. And why remind him if she didn't want him to use it to find her? Ronan's heart sang for a pulse before he sobered, wondering if he was reading more into it than was there. Yet even if she no longer loved him, she was clearly asking him to search. And as surely as *he* still loved *her*, that's what he'd do.

As the need for action gripped him, Ronan ran through the message again, on the verge of panic, afraid he'd missed something. But there was no inkling of urgency or peril.

Breathing deep, he reminded himself she was more than clever enough to have included alarm in the coded message. But it was the calming rune, as much as reasoning, that convinced him she wasn't in danger. Regardless, he couldn't bear the thought of someone with Saoirse, vetting everything she said, or worse. Nor could he accept she didn't trust her best friend. Without thinking, he flicked a glance at Caitlin.

"What?" Her tone held a defensive edge.

"I was wondering, why send a coded message if neither of us knows what it means?"

"Perhaps it's a substitution cipher," she said, frowning.

"A what?"

"Substitution cipher. You know, where you substitute other letters for the ones you have ... just need to crack the puzzle ... I'll work on it."

Caitlin's confidence drove a wedge of doubt into Ronan's certainty. He replayed the message and it still said: 'Ronan, use your rune to find me'. It couldn't be a substitution thingy, but he played along. "How long will it take you to crack it?"

Caitlin shrugged. "No idea," she said, swiping at fly-away strands.

As he watched the futility of her action, Ronan couldn't believe she had any connection to Saoirse's situation, but until he was sure, he'd keep things to himself.

While his concern for Saoirse persisted, rune confidence tempered it, buoying his spirits. And his heart dared to hope.

8

———

SKIRMISH

Now that Ronan was positive Saoirse wanted him to find her, he struggled to think of anything else. The obvious strategy would be to pinball back through time until he found when she'd left Raven's Roost, but how many flytjas would that take? He didn't know if he could survive *one* more fiery flytja, let alone several; the torment was too fresh. And the couple of painless same-time jumps between cottage and stables only confirmed the pain was linked to those with a time change. The mere thought of what that meant was crushing. To avoid it, Ronan concentrated on other options.

Calling Saoirse was impossible. Not only was there zero chance of Caitlin revealing the number, Saoirse's calls were intercepted and controlled, of that he was positive. Ronan saw no alternative but to start searching, and until certain about Caitlin, he'd do it alone.

"Thanks for doing that," he said. "It's good to know she's okay, even if I don't know what the hell's going on."

"Well, if it's any consolation, neither do I," Caitlin replied. "I only know what Saoirse has told me."

"That's more than she's told me," Ronan grumbled, feigning hardship.

Caitlin's compassion was consumed by a sudden blaze. "Don't be so damned petulant!"

Startled by the ferocity of the rebuke, Ronan bit his tongue, dropping his gaze, berating himself for overacting; the last thing he needed was an aggravated Caitlin. "Sorry," he said at last, staring out over the nearby field. Attempting to lighten the moment and compensate for his overacting, he added, "I need a dog."

Caitlin looked blank. "What?"

"A dog," Ronan said with a crooked grin, "I need a dog to kick."

She glared.

"No, not literally," he assured her. "It's just a saying we use at home for when we're really frustrated. You know, you vent your frustration by kicking the dog." Ronan's humour wilted in the face of Caitlin's censure.

"I think that's an appalling saying." She threw her chin in the air, turned and crutched into the cottage.

"It's harmless," he told her retreating back. "I was trying to be light-hearted. I'd never *do* it."

"Then don't *say* it!" Caitlin halted in the shadows of the doorway, presenting a stony profile. "Just by repeating something like that, you help make it acceptable."

Ronan's jaw dropped. "What? ... How?"

With an exasperated sigh, she said, "What if it was a girl?"

"What?"

"The dog."

"The dog?"

"Yes."

"A girl?"

"That's what I said."

"What do you mean?" Ronan fought the urge to throw his hands in the air.

Caitlin let out another sigh. "Suppose the saying was that you want a girl to slap when you get frustrated?"

"That's ridiculous," he shot back.

Her exasperation sent blonde tendrils into chaos. "I don't know what she sees in you."

Heat rose in Ronan's cheeks. "It's just a harmless saying," he repeated, but he was talking to an empty doorway.

He stood there, thinking on what she'd said and wondering why she was so combative about a stupid saying. Swallowing frustration, he followed her into the cottage. She was propped on the crutches at the open refrigerator, transferring perishables into a couple of shopping bags.

"Caitlin?"

She continuing sorting, throwing the occasional reject into a bin bag with particular vigour.

"Caitlin?"

She paused at his insistent tone, back rigid.

"Caitlin?" he repeated.

"What?"

Ronan took a deep breath. "Look, I'm sorry ... I know it's a stupid thing to say ... now." He paused, not wanting to overdo it, but needing to do more to rebuild bridges with his only conduit to Saoirse. Besides, by Saoirse's estimation, there was a lovely person beneath the prickly personality. "I'd never thought about what it implied before ..."

"Don't push it, boyo," she said, reaching for a block of cheese.

"I'm serious. I'll never use it again." Ronan detected a minute thaw in the tension between them, and decided to ride his luck. "What can I do?"

"Leave."

Ronan baulked. "What's your problem?" he snapped. "It's a simple offer of help."

"I don't need your pity," she retorted.

"Well, if you get any, it'll be for your attitude, not those bloody crutches," Ronan fired back.

Again, Caitlin went still.

"And the offer was for Saoirse," Ronan said. "You're obviously doing this for her, and anything she needs, I'll help with. You may not believe this, but there's nothing more important to me than Saoirse, so any help I give you is for her." Irritation pinwheeled inside him. "So get over yourself!"

Before she could respond, he stalked from the cottage.

9

────────

LONELY

Ronan's multi-front spat with Caitlin left him with a hot face and tight jaw; he sought the calming influence of the stables. Viking's soft nicker was a non-judgemental greeting. "Hey big fella?" Ronan murmured, rubbing the muscular neck. The inquisitive ears of the other horses pricked toward him. Ronan sensed boredom—there were bite marks along the top of several of the half-doors.

Viking nuzzled Ronan's shirt, trying to gather it between rubbery lips. Ronan dragged a hand down to the horse's velvet muzzle, nudging it aside.

"What's happened, boy? Where is she?"

Viking turned large, liquid orbs on Ronan.

"*You'd* tell me if you knew, wouldn't you?"

Viking nodded his head, blowing moisture with a deep sigh.

"I miss her too," Ronan said, absently picking pieces of bedding straw from mane hair. He frowned. "When were you last groomed?" He entered the stall with a broad brush, launching into long, practised strokes. Viking's skin rippled with pleasure under the firm bristles as Ronan worked the brush along the large, grey body and down each muscular leg. As he brushed, he pondered Saoirse's message, reassuring himself it contained no urgency, only clear permission to search. And with every stroke, his annoyance at Caitlin's attitude faded. By the time the last of it was brushed away, Viking's coat gleamed, but a strategy for finding Saoirse that didn't involve an unknown number of flytjas through time, remained elusive.

Nothing in the house gave him a clue to how long it had been deserted, but the stable dust on the saddles was another matter. Ronan guessed it was perhaps four days since Saoirse had used hers, which made it Tuesday. Having already tried and failed to go back three days, it was more in hope than conviction that he aimed for Tuesday, only to abandon the attempt as a constellation of red-hot embers showered his brain. Sinking to the bedding hay, he huffed against the agony, wondering for a crazy moment if there mightn't be scorch marks on the inside of his skull. Viking nuzzled his back as he crouched there, devastated by the prospect of never doing another time-flytja.

While Ronan was confident of finding Saoirse without time-flytjing, he only had nine days to do it in. When he'd asked Freyja why the rune only allowed nine days in any time apart from his own, she'd smiled serenely and said, "Why are there nine realms? ... and nine heim rúnar?" In other words, she didn't know, and put it down to another mystery of the gods.

And when the nine days were up, regardless of whether he'd found Saoirse or not, the rune would heim him to 891. Without the ability to cross the centuries, he'd be trapped there for the rest of his life, unable to return to Saoirse's 2004, or his mother's 2021. As fond as Ronan was of Freyja, the thought of never again seeing the two most important people in his life made the air suddenly too thick to draw into his lungs.

But the solution revealed itself like a shaft of sunlight bursting through overcast: if he hadn't found Saoirse by the ninth day, he would cut the rune from his scalp, and stay in Saoirse's time forever. The confidence that he'd find her eventually, did little to quell the stirring grief for his mother.

With a settling breath, Ronan headed back to the cottage, trying to draw comfort from his decision.

The kitchen was empty; he followed the buzz of activity to Saoirse's room, finding Caitlin fussing about, tidying the drawers, straightening the bed. Thankfully, she hadn't turned the pillow to see the patch of dampness from his sweaty head.

"Is Darragh sick?" Ronan asked neutrally as he entered. "Has he had an accident?"

She shot a sharp glance. "Why do you say that?"

Ronan considered his options. Without a doubt, Caitlin could be fiery, but she was nimble-witted. The wrong word might trigger fireworks, while digging too much could make her clam up, not that she was exactly gushing to begin with. "Well, you said Saoirse was okay, so the reason they left at such short notice must be because something happened to Darragh."

Caitlin remained silent, unmoving.

Ronan had a sudden thought. "Or was it her mother? ... or brother?"

"Nothing to do with Niamh or Niall."

"So it's Darragh."

"Saoirse said you don't miss much." Caitlin contemplated him with the merest hint of approval. "They've had to go away, and won't be back for a while, and that's all I can tell you." Her tone was a gigantic punctuation mark.

Taking her response as a concession of sorts, Ronan decided not to push any further for the moment. Instead, he said, "Thanks. Now, what can I do?"

After a long hesitation in which she seemed to struggle with how to respond, she handed him Saoirse's lunch box. "Empty this into the rubbish bag in the kitchen, then put it in my car. I'll drop it at the waste station on my way home." She followed it with a grudging "Thank you."

While the gratitude was reluctant, Ronan accepted it as progress that he had to be careful not to undermine. "No worries," he said lightly, leaving her to it.

Whatever had happened to Darragh occurred before Saoirse left for school, so early in the day and early in the week. But how did that knowledge help if he couldn't time-flytja? With a clutter of different scenarios ricocheting through his mind, Ronan felt utterly inadequate for detective work. Doubly so when he could see no way of narrowing it down. He took a calming breath. What would Freyja do?

Speak to me, Grandmother. He closed his eyes, focusing on his ancestor's face. It dissolved into Saoirse's, tear-streaked as they parted. And Caitlin's words returned to haunt him: "... if you really care for her, you won't try to find her." It was a vain hope his path forward might become clear with a plea to his Norse forebear. If anything, she was becoming more distant, his rune less active and reassuring.

Ronan ran through the rune's poem, wondering, as he did, whether he was no longer 'true of mind and pure of heart', and if the rune was rejecting him, finding him unworthy, withdrawing its power. Without Saoirse, or the rune's warmth, he was lonelier and more uncertain than ever.

PROGRESS

Filled with thoughts of Freyja and Saoirse, Ronan lumped the bulging rubbish bag to Caitlin's car. Bottles clinked as he stowed it in the boot, setting off a chorus of whinnies from the stables. Ronan pictured equine heads leaning over stall doors, bedding straw tangled in unkept manes.

"Who's looking after the horses?" he asked when he re-entered the cottage.

Caitlin shot a glance. "Why?"

Sensing peril, Ronan proceeded with caution. "I don't think they're getting enough exercise."

"Why wouldn't they be?" Caitlin's sharp response declared she was priming for another skirmish.

"Don't be so damned prickly," he retorted, visualising an echidna. "It's a simple question ... I wasn't criticising anyone."

"Never said you were."

"No, but you're acting as if I was."

"Well, weren't you?" She simmered with challenge.

Ronan heaved a sigh. "No." He failed to keep all the shortness from his tone. "Look, Saoirse has been gone for quite a few days an—"

"Who told you that?" Caitlin fired back.

Ronan rolled his eyes and took yet another deep breath; her belligerence was wearing thin. "Dust," was all he said. *If she wants more information, she can damn-well ask.*

Caitlin scanned the cottage. "What dust?"

"Saddle."

"Saddle?"

"Work it out."

"You're just being difficult," she complained.

"Wow!" Ronan snorted. "Pot, meet kettle."

Caitlin fell silent, but the faintest twitch pulled at her lip. As if attempting to regain the advantage, she said, "How do you know someone else hasn't been riding them?"

"I know horses," he said, deciding to remain uncooperative—two could play that game.

"That's probably why she likes you."

"That and my awesome sense of humour," he said, unable to maintain his bloody-mindedness in the face of a suspected thaw.

Caitlin shook her head, chuckling. "No, definitely the horses."

"Aha. Now I see why you're her best friend."

"Touche," Caitlin responded, with a glimmer of humour that started in the odd-coloured irises, floating downward, displacing the weight of constant pain.

Arms folded, Ronan leant back, squinting at her. "Yes, I can actually see it now."

"Sorry," she said wryly. "I've been a right little shite, haven't I?"

"No comment." Ronan raised his hands in mock defence against a renewed verbal assault.

That drew a broad grin from Caitlin, transforming her features, highlighting the elfin uptick of her nose. She must have lost considerable weight since her accident, for her clothes draped as if from a coat hanger, except for the swell of blooming womanhood against her cardigan.

Heat kindling in his cheeks, Ronan chopped his glance away, hoping she missed it. When he dared check, she was gazing toward the stables; relief surged through him.

"I asked Fionn to do it."

"Fionn? Egan?"

With a sardonic laugh, she nodded. "He won't be enjoying getting his hands grubby."

"No!" Ronan gaped at her. "That mongrel should never be allowed near horses ... ever."

"I know"—she flapped a hand—"but someone has to do it and they're all Egan horses ... except Viking."

Saoirse would never let Egan anywhere near Viking, she just wouldn't. Adopting the most neutral tone he could manage, he said, "What does Saoirse think?"

"She has enough on her mind."

Ronan agreed it would only add to whatever Saoirse was currently dealing with, but he was surprised Caitlin didn't know her best friend's view on Egan and horses.

As if reading his thoughts, Caitlin said, "I know Saoirse would hate it, but it's not like there are any alternatives."

Ronan couldn't stop shaking his head; it was the worst possible option. Egan terrorised his former horse, Duke, chasing him up and down the yard with the farm Land Rover. After that, whenever a vehicle came close, the poor animal trembled in fear and sought escape. And all because Egan fell into the mud when Duke baulked at a water jump.

"There's got to be a better option than Finnegan," Ronan growled.

Caitlin stared. "What did you call him?"

"Finnegan."

She chuckled. "Don't let *him* hear that."

Ronan mimed an exaggerated 'oops!'

"Why? What happened?" She leant forward, eyes gleaming.

"Well," Ronan began, "Finnegan was being obnoxious—"

"No surprise there," Caitlin cut in.

"He tried to pull me off balance, so, I let him"—Ronan enjoyed the memory—"and my forehead happened to catch him on the nose ... caused quite a bit of blood ... and ungentlemanly language."

Caitlin tossed her head, squealing with delight, giving Ronan a glimpse of the attractive, carefree girl she must have been before her accident.

A thumping bang from the stables interrupted his thoughts.

Caitlin flinched. "Jaysis! What was that?"

"*That* is a bored horse."

"But what ...?"

"I'd say one of them let fly, both barrels ... at the wall."

Head tilted, Caitlin frowned.

"Both back feet," Ronan explained, "... into the side of the stall, I'd reckon." He grimaced. "Those horses need exercise and decent care ... which rules out Finnegan."

"Oh, I love that name."

It's such a pleasant smile. Ronan absorbed her amusement. "Yeah, well Finnegan doesn't."

"Which makes me like it more."

"Why don't you like him?"

"Probably the same reason as you."

"Because he's a bully?"

"Yep."

"And arrogant, pompous and entitled?"

"All of the above."

"I'm guessing there's more."

"You really should be a detective."

With a pang, Ronan realised how much the lilt of her voice reminded him of Saoirse. But he was getting side-tracked again; they needed a plan for the horses that didn't involve Egan. "You never know"—he rubbed his chin—"I might try it one day." When she didn't respond, he prodded: "Finnegan?"

She looked like she'd bitten into a grapefruit. "Vindictive ... cruel."

"Right." Ronan was unsurprised by her assessment.

"Interesting clothes, by the way," Caitlin said, scrutinising his ill-fitting attire.

"Long story," Ronan replied, "... for another time."

"Okay," she said slowly.

Ronan could almost feel questions forming in her mind. "I've been thinking about the horses," he said, guiding the conversation back on track, "or Viking at least. There's no way I can leave him with Finnegan. I'm wondering if there's a farm round here that would let him run in their paddock." In response to Caitlin's blank look, he added, "Field."

"Mmm ... no idea."

"We rode through a heap of fields when I was here last time ... Saoirse said the farmers were happy as long as she kept the gates closed. Maybe, there's one where Viking could have a little holiday?"

"Possibly." She dragged the word out, any confidence it held leaking away between syllables.

"Well, would you mind asking round? It'd be better coming from you ... you know them."

"Not really ... hardly know anyone this side of the harbour ... apart from Saoirse."

"Okay ..." Ronan paused, searching for an alternative. "What say I ride Viking through those farms where Saoirse took me? Maybe one of them could help. Anything would be better than Finnegan."

"If that's what you want," she said without enthusiasm, "... might work."

"Won't know till I try." Ronan wasn't sure whether his newfound enthusiasm came from the prospect of riding Viking, the fact that he was now on a path of action, or the hint of radiation from the rune. Finding lodgings for Viking wouldn't get him any closer to Saoirse, but at least it would occupy him while he worked out his next move. It never occurred to him that he might not find her.

Caitlin brightened. "Right, that's settled, then." After locking the cottage, she crutched to the car, halting at the driver's door, frowning across the low roof to Ronan. "How did you get here?"

The question caught Ronan off guard for a heartbeat. Suspicion sharpened her gaze; Ronan feared withdrawal. Thankfully, the back-story he and Saoirse had concocted leapt into his recall.

"Over the hill from the cafe," he offered.

"Why would you do that?"

"Mum's having coffee with a friend ... I said I'd walk."

"That's a fair hike," Caitlin pointed out. "Why not get her to drop you here?"

"Given our past encounter, I didn't want Finnegan seeing me."

"Oh, I see." Her shoulders relaxed. "Can't say I blame you. I'd walk a mile to avoid him too."

Ronan sobered. "If Finnegan ever asks, I came with you."

"Okay ..." she said, as if digesting the request and finding it acceptable. "So, can I drop you home now?"

"Actually, I thought I might take Viking out ... try a few of those farms. How long should I ask them to keep him for?"

Caitlin squinted at him. "Nice try, Sherlock."

For a split second, Ronan wondered what she meant. "No." He raised a hand in denial. "I wasn't trying to trick information out of you. They're going to want to know. I would if I were them."

Ronan's sincerity worked; Caitlin's suspicion faded. "Oh. Okay, then." She balanced on her good leg, thrusting the crutches into the passenger space. "Tell them it might be as long as a month, but I really don't know. Now, do you want to put my number in your phone so you can let me know how you go?" She slid into the driver's seat, calling out the open door, "And I can tell Saoirse ... I'm sure she'll be pleased."

Despite the familiar pleasant stirring in his chest at the mention of his girlfriend's name, Ronan faked annoyance. "I left it at home." While it wasn't a lie, it was a deception, so he ploughed on: "But please tell Saoirse that I hope her dad gets better soon, and ..." He paused, trying to find the best disguise for what he so desperately wanted to tell Saoirse. Then he realised there was no need to conceal his message. So, cheeks warming, he added, "Ah ... tell her I still love her, even if she doesn't want to see me."

"That's sweet." There was enough tease in Caitlin's tone to inflame the colour climbing Ronan's neck. "But how am I going to get any updates to you ... if there are any?"

Ronan was too focused on quashing his embarrassment to respond.

"Come on, Romeo, get with the program." She was enjoying his discomfort. "What's your number? I'll call you this evening."

Ronan smiled ruefully. "No, it's back in Australia."

"Ah, you eejit!"

"Yeah, don't I know it. But give me your number ... I'll call you when I'm near a phone."

Caitlin scribbled on a scrap of paper from the glove box, handing it to Ronan as she fired up the engine. He barely had time to grab it before she released the brake and sped off, the squat vehicle's belly skimming the ground.

II

———

ENCOUNTER

Soon after, Ronan was trotting Viking down the lane from the cottage. To the right, a stone wall crowded the gravelled surface, while on the left rose a privet hedge sculptured to within an inch of its life. Beyond the angular shrubbery rose three stories of stone and glass, the Egan family home. They also owned the Raven's Roost cottage, the stables, the farm, the Detencin Boot Factory, and half of southern Donegal's real estate, according to Saoirse.

Ronan hadn't met Dooley Egan, but Fionella was a piece of work. A small woman with fine features and fading auburn hair, she might have been attractive except for cold reptilian eyes, which seemed apt given the encounter in the cottage yesterday evening.

An asphalt strip swept from the Egan mansion, through a scalpel-sharp incision in the hedge, shouldering the gravel aside to take over the laneway. The opening provided an unimpeded view of a modern-day castle surrounded by a moat of manicured lawn. Ronan tried to ignore it; he wanted nothing to do with that family. Fionella had blasted him from under Saoirse's bed with such murderous ease, Ronan wasn't sure how he'd react if he encountered her.

Viking plodded along, sixteen hands of gentle giant. Ronan latched onto the diversion, wondering why horse height was measured in hands. Viking should be one-point-six metres tall. Ronan vaguely recalled something about Ancient Egyptians and Henry VIII, but couldn't remember specifics. Regardless, he was perched high.

The laneway emptied onto the Sliabh Liag road and, as they approached, Viking's ears toggled between traffic and rider, as if trying to divine the plan. Ronan intended to retrace the first part of the route he and Saoirse took on their ride to Sliabh Liag a couple of weeks back. Their path had taken them through several farms and Ronan thought that, today, he'd veer across to the farm buildings, ask about a spot for Viking, anything to keep him out of Egan's suspect care.

While they were still a good fifty metres from the road, a vehicle's familiar rumble rose from behind. The hairs on the back of Ronan's neck stiffened; he'd not long ridden past the spot where Egan had run him down with those same two tons of gleaming steel.

He snatched a glance over his shoulder, catching a flash of auburn behind the wheel. Amid jangling nerves and lifting heart rate, Ronan's mind filled in the features of Egan's mother. Surely she wouldn't try the same thing as her son? Unwilling to risk it, he heeled Viking forward, desperate to clear the confines of the laneway before the vehicle could catch him.

Every stride took horse and rider closer to escape; every second brought the Range Rover closer. Even though his mind registered the lack of urgency in the engine's pulse, Ronan didn't relax until he reined Viking round the protective end of the stone wall. He spun as Fionella Egan brought the four-wheel-drive to a halt adjacent, its engine throbbing with raw power, an attack dog straining for release.

"Why, Ronan Ryan, how pleasant to see you," she gushed, cardigan-clad elbow hooked out the open window, grey eyes several degrees cooler than the autumn air.

"Mrs Egan." He nodded, stroking Viking's neck.

"Oh, please," she simpered, "... Fionella."

Ronan studied the women who 'murdered' him the previous day.

"My, you are the strong, silent type, aren't you?" The calculating appraisal and mocking tone undermined her attempt at radiating friendliness.

Ronan was unmoved by the banter, but the woman herself was poison; there may as well have been venom dripping from fangs. Someone who shot first and asked questions later, if at all, was not to be trifled with.

"Mrs Egan ... Fionella ..."

"That's my boy." She smiled. It was a gust of winter.

Caution had Ronan pausing, analysing everything about her; Fionella ran out of patience. "You were saying?" she prompted, the words curling round his arm like a strangler fig, reaching toward his throat.

Ronan stifled his imagination. "I'm wondering why you drove down here."

Fionella tut-tutted. "Such a clever young man ... handsome too." Her tongue tip laid a trail of moisture across artificially red lips.

Ronan fought a sudden wave of distraction. And while he'd prefer to stay silent, he was becoming annoyed. "It's what's inside that counts," he said, paraphrasing his Grandpa Paddy.

"And wise as well." Her chuckle never reached her eyes.

"What do you want, Fionella?" Tired of the games and the pretence of civility, Ronan was sharper than good manners dictated.

She gave the steering wheel a triumphant bop with the heel of her hand. "Good boy, I *am* getting you trained."

Viking fidgeted. Ronan settled him with pressure on the reins, and waited.

Fionella sobered. "I saw you ride past and wanted to know what you are doing with Saoirse's horse."

"Exercising him," Ronan said. "I came over with Caitlin and thought I'd stretch his legs … as a favour to Saoirse."

"Have you spoken to her?" she asked.

Ronan saw no harm in being honest. "No. Apparently, she doesn't want to talk to me."

She stared across the road into the distance, shaking her head. "Young girls … they don't really know what they want until it's pointed out to them." Returning her attention to Ronan, she added, "I'm sure it will all work out for the best."

"I'm sure it will," Ronan murmured, pondering her words.

"Now don't be late back with that horse; Fionn feeds at five." With that, she pulled out into a break in the sparse traffic, executed a precise, three-point-turn, and accelerated up the laneway with an imperious wave.

While unsettling at first, the encounter left Ronan intrigued.

12

GOSSIP

Viking ambled across the road and stood patiently, cars zooming past his tail, as Ronan spun Saoirse's code into the combination padlock. It stuck in his brain because of its simplicity: the Teelin postcode—F94—with the *F* becoming a *6* to reflect its position in the alphabet. The recollection of her explanation rekindled his anxiety and longing. But as Freyja had said when teaching mastery of the blood rune, he must learn patience.

Saoirse's big grey stepped out eagerly through the first field, grazing sheep nibbling their way from his path without lifting their sooty faces. As he rode, Ronan replayed the encounter, wondering why Fionella was interested in whether he'd spoken to Saoirse, or was he only imagining it. The woman disturbed him. Her immaculate grooming disguised a murderous ruthlessness wrapped in a swirling undercurrent of calculation and cunning. She always appeared to be several steps ahead. He shivered.

Horse and rider were well into the third field when their route topped a rise, revealing a nearby farmhouse and barn. Ronan reined his mount down-slope toward them.

As they approached the yard, a scatter of hens scratching in the dirt clucked from their path, and an obese black and white pig came grunting round the side of the barn. It jumped, let out a strident squeal and waddled from sight.

A grizzled old man, muffled against the cold, met them between the buildings. "Howya," he said, subjecting Ronan to rheumy scrutiny.

"G'day, sir," Ronan said, reining Viking in, sitting easy in the saddle.

"What ya be doing riding over the farm?" The man's challenge had his bushy grey brows bunching.

"My name's Ronan ... I'm a friend of Saoirse and Darragh Kelly," Ronan began, but before he could continue, the old farmer shook his head.

"Aye, and tis brutal what happened to poor Darragh."

Ronan's pulse skipped, but he sat motionless and silent, sensing a door of opportunity opening.

"Construction lorry, the guards think, you know ... rammed him off the road."

"Really?" Ronan couldn't help himself.

The grey brows were like excited caterpillars. "Aye, and they can't find it ... disappeared into thin air."

That explains the empty cottage, but not Saoirse's mixed messages. Aloud, Ronan repeated Caitlin's words, "At least Darragh is in good hands."

"Aye, nothin' but the best in Dublin."

Ronan couldn't believe his luck, and with a droll thought, wondered if the man had the hospital name and bed number as well.

"Now tell me, how is the poor divil?"

Ronan used a judicious pause to construct a suitable non-committal answer. "As good as can be expected."

"Tanks be to God," the old man intoned, lifting and dropping his hands without taking them from his coat pockets.

"Yes," Ronan agreed.

The farmer squinted up at Ronan. "What did ya say ya name was?"

"Ronan. Ronan Ryan."

"Eoin Duffy," the man said, giving Ronan's extended hand a firm grip.

"Pleased to meet you, Mr Duffy."

"Eoin, lad, Eoin. And climb down ... you're welcome here."

"Eoin," Ronan repeated, dismounting.

"Ryan, eh?" Eoin studied him. "There's Ryans over Killybegs way, but you're not one of them?"

"No, I'm from Australia."

"And fortunate that is, lad." The man's features were sombre. "The Killybegs Ryans lost a lad off Sliabh Liag a few weeks back ... never even found the poor soul's body."

Ronan no longer felt any pang at the mention of his father's supposed death, but he still had gnawing impatience to find why Paidin never returned to his own time.

Something serious must have happened, for nothing else would have stopped his father getting back to his mother. Nothing. But for now, his priority must be Saoirse.

Eoin's head swung as if banishing sad thoughts. "Australia, eh … what ya be doin' in Ireland, lad?"

"Visiting friends with my mum," Ronan said. Before another question came his way, he added, "Ah, Eoin, Saoirse told me about your farm"—which wasn't strictly true—"and I was wondering if you'd have space for Viking for a month or so."

"Ooh, don't know about that … me barn's full." Eoin's callused palm sandpapered across his bristled chin. "Anyway, why would you be wanting him over here?"

"Because Fionn Egan is looking after the horses while Saoirse is away."

"Ach! Say no more. I wouldn't want that one tending any animal of mine … heard what he did to that poor horse what dropped him in the mud. Got a vindictive streak a mile wide, and devious too … just like his mam."

"Mmm," Ronan intoned, not wanting to interrupt the flow.

"Young Dooley's harmless enough … always got his nose buried in the cashbook at the factory they say, but the son, well, he might look like Dooley, but he's his mother's lad for sure." Eoin gestured toward Raven's Roost and dropped his voice. "There's stories I've heard 'bout em that would curl ya hair, even if they was only half true. Best stay clear of them Egans, lad. As nice as they like to play in public, there's evil in their hearts, nothin' surer."

Ronan tingled with anticipation. "What sort of stories?"

"Well," Eoin began, leaning close, "I'm not one for the gossip, mind, but it's more than gossip when you keep hearin' it. Isn't it?"

Ronan didn't follow the logic, but indicated agreement, keen to learn more. Before shooting Ronan, Fionella had said to her son, "When you play for high stakes, you don't leave anything to chance." *What the heck did she mean?*

"It just seems strange," Eoin continued, "that Dooley Egan, a Dubliner no less, comes to Killybegs as the new accountant for old Donal O'Mahony at Detencin Boots and, in no time a'tall, Dooley was part-owner … lord knows where he got the money … they was living in a tiny rental, driving an old rust bucket … some say he musta been skimming the profits, but who knows. And word is, Fionella wove a web round poor Donal, a lifelong bachelor, so he couldn't think straight. Then the hapless sod goes and dies of heart failure, he does, and leaves his share of the company to her … devious schemer."

Duffy's caterpillar eyebrows convulsed as though preparing to walk to another face. While the furry antics were mesmerising, it was the information that fascinated Ronan.

"But wasn't that his choice?" Ronan asked, puzzled by Eoin's intensity, unsurprised by the story.

"Aye, but before the Egans showed, Donal had made it well known he was leaving the business to the workers, in equal parts. All those who'd been loyal to him through the rough patches, and what made Deetees the boots they are today, they was all going to get a wee piece of Detencin ... then fecking Fionella comes along."

Ronan gawped. Eoin fired spittle into the dirt.

"And people like Darragh, and my lad, Colm, got nothing!"

A heavy silence settled. Ronan kept his tongue still, eager for further enlightenment.

"Anyway," Eoin said at last, dragging his gaze from the direction of the Egan's green-moated mansion, "that's all bye the bye."

Disappointed that the well of resentment and information had run dry, Ronan returned to the purpose of his visit. "Anyway, would you have room for Viking in one of your fields?"

"Ah, well, that's another matter." Eoin stroked his whiskers again, brows twitching as he pondered. "Aye, we can do that, lad."

The response buoyed Ronan further—it had almost been too easy, getting information on Darragh *and* finding a place for Viking at the very first farm. But when he thought about it, he supposed small communities were the same in Ireland as Australia: everyone knew everybody's business, and they always rally to help those in need. And one extra mouth wouldn't affect a pasture as rich as Eoin's.

Ronan turned the horse loose into the allocated field with murmured reassurance; Viking tossed his head and trotted off to explore his new home.

With the saddle and bridle stowed against a canvas-draped tractor deep in the barn, Ronan took his leave of farmer Duffy, heading for the Sliabh Liag road. Once there, he turned toward the mountain itself, navigating the right-hand side of the road, against the traffic flow. It was slow going, often having to take to the weeds as a procession of cars, RVs and small buses meandered past.

As he walked, he pondered Darragh, Dublin and hospitals, and when he put it together with a hit and run, Saoirse and a coded message, it smelt fishier than a Killybegs trawler. By the time the road took him past a knoll of exposed granite to the Raven's Roost entrance, Ronan was positive that shotgun-toting Fionella and her son had fish all over them. He also knew he was going to Dublin, just not how, when, or precisely where.

Taking a deep breath and squaring his shoulders, Ronan strode up the laneway, the pretentious dwelling rising like an omen to meet him.

13

———

CONFRONTATION

Confidence bubbled through Ronan as he strode up the centre of the tarred lane. With Viking sorted, he was eager to see if he could glean further information to add to the trove from the affable Eoin Duffy. Besides, he wanted to watch Fionella's reaction when he told her Viking wouldn't be returning to Raven's Roost until Saoirse did.

Before hearing Eoin's story, Ronan thought the woman's aura of villainy was as malevolent as possible, but the ruthless cunning and biblical patience required to hoodwink the previous owner of Detencin Boots added layers of wickedness. And to think that she'd transmitted her genetics. He shuddered, certainty faltering.

By the time he navigated the gap in the hedge, caution was whispering in his ear; he sought the reassurance of the rune's warmth. A moving curtain added menace to the building's inscrutable stare.

A covered portico, currently filled with the coiled power of the gold Range Rover, protected the entrance from the elements. Several expansive steps climbed to a sprawling porch festooned with potted plants almost dense enough to need a machete to navigate. Ronan clunked the hefty brass knocker and waited. Solid footsteps drifting through the imposing oak doors had him tensing, the rune warming. The catch snicked open and the door swung inward, revealing the well-fed features of Fionn Egan, instantly turning ugly.

"What do *you* want?" he scowled from beneath snow-white hair precise enough to have been trimmed by their gardener.

"Hello to you too, Finnegan." While Ronan's tone was pleasant, the words were meant to irritate—he wanted to keep the oaf off balance, and perhaps, more prone to an unguarded remark.

Egan's fists balled but stayed by his side. He was shorter than Ronan, and much heavier, but there was no hardness in the extra weight, and despite his two-year advantage, he exuded wariness. Perhaps he was recalling Ronan's effortless dispatch of a couple of hired thugs in a blur of karate.

Before Ronan could needle further, Fionella swept into the entryway in a rainbow swirl of woollen scarf. "Ronan," she exclaimed, teeth gleaming through a red gash, "how wonderful to see you again so soon. Do come in … come." She hooked eager, vivid talons at him, but her son remained steadfast, unmoving.

"Finny, where are your manners?" she chided. "Bring our guest through." She retreated, trailing perfume as sharp as her nails.

Egan stepped aside, glowering. Ronan mouthed 'Finny' as he passed. The silent barb drew an angry mutter, and he wondered if his deliberate unsettling tactic made him as bad as the bully behind him. With a mental shrug, he followed the woman's green pants and cream jumper into the same sitting room he'd visited with Saoirse, not much more than a week earlier.

In the midst of warm wood and expensive leather, Fionella swung to face him. "Now," she said, "to what do we owe this unexpected pleasure?"

"I didn't bring Viking back," Ronan stated. But then, she already knew; he'd seen her blood-red claws clutching an upstairs curtain.

"Oh, well that's a surprise," she said dryly. "Have you stolen him?"

"He's Saoirse's horse and I've found him a …" About to say 'better', Ronan decided against further prodding. "… more suitable home."

"Whatever for?" she said, unblinking, throwing her arms wide.

The scrape of shoe leather sent a prickle up Ronan's spine. Pretending the adjacent painting of a rural scene held mild interest, he took a couple of steps toward it before turning so he could watch both mother and son at the same time. Egan seemed not to notice; his mother's mouth ticked upward at one corner. Not that it bothered Ronan, he was running on adrenaline and rune power. Both were coursing through his veins, heightening senses, sharpening wits, flooding muscles with energy.

"Mrs Egan, I—"

"Fionella, please."

"Fionella … what do you know of a horse named Duke?"

Her son stiffened; she assessed Ronan. He felt sure she was about to pass a comment on his leanness. Instead, she drawled, "You really should change your fashion adviser."

The mockery of Darragh's ill-fitting clothes had no effect on Ronan. He was comfortable and warm; it was all that mattered. "Duke?" he repeated, wondering if she was avoiding the question.

"Ah, Duke. Fionn's jumper ... quite promising ... until he wasn't."

"And do you know why?"

Egan fidgeted again. Ronan wondered whether Fionella was even aware what her son had done to the horse. Her calculating gaze bored into him.

Ronan took a breath. "After Duke sent Fionn into the mud, your son decided to teach him a lesson, hounding him round the yard with the Land Rover. He now has a phobia of cars and, I reckon, for your son."

Fionella's silent appraisal continued.

"Do you really think Saoirse would want Viking under that *care*?" Ronan added.

Puce blotching his cheeks, Egan shifted his weight for the umpteenth time.

"Even if that were true," Fionella said, "where Viking is kept is not your decision to make. He was left with us."

Ronan folded his arms. "I know Saoirse, and I know how much she loves that horse ... she would only leave him with Fionn if there was no alternative."

Egan appeared to have swallowed his tongue, while his mother assessed Ronan like a cobra deciding whether to strike, or leave the mouse for another day.

"Well, I found an alternative," Ronan continued before she could respond.

"And where is that?" she scoffed.

"I'd rather not say."

"Now, aren't you just a ball of business."

Ronan ignored the gibe. "This is what Saoirse would want."

"If you know so much, smart arse, where is she?" Egan had exploded into life, words dripping enmity.

"Fionn!" his mother snapped. "Control yourself."

"I don't think that's his strong point," Ronan quipped.

"And you," she hissed, stabbing a blood-red nail toward Ronan's face, "keep your mouth shut."

Fionella's scrutiny was unwavering. A fleeting tremor swept Ronan.

"Did Saoirse ask you to move the horse?" she asked icily.

"No."

"Have you even spoken to her?"

"No."

"Do you know where she is?"

"No." It was an honest answer, but Ronan was now certain Saoirse was in a Dublin hospital, sitting at the side of her injured father.

"You haven't a bloody clue what she wants." Egan's voice bristled with hostility.

"Fionn!"

Ronan ignored him. "Like I said before, I know horses and I know Saoirse."

Fionella straightened her scarf. "You think you know a lot, young man? What else do you know?" Again, she raked him with an appraising stare.

"That, Fionella, is my business."

"Well, that horse is *my* business"—her voice crackled—"and I demand you return him!"

Ronan shook his head with as much bravado as he could muster.

The woman snorted. "Well then, expect a call from the garda."

"We both know that's not happening, Fionella." Ronan's confidence ignited her gaze. Something was off, and he was betting she didn't want scrutiny any more than he did. With a curt nod to her stony features, he strode from the house, ignoring them both, their glares boring into his spine like lasers.

14

———

DECEPTION

Slanting rays from the dying sun followed Ronan down the laneway toward the Sliabh Liag road. Determined not to give the woman the satisfaction of knowing she unsettled him, he maintained a steady stride, focused ahead. The venom and threat oozing from every word she uttered prickled him with unease. Even without looking, he sensed surveillance from an upper-storey window.

The evening breeze created further disarray with his hair. Combing his fingers through it, they passed over the reassuring lump of his blood rune. With its power came the constant sobering thought that whatever he said or did, could have consequences for those without the rune's protection. The liberation he'd felt at the touch of the stone dissolved.

Hunger pains interrupted Ronan's contemplation; he couldn't remember the last time he'd eaten. Once out of sight of the Egan mansion, and there were no cars in view, he blanked his mind and aimed for the takeaway at The Leaky Bucket pub.

Next moment, he set down on the blind side of a solid building on the edge of Teelin Road. There was no discomfort, but it had only been a space-flytja, a simple jump from one place to another, without any time change. While it was some consolation, it did little to ease his time-flytja misgivings.

Jiggling a handful of Darragh's coins, he entered the dining room, sunset glinting off the windows. The clock above the menu board had just gone 4:45, still too early for the evening customers. Apart from the ruddy-faced woman behind the counter, Ronan had the place to himself. The aromas of cooking drew a growl from his belly, but the prices made him baulk. While it had been a stroke of luck, rune-driven or not, to learn that

Darragh and Saoirse were in Dublin, they were still two needles in an enormous haystack. If he didn't find them fast, he ran the risk of starving.

Briefly, he contemplated using the rune to win bets, just enough to get by. But even if his conscience would let him, the rune wouldn't; Freyja had made that crystal clear, as did the poem. Should he cease to be 'true of mind and pure of heart' the magical pebble would desert him.

So, with only twenty-three euros, and scant likelihood of any more, Ronan changed his mind, deciding to dine on tinned food from the Kelly's kitchen.

As he turned to leave, an appeal on a small notice board snagged his attention. Sandwiched between one for a lost cat named Puss and an offer for washing and ironing services, it read: 'Reward, €500'. Five hundred euros! He'd be happy with fifty! With ballooning interest, he read on. The reward was for information leading to the recovery of a stack of brand-new fishing equipment. According to the note, brazen thieves had boarded *Fair Winds* in the middle of the night and made off with the recent purchases of the poor owner who was now willing to part with considerable money to get them back. An idea formed as Ronan tore a finger of paper from the bottom of the sheet. He considered the hand-written phone number before flicking it with a nail and tucking it in a pocket.

Hunger forgotten, he asked directions to the nearest public phone, and set off to see if his sketchy plan would fly. On the second attempt, he got a gruff hello.

"Ah," Ronan began, fighting his fluster, "I'm calling about your stolen fishing g—"

Belligerence exploded down the line. "Are you one of the little shites what ransacked my boat?"

Ronan winced, whipping the handset away from his ear. "No," he said, struggling to remain calm. "I'm after details so I can find out who did."

"And how are you going to do that?" The voice remained combative. "The guards haven't found any clues ... what makes you think you will?"

Ignoring the sarcasm, Ronan said, "I have the advantage of not being a guard."

"Meaning?"

"Well"—Ronan adopted his most neutral tone—"people tell me things they wouldn't tell a copper ... er ... guard."

"Yeah ... right."

Ronan stifled annoyance, ignoring the scepticism bouncing down the line. "Your notice said the reward was for information leading to the recovery of the stolen goods. If that isn't right, I won't waste your time."

"No, I suppose that's right ... but you sound like a kid, and a foreigner to boot."

"Yeah, well things aren't always as they seem."

"Whatever."

Rune-driven confidence pushed Ronan on. "I might be young, but I'm very good at what I do." What that was, he wasn't sure, but the words kept coming: "But if you're not interested ..."

"Hang on, hang on, no need to get precious."

Ronan remained silent, letting the silence grow. Finally, the man exhaled and said, "What do you need?"

"A list of what was taken and when, and where *Fair Winds* was moored."

"Do you have a pen and paper?"

The voice remained doubtful, so Ronan fibbed. "Yes, fire away." He was only interested in the when and where.

As the man recited the list, Ronan understood the size of the reward. There were nets and floats and pots and buoys, as well as a state-of-the-art fish-finder, a heap of electronic sensors and a marine laptop. Much of it was foreign to him, but must have cost many thousands.

Keeping his ignorance to himself, Ronan punctuated his listening with the occasional uh-huh or mmhmm. Even if he wasn't a sleuth, he'd better act the part. As soon as he had the time and location of the theft, Ronan asked, "And who am I speaking to?"

"Sean, Sean Hagan. And you are ...?"

Ronan froze, suddenly unsure about the whole deception, and reluctant to give his name. While he couldn't think of a good reason not to, something told him he shouldn't.

"Owen Doyle," he said, hoping the hesitation would go unnoticed. Owen was his mother's brother back in Australia; he'd never know his identity was being borrowed on the opposite side of the world.

"And what's your number, Doyle?"

It was a simple question, but it threw Ronan into a spin. "Ah ... I lost my phone earlier and, ah ... haven't got a replacement yet." The words were no sooner out, than he knew it was the wrong lie.

"Ha! Can't find your own bloody phone! What good are you?" The receiver slammed down.

I5

DOUBTS

Ronan was stung; his fib had opened a credibility gulf. Had he not been burning with irritation, he might have been amused by the thought of a detective not being able to find his own phone. As it was, he jabbed another coin into the pay-phone slot, punching in a number.

As the connection clicked through, Ronan's thoughts were moths circling the candle of reward money. It was his passport to Dublin, to Saoirse, but impatience gnawed. As well as a phone, he needed a full outfit. By the dim overhead light, his baggy britches, sloppy cardigan and scuffed Deetees trumpeted country yokel. While he might blend with the local Donegal farmers, he'd be a beacon in the Irish capital. The number began ringing.

Without knowing what lay ahead, five hundred euros mightn't be enough, but at least it would be a good start. About to chide himself for his cockiness, Ronan recognised it as rune-driven confidence. The magical stone would help him find the stolen fishing gear, he simply needed a sound strategy to harness its mysterious power.

Standing in the booth, handset cradled on his shoulder, his mind circled from the rune to Freyja, to Paidin, to Saoirse. They were all missing, but the first two had runes, and there was only one of him. Saoirse was his priority, yet Paidin, and to a lesser extent Freyja, clamoured at his conscience. Ronan's earlier certainty drained away, his previous clear-headed resolve swirling into a vortex of doubt.

As he listened to the burring coming down the line, Ronan wondered about the pain. Was it a warning, or a sign the rune's bond was weakening? He tried reassuring himself: he was worthy when the rune first bound to him, and he'd done nothing to change that since. Whatever the cause, he was going to test it; it was the quickest way to get to Saoirse.

Before he could ponder further, Caitlin answered with a hesitant, "Hello?"

"Hey, it's Ronan."

"Sorry it took me a while. I was in the shower."

"No worries. Should I call back?"

"Yeah, give me ten."

"Okay, bye." The words echoed in his ear; she was already gone.

Twilight had crept up unnoticed, greeting Ronan with chill air as he left the glass-panelled box. Beating his arms across his chest, he strode along the roadside, figuring a brisk walk round the corner and back, would warm him.

Despite the exercise, his return to the public telephone saw his shoulders hunched, hands driven deep into cardigan pockets.

To his dismay, a battered Corolla sat in the pool of light thrown by the solitary street lamp. It might have once been blue—or grey—but the caked dust and grime made it impossible to be sure. At some stage, an altercation with a solid object had punched a hole in the grill, the lopsided maker's name hanging like the final autumn leaf. The vehicle remained half on the road, as if rules didn't apply to it. Both front doors gaped, the meaty arms of a rugged man draped over the driver's side one, a glowing cigarette dangling between sausage fingers.

Even from a distance, Ronan could hear the man's companion in the phone box, staccato babbling in a foreign language. Without knowing why, he thought central Europe. Hanging back out of sight, he stamped from one foot to the other. Impatience gnawed—Caitlin was expecting his call—but the chill had sharper teeth. Emboldened by the painless space-flytjas, he blanked his mind.

Not long after the last of him was sucked into a slit in the air, he curled outward from a similar fissure, but wearing a thick green overcoat over his motley attire. It was a woman's garment, but Ronan didn't care, he pulled it tighter. He'd found it by touch in the entranceway of the Raven's Roost cottage. Not daring to use the light, he'd groped in the gloom; it was a bonus when he'd caught Saoirse's scent on it.

The smoking man straightened when Ronan strode into view.

"G'day, mate," Ronan called as he approached. "Will your friend be long?"

Unmoving, the man dribbled smoke from flattened nostrils. His face might have been shaped from clay thrown onto an oversize skull by a drunk sculptor. Either that or he had lost many fights. The street lamp threw misshapen shadows from uneven brows, crooked nose and lopsided lips.

Instantly wary, Ronan halted and added in his friendliest tone, "Just wondering when your mate will be done?" He inclined his head to where man-number-two still jabbered away, evidently getting worked up over something. "... need to make an urgent call."

Ronan's amiable manner made no impression on man-number-one, who squared enormous shoulders, dropping hefty arms from the door. "You no use," he said, hooking a thumb at the telephone. "We use many times ... long times ... much." He cracked his knuckles, then pointed a thick finger at Ronan, saying, "Go." The instruction was punctuated with a brusque hand-wave up the road in the direction Ronan had come.

While the man's English was rudimentary, his sign language was fluent. So, Ronan went. Once hidden in the shadows, he filled his mind with the phone box he remembered near the Killybegs information centre on a recent visit with Saoirse. The air split and he folded inward to nothing.

16

———

CLARITY

Caitlin answered on the second ring. "I thought you'd stood me up," she said, without even a hello. Gone was the prickly demeanour of earlier in the day, and her playful inference that the phone call was some sort of date caught Ronan off balance.

"Couldn't get a better offer," he quipped, agile tongue swinging into action.

Caitlin laughed. "I really can see why she loves you."

Her musical lilt was achingly like Saoirse's. And he definitely preferred this version of the girl to the earlier one, although, considering the crutches and gammy leg, the testiness was understandable. Without thinking, he tried his luck: "I don't suppose you'd consider telling me where she is?"

"No, I wouldn't ... but points for trying, Ronan Ryan."

Using a person's full name must be an Irish thing to do. Saoirse did it often; now Caitlin was doing it. It was strangely magnetic. "Worth a try," he said, pausing, refocusing on why he'd phoned. "Hey, do you know the High-tide Pier?"

"In Teelin?"

"I think so."

"Mmm, I think it's the concrete one where the boats end up lying in the mud at low tide."

"Okay," Ronan responded hesitantly. He recalled driving past such a spot with Darragh Kelly, but wasn't aware of its name. "Is there any way to find out for sure?"

"Isn't my word good enough for you, Ronan Ryan?" she teased.

Ronan wished she'd stick to his first name. "Of course it is," he said, "but you didn't sound positive ... it's fine if you are."

"Hang on, I'll check."

After earnest background murmuring, Caitlin returned to the line. "Dad says I'm bang on."

"Thanks, Caitlin ... appreciate it."

"What are you up to?" Suspicion edged her voice.

Ronan didn't want the delay of explaining, he just wanted to get it done. "Look, I've got to go now, but can we meet tomorrow? I'll tell you then." Which was a straight lie. There was no way he could share his plans, but he needed time to concoct a plausible tale. Thinking back on the disastrous lost-phone fib to Sean Hagan, Ronan realised he had to improve at weaving believable stories to cover his secrets.

"Okay," Caitlin said. "I'll pick you up. Where and when?"

"I'll be out and about early," Ronan said. "Would the Carrick supermarket suit?" It was the only place he could think of in a hurry. "At ten?"

"That's grand." There was nothing in her voice to suggest it was. "See you then." The connection cut.

Ronan hated the deception, but he couldn't tell Caitlin the truth. Even Saoirse had struggled with it at first, and that was after she'd heard his full story. She only accepted it after seeing him run over and disappear, then reappear unharmed minutes later. Although he'd lost his earlier misgivings about Caitlin, the fewer people who knew his secret, the better. He hadn't even told his mother.

But that was a distraction; he focused on the reward. An aching weariness seeped into his bones, but he'd sleep when he could; what he needed most was a way to discover the whereabouts of the stolen goods without time-flytjing, but nothing came to him.

With a despondent sigh, Ronan slid down the wall, ignoring the chill through the seat of his pants. His forehead sank onto his bent knees as he hugged his thighs. "Saoirse," he breathed. "Mum." He was alone, caught in the year before his birth, with no prospect of anything but a one-way ticket to 891 in less than nine days. "Freyja ... Freyja." Time was speeding up.

There was no help from his Norse grandmother, and again, Ronan found himself reciting the rune's poem in Norse *"The bearer of the living stone, in solitude is ne'er alone; the gods shall let no ill befall its keeper with eternal thrall. Its power burns if blood enfold the lightening rune, and wealth untold awaits the one who stands apart as true of mind and pure of heart."*

Annoyance bubbled through him. If, as Freyja said, his blood rune was exceedingly powerful, where was it now? Why had it deserted him? As if in response, her words echoed in his head: "… the rune has much power, but never assume it is infinite." Was that it? Was he expecting too much?

Ronan's search for answers amongst the memories of his time with Freyja proved fruitless, so he went through every time-flytja he'd done. At first, he wondered if the fiery onslaught only happened with forward time-flytjas. But it couldn't be; he'd done several forward ones with no ill effects. Could it be related to the distance or amount of time difference? If that was the case, why didn't he get it the previous time he flytjed from 891 Norway to 2004 Ireland? Nothing made sense. Then it hit him.

Of all the ones he'd done, it was only the last one that he felt might kill him, and it was the only one he'd done so soon after another. What if he needed a certain recovery time between each one? It had been over six hours since his last successful time-flytja, so if his theory was right, there should either be less pain, or none at all.

There was only one way to find out; the prospect of agony-filled helplessness had Ronan flytjing into the locked Raven's Roost cottage. He wanted all the help he could get so, lights blazing—to hell with the Egans—he searched for Saoirse's Panadol and his own motion-sickness medication.

The headache tablets were easy to find—on the bench in the kitchen; he swallowed two. The Kwells proved more elusive, and by the time he'd scoured the bathroom without success, an engine's roar penetrated the walls. Ronan tried thinking like a girl, but failed. Tyres skidded. He ducked into Saoirse's bedroom, hoping for inspiration. A door slammed. He scanned the room—nothing. A key rattled in the front door.

A pulse later, Ronan was peering from the stables as the green door closed behind Egan's bulky frame. As the minutes dragged, he imagined rising blood pressure as Egan checked in cupboards and under beds.

Ronan continued to wait after Egan left. Even though he only had a few hundred metres to drive, Ronan wanted to give him long enough to get back to the mansion, park the car, go inside, and settle into whatever he was doing earlier. When Ronan judged the time right, he flytjed back into the dark cottage.

He stepped from the air, flicking on the same lights, striding straight to Saoirse's room. The dresser's small drawers turned up nothing; uneasiness prickled him like a grass rash as he snooped beneath knickers and bras. Nothing. The main drawers, so recently tidied by Caitlin, also yielded nothing. The growl of the approaching Range Rover reverberated through the cottage walls. Ronan spun, scanning. Tyres skidded. His frantic search snagged on the cluster of childhood mementos on the dresser. A car door slammed. And there, between a beaming brown monkey and a pink pony with an impossibly long mane and tail, was the corner of a small packet. The lock rattled. Ronan grabbed the Kwells, visualised the nearby stables, and cleared his thoughts.

After finding the water tap in the dark and washing down a couple of tablets, he settled in to wait for them to take effect, enjoying the thought of Egan's futile activity. Curses and frustration echoed through the rooms before the oaf finally stormed away.

With wicked intent, Ronan flytjed back to the living room, flicking on several lights. Then, holding a vision of the High-tide Pier, he set the target to a quarter to midnight the previous night. A burgeoning flare made him give up, but it wasn't as bad as it could have been, so he tried again. And despite the fire igniting in his skull, he drifted into ró.

17

———

HEIST

The High-tide Pier began at the edge of Teelin Road where the loose gravel of the verge gave way to the concrete platform thrusting into the harbour. A lone street lamp stood sentinel, its floundering bulb little more than a jaundiced flicker, morse-coding its existence to the world. The darkness swallowed its feeble attempts to radiate more than a handful of metres.

The rune had set Ronan down behind the corner of a large stone cottage opposite the pier. Which was fortunate, for he was doubled in misery, clutching his temples, holding his head together. The fact that it wasn't the same level of searing agony as his return from Freyja's longhouse, was a sliver of hope. Even so, anxiety gripped him. If he could only do short or occasional time-flytjas, where would that leave him? But Saoirse was waiting, and he only needed one more short jump through time to bankroll the search. He could do that for her.

As the torment eased, the salty tang of the harbour assaulted Ronan; he wondered if the locals even noticed it. Across the road, a dark van sat silhouetted against the half-moon's reflection off the water. It was backed onto the pier at a strange angle, obscuring most of *Fair Winds*; only an insipid glow from the wheelhouse windows and the stubby prow were visible past the vehicle's front bumper. The modest boat rocked on its moorings, scraping against buffers of old car tyres lining the pier's edge.

Sean Hagan claimed his son, Jamie, had left *Fair Winds* at five after midnight, locked and secure. So, the theft of the gear happened sometime between then and daylight, when Sean arrived. Ronan recalled stories he'd read of armies attacking at three in the morning when sentries were at their weariest; he hoped the thieves didn't keep him waiting that long in the chill. He was also curious what Hagan junior was doing at such an hour—something quiet and below decks, otherwise the nearby residents would be irritated. Although, if late-night activity at the pier was normal, it would explain why the locals hadn't noticed anything untoward.

Ronan emptied his mind and visualised the driver's side of the van—he was there in a pain-free instant.

The van's window gave him an unimpeded view out the open cargo door, and onto the dark rear deck of the boat where a bubble of illumination erupted from below. A hatch hinged upward and a capped head emerged, then swung back, hissing, "Shut the fecking light!"

A burst of guttural cursing was followed by compliance, but the low half moon and the wheelhouse glow were enough for Ronan to see what was going on. The capped figure uncoiled from the hold with a familiar ease, confident and sure-footed in the gloom. It could only be Jamie Hagan. In each hand, he carried a sturdy black briefcase large enough to hold a laptop on steroids. Behind Hagan, a blocky frame lurched from the darkened hatch, then a lean figure, both festooned with bundles of pots and buoys. They trailed Hagan as he stepped ashore and crossed to the van.

Baffled, Ronan studied them for as long as he dared before ducking. Gentle thumps came through the van's metal skin as the three placed their loads in the vehicle, their baritone murmurs resonating in the night.

Twice more, the trio returned empty-handed to the hold; twice more, they left the boat laden with articles for the cavernous van. By that time, and much to his astonishment, Ronan knew he was watching the theft in progress. Once he saw the pots, buoys, nets and floats coming out in massive armfuls, he realised Jamie Hagan was thieving from his own father; the two briefcases must be the marine laptop and the fancy fish-finder. Ronan now understood why the guards found no leads. No vehicle but Jamie's visited the High-tide Pier that night, so there had been nothing out of the ordinary to arouse the suspicions of late-night drivers or sleepless residents. And the van's strategic positioning masked the moored vessel from passing traffic, or busy-bodies in the cottage. The perfect crime.

As the cargo door slid closed, Ronan fought the adrenaline-fuelled urge to flee. He had to stay; the reward was for 'information leading to the recovery' of the stolen goods. Knowing who took them wasn't enough; when they drove off, they could go anywhere. Ronan needed a plan, and he needed it now.

He dropped to the ground, rolling under the vehicle, holding his breath, scrambling for options. Two sets of feet waited while a third returned to the boat. Ronan caught a flash of Jamie Hagan when he opened the wheelhouse door to flick the switch. In the instant before the light died, it cut across the man's shadowed features, level with the top of the pier. Ronan could have sworn Jamie stared straight at him.

After locking the door, Hagan bounced lightly ashore. "Get in," he ordered, as he passed the front of the van.

The vehicle rocked as the three men climbed in. The engine fired and the drive-shaft started spinning, mere millimetres from Ronan's nose.

18

———

CACHE

As Ronan set down in the rear of the van's cargo bay, it lurched backward, throwing him face-first into the pile of nets.

"What you do!" The voice was thick with accent; Ronan's memory stirred.

The vehicle jerked to a halt, its rear wheels flirting with the edge of the pier. Ronan was flung backward in a jumble of nets and pots.

"Madman!" Another accented voice, different but also familiar.

"You crazy," added the first.

"I thought I saw eyes under the van when I locked up," Hagan said, scanning the bare concrete in the headlights. "Must've been a cat."

"You one crazy bastard," chuckled the second man. Hairs rose on Ronan's neck—it was Smoking Man from the Teelin phone box. Despite the proximity of the three men, Ronan appreciated the irony of the man's statement.

Hagan eased the van off the pier, working up through the gears along Teelin Road toward Carrick. His involvement put an interesting twist on things, but it was up to his father to sort that out. Once Ronan knew where they cached the stolen goods, he'd flytja away—he only needed a location for the reward. And the sooner he put distance between himself and those two foreign thugs, the better; even looking at the back of their heads shot warning tingles through him.

The vehicle had settled into a rocking and swaying gait when Smoking Man growled, "Boss want money, Jemy, when you have?"

"For Christ's sake, Vítek, I'll have it as soon as I get rid of this gear. Okay?"

"You better ... Boss not like waiting," Vítek responded.

"Just give me the bloody week."

60

"No more," Vítek warned.

A brittle silence settled; Ronan took advantage of it to concentrate on their route.

When he'd driven the road with Saoirse and Darragh, it seemed smooth, but lying on the hard metal floor at the back of the van was like riding a pogo stick. Every tiny flaw in the pavement magnified up through the wheels and suspension, jolting Ronan's bones. He kept moving position to relieve the pressure one hip or the other, timing it with the clunks and bumps of the shifting load.

They negotiated several gentle turns before slowing, the vehicle's rumble swelling and echoing as though entering a tunnel. Ronan stole a peek above the nets as they negotiated the close-pressed buildings of Carrick, turning left onto R263.

At last, the enveloping sound dissipated and the van gained speed. Soon after a sweeping right-hand bend, it braked hard, lurching the opposite way onto loose gravel and coming to a halt. A brief backwash from the headlights bathed the interior, then darkness.

"Come, Ylli," Vítek said, "we unload and go."

A dim cabin light came on and the vehicle rocked as the men alighted. Ronan pictured the drive-shaft sitting at the end of his nose, and was instantly beneath the van, back pressed onto the cold, lumpy ground. Above him, the cargo door slid open. They were plainly in an isolated spot, for while the men kept their voices low, the occasional scrape or clunk as they unloaded their haul drew no rebuke from Hagan.

As he watched the three sets of boots trudge off in bobbing torchlight, Ronan pondered why someone would steal from their own father. His mind went to Bruno Masters, the stepfather whose notebook and rune Ronan had taken. But he told himself that was different because Ronan had already been sure that neither belonged to Masters. Was Jamie Hagan also trying to right a wrong? Or was he simply a thief?

Ronan rolled from beneath the vehicle and peered through the side window. Like before, the open cargo door gave him a clear view, this time of a ramshackle shed with a low iron roof and walls of mortared stone. When the men returned for another load, their lights played across a two-storey building behind Ronan. It was lifeless, with missing windows and patches of plaster fallen from unpainted masonry. A gravelled space sprinkled with weeds separated the house from the outbuilding. If squealing children had ever used the yard as a playground, they were a dim memory.

The murmuring swelled as the men approached the van. "When you want more?" Vítek was asking.

"Not get more until pay Boss for last lot," Ylli cut in.

"He pay," Vítek said. "That right, Jemy?" There was nothing jovial about the man's sharp back-slap.

"I'm taking this to Sligo on Sunday," Hagan said, gesturing to the load. "I'll have the money then, okay?"

"Okay, friend." Vítek's second back slap was less forceful, but it still carried menace, as did his choppy accent.

"And tell the boss I need more transport work," Hagan said as they retreated with another load.

Ronan had seen and heard more than enough. As soon as the trio disappeared into the shed, he flytjed to the end of the building, ducking from sight, but the smooth slide of the cargo door drew his gaze back round the corner. Amid more murmuring and crunching gravel, Vítek and Ylli strode diagonally away. Parked beneath adjacent trees, and dappled by weak moonlight, was the same battered Toyota Corolla he'd seen at the phone box.

Hunkered in the deep gloom beside the wall, Ronan watched them climb in and drive off. He followed their unlit progress as he circled the building to an enclosed front porch. They might be out of inquisitive earshot, but the lights-out departure suggested there were other houses within sight. The car, still in darkness, turned onto the road, away from Carrick, accelerating, its shape flickering through a straggle of pine trees. Ronan let out a slow breath.

As if in response, the brakes lit up, one a beacon, the other a glow-worm. The Corolla spun and beetled back into the drive, intercepting Hagan's vehicle.

Within a blink, Ronan was crouched beneath the van's passenger door, palms pressed against its cold skin.

"Ylli see someone in shadows," Vítek murmured.

"Where?" Hagan asked.

"Near porch," Ylli said with the eagerness of a hunting dog.

Ronan cursed his carelessness.

"You sure?"

"No, but you want risk?" Ylli snapped.

"Okay," Hagan said, "best check. You two split up, circle the house ... I'll keep a lookout.

Crouching, Ronan considered his options. He should leave, but he didn't have a location to give to Hagan's father, so he'd let them conduct their search before working out where he was. The van was still swaying from Jamie's exit when Ronan set down inside it.

The men tramped off, but soon returned. "That was a waste of time," Hagan grumbled.

"But weeds crushed where Ylli see person," Vítek said.

"What did they do, sprout wings?"

Muttering drifted in the night.

The van rocked again and Ronan flytjed to the other side of the house.

From there, he watched the blacked-out car trundle up the road. It was almost out of sight when the lights flicked on and it sped away. As it did, the van idled off in the opposite direction, back toward Carrick.

Ronan eased through the yard, heading for the driveway. A faint pebble click reached him, lifting neck hairs. Hugging the wall, he edged backward round the corner, away from the sound. Too late, he registered an air current. A rock-hard fist smashed into the side of his head. Darkness engulfed him.

19

———

TAKEN

Misery consumed Ronan; vicious throbbing hammered through his skull. He wanted to check that it was in one piece, but he couldn't move. And no matter how wide he stretched his eyes, the world remained dark.

He remembered the three men, the derelict house, the car and van leaving. Then nothing.

As his head cleared, panic swamped him. His hands were numb, face taut. He couldn't move his limbs. For a heartbeat he feared paralysis, but his frenzied thrashing said otherwise. Breathing deep, he embraced the rune's radiating calm, assessing the situation as his pulse steadied. A broad strip of tape made his lips feel paralysed; his wrists were trussed behind his back; and his legs would only move like a butterfly swimmer. The floor against his cheek wasn't cold enough for concrete or stone, and a pungent odour bit at his nostrils. The door swung open before he could identify it; a light flicked on. Ronan feigned unconsciousness.

The burst of brightness needled his lids; he struggled to still them. A rough boot nudged his ribs, and Vítek said, "You always hit too hard."

"No matter, we get rid of him," Ylli replied, as if talking about discarding rubbish.

Ronan goose bumped before rune warmth stilled an involuntary shudder. While it was comforting that the rune would heim him from mortal danger, the prospect of the searing torment from a return flytja almost had him twitching.

"Maybe," said Vítek, "but Boss wants to question ... see what he knows."

"When Boss come?"

"Later, so no hurt. Come, Ylli, leave boy alone."

64

Not daring to crack an eyelid, Ronan imagined Vítek shepherding Ylli away. The door clunked shut, muting the latter's mumbled protest.

As he listened to the fading footsteps, he tried to recall a sharp edge at the derelict house, something on which to cut his bonds, a target to flytja to. He had to get back there so he could identify its location and claim the reward money. But the panicked urge to get far from Ylli's menace clouded his mind.

Ronan was appealing to his rune when the door breathed open. He froze. Hinges whispered closed; the light flicked on. Amid popping knee joints, Ronan sensed someone squatting beside him. Then a sourness washed over him—stale sweat and something else. With apprehension cloying his lungs, he embraced his rune, beseeching it to still his twitching lids and calm his pulse. Warmth flowed from the stone as cold steel pricked his cheek. Consuming tranquillity quelled the urge to recoil.

Ylli's familiar voice breathed garlic over Ronan and turned his blood to ice. "Wake up little rabbit ... I want sport."

The breath and knife retreated; the bonds parted, sliced by a blade so sharp that it met no resistance. Ylli had a knife and wanted sport. Terror stirred, but Ronan continued to fake unconsciousness, surrendering to the rune.

Ylli rolled him onto his back, slapping his face, saying, "Wake up rabbit. I not hit so hard."

Ronan moaned past the tape across his mouth.

"This is good rabbit." A fresh wave of garlic surged.

Through slitted lids, Ronan saw Ylli rise, straddling him. He rolled his eyes backward.

Ylli toed him in the ribs. "Wake up, rabbit. I want to see you scuttle ... see fear ... smell it on you." He leant down, sitting the knife point on Ronan's cheek, letting the weight of the weapon break the skin.

Ronan didn't flinch; he was as one with his rune. A red bead appeared round the blade, swelling into a warm trickle. He ignored it, allowing his lids to flicker.

"Wake up," Ylli hissed, clearly running out of patience.

Ronan groaned, making small movements with his limbs. Ylli straightened, one foot either side of his victim. Ronan needed him further away; he worked his arms.

Anticipation blossoming, Ylli eased backward. As he did, Ronan kicked up with everything he had, sinking his foot into the other's groin. The knife clattered to the floor. Ylli clutched his crotch with both hands, grunting as his knees sagged. Ronan erupted off the floor, driving a karate punch into the man's ribs, following it with a rigid hand strike to the base of the neck.

None of the moves were elegant or smooth, but they put Ylli on the floor against a steel-framed bed. Yet he was already rising, shaking off the effects. Ronan rushed him like a Norse warrior, delivering a ferocious kick to the head. Ylli toppled.

The reverberating thud of Ylli hitting the floor must have alerted Vítek, for a chair scraped deep in the house and urgent footsteps echoed. Ronan stood, chest heaving, attention glued on a chain lying beside Ylli's still form. It was anchored to the metal bed frame, and ended in a single gaping manacle. As its meaning sank in, it triggered the identity of the biting smell: urine, mixed with excrement, sweat, blood and bile, the stench of fear and hopelessness. Ronan chilled.

"You better not be hurting boy," Vítek called as he neared.

The rumbled threat broke Ronan's trance.

"Ylli, you bastard, get out of there," Vítek growled through the door.

Although adrenaline still coursed through Ronan's veins, a Freyja-like calmness settled over him. With grim satisfaction he snapped the manacle round Ylli's wrist. The latch clicked; the door swung inward. He visualised the derelict house, and folded away.

Striding from the air, Ronan headed down the driveway, ripping the tap from his mouth as he went, grimacing, checking his lips were still attached. By the time his feet found the paved road surface, he was satisfied his face was unscarred.

As he picked up the pace and trotted toward Carrick, he counted the strides, seeking a feature he'd recognise later. But the gloom hid the landscape, and the few houses he passed looked the same. His count had almost reached three hundred when he drew abreast a driveway on the left. It was bracketed by twin horse jumps.

Stopped in the centre of the empty road, Ronan thought of Egan and Duke; he would remember this entrance, and that was all he needed. Filling his head with the target of sixteen hours later, he banished all other thoughts; fire blossomed. With gritted teeth, he refocused, clamping down on the pain, folding into its embrace.

20

———

SUNDAY DRIVE

Visions of Saoirse filled Ronan's sleep. Her scent was his last memory before exhaustion overcame flytja torment. Snippets of her, hair flowing, eyes aglow, swirled through his slumber: astride Viking; lifting him, clothes soaked, from the floor of the shower; turning her back when he'd insulted her old mobile phone; her feather fingertips tracing the arrow-wound in his chest; lying in his arms on the couch, apple-scented hair tickling his nostrils; sending a message via Caitlin that if he cared for her, he wouldn't try to find her.

Then there was the weight of manacles round his wrists and ankles, the rattle of chain with every movement, and the stink of fear. Each time the door to the darkened room opened, light fell across the sinuous Ylli. The cruel features and dead gaze turned Ronan's bowels to water.

In the Saoirse dream, he never received her coded message; he thought he might die, collapse in a heap and shrivel to nothing. In contrast, the imprisonment nightmare was an arctic warning. The competing illusions looped throughout the night until daylight ruptured the dreams. He lay there, washed out, woolly headed and unrested, but feeling closer to understanding the flytja fire.

The return flytja in the wee hours had been far worse than the outward one, even though there was about a four-hour gap between the two. He clung to the hope that all he needed was a longer recovery time before attempting another.

And because he'd suspected a worse reaction, he'd aimed for behind the stables. Just as well, for the agony had him vomiting into the grass within moments of tumbling from the air. When he'd eventually jumped to Saoirse's bedroom, he'd been too pain-wracked and fearful of showing a light to raid the kitchen, so he took his hollow stomach to bed. Now, with sunlight clamouring at the curtains, he wondered whether his belly button might have become stuck to his backbone during the night. He was as tucked up as a starving greyhound.

Head fog clearing, he reluctantly rolled from the warm sheets, taking Saoirse's lingering fragrance with him. He'd slept fully clothed, and her scent had permeated the fabric, for it was still with him when he entered the kitchen. It set his heart aching and his arms longing, concentrating his focus on reward money, clothes, phone and Dublin.

While his misadventures with the foreign thugs were still very much in his mind, Ronan's thoughts of food dragged him toward the cupboard. The angle of the light streaming through the window suggested about six, but the clock told him it was after nine. When he'd left home a couple of days ago, the sun was up by five, but with the sudden change from Queensland to Donegal, his in-built clock was in turmoil. He'd cope.

After polishing off a main course of baked beans, and dessert of tinned peaches, Ronan was ready to tackle the day. He palmed away all evidence of his presence from Saoirse's bed and took a quick shower, forgetting about not leaving telltale signs. As he slipped back into Darragh's clothes, he remembered and, frowning with irritation, hurriedly wiped down every surface with his damp towel—he didn't want to be late for Caitlin. From their brief phone conversation, he feared she was already prickly with him.

With the damp towel buried in the laundry hamper, Ronan gathered the breakfast empties, and flytjed to Carrick, stepping from a rent in the air behind the Post Office. The street was empty, but as he approached the supermarket, Caitlin's beige Mini burbled into sight. It crossed to the wrong side of the thoroughfare, pulling into the kerb beside him, facing potential oncoming traffic. The Sunday cars parked in either direction on both sides of the street reminded Ronan of his hometown, Killarney, where the pace was slow and road rules equally flexible.

Caitlin dropped the window, glancing at the cans, an eyebrow almost disappearing under a plaid cap. Ronan ignored the silent question, dropped to his haunches beside the door and said, "Any word from Saoirse?"

"We spoke briefly last night, and she said her dad was comfortable, whatever that means."

"How was *she*?"

"Said she was grand, and not to worry"—Caitlin paused—"but she sounded tired."

The urge to find Saoirse made Ronan want to jump in and tell Caitlin to drive out past the sweeping bend so he could confirm the location of the dilapidated house. "I wish there was something we could do," he said.

Caitlin threw a sharp look. "Well, there isn't."

"Yeah, I know." Ronan drooped his shoulders. "Did you get anywhere with the coded message?"

"No," she said, visibly frustrated. "I can't make any sense of it."

Ronan faked disappointment. "Morning, by the way," he said, rising to drop the cans in a nearby rubbish bin.

Caitlin said nothing. As he returned to the driver's door, her eyebrow shot up again, her gaze flicking to the bin.

"Just cleaning up," Ronan said.

She eyed him askance. "I didn't pick you for a housekeeper."

"I'm full of surprises."

Caitlin ignored his smirk, reaching out, pushing his chin to one side. "What did you do to your face?"

"Accident with a knife," Ronan said, touching the broken skin.

"Eejit."

"You don't miss much, do you?"

"Doesn't pay to round you."

Ronan huffed with affected offence. Her dour and combative mood of the previous day was gone, as was the constant discomfort etched into her features and body language. Whether from rest, medication, or both, Ronan wished her more of it; he couldn't imagine losing the use of a leg and being in constant misery. Norse anger stirred. The brute who attacked Caitlin deserved retribution.

"Fancy a drive?" Caitlin asked, interrupting Ronan's dark thoughts.

"Sounds good," he said, embracing the good-mood Caitlin—it was next best to being with Saoirse. Guilt needled him like wind-blown sand. Saoirse was waiting for him, and he was taking a Sunday drive with Caitlin. He kept telling himself the drive was critical. Once he'd located the deserted house and passed the information to Sean Hagan, the reward was his, but he couldn't expect the money before tomorrow; then there'd be no holding him back. He swallowed impatience.

"Okay." He circled to the passenger door. "Let's go."

21

———

EEJIT

The passenger seat of the Mini was so close to the ground, Ronan thought his butt might scrape the road.

"Which way?" Caitlin said, flicking on the indicator, pulling the transmission into drive. Her left foot pressed the brake pedal, her right sitting useless on the empty floor. The accelerator had been moved to where the clutch would be in a manual version of the car.

"Straight ahead is as good as any," Ronan said, gesturing indifference, delighted they were facing the direction of the derelict building from last night's 'last night'. He almost snorted at the contorted logic.

"Okay then." Caitlin checked for traffic before easing away from the kerb, across the oncoming lane and onto the left-hand side of the street. "Let's see where this leads."

Ronan watched her practised left foot in action as the houses began sliding past. "Who changed your pedal?"

She stiffened. "Dad."

"He did a good job," Ronan said neutrally, admiring the workmanship and stealing a peek at the odometer.

She nodded but remained silent, focused on negotiating a snarl of pedestrians disgorging from an old stone church, square bell tower connecting it to the heavens.

With the throng of worshippers behind them, and Sliabh Liag looming large in front, they trundled past a road sign with 'Málain Bhig 15km'.

"Mum's family comes from Málain Bhig," Ronan said.

Caitlin shot him a probing look. "Where did you learn to say it like that?"

"Like what?"

"You just said Malin Beg in Irish."

Bloody hell, have to be more careful. There's no way he could tell Caitlin about his blood rune and how it gave him the native tongue of wherever he was. "Oh ... Mum," he said. "She studied at University College Dublin ... worked as an archaeologist in Ireland for a while. And her family came from round there ... long time ago."

"You *are* full of surprises, Ronan Ryan," Caitlin murmured.

The Mini gathered pace past an eighty-kilometres-per-hour sign marking the beginning of farmland. They overtook a flock of sheep nibbling through a field of luxuriant pasture, and entered a sweeping right-hand bend. If Ronan's memory of his bouncing journey in the rear of the van, and his subsequent reconnaissance, was accurate, they should be close to a pair of horse jumps on the right. He almost missed them; they weren't much like jumps in daylight. There was one either side of a driveway, each comprising two horizontal rails set between pillars in a stone wall.

"Interesting entrance," Ronan said as they passed.

"Looks like jumps," Caitlin replied, after a lightning glance.

"Mmm." Ronan swallowed the irony as he scrambled for a reason to stop in three hundred metres.

Before he could think of one, he spied the house. Penetrating daylight stripped away the flattering shadows of night, leaving only the harsh reality of abandonment and broken dreams. Their current angle offered a fleeting glimpse through a grove of ash, limbs bared by approaching winter. "Hey, cool," he said, enthusiasm only half forced. "Can we stop, Caitlin? Please?"

"What for?" She kept driving. The house disappeared as they came abreast of a tangle of conifers.

"Please?"

Caitlin sighed and pulled into a convenient lay-by. "What's your problem?" Her voice straddled the boundary between light-hearted and annoyed.

"Can we take a closer look at that house we just passed?" As he spoke, he read the odometer: one-point-four kilometres from the supermarket.

"We can't sticky beak at people's houses."

"No, this one's abandoned ... looks really cool," he insisted, hooking his thumb over his left shoulder.

"Oh, that one. Why? It's an old dump."

"Precisely." Ronan twisted in his seat, peering back with genuine interest. "My mum loves them ... says they all have stories to tell," he said truthfully. "Can we go back?"

Caitlin considered him with pursed lips before checking the rear-vision mirror, hitting the indicator, and swinging the little car in a tight U-turn.

"Looks spooky," she said, pulling into the weed-fringed driveway, stopping short of a gravelled area between house and shed. "It doesn't look like anyone's lived here for years."

"But someone has been in here recently," Ronan said, pointing to where Vítek's tyres had crushed the grass.

"Are you sure you're not a detective?"

"I'm thinking about it," he responded, only half-joking. Then he explained: "When you live in the bush, you have to read the land ... you notice crushed grass, broken twigs, strange tracks." He waved his hand at the tyre prints. "Things that are out-of-place catch your eye. It's how you know what's going on round you."

Caitlin regarded him, sidelong. "You're very practical, aren't you?"

Ronan took it as a compliment, enjoying a pleasant glow.

The building was even more forlorn up close: window frames askew, absent shingles exposing the bones of the roof, and missing chunks of drab render showing angry welts of underlying red brick. Weeds clamoured about the stoop, held at bay by the demoralised sadness and pining for when the house had glowed with the pride and love of a lost family.

"Coming?" he said, uncoiling from the car.

Whether it was because he wasn't giving her special treatment, or she was truly interested, Caitlin sprang to life. "You don't think you're going to have all the fun, do you?" Grabbing the crutches, she threw her useless leg out the door. "Race you!"

Ronan grinned. "I can see why you and Saoirse get on so well. Mum would call you kindred spirits."

"Where's your mum today?"

"She's gone up to Portnoo," Ronan said, averting his lying eyes, "... meeting up with more friends.

"Why didn't you go with her?" Caitlin crutched beside him, past the corner of the house and into the gravelled space at the rear.

"And miss your company?" Ronan's expression was overdone disbelief.

Caitlin gave him a dose of side-eye. "I'm serious."

"Yeah, I know," he conceded. The web of his fibs would get him into trouble eventually, but as Grandpa Paddy used to say, a secret shared is a secret no more. Even if he wanted to tell her, she wouldn't believe him. It had taken a lot for Saoirse to accept the truth. "But they talk about boring stuff all the time," he added.

"You might learn something." Caitlin's glance held a teasing twinkle.

"More than likely," he said, enjoying the banter. Ignoring the shed with its gleaming padlock, he threw all his attention at the house. "Hey, cool … look at this."

"I'll wait out here," Caitlin said, turning her attention to the outbuilding.

Ronan stepped over the threshold, pushing past the lop-sided door. At his touch, it parted company with the frame, toppling with a clatter and billowing dust. Ronan emerged from the enveloping cloud, fanning at his face and hacking with great exaggeration.

"How did that go for you?" Caitlin asked dryly.

Ronan coughed past a layer of dust. "Yeah … good."

Caitlin chuckled. "You look like you've been slathered with pancake foundation."

"Huh?"

"Never mind." She sobered, pointing to the new padlock. "Someone's using this shed."

"Yeah, looks like it." Even as Ronan feigned disinterest, an idea came to him. "I'm going back inside"—he was already turning—"I'll never get another chance for a good look."

"Don't be daft," Caitlin admonished, voice lifting. "Something else might collapse on you."

"I'll be extra careful." He stepped across the fallen door, calling over his shoulder, "Don't go anywhere."

"You're an eejit," she called after him.

22

———

MALIN BEG

Ronan picked his way to the second floor, testing each stair tread for strength before transferring his weight. He found himself on a landing separating a large bedroom on one side from two smaller ones on the other. The floorboards appeared sound enough, although occasional squeaks of protest sharpened his caution. Dust thick enough to grow vegetables coated everything, and the remnants of furniture were splintered and scattered—vandals had been busy.

All the windows were empty frames; two of the three doors had holes kicked in the lower panels. Many of the spindles were smashed from the balustrade round the stairwell, with nothing but the intact top rail to stop a plunge to the floor below.

Finding himself in a small, rear-facing bedroom, Ronan leant from the window, sending a low whistle Caitlin's way. She spun on her crutches, flipping a hand in a casual wave.

"Come on, Ronan." Her words were woven with disinterest, verging on impatience.

"Won't be a minute," he called back.

"Good. I want to show you something, and we haven't all day." She swung toward the Mini.

"Okay ... be right down." Ronan withdrew to the depths of the room, and cleared his mind.

"The sun doesn't hang about for curious Aussies, you know," she said, but he was gone.

Next moment, he bundled into the Teelin phone box. "Sean, it's Owen Doyle," Ronan said when the man answered. Before Hagan could respond, Ronan continued, "One-point-four kilometres west of the Carrick supermarket on R263, there's a derelict, two-storey house tucked in behind some pine trees on the left. Your stuff's in a locked shed behind the house."

This time, Ronan waited for a response, but there was none. "Hello? Sean? Are you there?"

There was no 'thanks' or 'good work', only a brusque grunt and, "How do I know you're right?"

Ronan exhaled. "You won't pay me otherwise, will you?"

There was silence at the other end. Hagan should be pleased; maybe he didn't get excited over anything.

"Look," Ronan continued, on the verge of exasperation. "Take the guards out there, but do it before they can move the stuff. I'll call you later to organise my five hundred euros."

Ronan was folding away as he rang off, and was soon peering down from the window of the dusty bedroom; Caitlin was reaching for the Mini's door handle.

Bloody cool. The thrill from his two silken, rapid-fire flytjas had him light-headed on rune power. He floated down the stairs, catching himself, taking a deep breath, composing his features and stepping into the sunlight.

"Took you long enough," Caitlin said, her smirk transitioning into a penetrating gaze. "What did you find up there? You're looking very satisfied with yourself."

"Lots of dust," he said, walking toward the Mini, "and someone's broken dreams."

"Ach, you have an Irish way with words, Ronan Ryan."

He put on his best Grandpa Paddy voice. "Ah, 'tis me Irish heritage, so."

Caitlin chortled. "That's a horrid accent."

Ronan made a face, disappointed. Thanks to his rune, he was now fluent in Norse and, as he'd discovered earlier, Irish, but his native English must still carry the Aussie accent. He'd have to ask Saoirse if he spoke Irish with an accent as well. The thought of her set up a renewed internal tug-of-war. *Patience.*

"Ronan?"

"Huh?"

"I said, are you getting in, or are you going to stand there all day with that vacant look?" She followed her crutches into the Mini as she spoke.

"Um ... sorry," Ronan said, lowering his backside onto the seat. "Where are we going?"

Caitlin ignored his question. "She doesn't want your help, Ronan."

Although she eased the words toward him, they needled. And not because they were true; Saoirse's coded message told him they weren't. Not for the first time, he wished he could find a strategy that didn't need money, or time-flytjas. *Stick with the plan.*

"But she needs it," he said without thinking.

"Ronan, stop!" Caitlin's eyes bored into him. "Promise me you won't try to find her."

He was about to say he couldn't do that, but knew he had to fib again. "Okay," he said.

Caitlin gathered herself as if to speak, but relaxed, turning the ignition instead, guiding the ground-hugging Mini back onto the road toward Malin Beg.

As fences, farms and signposts slid past, Ronan struggled with his conscience, longing to be rid of deception. Caitlin hunched forward, gripping the wheel in concentration as she navigated the sinuous ribbon of bitumen, at one stage having to leave it to make room for a battered farm vehicle carrying several bemused sheep.

The road led them over a rise into a shallow valley, the far end framing a distant wedge of North Atlantic. A straggle of conifers beside the road hunched inland, as if expecting a gale-force assault from the ocean. The razor-slash horizon was all that separated ocean and sky, both grey and bleak, and stretching forever.

As they swung onto the coast, the character of the ocean came into focus. The pewter surface heaved and boiled over fringing rocks and reefs before smashing against the stoic Donegal shoreline. Along the cliff-tops, scattered sheep grazed, oblivious to the herculean battle raging below.

The pitching waves and the car's continuous changes of direction stoked Ronan's bubbling motion sickness. Before it could blossom, an unassuming village opened its welcoming arms to save him. There seemed to be as many tractors as cars scattered among the cluster of houses; Ronan wondered what they farmed. While green tinged the surrounding landscape, it was harsh and windswept. He shivered.

At his insistence, Caitlin pulled into the park of a small shop—he needed something to settle his stomach.

"Do you want anything?" Ronan said, unwinding from the seat.

Her fingers stretched toward the radio. "No thanks."

While reluctant to spend his meagre euros, Ronan was confident he'd soon have another five hundred, so he bought two lots of sandwiches, bottled water, and ginger beer.

As he handed coins to the cheery-faced lady behind the counter, he asked for the nearest toilet.

She hooked her head to the rear of the building. "Out the back and to the right. Mind you close the door, now ... the sheep think it's a water trough." The woman smiled, either at the animals, or her own wit.

Ronan nodded, gesturing to his purchases. "Can I leave these here for a minute?"

"Of course, lad."

The sweet zingy tang of the soft drink was calling but Ronan had an urgent job. Once inside the toilet, he locked the door, blanked his mind and folded inward to nothing.

23

SHAFTS OF FIRE

The empty air delivered Ronan into the rear bedroom of the deserted house. He tried dismissing the prickling in his head as imagination; it was only a space-flytja, after all.

While it hadn't been necessary, he wanted to be there when Sean Hagan arrived with the guards. It was what Grandpa Paddy would have called dotting *T*s and crossing *I*s, always saying it back-to-front to goad Ronan into correcting him. He'd then chuckle and say, "And so it is, lad ... so it is." A pang of grief hit Ronan, and he wondered how long it took to get over losing someone you loved.

As the minutes dragged by, Ronan began fidgeting. Each tick of the clock took him further from when he'd left Caitlin at the store. He contemplated jumping forward in ten-minute intervals until Hagan arrived, but how many would it take? And he still needed to time-flytja back to Caitlin so there was no time gap to raise suspicions. Even though it had been more than ten hours since his last time-flytja, the tingling residue of the space-flytja's warning was undeniable. He decided to wait.

Just when Ronan had convinced himself that Hagan wasn't coming, a purring engine rolled into the yard, gravel scrunching beneath rubber tyres. It was the same van Jamie drove two nights ago; they obviously shared its use. To Ronan's astonishment, it was also the same driver. A middle-aged version of Jamie, but carrying a generous paunch, alighted from the passenger side. Sean turned a sour glare to his son in response to a mumbled remark Ronan didn't catch.

After the initial shock of Jamie's presence subsided, Ronan realised that of course Sean, not aware of his son's actions, would bring him to help recover the stolen gear.

Perhaps Jamie's shame caused the simmering tension between them. But none of that explained the absence of the guards.

Sean mumbled at Jamie's back as the latter released the padlock and opened the shed door. Something niggled at Ronan's thoughts, but before he identified it, Jamie spun on his father and snarled, "For god's sake, Dad, I didn't tell anyone. The only way he found out is from Vítek or that psycho Albanian ... my money's on Ylli."

"They wouldn't," Sean said. "The boss would have their guts."

Ronan's jaw sagged. That was it! The key! The only reason Jamie would allow his father to know he had the key to the padlock, was that it didn't matter. Sean was in on the whole thing! That's why there were no guards!

The exchange between the two men became inaudible when they entered the shed, but he'd ceased listening, his mind whirring through the possibilities of what they were up to. Irritated, he stopped and took a breath. While it wasn't his mystery to solve, he now understood that the only way he might ever get the reward was to have leverage.

Hugging the shadows, straining to pull quiet words from midday air, Ronan plotted. If Hagan refused to pay, Ronan would take the information straight to the guards. But that's where his planning lurched to a halt. If he reported them, he'd get entangled in awkward garda questions. He was in the country without parents, passport, or any record of entry. Definitely no guards.

As the Hagans worked, Ronan caught snatches of their tetchy conversation. Apparently, Jamie had already sold the gear for nine hundred euros to someone in Sligo, but given the breach of security, he was delivering it immediately. Meanwhile, Sean would talk to the boss about Ylli, finalise the insurance payout for the gear, and deal with Sherlock Holmes, who Ronan assumed was himself. He didn't much care for the prospect.

While mulling it all over, he kept returning to the payout Sean mentioned. What a cosy deal to steal and sell your own stuff, then claim insurance for replacements. And the reward made sense, showed Sean was serious about finding the thieves, and diverted suspicion. With that thought, Ronan's confidence of getting the money lifted; Sean Hagan wouldn't want the truth to get out. Yet there was still a gulf between offering a reward and actually paying it.

Regardless, Ronan decided to drop a rock into the Hagan puddle of wrongdoing before returning to Caitlin.

With mischievous intent, he threw pieces of broken furniture about, hurling some through the open window, clattering onto the ground beside the van. He chuckled to himself as they rushed into the house from front and back: they'd find it empty with boot-prints everywhere.

As lumbering footsteps climbed toward him, Ronan flung a dresser drawer out the door to splinter across the landing at the top of the stairs, and visualised the locked toilet at Malin Beg. The air sucked him away with shafts of fire scorching his brain.

24

SILVER STRAND

Caitlin and her Mini were where Ronan had left them. While he wanted to wait in the toilet until his head eased, any delay would raise questions, so he staggered through the shop collecting his purchases on the way. "Are you alright, lad?" the shopkeeper said when she caught sight of his ashen face.

"Headache," Ronan replied. "Be right in a minute."

He took a slug of the ginger beer, hoping it might help. It generated a hearty belch but little else. He was about to take another gulp when he noticed Caitlin's fingers drumming on the steering wheel. Her impatience puzzled him—the frosted drink in his hand told him he'd only been minutes. When he opened the door, Saoirse flooded through him with the tinkling piano and breathy tones of Britney Spears: *"And every time I see you in my dreams I see your face, you're haunting me ..."* For a pulse, it was Saoirse sitting behind the wheel. Ronan's heart lurched.

"That was quick," Caitlin said, clicking off the song, halting Ronan's daydream.

On the back of a micro-pause he quipped, "I don't muck round." He thought of what he'd done while she listened to half a song, and had to stifle a rising urge to confide. As he climbed in, he hoped she wasn't as sharp-eyed as the shop lady. It was too much to ask for.

Caitlin frowned. "Are you okay?"

"Just a touch of motion sickness," he lied, fidgeting under her scrutiny. Holding up the soft drink, he added, "This'll fix it."

"Mmm."

Ronan took a long swallow, smothered a burp, and said, "Now, what did you want to show me?"

"I thought you must have forgotten," she said, accepting the offered water. "Thanks."

"I don't forget, especially when someone cuts into my exploration time," Ronan said, referring to the deserted house.

Caitlin rolled her eyes. "Ach, we know that's not true."

"What do you mean?" The inferno in his head had calmed to a hammering throb at the back of his eyeballs.

"'I need your help, Caitlin.'" Her voice dripped mockery. "'Where's the High-tide Pier, Caitlin?', 'I'm sorry, I'm too busy to tell you what I'm up to, I have to go ... I'll tell you tomorrow' ..."

Ronan wasn't sure what was worse, the derision, side-eye or snort. "I forgo..." He stopped, defeated, laughing at the corner she'd painted him into or, rather, he'd done the painting, Caitlin merely handed him the brush. And she did it with such ease.

Raising his hands in surrender, Ronan said, "Okay, I'll tell you over lunch." He held up each sandwich packet in turn. "Corned beef and cheese, or tuna salad?"

"Half of each?" Caitlin suggested, but declined the offered packet. "In a minute." She fired up the car, engaging the transmission, pulling onto the street.

As they idled along between houses and barns, fences and walls, Ronan wondered what in this remote tractor town was special. In his urgency to observe Sean Hagan's arrival at the derelict house, he'd forgotten they were in the ancestral village of his mother's family. He should have asked the lady at the shop if there were any Doyles still in the area. The surrounds changed in a blink, becoming softer, less daunting.

Ronan's reverie was interrupted by their arrival in a sprawling car park. Caitlin nosed the Mini against the safety rail, killing the engine, sitting back with a contented sigh. They were perched near a cliff edge, high above a perfect crescent of sand marred only by an occasional, ant-like human figure. It was as if a gargantuan celestial stallion had left its first hoof-print on a new world in the soft Donegal coastline.

"Wow," Ronan breathed, marvelling at the symmetry and elegance of nature. The sand wasn't nearly as white as a Queensland beach, but the encircling cliff-tops carried far greener grass than he'd ever seen at home. And the usual shaggy, black-faced sheep grazed contented, unaware.

"Silver Strand," Caitlin said with unbridled pride. "Come on," she added, flinging her door open, "there's benches across the way ... let's eat there."

The fragrance of fresh grass with sharp undertones of sheep pee invaded the Mini on a surge of salt-laden air. Uncoiling into the car park, Ronan lifted his collar. While the cool overcast had daunted most potential beach-goers, there were still half a dozen cars scattered across the asphalt.

'Across the way' turned out to be about fifty metres along a narrow concrete path bordered by a handrail, and swept by a blast fresh from the north pole.

The empty benches should have told them something, but they ignored it. Ronan dropped the sandwich packs on a table, and he and Caitlin sat, side-by-side, pondering the beach far below, shoulders hunched, wind needling their skin.

"It's a great spot," Ronan said, "but why would anyone go to the beach on a day like this?"

"Toughen up, Aussie."

Ronan stared down at the shapes on the sand, realising it was sheltered from the gusts, but still too cold for him. Admitting defeat, he said, "Which one first? Corned beef or tuna?"

"I don't care."

"Choose," Ronan growled.

She chuckled at his attempted severity. "Why don't you pick?"

"I paid, you pick," Ronan insisted.

"Fine"—she pulled the bottle of water from her pocket—"corned beef."

"There, was that so hard?" He took another swig of ginger beer.

Ignoring the gibe, Caitlin said, "Is it working?"

As he went to respond, an enormous bubble of gas erupted from his stomach, echoing through his mouth. He clamped his lips, the instant back-pressure sending bubbles fizzing upward, bursting from his nostrils. He sniffed in panic. Caitlin threw back her head, shrieking with delight.

Heat lifted through Ronan's neck as his fingers scrabbled for a handkerchief in Darragh's pockets.

Caitlin chortled at his fruitless quest. She managed enough control to drop car keys into his hand and say, "Tissues in the glove box."

When Ronan returned, nose dry, cheeks cool and head settled, Caitlin was already on her share of the tuna sandwich. "Looks like I've got some catching up to do," he said, taking a large bite of corned beef and cheese, swallowing his disappointment that it was tined meat, not fresh.

She gave him two mouthfuls of peace before reminding him, "Don't you have something to tell me?"

Now that the time had come, Ronan was unsure how best to say it.

"Oh, for pity's sake," she snapped, "spit it out!"

25

PROVE IT

Ronan squirmed at the prospect of weaving still more fibs and fabrications into his relationship with Caitlin. He wanted to tell her everything, get it all out and be damned with the consequences. Despite his earlier doubts, he was now as sure as he was of anything, that she wasn't involved in Saoirse's predicament, but how could he tell her about his blood rune? Yet without telling her, his alternative explanations must be half-truths wrapped in deception.

"What have you been up to, Ronan Ryan?" Caitlin asked with a penetrating gaze. Accusation flared. "Have you been looking for Saoirse?"

"Not yet," Ronan said, hoping his turmoil wasn't showing.

Caitlin's features tightened. "Saoirse has begged you to leave her alone, and so have I. You promised me you wouldn't!"

"I haven't looked for her," Ronan retorted.

"But you're going to, aren't you?"

"Let me explain ... please."

"I think I already know enough," she shot back.

"Caitlin ..." Ronan heard his own desperation.

She glared. "Is anything about you honest?"

"Caitlin." He leant closer; she retreated. "Caitlin," Ronan growled, "does Saoirse trust me?"

"I don't know why," she said with a gust of arctic.

"Because she's a good judge ... you know it." Ronan wanted to give her hand a reassuring squeeze, but the invisible barricade she'd thrown up may as well have been a brick wall. He swallowed frustration. "We both know something funny is going on and it's related to Darragh's accid—"

"How do you know about that?" Caitlin's shoulders sagged. "How can you possibly know that?"

"I'm a detective," he said wryly.

Caitlin stared across the Atlantic, ignoring him.

"Hey"—Ronan leant into her line of vision—"I need you to trust me ... like Saoirse does."

"But she asked you not to look for her," she moaned, resistance drained.

Despite her angst, Ronan was unable to stop. "At first, yes, but then she changed her mind and sent that coded message."

"The hedgehog?" She eyed him. "But you said you didn't know what it meant." There was no accusation, only resignation.

"I lied ... I'm sorry ... but I don't want to lie to you again."

"Why?"

"Because I was floundering ..." Ronan paused, searching for less dramatic words, they eluded him. "... and that first message from Saoirse broke my heart ... I couldn't think straight." The quaver in his voice appeared to melt Caitlin's barriers. She gave his forearm a brief squeeze. Connected through Saoirse, they sat in silence, staring down at the dull water, half-eaten sandwiches forgotten; contented visitors passed unseen, huffing and puffing up the last few steps from the distant sand.

Ronan swallowed. "The other reason I didn't let on was that I hadn't thought everything through."

"Meaning?"

Instead of answering, Ronan fired back his own question. "Why do you suppose Saoirse sent the coded message?"

"Because someone's listening to her calls?"

Ronan nodded again. "I also wondered if it was because you were involved, and—"

"I'm her best friend!" Caitlin's fire from the previous day exploded into life.

Recoiling as if his hair might singe, Ronan threw up a hand. "Whoa, that was before I got to know you and figured a few things out." His words had no effect.

"I would never do anything to hurt Saoirse," she blazed.

"I know ... I'm sorry."

"Harrumph!"

Ronan ignored her indignation. "I think whoever's listening is with Saoirse the whole time, otherwise she'd have been able to get an uncoded message to you by now."

Caitlin glared.

"Speaking of which," Ronan continued, "can you send her a text saying ..." He thought for a moment. "... Paidin's hedgehog is getting frisky."

The request was met with an arched eyebrow.

"Please, Caitlin?"

As if against her better judgement, she keyed in the words and pressed 'send'. "I suppose that means you're coming?"

"Yeah ... and thanks." The weight that he hadn't been doing enough to find Saoirse eased fractionally.

Caitlin remained silent, continuing to radiate displeasure.

"What would you have done?" Ronan's own annoyance rose before he realised he'd have reacted the same way. "I'm sorry ... I also lied because I wasn't sure how much to tell you." While he'd decided to share his secret, he figured his thoughts on how Saoirse was being controlled were best kept to himself, until he was certain.

"What do you mean, how much you should tell me?" Wisps of resentment still floated through her words.

"Okay," Ronan said, decision made. "Feel the back of my head."

"What?"

Ronan bent forward. "Feel it."

The instant Caitlin's searching fingers found the rune, they leapt away. "Urgh, there's a great lump. What is it?"

"You tell me."

She hesitated, swallowing. "It's not a tumour, is it?"

"No," he laughed, "nothing bad, I promise."

"I'm not sure your promises rate." Caitlin's deft fingers parted his untidy locks. She clicked her tongue. "You need a haircut."

The return of banter was a life-ring under the armpits of Ronan's spirits. "Yes, Mum," he said with relief.

"What is it?" Caitlin's fingers slowed, her words hesitant.

"What does it look like?"

Caitlin froze. "Jaysis," she breathed, "it looks like a black stone bulging out of your skull."

"Close," Ronan said, the weight of deception lifting. "It's a Norse rune ... bonded to me ... my skin's growing over it."

Caitlin's features curled with distaste; her hands shrank away. "What are you talking about?"

So, Ronan gave her a brief history of the rune, its discovery, the poem, the notebooks, and the episode with the tacks.

"Ah," Caitlin said, almost to herself, "so that's the hedgehog." She studied Ronan. "And you're Paidin." It wasn't a question.

"Ronan Padraig Ryan, at you service, ma'am." He flourished a hand in front of his face and dipped his head.

Unmoved, Caitlin took another swallow of water. "Sounds like a weird folk tale."

"Does the rune look like a folk tale?"

"No, it looks ... erm ... alien."

Ronan took a breath. "You don't believe it, do you?"

"Convince me," Caitlin challenged.

There was no other way; it was all or nothing. "Remember my father's notebook I told you about?"

She remained silent, her twin lie-detectors scrutinising him for falsehoods.

"Well, my stepfather had it, and when I took it and the rune, he shot me in the back."

Caitlin gasped. "You're lucky to be alive."

"That's the thing, I *should* be dead, but the rune saved me ... brought me to Raven's Roost."

She considered him, doubt tightening her features. "Does Saoirse believe you?" she said at last.

"Didn't at first," he admitted. "But then she saw it."

"Saw what?"

"Finnegan ran me down"—the memory triggered a fleeting shiver—"and Saoirse was there, but I just disappeared ... no body ... just clothes and boots. Then, a few minutes later, when she got back to the stables, I was waiting for her, as good as gold."

Shutters of disbelief descended across Caitlin's face. They were as plain as the group of returning beach-goers filing past, full of excited chatter. "I know it's unbelievable," he said once the throng was out of earshot, "but the rune saved me again."

Ronan was aware he was laying a lot on Caitlin, expecting her to believe an outrageous story about travelling through time with a shiny black stone. At least she had seen the rune. And now that he'd started down that path, he was determined to convince her.

"Saved you?" Her brown eye indicated she thought him deluded; the green one agreed.

"What would it take," Ronan began slowly, gaze flicking from brown to green to brown, "to convince you?"

"Disappear."

He paused, considering his options. "Want to go down to the beach?"

"Very funny," she said, hooking her head at the crutches leaning against the end of the table.

"I'm serious," Ronan insisted, pointing to the first turn on the long and winding set of stairs to beach level. "Can you make it down two-dozen steps to that first landing?"

"Stop trying to avoid the issue." Caitlin shot him suspicious side-eye. "If you want me to believe you, disappear ... prove it." Her tone dripped challenge.

"I will, but I can't do it where people might see," he said. "The landing?"

"Fine," she responded with a heavy sigh, "but you'll have to carry me back up."

"No worries," Ronan quipped, squashing the lunch debris into the voluminous pockets of Darragh's cardigan, and following Caitlin's awkward progress down the rough wooden steps. As he did, an idea germinated. It was so obvious, he wondered why he hadn't thought of it earlier. Or why Freyja hadn't mentioned it to him. Either she'd never contemplated it, or the rune didn't operate like that.

But the more Ronan pondered, the more convinced he was that, in theory, it should.

26

——————

DOUBLE UP

The landing was a metre-square patch of flooring where the stairs made a right-angle turn. When they arrived, Caitlin grimaced, massaging her forearms, rolling her shoulders. "This better be good."

Before Ronan could answer, squeals of delight dragged two young boys round the corner below the landing. Hard on their heels was a man laden with bulging beach bags, growling as he zombie-walked in pursuit. The boys stopped, radiant faces red from exertion, waiting for the pursuit to get close. With their undead father almost upon them, they squealed in unison and darted upward once more. Trudging behind the pantomime was a weary woman hip-carrying a grizzling toddler chewing a teething ring.

Ronan and Caitlin hugged the rail to let the little caravan pass, watching them out of sight beyond the tables. A quick check below confirmed they had the section to themselves.

"Can I pick you up without hurting your leg?" he asked.

Caitlin answered with a blank stare.

"I'm serious. Can I carry you without hurting you?"

"Oh, so you lure me down here with a promise," she said in mild rebuke, "then back out."

Ronan feigned coyness.

"What?" Caitlin paused, colour sweeping into her cheeks. "That's not what I meant, and you know it." Pursing her lips, she jabbed at his foot with a crutch.

Ronan grinned, dancing away from the determined prod. "I'm not backing out, and I'm not carrying you up, I'm carrying you down."

"What happened to disappearing?"

"Didn't you know patience is a virtue?" Ronan said, parroting his karate teacher.

"Yes," she shot back, "and like all virtues, is easily lost."

"Right," Ronan said, pulling the conversation back on track. "Can I pick you up without hurting you?"

Caitlin eyed him. "I suppose."

"Okay, here goes." He wrapped an arm round her shoulders, gathered her legs in the other and lifted her with ease, surprised by her lightness. Caitlin stiffened, attempting to draw away, yet death-gripping his neck, all while still clutching her crutches.

"Don't drop me," she warned with an apprehensive giggle.

"Just hang on," Ronan said, making a final check they were alone. In case his reasoning was flawed, he lowered himself onto the edge of the landing. Caitlin shrieked at the sudden movement, squeezing tighter. Her body was light on his lap; her right leg hung dead across his arm. Ronan emptied his mind, pictured the beach far below, and drifted into ró.

Next instant, he stood on powdery sand in a shallow alcove in the base of a steep, rocky slope, Caitlin's choked whimper buried deep in his collar. His elation smothered the warning ripple of discomfort.

Thankful the tweed cap kept her blow-away hair under control, Ronan eased her head from his shoulder, and her feet onto the sand. She clung to him. "You can open your eyes now," he said, prising her suffocating arm loose.

Face screwed tight, she panted and mewled.

"Caitlin," Ronan soothed, "you're safe ... it's alright ... we're on the beach." Self-reproach roiled through him: he hadn't even done a double-flytja with Saoirse. To be fair, he'd never thought of it, but now he knew it worked, as soon as he had the reward he'd find her and whisk her away from whatever bind she was in. But Saoirse would never leave her father.

A spreading numbness drew his attention to Caitlin's vice grip. Ronan peeled her fingers from his arm, one by one, edging away from her clutch.

She stood, good foot twisting into the sand. Her lids flickered, then flew wide. "Ah!" She shrank from the nearby water. "Wha ... what ...?"

"You've just done your first flytja," he said as if it explained everything.

Caitlin turned, bug-eyed. "Flytja?" she repeated, as though afraid the strange word might toss her back into the unknown.

Ronan nodded. "Controlled rune travel."

She stared at him.

"You wanted me to disappear ... I just took you with me."

"But how is that possible?" It was a plaintive tone that morphed into accusation and bi-coloured scrutiny. "Did you put something in my drink?"

"Seriously? The bottle was sealed."

"But ..."

"I know it's unbelievable, but if it's not a dream, it must be real."

"It can't be." Caitlin trembled. "It has to be a dream ..."

Ronan smiled wryly. "Been there, done that."

Caitlin lowered herself to the sand, gathering a handful, letting it dribble from her fist. "I was spinning ... tumbling."

"That's umrót, both the turbulence and resulting nausea of rune travel. Not much with a short flytja, but for longer ones"—he grimaced—"I need ginger beer ... or motion sickness tablets."

She gazed absently at grains stuck to her moist palm. "How is any of this possible?"

In response, Ronan touched his rune; she peered at him.

"Want to take a walk while we're here?" he said, extending a hand, pulling her upright. "Get your toes wet?"

"Not sure how I'll go," she said as the crutches sank into the soft sand. "But I'm not going near the water ... too damned cold."

"Toughen up, Irish."

Caitlin whacked his arm. "Very funny."

Ronan embraced the camaraderie and wandered off. A towel-draped couple climbed from sight round a turn in the steps. Apart from a lean lad in baggy clothes with a thin girl on crutches, the beach was deserted. Its elegant crescent of sand was a white lip embracing an aqua pond. Toddler waves rippled across the surface, curling into a line of bubbles that eased up the shore to peaceful oblivion. The access stairs meandered up a precipitous, grassy slope. On either side, cliffs curved out to rugged headlands, temple sentries barring the ocean's clamour from the tranquillity of the shallow bay. The breeze was fresh and tangy, triggering memories of fish and chips.

They walked in silence, immersed in the charm. But despite the going getting easier for Caitlin as the sand hardened closer to the water, it wasn't long before she halted, worked her shoulders and said, "I've had enough."

"Okay," he said, lifting her effortlessly, "time to go." She made a sound somewhere between a gasp and a giggle as Ronan cleared his mind and the air split open, sucking them away.

27

───────

SANDY EVIDENCE

The beige Mini sat at the edge of the car park above the Silver Strand beach. Ronan had aimed beside the car, hoping the rune would set them down close. As it was, they arrived in a tangle of arms and legs in the rear of the vehicle. Caitlin was half on the seat, but still in Ronan's arms, wedging him onto the floor. The jab of a crutch's hand grip skewering his neck was worse than the pinging sparks in his head. By the time they untangled, laughing and breathless, he'd forgotten both.

Ronan threw the front seat forward and climbed from the tiny car, helping Caitlin out. They were still chuckling and straightening their clothes when a haughty sniff cut through their amusement. The snooty disapproval came from an elderly man, bald as an egg and draped in a long overcoat, backside propped against a vehicle several parking spaces away across the otherwise-empty asphalt.

He was hung with cameras, no doubt capturing seascapes in the muted afternoon light. Beside him, a woman of similar age smirked past a woollen scarf, winking at Caitlin and firing a sly look toward Ronan, all while patting the man on the arm and making soothing sounds.

Ronan and Caitlin climbed into their respective seats, turned to each other and guffawed.

"That was fun," Caitlin enthused when she'd caught her breath.

Ronan grinned. "Did you see his face?" Then he sobered. "Why do people always make assumptions?"

"Evolution," she replied.

"What?"

"I read that jumping to conclusions is a survival mechanism," Caitlin explained. "You know, always assume a rustle in the grass is something wanting to eat you."

Ronan threw her a teasing scowl. "You read weird stuff."

Before she could respond, her pocket buzzed.

"Hi, Mum ... No, Silver Strand ... No, with Saoirse's friend, Ronan ..." Caitlin sighed. "Yes, Mum, sandwiches ... Just leaving ... Why?" Her features tightened. "What? ... What about? ... Oh ... Uh-huh ... Okay, well, we're leaving now." Her hand eased toward the ignition. "Yes, I'll drive carefully"—she rolled her eyes—"Love you too ... Bye."

At Caitlin's final words, Ronan's heart flew to his own mother, and Ruddi, his half-brother. But with this quirky Irish girl beside him, and their shared flytja behind them, his previous loneliness evaporated. The engine fired.

"What's wrong?" Ronan asked as she reversed in an arc and accelerated away.

"Eoin Duffy rang Mum ... looking for me ... to get a message to you. Fionn Egan was nosing about looking for where you hid Viking, and Eoin wanted—"

"I didn't hide him." Ronan's anger stirred at the knowledge of Egan snooping at the prompting of his mother.

Caitlin continued as if she hadn't heard, "—to talk to you, so she gave him my number ... we can sort out our own mess ... Mum's words."

"I didn't hide him," Ronan repeated, "I simply refused to tell Madam Viper and Finnegan where he was."

Caitlin whipped her gaze to him, holding it there for far too long given they were moving along a narrow thoroughfare between walls and tractors. "What did you call h—"

"Watch the road," Ronan yelped.

"What did you call her?" Caitlin repeated, returning her attention to the street.

"You heard me."

"I know what I thought I heard, but I wanted to make sure."

"You heard right."

"Why?"

"Haven't you even seen her eyes? She looks like a cobra deciding when to strike."

"Oh, I love your sense of humour, Ronan ... first Finnegan, now Madam Viper. What next?"

Her bell-like laughter was reassuring. Ronan felt their friendship was less brittle, their shared flytja a bond. "I'll think of something," he said.

She threw him a side-glance. "I'm sure you will." As they left the last of the houses behind, she added, "What have you named me?"

"Mmm"—Ronan rubbed his chin—"first thing yesterday I would have called you Róisín."

"Rose?" Caitlin frowned without looking at him as she steered through a tight corner.

"Cute but prickly."

"Very funny." Her tone was droll.

"But today you're the Boston Strangler."

There was an extended silence as Ronan let her mull it over. It wasn't witty, but the best he could come up with in a hurry.

"Okay," she said at last, "I give in."

"I thought you were going to choke me back there on the beach."

Caitlin laughed more than it warranted. "Yes, well, you deserved it ... frightened the bejaysis out of me. It's a wonder my hair isn't grey." She pulled strands from under her cap, inspecting them in the rear-vision mirror, leaving them dangling.

"Well, you asked for proof." He lowered his voice. "Do you believe me now?"

"I don't want to."

Ronan held his tongue, letting her draw her own conclusions.

"But, how else"—Caitlin pointed at the sprinkling of white sand on the floor mat—"can I explain that?"

28

———

IMPOSSIBLE WISH

On the drive back to Carrick, Ronan dropped the bombshell. Once Caitlin had accepted that he could vanish at will, he thought it was time to share the rest of the blood rune's mind-boggling powers. He eased into it by raising Sean Hagan's stolen fishing gear.

"High-tide Pier?"

"Yeah," he nodded, "and the deserted house." He waited for Caitlin's censure.

She didn't disappoint, flicking him a sharp glance. "So that story about your mother's interest in derelict houses was all lies?"

Ronan almost flinched from the sting of the accusation. "No, that part's true, but I've had to fib to cover up things I couldn't tell you at the time."

Caitlin stared ahead, silent.

Annoyance and exasperation needled Ronan. "What would you have done if I'd told you why I wanted to know?"

She ignored his question, instead shooting off one of her own. "How did the High-tide Pier help you find Hagan's stuff? Dad told me the robbery was Friday night."

Ronan hesitated, but she deserved honesty. "I can time-travel."

Caitlin gave no sign of being aware of his scrutiny, or anything else. It was only when the Mini wandered toward the side of the road that she snapped from her trance, lurching the car back on course with a sharp jerk. Ronan decided it would be safer to continue the conversation while stationary.

"Pull into the next lay-by, Caitlin ... please."

"Why?"

"I need to explain ... and I don't want us ending up in a ditch."

She was distant, detached. Silent.

They were back on the 263; the cheerful stream had rejoined them, on the right this time. Beyond it, Sliabh Liag loomed. Ronan concentrated on scanning ahead for a pull-off. He spotted one. "Your side ... right on the corner."

Caitlin hit the right-hand indicator, slipping across the opposing lane into the lay-by, her abrupt braking threw Ronan against the seatbelt.

"Good to see they work." His quip went unanswered.

After killing the engine, Caitlin twisted, leaning against the door, folded arms pulling the cardigan tight across her chest. She ignored the tassel of escaped hair against her temple. "Is there always something else with you?" The words were weary, burdened. "First the flitter, now—"

"Flytja," Ronan corrected, shoulder against the window. While the tiny car kept them close, a chasm had opened between them.

"Whatever." She studied him across the width of the Mini. "Time-travel? What's next?"

Her brittle voice told Ronan he was expecting too much, but what else could he do? He ached for her trust and friendship; besides, finding Saoirse would be loads easier with Caitlin as an ally. But more than anything, he didn't want her turned against him; that wouldn't be pleasant for either him, or Saoirse.

"This is the last secret," he said, not attempting to bridge the physical gap. "After this, there'll be no point hiding anything from you ... nothing left to conceal." She appeared unmoved. Ronan continued, "But you must promise not to tell anyone, except Saoirse, what I reveal. Caitlin? ... promise?"

"Whatever," she said again. "No one would believe me anyway."

"Promise me, Caitlin?" Ronan repeated. "Promise me and I'll honestly answer any question you ask."

Caitlin's offbeat eyes probed his; he held them, trying to convey sincerity.

Neither moved nor spoke for an age. Occasional cars trundled past, their slip-streams rocking the Mini on its springs. Ronan was determined not to speak; Caitlin seemed unable. It took a flower-adorned van pulling up in front of them to break the impasse.

"I promise," she said without expression, as the van's dreadlocked occupants alighted in a bubble of chatter and a mismatch of charity-shop fashions.

"Thank you," Ronan responded, relaxing. "Stop me whenever you want." He breathed deep. "This rune, basically, does two things: it enables me to flytja, and it protects me."

Caitlin raised an eyebrow; Ronan ignored it. "When my stepfather shot me, I knew nothing about this, but I was carrying the rune and a Deetee notebook … when the bullet hit my back, the rune heimmed me to the field behind the Raven's Roost stables … it always sets me down in a safe place, where no one can see me, so I can recover from the umrót without threat."

There was no further reaction, so he continued. "Normally, the rune would take me to the Home Stone, near Kaupang, in southern Norway, but in 891."

This drew a disbelieving snort from Caitlin.

"Just hear me out," he said, holding up a palm. "But it took me to Raven's Roost because that's where the notebook was made … Saoirse made it."

The mention of her friend jolted Caitlin from her torpor. "Suppose that's true, what's it got to do with time-travel?"

"I'll get to that later, but first, some more background. Did you hear about the accident at Sliabh Liag a couple of weeks ago? A man fell to his death?"

Caitlin hesitated for a beat. "You weren't involved, were you?"

Ronan sensed withdrawal. "No, but I saw it happen." He ignored the catch in her breath. "It was my father," he murmured, "Paidin Ryan."

"Oh, Ronan, I'm sorry," she said, stretching to touch his arm.

"It's fine," he said, waving the apology away. "It was before I was born and, anyway, he isn't dead."

Caitlin's hand recoiled as though he'd suddenly become a grotesque alien. Apprehension and suspicion chased each other across her features.

Outside, the charity shoppers were snapping selfies with a Sliabh Liag backdrop.

There was no going back for Ronan. "I didn't know he wasn't dead until Finnegan ran me down. The rune heimmed me to the Home Stone, and I discovered my father had been there just before me … he was carrying a second rune when he fell. When I was at the Home Stone yesterday, I missed him again."

Ronan's gaze followed the departing flower-van as he told Caitlin about Fionella shooting him, his father's message on the longhouse door, and his blood connection to Freyja, which was why the rune bonded so fiercely to him. He thought it best not to tell her that it sometimes made him think and act like a Norse warrior, or how it enhanced his mediocre ability at karate, and turned his well-honed archery skill into deadly accuracy.

As he related the story of the stolen fishing gear, the blood had drained from Caitlin's face. Shaking uncontrollably, she tried to cringe into the door's upholstery, her good leg and both hands lifted in defence. Gripped by hysteria, she panted, spittle flecking her lips.

"Caitlin? ... Caitlin? ... talk to me!" Ronan reached for her, but she screamed, clawing at his hands. His throat closed, but the rune surged and his head cleared. He'd seen similar reactions in television shows so, hoping he didn't make matters worse, he slapped her. As he did, he wondered if she'd hate him forever.

The blow cut the screaming like a knife. Her trembling transformed into shuddering sobs wracking her frailty. She collapsed into the seat. Ronan reached over, easing her into his arms, rocking, crooning. It was an awkward embrace with her in one seat, him in the other; regardless he hummed and soothed. When her weeping eased to sniffles against his shirt, she stiffened, shrinking away.

"Sorry," she said. A deep composing breath turned into a ragged shudder as she attacked the pack of tissues, blowing and dabbing.

Ronan replayed his words, searching for the trigger to her panic attack. He'd been telling her about watching Jamie, Vítek and Ylli steal the fishing gear. Despite stirring unease, he said, "Want to talk about it?"

Caitlin took another juddering breath. "My memory of what happened," she began, patting her useless leg, "has been blank until you said that name ..."

"What name?"

She swallowed. "Ylli," she forced out in a strangled whisper. Gathering herself, she continued, "I remember now ... I was looking for Lena, my friend, and I"—she screwed her lids tight—"saw her chained to a bed ..."

The image jarred Ronan as he listened, transfixed by the relived horror radiating from Caitlin.

"... there were people with her ... they saw me ... maybe a board squeaked. A woman screamed, 'Get rid of her, Ylli!' I tried to run ..." She paused as though gathering the strength to make it through the memory. "I woke up in the hospital ... I think this Ylli threw me down the stairs."

"I'm sorry." The words were inadequate, but all Ronan had.

"They left me for dead," she whispered. "By the time Saoirse found me, they'd cleared out … Lena was gone … the guards found nothing but rubbish … said it was human traffickers. Scum!"

The room where he'd been imprisoned, and the manacle-fitted bed now made sense. It all linked to Vítek and Ylli, and whoever they worked for. Ronan's jaw knotted. He promised himself that as soon as he'd found Saoirse, he'd track them down.

"At least you're okay," Ronan ventured.

"Am I?" she retorted, driving a fist into her gammy leg, unflinching.

Without warning, she started the car and shot off, no checking mirrors, no indicating. Ronan winced, bracing for an impact, relaxing when one didn't eventuate, thankful for the lack of traffic. By the time Caitlin broke the silence, the grassy verge was blurring past. "If you really can time-travel"—she glanced at him—"go back and stop me going into that house … please." There was no cunning or calculation in her eyes, only naked, desperate appeal. "Then I'll believe you."

29

———

ASTONISHMENT

Caitlin's desperate plea was a challenge Ronan couldn't meet. The rune forbade interference with the past. Besides, if he could do that for Caitlin, he could prevent Darragh's accident, save his father, stop disasters, wars, and even climate change. He'd be a god! No wonder the rune had strict laws.

Ronan braced himself—they'd just passed the derelict house, and would soon be back in Carrick. "The rune won't let me," he said, almost apologetic.

Caitlin's shoulders slumped. "I knew you were lying."

The accusation stung. "I said I wouldn't lie to you again," he snapped.

"No, you said you didn't *want* to lie to me again."

"Same thing."

"I beg to differ." Her lips tightened. "You gave me an expression of desire, whereas a promise is a firm commitment."

Ronan gaped. "Are you a lawyer or something?"

"I've been studying law as an elective."

The silver waters of Teelin Harbour appeared in the distance, shimmering under a break in the afternoon overcast.

"Well, the rune has a law that prohibits trufla."

"Trufla?"

"Interference in the past."

"How convenient." Caitlin's sarcasm sliced the air.

"It's not convenient," Ronan shot back, "it's the truth … I can't change the past. Don't you think I'd have gone back and stopped Darragh's accident?" As much as he tried to prevent it, his voice rose. "There are limits to what I can do."

Caitlin stared straight ahead, fingers white on the wheel. "What good is time-travel if you can't do anything with it?"

Ronan ignored her mockery. "I think you should pull over again."

She ignored him, continuing in silence. He was about to repeat himself when she swerved onto a narrow side road without warning. The sudden right turn flung him against the door. Pulling over was now impossible without blocking the thoroughfare: farm fences, stone walls, even houses, threatened to scrape paint from the car, forcing it one way, then the other. There was nowhere to stop that wasn't someone's driveway, front yard or farm entrance.

At last, the lane disgorged them onto Teelin Road, but instead of turning, Caitlin drove straight across into a large gravelled area wedged between the road and the rock-strewn River Glen. "Consider me pulled over." Without a backward glance, she climbed out and crutched away along a slender path, back rigid.

Ronan followed, wondering how to rebuild her trust. Caitlin lowered herself onto a grassy bank, lifting her face to the lingering sun; Ronan continued a dozen paces until a busy stream gushing from under Teelin Road barred the way.

"Owenwee River," Caitlin said curtly. "Same one as back there."

Glistening boulders studded the final reach of the Owenwee as it dropped into the Glen. Light played across the water where it bunched behind each rock, and curled free round either side. The hypnotic swirling and churning, the cauldrons of bubbles and patches of calm, soon had Ronan soothed, collected, and ready to convince.

He flopped down beside Caitlin, casually laying his trap. "Would you like a drink?"

She gestured indifference while surveying the eddies where the two streams met.

"Don't go anywhere," he chirped, bracing himself and folding into thin air.

Next instant, the same air spat Ronan onto the grass. Caitlin jumped. A couple of bottles of fruit juice tumbled from his hands, a strip of paper fluttered after them. The back of his head had ignited into a bonfire of searing agony. He moaned, clutching at the vortex of pain and rolling away, retching, wondering through the torment whether his skull might explode.

"Ronan. Are you okay?" She leant across, placing a tentative hand on his back.

He groaned in misery, huffing shallow breaths, willing the torture to end.

"I'm calling an ambulance," Caitlin said, reaching for her phone.

"No ..." Ronan's hand flapped like the wing of a dying bird, "... just give me ... a few minutes ..."

Afternoon tree shadows had almost engulfed them before the pain eased enough for him to grit his teeth and rise to his haunches. "Freyja never told me about flytjas hurting ... but those with a time difference are now agony ... the greater the difference, the worse it is ..." He clamped his lids, heaving a sigh. "And I just did two in quick succession ... only half an hour each way ... I thought it wouldn't be so bad ..." He grabbed the frosted bottles, pressing one behind each ear, almost purring with relief.

Caitlin didn't seem satisfied. "Ronan?"

"I'll be right in a minute." He hoped it wasn't wishful thinking.

She gripped his arm. "I don't think you should do any more."

Ronan couldn't anyway, not if it meant such fearsome torment. "I'm fine," he said at last, forcing cheerfulness, holding up the bottles, "Apple or orange?"

Caitlin remained unconvinced.

"Please don't make this"—he held the icy bottles against his temples—"all for nothing."

When her frowning scrutiny produced no reaction, she reached for the apple juice.

"At last," Ronan said dryly. The fire was receding; he was returning to normal. "Now," he said, picking up the cash register receipt from the Killybegs Supermarket, "check the purchase time." He took a swig of orange juice, revelling in the sweet chill lifting through his head.

Caitlin glanced at him, opening the folded docket, scanning until she locked on a spot, skipped to another, then back to the first. She stiffened.

"Well, what's it say?"

"It's ... like ... for right now ... and you've been back for half an hour ... it's impossible ..."

"Read out what it says," Ronan insisted.

"Why?"

"Because once you hear yourself say it, you can't deny it anymore."

Caitlin's focus flicked from Ronan to the docket, and back again. Eventually she whispered, "Killybegs Supermarket; 07-11-2004; 15:53." The whole time, her head swung in denial. "But how ...?"

"Once you come to terms with that," Ronan said, "you'll believe the rest of it." To increasing disbelief, he told her he was born in eight months' time, and that he came from 2021, and that his mother might be somewhere close, trying to accept the cruel blow of losing her fiancé off Sliabh Liag's cliff, wondering how she would ever put her shattered life back together.

For several minutes, they sat in silence, watching the Glen and Owenwee rivers weaving themselves into a larger, stronger flow to tackle a final rocky obstacle to the harbour's tide.

"Darragh's most likely in the Dublin Mater," she said without warning. Ronan's head whipped round; she rattled on, "I'm sorry ... I gave Saoirse my word, and I didn't know if I could trust you ... all those wild claims and strange lumps. But I believe you now."

Gratitude and a sense of release, of unburdening, swept Ronan; he touched her arm. "Thank you."

Caitlin waved a 'no problem' while continuing to study the water. Its persistent gurgle was a constant background to the chirruping of camouflaged birds and the occasional hum of a passing vehicle.

"You said, 'most likely'," Ronan pointed out after replaying Caitlin's words in his head.

"Saoirse's told me very little, but Mum says that's where the air ambulance would have taken him ... it's got the best trauma specialists."

"Right," Ronan said, mind whirring with the new information—he now had a target. "Thanks."

"It's where they took me ..." She tapped her gammy leg.

"Oh ..." Unsure how she would react, he proceeded with caution. "Does it hurt?"

"Not like it used to," she said. "But lately there's been some different sensations, so the specialist wants to review everything."

"That's positive, right?"

Caitlin gazed into the distance, as if trying to divine the future. "I'm trying not to get my hopes up."

Ronan understood; he felt the same about the prospect of finding his father. While he had a lead, he wasn't getting any closer. With a pang of guilt, he pushed Paidin from his mind. "Where's your appointment?"

"I wish it was only one." She grimaced. "Dublin ... the Mater ... like I said, they have the best trauma specialists." Caitlin fired off a sideways glance and, before he could say anything, added, "No, I won't be seeing Saoirse ... already asked her."

"When?"

"Tomorrow and Tuesday ... we're driving down in the morning ... Mum and I ..."

As soon as he had Sean Hagan's cash, he'd be on his way to Dublin as well. Ronan stared across the river at sheep picking their way up a brown hillside. They didn't register; all he saw was Saoirse, sitting by Darragh's side, someone standing over her as she waited to be found. Meanwhile, he was driving round the countryside with Caitlin as if he didn't have a care in the world. But he did: there were less than eight days left out of his allowed nine, he couldn't time-flytja worth a damn, and he still didn't have the reward.

"I'd better get you home," Caitlin said, interrupting his thoughts.

"I'm fine, thanks ... I'll flytja."

"But the pain?"

"No time difference, so it's only a prickle."

Her eyes searched his as if divining truth. "Where are you staying? I know it's not with your mother."

"No more lies," he responded. "Raven's Roost."

"The cottage?"

"Yeah, I slept in Saoirse's bed last night."

"But how? ..." She snorted at his crooked smile. "Right ... flytja."

"Now you're getting the hang of it." He sprang to his feet, reaching down for her hand. It was tiny in his, and cold from the unopened juice bottle. Her crutches, anchored by forearm cuffs, came up with her as he pulled her onto her good foot.

"You'd better come and stay at home," she said when they reached the car.

Ronan wanted to accept; he enjoyed her company, and didn't relish another lonely night in the cottage. But he saw problems.

"Thanks," he said, "I'd like to, but ... your parents?"

"They won't mind; they'll be happy that I've doubled my friends." She grinned wryly.

"But they'll ask questions and I'll ... we'll have to lie."

"Do you always worry so much?"

Ronan glanced at her. "Just thinking ahead." After a short silence, he added, "Where do you live?"

"Doonin," she replied. "Down by Portacowley Beach ... the other side of the harbour ... close to the entrance."

"Right." Ronan was none the wiser.

They drove into Carrick, crossed the River Glen, and turned toward Doonin. Once past the local high school, most houses drew back from the road, leaving it to find its own way through bulging outcrops and rocky ridges. In places, all that clung to the earth were hardy shrubs and tenacious grass.

As they topped a rise, a huddle of dwellings, glistening in fresh paint, greeted them. Ronan didn't notice: in the yard of the third one along, familiar fluid strides were heading toward a late-model sedan. Ronan whirled as they passed, gaze never leaving the man. A ripple of resentment and fear coursed through him.

"That's my stepfather ... Bruno Masters!"

30

———

CONNECTION

For an irrational moment, Ronan relived pain, anger, humiliation and hatred. Temples pulsing, palms moist, his body curled inward to reduce visibility. But a rune surge straightened him. He sat taller, hoping Masters would see him and recognise the figure from the ledge on Sliabh Liag, a boy on the verge of manhood. Ronan had stood there, only weeks ago, watching in horror as Masters slapped away the comforting hand of his best friend, and sat motionless as Paidin overbalanced, toppling backward, sucked from sight by the two-hundred-metre drop to the North Atlantic.

Caitlin peered at him. "Your stepfather?"

Ronan wished she would concentrate on the narrow road. "Well, not yet, at least," he admitted, proceeding to relate the whole sorry tale of how Masters wooed and won Ronan's mother after Paidin's death, his half-brother's arrival, and Masters' loss of his family fortune and the years of abuse. That led him to Grandpa Paddy, the notebook and the rune.

He'd almost finished the abbreviated version of the saga when they entered a long driveway. It wound out to a low headland and an understated two-storey dwelling in crisp white with green trim, clearly the colours of Ireland. A paved courtyard separated the building from a detached granny flat with its own garage. Caitlin pressed a controller; the door slid up to welcome the Mini home. Ronan completed his tale as they sat in the car, staring at the blank garage wall.

Story done, he followed Caitlin into a neat two-bedroom space with a masculine air, all warm colours and sparse furnishings. "It's my brother's." She waved a hand. "Declan's at university ... in Dublin."

Ronan found himself in the middle of a living room, three-seater couch facing a television against the wall, table and four chairs near an open kitchenette. In pride of place was a large framed photograph of a sporting team, fifteen young men dressed in green and gold, faces glowing with recent exertion and victory. Most held wooden bats, part hockey stick, part canoe paddle.

"Declan's high school hurling team," Caitlin offered. "That's him." She tapped the back of a fingernail on handsome features in the front row. "He scored five goals in that match," she added with pride. "Anyway, he said I can use his flat while he's away, as long as I don't change anything."

"He's a good brother," Ronan said as he took in the view across the harbour from the living room's panoramic window. The village lay along Teelin Road like a string of randomly placed Monopoly tokens. Cloud had rolled in from the ocean, killing the harbour's sparkle and shrouding the crest of Sliabh Liag. Far up the valley of the Owenwee River, a distant, sun-drenched ridge glowed under a hole in the overcast. Off to the left, boats queued at the Teelin Pier, awaiting their turn for adventure. "And what a great view."

"Try these if you want a close up of birds or boats." Caitlin passed a pair of sleek binoculars from the end of the windowsill.

Ronan lifted them. "Wow!" The skyline of the distant Sliabh Liag almost knocked him over. He steadied the instrument against three window frame as the image shimmied with huge magnification. "I can see walkers on the path!"

"Yeah, they're powerful. And if you look up the harbour, you can just see the High-tide Pier."

Ronan panned the binoculars, scanning the opposite shoreline before lowering the device with a sigh and peering up the harbour. "Where?"

Caitlin leant in close, lining her finger up in front of his nose. "There ... just past those last houses."

Warm, unsettling breath feathered the side of Ronan's neck, then it was gone. He swallowed. "Ah, yes," he said, examining the pier through the binoculars until the magnification became too much.

They stood in silence, watching the day fade from the harbour, lost in thought. At last, Caitlin turned to him. "How are we going to help Saoirse?"

Her use of *we* was almost like a rune boost to Ronan. Not only had she accepted his story, as unbelievable as it was, she now considered herself an active partner in finding Saoirse. Relief had him buzzing as though he'd shot a perfect score in archery—his hands ached for a bow.

He squeezed Caitlin's shoulder; she stiffened. "Thank you," he said, dropping his hand.

"What for?"

"Believing me ... trusting me."

"No problem." Insistent burring erupted from her pocket; in one continuous motion, she retrieved the phone, thumbed it open, and had it to her ear. "Hi, Mum ... Yes, about ten minutes ago ... Mum, is it okay if Ronan stays? ... His mum's been delayed ... I thought it might be nicer for him here than sitting at home alone."

Ronan's gawped; she was an even smoother liar than he was. He waggled a finger and smacked the back of his hand.

She poked a tongue.

Her mother was saying plenty; Ronan frowned, holding up his palms like a traffic cop.

Caitlin turned her back. "Mum, he's *Saoirse's* boyfriend ... In the spare room ... At least meet him, please ... Thanks, Mum. See you soon."

"I don't want to cause trouble," Ronan said as she closed the phone.

"Too late," she quipped.

He absorbed her humour, liking her more. But he wasn't satisfied. "I'm serious."

She waved him away. "It's grand ... Mum's grand. She said you can come to dinner and she'll decide after she's met you."

Despite his reluctance, Ronan was grateful, yet he couldn't help feeling they were courting disaster. One unguarded moment could unravel everything; he wondered how undercover agents coped.

Despite his gratitude, Ronan's every fibre strained for action, desperate to be doing something. Yet he had to wait, so he sat with Saoirse's best friend, planning, discarding, planning some more. By the time the light began to fade, their conversation had descended into idle chatter.

Caitlin stirred, pulled herself upright and crutched into another room, calling over her shoulder, "Come and see if Declan's clothes fit ... you look a wee bit shabby."

Ronan gasped with feigned indignation. "Darragh would be thrilled to hear that."

"Oh, they're grand on him, but on you, they're ... ah ... untidy."

"Untidy, am I?" Ronan halted in the doorway with an injured slump. It didn't last long. An over-sized single bed was bracketed by a bedside table and a large set of book-shelves that held far less books than sporting trophies. They drew Ronan like magnets. There were a couple for tennis, and quite a number for cricket, mostly batting—a few for wicket-keeping—but the majority were for hurling. Ronan had immediate admiration for Declan O'Toole.

"There should be everything you need in here," Caitlin said, throwing open the doors to a cavernous built-in wardrobe. When there was no response, she turned to find him engrossed in the trophies. "Boys," she muttered.

Ronan snapped out of his awed scrutiny of the sporting accolades. "Huh? ... What? ... Sorry, what was that?"

"Oh, never mind." She rolled her eyes. "When you've finished trophy worshipping, help yourself ... get respectable for dinner." She swept a hand along the front of hanging clothes.

Before she'd finished, her phone began protesting—it was Eoin Duffy: Fionn Egan had arrived with a horsebox to collect Viking. "Hang on, Mr Duffy," Caitlin said, covering the phone with her free hand. "What are we going to do?" she whispered.

After brief thought, Ronan said, "Tell him we're close and you'll drop me."

She frowned at him, mouthed 'oh', and put the phone back to her ear. "Mr Duffy, we're close by and Ronan said he'll be there in a few minutes ... No, I'm sure it'll be grand. Thanks, Mr Duffy, bye."

Ronan cocked a brow as she cut the connection.

"He wanted to know if he should call for help." Her face said she thought he should.

"No," Ronan said, buoyant with rune confidence, "I'll flytja there and sort it out."

"But dinner is in twenty minutes," Caitlin grumbled, perhaps thinking her plan to showcase her new friend was falling into tatters.

"I'll be back before you're ready," he assured her, glancing at the wall clock. It was bravado he'd soon regret.

31

ANOTHER SHOWDOWN

The lane to Duffy's farm was deserted, the shadows deepening. Ahead, the old farmer walked across the yard with a rolling, stiff-jointed gait, heading toward a gold Range Rover and matching horsebox. The ramp of the empty trailer was down; there was no sign of Egan. Eoin turned when Ronan called a greeting.

"Howya, lad."

"Where is he, Eoin?" Ronan asked, swallowing the last of the flytja discomfort as he drew up.

Eoin's eyebrows came alive. "Gone off to the field with a halter. Means to take the horse home, he says."

"We'll see about that." Ronan clenched and set off after Egan, but stopped when he caught sight of Viking through the fading light. The gentle, trusting animal, ears pricked, walked straight up to Egan, who slipped the halter on and led him from the field.

Ronan eased Eoin from sight behind the horsebox. "How do you think Egan found him, Eoin?"

Eoin shrugged. "I s'pose he asked round and put two and two together."

Egan's persistence puzzled Ronan. He couldn't understand why he and his mother were so determined to have Viking. Before he could contemplate further, the horse's relaxed plodding approached.

Ronan held a finger to his lips; the caterpillars screeched to a halt. When he judged Egan to be nearing the back of the horsebox, Ronan emerged, saying, "Thanks for bringing him in for me, mate."

Egan, attention on the farmhouse, leapt backward with a high-pitched squawk. The lead rope ripped from his hand as Viking skittered away in a sideways shuffle, snorting, turning dark orbs to the newcomer, as much as to say 'Huh, didn't expect to see you.'

After his initial fright, Egan skewered Ronan with a vicious glare. He snatched at the lead rope, but Viking recoiled from the sudden movement, sending the rope arcing away from his clutch and into Ronan's open palm.

"Nice work, old boy," Ronan said nonchalantly, stroking Viking's neck while eyeballing Egan.

"You ..." Egan breathed, turning into a human beetroot.

With a wry grin, Ronan spread his arms. "What can I say?"

As if remembering who he was, Egan sneered. "Always sticking your nose in where it's not wanted."

"Ah, Finnegan," Ronan began with exaggerated disappointment, "Eoin called me ... it's you, sadly, who wasn't invited."

Egan chewed on his frustration, spitting out raw hostility. "Give me the damned rope!"

With a great show of reluctance, Ronan dropped the lead into Egan's grasp with one hand, while he slipped the other under the halter behind Viking's ears, easing it up and over.

Egan was oblivious; he gave the rope a vicious, triumphant jerk. With the top of the halter clear of Viking's head, it ripped away; the bully sprawled backward into the mud.

"And that, Finnegan," Ronan said quietly, "is why you're not taking Viking any-where."

"Like hell I'm not," he snarled, bounding to his feet, flinging the halter aside, stalking to his vehicle.

"He won't get far like that." Eoin gestured to the trailer's open ramp.

"Leave, Eoin," Ronan hissed when he heard a chilling click of a shotgun breach closing.

Eoin hesitated. Adrenaline zinged through Ronan. Instinct said flee, but he couldn't desert Eoin, or Viking. So he stepped out, determined to talk sense to festering rage and an itchy trigger finger. As he did, Eoin stooped, collected the discarded halter, and disappeared up the blind side of the horsebox.

Egan strode into view, weapon at waist level, American-gangster style, barrels yawning at Ronan. "Now smart-arse, get the damned horse into the trailer." He motioned with the gun in the desired direction. "Move!"

Ronan's mouth dried in an instant; he held up a placating hand. "Think about this, Fionn."

"Oh, *Fionn* it is now," Egan sneered. "Boot's on the other foot now, isn't it?"

"Pulling that trigger won't achieve anything," Ronan told him, struggling to keep his voice even.

"It'll give me great satisfaction," Egan retorted, sweat beading across his brow.

"But land you in jail."

"Not if there are no witnesses." Egan glanced round.

"Too late … Eoin's already on the phone to the guards."

The gun wavered. Egan's short, shallow breaths bordered on an asthmatic wheeze; sweat trickled from his temple. "Won't matter," he scoffed with nervous volume. "By the time those retards get here, I'll be long gone … with the horse." The rivulet gathered pace, heading for his collar. "Besides, it's you the guards will be after … you and Duffy … horse thieves."

Ronan swallowed. Fionella was well-connected and had plenty of tricks up her sleeve; her word would count for more with the garda than that of an old farmer and an illegal visitor.

Even as the rune warmth flowed, he adopted a less confrontational tack. "Why do you want Viking at Raven's Roost?" The gaping barrels remained trained on Ronan's chest; he tensed, anticipating a crushing impact. In the background, Eoin crept between the vehicle and trailer, positioning himself behind Egan. Ronan fought to keep his focus on the sweating features before him.

Egan's lip curled. "You have no idea what you're interfering with, Aussie."

He was right. But whatever it was, Fionella was central to it, nothing surer. Yet where did Viking come into it? Perhaps it was only pride. Regardless, he'd be safer somewhere else.

The other puzzle was the change in Egan. Two weeks ago, the lad had been a soft bully boy, easily bluffed; now he had a harder edge, if still on the brittle side.

"Get that damned horse in the trailer," Egan repeated, hooking the gun at the horse-box.

The whole time, Viking stood by Ronan's shoulder, unconcerned. He had to be the most relaxed horse Ronan had ever met. "Okay," he said, raising an appeasing palm toward Egan before taking hold of the horse's mane and leading him to the bottom of the ramp.

Egan stepped back; Eoin seized his chance, swinging as though at a snake. Ronan dived. The weapon exploded. The rope halter's momentum had dragged the barrels downward. Lead pellets peppered the damp ground where Ronan had been standing. Viking launched backward, away from the blast. He halted, halfway across the yard, ears pricked, eyes beaming confusion.

With a savage curse, Egan reefed the gun free from the entanglement, breaking it open, reaching into his pocket for fresh shells. But Ronan was moving. In half a dozen rapid strides, he closed the gap. Glancing up, Egan fumbled the reload. In panic, he swung the open shotgun at Ronan's head. Ronan swayed aside, then came in close while his opponent remained off balance from the impetus of the swing. A sharp chop to the base of Egan's neck with the side of a stiffened hand sent the weapon clattering to the ground. Egan followed it with a soft thud.

"Jaysis, lad, what was that?" Eoin asked, open-mouthed.

"I don't know, Eoin ... maybe he's deranged."

The old farmer squinted. "No, lad, I mean you. Are you the belly Karate Kid or something?"

"I only did what I had to."

Eoin toed Egan's inert form. "No more than he deserves."

Not wanting to overdo it, Ronan had pulled the power from his blow at the last second. He hoped it was enough. A cursory check showed Egan's breathing was strong and regular, so Ronan dragged the limp form up the ramp, threw a couple of smelly horse blankets over him, and locked the horsebox from the outside. Turning to Eoin, he said, "Any thoughts on a safe place for Viking?"

"Funny you should ask ... I've been turning me mind to that very problem while you were tucking young Finnegan into bed." The grey caterpillars cavorted their way through the sentence. "Can you follow directions in the dark?"

32

———

PLAN B

Eoin Duffy led the way into his modest farmhouse. There he explained the lay of the land to the east of Sliabh Liag, pencilling features and tracks on a ragged scrap of paper. "Once you get to here," he said, stabbing his finger at a squiggly line, "listen for a wee brook ... turn up beside it, keeping it on your left. It's a steep climb for a bit, but you'll strike a narrow path leading east. That'll take you round the flank of the mountain and onto a feeder of the Owenwee. Cross the stone bridge, and bear right where the track forks ... you'll soon be in Garret McGinley's yard."

Ronan concentrated on committing the instructions to memory, visualising the landscape as Eoin talked, pulling it together into a single cohesive picture in his mind.

"At the brook, let the horse have his head ... he knows the path ... Saoirse rides it often." He paused. "And don't mind old Garret, his bark's worse than his bite, but he'll see you right."

"How long will it take?" Ronan asked, stowing the folded map in a pocket.

"In the dark?" Eoin frowned. "Three, maybe four hours at most."

Ronan's stomach, already hollow as a drum, protested. While reluctant to ask any more of the man, his hunger pangs left him no choice. "Ah, Eoin ... could I trouble you for a bite before I leave?"

"Oh, aye, lad." The caterpillars bunched, then stretched. "I wouldn't be sending you into a night like this without food in your belly." He piled a plate with chunks of bread, a slab of cheese and several generous slices of beef before fussing over the kettle and mugs of steaming tea.

"About Finnegan ..." Ronan said past a mouthful.

The old man chortled, rounded shoulders quaking. "Now that's a grand name you've given that worthless whelp ... I like it ... a lot." He sobered. "He can stay where he is for a wee while, then I might deliver him back to the she-wolf."

"Well, when you do, make sure you tell her it was all my doing," Ronan insisted. "You only used the halter to save Finnegan from himself, and because you didn't want the guards crawling round ... right?"

Eoin's watery eyes hardened. "I can look after myself, lad ... but thanks."

"I know you can Eoin"—Ronan held the man's gaze—"but you have to live here ... I get to leave. Besides, the Egans are up to something where they're likely to shoot first and ask questions later; neither of us wants to be caught up in whatever that is." He drained his mug. "What say you ring Fionella as soon as I'm gone, give her your side of the story, then let Finnegan out ... leave him to his own devices?"

Eoin scrutinised Ronan. "You're far wiser than your years, lad." He rasped a callused palm across chin bristles. "There's something about you ... you're one to watch." The words sounded more prediction than observation, as if Ronan was the new player on the local hurling team.

Ronan ignored them, concentrating on devouring the food. Eoin made a generous sandwich, wrapped it in newspaper and placed it on the table with a miniature torch and a thick, waterproof overcoat.

"Thanks for this," Ronan said, standing and gathering his supplies. "I'd better be going."

As they stepped into the night, the motion-sensing yard lights sprang to life, triggering loud thumping from the horse trailer, along with sullen threats of retribution.

"At least we know he's alive," Eoin muttered.

Without responding, Ronan scooped up the open shotgun where it had dropped from Egan's unconscious hands, snapping it closed, anger reigniting. "He was too damned keen to use this bloody thing," he growled. He stalked to the trailer draw-bar, threading the end of the barrels through a gap so the weapon was close to horizontal. Climbing up, he balanced on the gun's wooden stock, a diver on a springboard, and with a tiny bounce, drove downward with both legs. The thin-walled twin pipes designed to guide pellets of death, kinked into a malformed L-shape. Ronan threw the mangled shotgun into the Range Rover with a grunt of satisfaction.

"Shame about that," Eoin said without regret, "... must've cost a small fortune."

Perhaps set off by their voices, Egan renewed his complaints. "Let me out of here or you'll damned-well pay for it ... you hear?" Thump, thump, thump. "Let me out!" Thump, thump, thump.

Ronan slammed his palm onto the metal flank of the horsebox. "Shut up, Finnegan! And you might get out this side of breakfast." With that, he led Viking into the barn and readied the big grey for their night ride.

"Black as boots out there, lad. And there'll be rain if I'm not wrong." Eoin's assessment of the night blanketed Ronan's mood like the overcast shrouding southern Donegal. Not even a sliver of moon or pin-prick of starlight pierced the gloom.

Ronan squared his shoulders and led his mount across the yard. To ensure Egan remained unaware, he shook hands with Eoin in silence, donning the overcoat, stuffing map, torch and sandwiches into pockets, and swinging astride. Viking shuffled, eager to be off despite the late hour and glowering clouds.

Following Eoin's pointed finger, Ronan eased Viking from the yard and into the embrace of the waiting night.

33

———

GREY MOUNTAIN

The tall grey gelding and its rider made good time up the mountain's flank. Eoin's coat was warm, but its water resistance not yet tested. The fresh breeze coming off the ocean was laden with moisture, none of it falling—yet. Viking's stride was full of purpose, as though he sensed a mission. Behind them, and far below, the lights of Raven's Roost shrank before disappearing round a turn in the path.

On the surface, the Egans' fixation on Viking didn't make any sense, but he suspected there was more to it. Going by his brief interactions with Fionella, and from what Eoin related, the woman was only ever interested in two things: what she wanted, and how to get it. The thought of thwarting her gave Ronan great satisfaction.

Several times, he stopped to consult Eoin's map with the borrowed torch. No bigger than his little finger, its glow withered on the paper; yet every use killed his night vision. Each time his sight recovered, the mountain loomed, towering into the overcast, foreboding.

Ronan's third map-consultation showed he was nearing the marked stream. Clicking off the light, he nudged Viking forward with his knees, straining to hear the tune. There was music to running water that his dry Australian soul never tired of. It was the sound of life and hope and energy, and he wondered if those who lived with so much of it, truly appreciated what they had.

And there it was, cutting through his thoughts with its melodious gurgling as it raced itself down the mountainside.

Ronan turned Viking upslope. The horse grunted, taking to the steep incline with gusto, muscular hindquarters driving them upwards. Steel shoes scrabbled for grip, ringing loud on the grey rock that gave the mountain its name. Nothing was more than a vague shape in the gloom.

After a laboured climb, Viking stopped, blowing from exertion. Ronan stroked the horse's neck in appreciation, happy to let him rest. His coat was damp with sweat, body heat lifting its familiar sour smell before the wind whipped it away.

Eoin's instructions had sounded so simple in the warmth of his kitchen, but on the cold exposed slopes of Sliabh Liag, niggling doubt gnawed at Ronan's confidence. Eoin said to follow the brook upwards to a path, but not how far that was, or how to recognise it. The imprecise nature of the old man's directions began haunting Ronan. Anxiety stirring, his fingers sought the rune. The jitters eased, and he settled deeper into the saddle.

A tiny cluster of distant lights had popped back into view, courtesy of more elevation and the changing profile of the mountain. Ronan focused on them, his last connection to civilisation. They blurred; he blinked several times. But it wasn't his vision; low, broken cloud was scudding in on a stiff breeze. The pinpricks brightened for a beat before fading to nothing. Ronan may as well have been a lone astronaut on the way to Mars. He shivered, urging Viking forward under thigh pressure and a tongue click.

Instead of heading further up the mountain, the horse turned right. Ronan eased back on the reins, pulling out his map, thumbing the torch to life. A glance was all it took to verify they were on the right path. "Good boy," he murmured, stroking the sweaty neck again. Giving Viking his head, Ronan sat easy, content to let his mount take him to Garret McGinley's isolated farm.

The turn had put them on an easterly course and, with the wind at their backs, the going became easier. Although narrow, the trail was firm, and Viking's long, confident strides devoured the distance. With hunger raising an urgent clamour, Ronan tucked into Eoin's enormous sandwich, thankful for the man's generosity.

But the smooth run didn't last. As the track rounded the mountain, gusts swirled in Ronan's left ear, bringing with them a light drizzle. The wind flayed the droplets into sharp-edged projectiles, flinging them against his bare skin. He turned up the collar of Eoin's overcoat, hunching his shoulders into its warmth. Viking snorted discomfit but continued striding into the night.

Before long, the rain was sheeting down in curtains of misery. Ronan pulled the coat's built-in hood up, tightening the drawstring round his face. Regardless, squalls eddied the downpour past the barrier, sending icy trickles meandering down his neck.

With the deluge, the path was easier to see, the puddled water reflecting what little moonlight penetrated the cloud. Even though Viking's hooves pugged in the occasional pocket of shallow soil caught between rocks, the tracks would soon melt away. An expert tracker wouldn't find any sign of their passing.

Rocking in his seat, Ronan dreamt of a cosy fire and dry clothes, hot food and a warm bed. His head lolled, then jerked upright. *Mustn't sleep… keep going… can't be far now.* He fought leaden eyelids. But darkness claimed him. He toppled from the saddle, tumbling down the mountain.

34

———

GARRET MCGINLEY

Ronan's dream stopped with the motion of the horse. Despite being mired in a fog of fatigue, his ears registered a distant roaring, getting closer. While his brain messaged him to move, his body wanted to stay enveloped in the arms of oblivion. He tried tugging the reins but they slipped through numb fingers. For a moment, he didn't know where he was, but the smell of horse sweat activated wisps of memory: Viking, the ride.

Viking tossed his head, pawing the ground, sending up fans of water. Ronan realised he was slumped along the horse's neck. Something was wrong; wind was roaring off the mountain to his left, swelling in volume.

Straightening in the saddle, trying to shed brain fog, Ronan peered into the darkness. The trail was dipping, hopefully to the tributary of the Owenwee that Eoin had told him about. Not far now. But stretching across before him was a band of luminous movement, broken only by a dark rectangle.

Ronan blinked, vision and thoughts gaining clarity. The path, the Owenwee feeder stream, the bridge. He squinted. *The bridge! That's it!* He was looking at the bridge, and it wasn't a minor tributary across his track, it was a raging river. And the noise? Not wind, a flash flood! The torrent coming down the mountain would cut him off from warmth, leaving him stranded in the cold.

Without thinking, he heeled Viking into action, sending him clattering over the bridge as a wall of water descended. It hit Viking's legs as he climbed the rise on the far side. The horse stumbled, slipped, his rump dropping into the clamouring surge. Viking squealed in terror, muscles pumping against the pull of the flood. His body swung with the current. Then his powerful hooves found purchase and he lifted clear, surging from the river's clutch, scrambling up the slope.

Ronan reined in, hands trembling. He stared back in disbelief at the boiling strip of luminescence that had doubled in width in a blink. The small stone bridge had vanished beneath the tumult. He should have waited; being so near the headwaters, the flood would be short-lived. Impatience could have cost Viking's life. Tremors rippled through the normally unflappable horse. Ronan leant forward, rubbing the quivering neck. "Sorry, big fella ... and well done." With a final glance at the swirling stream, he jiggled the reins. "Let's get out of here."

From there, the track down to McGinley's farm was easy. Although laced with rivulets and muddy patches, there were no more enraged streams hungry for victims. Before long, a pinprick of light appeared, uncertain, dissolving, returning, the wisp of a dream, but growing stronger until it became a hooked finger beckoning them in from misery.

As horse and rider slushed into the yard, a deep-throated bark echoed from house to barn and back again. Several elevated floodlights blazed into action, bouncing off the water-logged ground, slashing across Ronan's face. A door swung open and a broad-shouldered man with a shotgun nestled in the crook of his arm filled the rectangle of brightness. And cutting in front of him was an enormous dog, a lean tawny-brindle animal that came to the man's waist.

"Cú, sit," the man growled. The great hound dropped to its haunches. The man set the gun aside, reached behind the door for a rain jacket, and trudged out into the slop as Ronan swung down. "You'd be Ronan," he said gruffly, extending a gnarled hand. "Garret McGinley." His grip was a vice; Ronan stifled a wince.

"Pleased to meet you, Mr McGinley."

"Garret," McGinley said.

Ronan was unsure if it was an order, request or statement.

"We'll tend to the horse, then you."

An overwhelming sense of intrusion caused Ronan to wonder what favours Eoin had called in to organise this hideaway for Viking. Whatever they were, the dour features and curt words made Ronan doubt he'd find out from his host.

Garret led the way into a modest barn, dog by his side. Viking stretched down, giving the dog's tawny hide a familiar nuzzle, receiving a welcoming sniff in return.

The man watched without a word while Ronan rubbed Viking dry, then pointed a sausage finger twice, saying, "Oats ... hay."

Ronan gave the horse a generous measure of each before following Garret's solid frame into the farmhouse. The low ceilings held in the warmth and aroma of a peat stove, but made the owner appear too large for the space. The wall clock ticked toward nine-thirty. *Three-and-a-half hours ... not bad going.*

As the door cut off the cacophony of wind and rain, a veritable torrent of words hit Ronan.

"You must be starving, lad, and you're blue from the cold." Garret McGinley's voice matched his face; as hard and rough as crushed stone. He clearly lived outdoors, the elements having shaped his features and set them into dogged resolve. Piercing blue eyes were twin pools nestled beneath thick brows and a matching thatch of brown hair.

They fixed on Ronan. "Eoin told me what made ya ride Sliabh Liag on a night like this," he said. "And you're a friend of Saoirse's ... no more to say." He gestured to an adjacent room. "There's the bathroom, run yourself a hot tub, but throw ya wet stuff out before ya get in, hear, an I'll set it to dry."

Head spinning from the sudden change of demeanour, Ronan complied mutely, too tired to resist. Minutes later, immersed in warm water, his thoughts cleared and he remembered Caitlin waiting for him to go to dinner. *Damn, why couldn't anything be simple?*

A tap on the door was followed by a gruff, "There'll be hot broth ready shortly. And use the pink robe ... Abby won't mind, and I won't laugh." Garret's chuckle belied his words.

"Be with you in a minute," Ronan called, wrapping Abby's robe tight. With gritted teeth, he pictured Declan's flat, set his mind's clock for five minutes after he'd left, shutting out everything else.

35

WEB OF DECEIT

Ronan bit down on the fiery onslaught. It wasn't quite as bad as the previous time-flytja, even though it was a longer time jump. Perhaps the extended recovery time helped.

The empty living room had Ronan fearing he'd miscalculated, then he heard the running shower. The wall clock confirmed his timing was good, but he wasn't sure Caitlin's was, or if another quarter hour would see her ready. He was wrong. Eight minutes later, she emerged in an ankle-length, soft-green woollen skirt, with a red jacket over a white blouse, and while he was dressed in Declan's clothes, he was struggling to pull a comb through wet hair.

She stopped, almost overshooting her crutches. "Oh, you're back … I didn't expect you so soon." With an exasperated tongue-click, she snatched the comb from his hand and began dragging it through his hair.

"Oi, go steady," Ronan said, grimacing. "It's attached, you know."

"Don't be such a baby," she admonished, grinning.

"Any response from Saoirse?" Ronan turned so she could reach the back. Her touch became Saoirse's; they were on the couch at Raven's Roost, Saoirse snuggled into his neck, soft fingers in his hair. He squirmed, thankful his face was hidden.

"Not yet," Caitlin said.

The comb snagged a tangle, reefing his head backward. Ronan gasped, all thoughts of Saoirse gone.

"Sorry. What have you been doing to your hair?" Ronan was about to deny doing anything when she added dryly, "Obviously nothing." Before he could respond, she continued, "Now, tell me, did you sort Finnegan out?"

Ronan snickered; the nickname was taking hold. "Finnegan sorted ... Viking sorted."

With a shadow of impatience, Caitlin said, "Details ... don't make me beg."

"I might want you to," he teased.

"In your dreams, boyo," she shot back, tossing the comb in his general direction.

As he plucked it from the air, he wondered if his smart mouth had overstepped. "Thanks for that," he said, hoping for the best. When there was no response, he added, "You look really nice, by the way." Before the rune, he wouldn't have dreamed of voicing such a compliment; now it seemed natural.

"Why, Ronan Ryan"—eyes alight, she graciously inclined her head—"thank you."

The sudden colour in her cheeks surprised him, and he wondered for a second time whether he'd overstepped. To hide his uncertainty, he tossed the comb from hand to hand a few times before turning to replace it. As he did, the framed photo of a cricket poster caught his eye. Under the headline, *Hot Property!* was an athletic young man in white executing a textbook cover drive: left foot forward, head over the ball, concentration intense. The creativity of a graphic artist had transformed the red ball into a meteor trailing a sonic boom from the face of the bat. The clever artwork detracted from the purity of the shot. But it was the cricketer's features that transfixed Ronan.

A small inset of the batter in the top corner amplified the thrill of recognition.

It was almost a mirror. The sandy hair sprouting from beneath an emerald cricket cap could have been Ronan's, as could the chin, nose and facial proportions. However, Paidin's eyes were blue where Ronan bore his mother's green; he had her mouth as well.

"What's wrong?" Caitlin said, studying his reaction.

Ronan was glued to the man who, even in concentration, appeared on the verge of smiling. "That's my dad," he murmured past the catch in his throat.

Caitlin gawped from Ronan to the poster and back again. "Jaysis, Ronan," she breathed, "you could be brothers."

"Thanks," Ronan murmured, swelling with pride. Then he snapped from the trance. "We'll be late for dinner," he said, leading her to the door, holding it open. He followed the ripple and flow of her skirt as it brushed past her crutches with each step. A pang of regret stabbed at Ronan as he wished he could go back and stop her assault. But that would be an exercise in futility. At best, the rune would whisk him to another spot to prevent trufla; at worst, he'd find himself in Freyja's time, with massive umrót. He swallowed frustration.

A stiff breeze laden with moisture swept the courtyard, a harbinger of the rain and high wind of later in the night. Ronan shivered, thankful the ride was behind him. Caitlin led him to a side entrance between a pair of lamps that might have come from a nineteenth-century carriage. Beyond the door, the atmosphere was cosy with warmth, chaotic conversation, and the enticing aroma of home-cooked food.

Their entry froze the hubbub. A woman with a sunny face stood over a steaming pot, dripping spoon caught mid-air; an aproned man's carving knife halted midway through slicing a joint of beef; a boy with Caitlin's eyes and Declan's mouth, and balancing stacked plates, stopped mid-stride; and a long-haired miniature of Caitlin paused her napkin folding. Four curious gazes locked on Ronan.

As if on a signal, the tableau thawed, descending into babble as everyone spoke at once. The woman dropped her spoon and clapped twice, staccato smacks that stilled the family again. "That's no way to greet a guest," she chided. "Now, Caitlin," she continued, with the tiniest dip of her head, "please introduce your friend?"

Caitlin's cheeks coloured, her usual strength and independence melting in the midst of her loved ones. "This is Ronan," she said, then pointed to each in turn, "and this is Mum, Dad, Conor and Eireann."

Caitlin's mother wiped her hand on a towel and clasped Ronan's. The power of the grip took him by surprise, as did the calluses. "Pleased to meet you, Mrs O'Toole," he said.

"Likewise, Ronan." The woman's smile morphed her into an older version of Caitlin. "But please call me Bridget."

"Bridget," Ronan repeated, thankful for Irish informality.

Dropping his knife, Caitlin's father stepped across the room with an extended hand. "Cormac, lad ... welcome." The handshake was like Bridget's; Ronan wondered what they did for a living.

Conor, who looked several years older than Ruddi—maybe thirteen—waved fingers from under his load. "Howya, Ronan."

Meanwhile, Eireann patted a folded napkin into place, swept serenely past the table and extended a royal hand to the visiting prince. Ronan caught the challenge in Caitlin's glance. He clicked his heels, took the offered hand and bowed low to brush it with his lips, saying, "M'lady." Eireann performed an exaggerated curtsy, giggled, and ran to the opposite side of the table.

"Eireann Louise," Bridget said. The grateful nod directed at Ronan undermined the reprimand.

"Now, lad, I hope you're hungry," Cormac said, resuming his carving.

"I'm famished," Ronan admitted. Eoin's sandwich was a dim memory.

Once they began demolishing plates piled high with meat, gravy and vegetables, the O'Toole family launched into an interrogation.

"Tell me, Ronan," Bridget began, "What brings you to Donegal?"

Ronan would have been more relaxed in a field of rabbit traps. If he and Caitlin had their wits about them, they would have organised a story before coming to dinner. He should have seen the danger. His normally clever tongue almost deserted him. In the company of this open, welcoming family, untruths swirled into a thick fog, threatening to trip him up at any moment. "Mum's visiting friends," he said at last, deciding to stick with the fib he'd told Caitlin. A sharp kick to the shins made him wonder whether it was the wrong choice. He coughed hard to give himself thinking time.

"Conor, could you get Ronan a glass of water, please?" Caitlin asked, unruffled. Turning to her mother, she said, "His mum went up to Portnoo today and was delayed."

Ronan was happy to let Caitlin take the lead with the lies. Sipping water and clearing his throat, he marvelled at her glibness.

"When Ronan told her about coming to dinner," Caitlin continued, "she said she wouldn't come back until tomorrow."

The last was a new fabrication, flowing with ease from her tongue. Under the scrutiny of attentive listeners, shame haunted him.

Whatever explanations Ronan used to cover his secret, they were simply more threads of untruth in the expanding web of deceit clinging ever tighter to him. Yet, he couldn't see any alternative. And now Caitlin was being dragged into it with him, lying to her family. Dinner with the O'Tooles was a mistake.

36

FAMILY INQUISITION

The O'Tooles didn't question Caitlin's explanation of Ronan's situation, and kindly offered for him to stay the night. Once that was settled, the normal clamour of family meal time resumed. Questions about the day's activities centred on the older daughter's trip to Malin Beg with her new friend, and that she'd walked on the beach.

"You what?" Bridget almost dropped her fork.

Caitlin glowed with remembering. "It was slow, but Ronan carried me down and back." She gave Ronan a teasing nudge beneath the table.

"That's impressive," Cormac said, appraising Ronan's wiry frame.

"Wow!" Conor gaped. "There's like hundreds of steps."

"One hundred and seventy-four." Eireann's contribution to the conversation grabbed everyone's attention.

"Good lord," her mother breathed. "How do you know that?"

"I read it," came the straightforward reply.

"She reads anything," Caitlin told Ronan from the side of her mouth.

"Wow!" Conor repeated, with the beginnings of hero-worship. "Your legs must be ripped."

Ronan stayed silent, prodding Caitlin in return, harder than he needed to. She smirked, but no one seemed to notice.

"What sports do you play?" Conor continued before anyone could cut off the important questions. "Hurling? ... Rugby?"

"Conor," his father said with an indulgent smile, "they don't play hurling in Australia ..." He turned to Ronan. "Do they?"

"I think we might," Ronan admitted, "but I've never tried it ... too rough for me."

"Ach," Cormac said, "if you can carry my girl up a hundred and seventy-four steps, there's plenty of toughness in you."

"She didn't give me any choice," Ronan said with a lopsided grin. "Said she wouldn't drive me home otherwise."

Laughter greeted Ronan's self-fulfilling logic, although Conor's held uncertainty, and Eireann's was automatic.

"So, what sports?" Conor's interest was dogged.

"Cricket, mainly, but also karate, archery and a bit of tennis."

"Cool." Conor's eyes were alight. "Can we play tomorrow?"

"I'm sure Ronan has other things to do," Bridget cut in. "Besides, it's a school day. Now, eat up."

As the meal drifted through main course, Ronan glanced round at the cheerful faces, impatience and remorse tugging at him. Was Saoirse eating bland hospital food beside Darragh's bed, or sitting in a hotel room with an unknown person holding her phone and watching her every move? No matter how many times he told himself to stay calm and stick to the plan, he itched to be doing something, anything.

He was still trying to soothe his conscience when Cormac unwittingly changed the room's atmosphere. "And what about your father, lad?" he asked. "What does he do?"

Caitlin stiffened; Ronan pressed reassurance with his knee. "My dad died before I was born." His blunt words hung in the air.

"Oh, I'm sorry," Cormac said, waving a fork in apology. Bridget's cheeks reflected her husband's discomfort; Conor studied Ronan with revised interest, an oddity; Eireann stared dreamily at the back of her hands.

"No worries," Ronan responded, eager to quash the awkwardness. "I have an amazing mum, and a brother ... half-brother, actually ... my best mate ..." He stopped, not wanting to go any further down the family road. There were too many things to trip him up. He'd been a heartbeat away from bursting forth on Grandpa Paddy, but for all Ronan knew, Cormac might even know Padraig Ryan. After all, Killybegs was only over a couple of hills from Doonin.

"What about your stepfather?" Bridget urged, missing the warning glance Caitlin shot across the table.

Ronan concentrated on skewering a large bean onto his fork. "I wish there was something good to say about him," he said without expression.

"Oh, pardon me." Bridget flicked her gaze between her husband and older daughter.

"No worries," Ronan assured her, swinging the discussion in another direction. "This is a lovely dinner, Bridget, thank you."

"This is Cormac's doing," she said, spreading her arms over the table, "but *I* made apple tart for dessert."

"Yay!" Conor raised a fist.

Eireann clapped. "Goodie!"

Ronan shot a silent appeal to Caitlin for help with the conversation, but she seemed engrossed in her sister's glee.

Cormac took up the questioning again. "What's your last name, Ronan?"

"Ryan," he said, bracing for what might come next.

Cormac flashed a glance at Bridget, who mirrored his apprehension. "Do you have relatives round here, lad?" he asked, as though dreading the answer.

"Not that I know of," Ronan lied.

"Now that's a relief," Cormac murmured. "There was a young Ryan fell to his death from Sliabh Liag a few weeks ago ... Paidin ... very sad thing ... no way anyone could survive the fall, or the water ... the guards gave up their search after a week ... only found some scraps of clothing."

Beneath the table, Caitlin pressed her knee against Ronan's. While he appreciated the gesture, it wasn't necessary. Talk of his father's death had become quite abstract since he discovered Paidin's rune had saved him.

Cormac fell silent, eyes distant, sad. "But those poor people, they're still searching ... wanted to engage us to help ... but we couldn't take money from a grieving family with no prospect of good news ..."

"So," Bridget continued in a soothing lilt, "Cormac and I have been taking them out for free ... only a small thing in the scheme of things ..."

At Ronan's puzzled glance, Caitlin said, "Mum and Dad run a tour boat ... "*The Moods of Sliabh Liag.*"

"That must be interesting." Despite a lifting heart rate, Ronan forced an unruffled facade. The thought of the O'Tooles taking his mother, or grandfather, out searching for his father's body in the ocean was stirring his emotions.

"Well," Cormac said, "we love being on the water."

"And we love people," Bridget added, launching into the quirky characters and peculiar individuals they'd met on their tours. With Cormac joining in, they descended into the warmth of conversation, good humour and full bellies, which carried them well beyond the end of the meal. Ronan felt a sudden pang of homesickness and, if he were honest, envy for this complete and normal family.

"Goodness," Bridget exclaimed, glancing at the clock. "Will you look at the time, now?" Her decisive double handclap was a signal everyone understood. Eight o'clock saw the dishes cleared, washed and packed away; Ronan and Caitlin said their good-nights and made for the door.

"Are you Caitlin's boyfriend?" Eireann piped up as Ronan opened it for Caitlin.

"Eireann Louise," Caitlin scolded, before her mother could.

"I already have a girlfriend," Ronan said solemnly to the youngest O'Toole. "But if I didn't, your sister would be the first person I'd ask." Stunned by his rune-induced flattery, he stole a glance at Caitlin. Her cheeks were glowing.

"Can I be second?"

"That would be my honour," Ronan assured her.

She squealed with delight.

"I'll write your name in my book as soon as I get home," Ronan promised.

"Goodnight, Ronan," Eireann said, curtsying from across the room.

"Goodnight, m'lady," Ronan replied with a bow, before following Caitlin into the chill drizzle.

37

ANOTHER MYSTERY

They hurried across the courtyard, eager for indoor warmth. "Thanks for inviting me to dinner," Ronan said, shutting out the weather. "It was fun ... and you have such a lovely family."

Caitlin brushed moisture from her sleeves. "They *are* very special ... and you'd like Declan ... you'd hit it off."

Ronan glanced at the trophy shelf. "I'm sure we would."

"And, sorry about Eireann ... she lives in her own little fairytale world."

"She's so cute." Ronan paused in thought. "It's funny ... before the rune, I would have been embarrassed ... wouldn't have said half the things I said tonight." Despite her raised eyebrow, he continued, "It's made me different ... more confident ..." The rising warmth in his face undercut his words.

"Mature?" Caitlin prompted.

He shrugged. "Others can judge."

"They were ... you're way more grown-up than any of the boys my age."

"I'm sixteen," he said, assuming she judged him younger.

"Exactly," she shot back.

Ronan frowned. "How old are you?"

Caitlin's chin dropped, her lashes fluttered. "Ronan Ryan ... a gentleman doesn't ask a lady her age."

"I'm not a gentleman, and you're ..." He paused for dramatic effect.

"Don't say it!" she squawked.

With a faint smirk, Ronan continued, "... certainly a lady."

Her laughter tinkled. "Nicely done ... and that proves my point."

"I assumed you were the same age as Saoirse?"

Caitlin shook her head. "Seventeen last month."

"And you don't look a day older," he quipped.

Eyes sparkling, she said, "How old is your brother?"

"Ruddi is a bit young for you," Ronan teased. "He's not quite ten."

"I can wait." With an impish grin, she tossed the crutches aside and flopped onto the couch.

Caitlin's mood was so buoyant, Ronan wondered if she'd taken something. Perhaps she was merely relieved that dinner had gone so well. And while he hated to ruin it, he had to get back to Garret McGinley's farm—there was broth waiting. He groaned at his already-stretched belly.

"What's wrong?" Caitlin asked. When Ronan told her, she gawped. "You took Viking to McGinley's farm?"

Ronan hesitated, wondering what Pandora's box he'd opened. "Er ... yeah ... Eoin Duffy organised it."

"Round the Sliabh Liag path?" Her voice kept rising. "At night?"

"Viking knew the way ... it was fine."

Caitlin's features tightened. "Don't be so damned blasé!"

Ronan lowered his backside to the edge of the coffee table, wary; he couldn't tell her how close he and Viking came to being swept away. "I didn't mean to be flippant ... it wasn't a breeze, especially with the rain, but Viking knows the track ... and we made it in one piece."

"Saoirse has told me about that path ... it sounds dangerous, even in daylight." She gestured to the drizzle drifting against the window, distorting the village lights across the harbour. "How did you do it on a night like this?"

"Viking," he said.

Irritation fading, Caitlin scrutinised him in silence.

Ronan continued, "Why does Saoirse ride that path?"

"If she hasn't told you, I'm not sure I should." Caitlin held up a hand to stifle Ronan's protest. "Not many people know."

"Know what?" he asked, ignoring the hand. "No secrets ... remember."

Caitlin nibbled her lip. "There are some things only Saoirse should tell you, if she wants to ..."

There was enough uncertainty in her tone to stir Ronan's curiosity. Regardless, he backed off. "Okay."

"All I can say is, it's nothing bad." Caitlin declined to elaborate, but insisted on driving to McGinley's farm to pick Ronan up. Even when he told her he wouldn't be there for another hour and a half, she was adamant.

"Thanks, Caitlin," he said. "And please drive carefully ... it pours later."

"I'll be grand," she assured him, pushing him toward the door. "I know the road."

In the bedroom, Ronan slipped into Abby's robe, excluded his surrounds, and concentrated on the inside of Garret McGinley's bathroom. His head ignited.

38

WOLFHOUND PUZZLE

Ronan had aimed for the instant after he'd passed his saturated clothes out the door to Garret. He stumbled to the bath, sitting in the warmth, massaging his temples, then the base of his thumb, anything to ease the torment. He dallied for as long as he dared, but the bonfire was still raging when Garret knocked a second time.

When Ronan stepped into the kitchen, he met a steamy fog rising from wet clothes spread round the modest peat stove. It occupied a converted fireplace scrubbed clean and whitewashed beneath a stained mantelpiece of knotted timber. Hooks round the sides of the recess sprouted mismatching ladles, spoons, pots and pans, all in various states of repair. Some owed their longevity to strategic twists of wire, others to a cleverly placed bolt.

"Are you okay, lad?" Garret asked, raising an eyebrow.

"Just a sharp headache"—Ronan couldn't smother a grimace—"but it's almost gone."

Garret remained silent as he set a brimming bowl on a scarred wooden table with mismatched chairs. A short bench and tiny sink hunkered beneath the single window, while on the opposite wall, a low cupboard sat under a purpose-made rack cradling a glorious recurve bow and five target arrows.

"Beautiful bow," Ronan murmured.

Garret grunted. "Abby's."

Appreciation lingering on the weapon, Ronan lowered himself in front of the steaming brew. "Nice soup," he said after the first spoonful. As well as being tasty, its spreading warmth soothed the embers of his flytja fire. The pungent peat smoke had found its way into the food, giving it a mysterious tang, adding to the atmosphere of the remote farm.

"Broth," Garret said.

"Broth," Ronan repeated.

Garret grunted again, flipping pants and shirt on the stove top.

"My friend should be here soon to pick me up," Ronan said, shooting a silent question at the drying clothes.

"They'll be dry enough," was the gruff response.

Conversation was too much effort, so Ronan concentrated on chasing unidentified flotsam round the watery concoction. The last few spoonfuls threatened to pop his stomach, still distended from the enormous meal with the O'Tooles.

"Thanks for that," he said, suppressing a belch. "And thanks for taking Viking ... I know Saoirse will be grateful."

"Ach, he can stay as long as she needs," Garret said in a chatty display. "And tell her if she needs anything, anything at all"—his demeanour softened—"to give me a call."

While reluctant to quiz his taciturn host about Saoirse, Ronan could help probing. "If it wasn't for Viking, I wouldn't have made it tonight ... he knows the trail well."

"Aye."

Ronan tried being more direct. "Saoirse must ride it a fair bit."

"Aye."

Ronan stifled a sigh and tried a different angle. "Why do you think the Egans are so determined to have Viking at Raven's Roost?"

"No idea, lad," Garret replied, "but anything the Egans want, I'm against."

Ronan had yet to meet anyone with a good word for the Egan family; they'd evidently ruffled feathers since coming up from Dublin. The mere mention of them stimulated Garret's vocal cords. "You probably don't want my advice, lad, but stay clear of them Egans."

"Too late," Ronan said with a lopsided grin.

Garret actually smiled. "Yeah, Eoin told me ... wish I coulda seen that." Then he chuckled. "You really leave him locked in the horse trailer?"

Ronan nodded. Even as he wondered why there was so much enmity toward the family, the answer hit him: Fionella. The more he learnt, the more she seemed to be at the heart of everything. Perhaps the Viking tug-of-war was simply a power thing. Ronan had dared to take the horse away, and now she wanted it back, regardless of cost. He shuddered. He wasn't keen on finding out how far she'd go.

"And Eoin also tells me they don't make shotguns like they used to." Garret looked impressed. "You've got spirit, lad ... I like that."

A deep-throated woof erupted from beyond the door, saving Ronan from having to respond. Cú's presence was reassuring: if Egan ever discovered where Viking was, he wouldn't get close with an Irish Wolfhound called Hound guarding the place. And as the dog barked, floodlights burned a hole in the night, illuminating Caitlin's squat Mini sloshing into the yard. Ronan pondered on the need for motion-activated lights when there was Cú.

A neat U-turn put the driver's side closest to the front door. The rain persisted, and Caitlin stayed where she was, cracking the window, throwing a casual, "Howya, Garret," through the gap.

"Howya, Caitlin," he returned. Cú pressed a slobbering muzzle to the window slit, tasting her scent, tail wagging in recognition.

Still wrapped in Abby's pink robe, Ronan stood behind Garret, puzzling over Caitlin's obvious familiarity with the isolated farm and its occupants. It promised to be an interesting ride home, if he could stay awake.

"Frightful weather," Garret offered.

"A beast," Caitlin agreed.

"Ya know this lad?" the man asked, hooking his head toward Ronan.

"Never seen him before," Caitlin said, expressionless.

"Well, can you do me a favour and get rid of him?"

Ronan couldn't believe the change in the man; he was almost jovial.

"Ooh, don't know 'bout that," Caitlin replied, clipping her words.

Ronan left them to their good-natured banter, donned the toasty clothes from the stove-top, and returned Abby's robe to the bathroom hook. Holding Eoin's overcoat aloft, he thanked his host once more, and slipped into the Mini's passenger seat.

"Thanks, Garret, we really appreciate this," Caitlin said. "See you later." Then, dabbing a finger to a wet nose, she added, "Bye Cú," wound the window tight, and drove into the slanting rain.

39

———

LEGALLY ROBUST

Cocooned in the Mini's warmth, Ronan and Caitlin drove into a hole punched through the darkness by the headlights' twin beams. Wipers slapped at the downpour, providing brief glimpses of clarity in a blurred world. They crossed a Lilliputian bridge over the Owenwee River, and joined the Malin Beg road, the only beings on the planet. A few dark-windowed cottages ghosted past, but once on the 263, they were alone again. Occasionally, the extremity of the lights caught the Owenwee rattling along beside them, swollen and sullen, surging toward the harbour.

Lids drooping, head lolling, Ronan only registered snippets. A sharp head-clunk against the window convinced him he must talk to stay awake. He glanced at Caitlin peering ahead, features eerily up-lit by the dashboard's glow. Her driving was cautious, the night thick with rain.

"So," he ventured, "what's the story with Garret?"

Caitlin shot him a lightning glance. "What do you mean?" she asked with forced innocence.

Allowing his annoyance to show, Ronan responded, "Oh, come on, Caitlin, you've said nothing about Garret, and there's obviously something there."

"I told you," she said crisply, "it's Saoirse's story to tell."

"I know that," he said, not caring that his voice had risen, "but you've got a story there as well." Sensing her sudden tension, he inhaled, forcing calm neutrality. "Look, I thought we agreed, no secrets?"

Caitlin's lips were set, and the woollen beanie pulled low made her face smaller, more fragile. Ronan chided himself for getting short. Apart from her initial frostiness, she'd been nothing but helpful.

They said each other's names together, paused, then in unison said, "You go." They laughed.

"Ladies first," Ronan said.

"You're right, I could have told you more. My connection with Garret is really part of Saoirse's ... I guess I hadn't separated them in my mind."

"So, what's yours?"

"Nothing much, really. Nearly every holiday, Saoirse rides round to Garret's farm, sometimes twice. She'll spend the afternoon ... I pick her up and drop her back the next day ... or the day after."

"She leaves Viking there for a night or two?"

Caitlin nodded.

"That explains his familiarity with the trail, and the farm ... and Cú, but why does"—Ronan caught himself—"I know, Saoirse will have to tell me." He sank into the seat. "I'm so tired."

"We'll have you home soon."

Saoirse and the reward swirled in Ronan's thoughts. "What can you tell me about Sean Hagan?" he asked, not lifting his head.

"He won't pay," Caitlin insisted.

"But I *need* money ... new clothes ... ph—"

"I'm sure Declan won't mind you borrowing some of his," she cut in. "And we might have an old phone somewhere ... I can buy you a SIM card."

"Thanks, but I already owe Saoirse, and I borrowed from Darragh, and now I owe you for fuel." Resentment toward Sean Hagan flooded Ronan as he sensed the money, the one part of his plan he'd been sure of, slipping from his grasp. "I'm depending on that reward," he growled.

"We'll come up with a new strategy."

Ronan's irritation ebbed as he studied her profile in the dash lights. "So it's *we* now?"

"I'm not sure you can be trusted by yourself," she responded wryly.

Relief that he was no longer dealing with the unknown by himself was like a tonic to Ronan; his shoulders straightened, his chin lifted. "Has she tex—"

Caitlin shook her head. "No ... and it's too late now ... won't hear anything until tomorrow."

While disappointing, Ronan wouldn't let it dampen his renewed optimism. "What do you think is going on ... with Saoirse?" he said, hoping her thoughts would lend clarity to his.

"There wasn't any hint of urgency in that coded message, was there?"

"Nope."

"She'd have found a way of telling me if she was in danger, wouldn't she?"

"Absolutely." Whether it was the rune talking, or wishful thinking, Ronan had never been more certain of anything.

"Then someone must be threatening Darragh to keep her quiet."

Ronan glanced at her. "Wouldn't he be safe in hospital?"

"Yeah, I suppose so."

"Could it be Niamh and Niall being threatened?"

"Mmm ... maybe."

"It's the only thing I can think of," Ronan said.

"But why?" Her voice caught.

"Million-dollar question." Every angle Ronan examined slipped from the grasp of logic, like the shadows washing past in the night. "To prevent Saoirse from talking openly?"

"But wh—"

"Fionella!" Ronan gasped. And it suddenly made sense.

"What?"

"Madam Viper! When I spoke to her yesterday, she seemed pleased that Saoirse didn't want to talk to me."

Caitlin stared at him for far too long: the Mini drifted off course.

"Watch the road!"

The vehicle swerved as Caitlin corrected. "Sorry."

Ronan didn't respond, his mind whirring away at why Fionella wouldn't want him speaking to Saoirse. Only the previous week, Saoirse had warned him that Fionella was a manipulative witch who already had her married off to Fionn. Ronan had thought it amusing; now it appeared sinister.

"I said I was sorry." Caitlin's glance was so fast it risked throwing her neck out.

"What? Oh ... no ... I was just ..." Ronan hesitated. "I think Madam Viper wants Saoirse for Finnegan."

"Ha! Fat chance!"

"I know, but—"

"Saoirse loves you," Caitlin stated with finality.

A warm glow swept Ronan. "I still reckon Fionella is taking advantage of Darragh's accident."

"Mmm."

If he could only get to Saoirse, Ronan was sure he could put an end to the stupidity; all he needed was the reward money. "Can you show me where Sean Hagan lives?" he said.

She shot him a sharp look. "Ronan, he won't pay."

"Doesn't matter. Where does he live?"

"What's the point?"

"The point is, he owes me"—Ronan thumped his thigh—"five hundred euros."

Caitlin's eyes narrowed, but never left the road as she banked into the sweeping left-hander approaching Carrick. "Are you going to steal it?"

"No, I'll ask. And when he says no, I'll tell him I know what he's up to, and that I have the details all parcelled up, ready to go to the guards if he doesn't pay." He finished presenting his quickly cobbled-together plan with satisfaction.

She gaped. "You're going to blackmail him?"

"I'm merely laying out the case why he should pay what he agreed to in the first place ... what he actually owes."

"Justify it however you like, Ronan, but it sounds like blackmail," she said, chin jutting.

Ronan exhaled. "If everything was legitimate with that theft, if that even makes sense, he would owe me that reward, right?"

"Yes, but it wasn't."

"But that doesn't alter the fact that he offered money for information on the stolen goods ... I gave him the information ... he owes me ... simple."

"If you say so." She slowed the Mini as Carrick emerged from the rain.

"Don't you see my point?"

"I do, but I'm not sure it's a legally robust argument."

Ronan rolled his eyes. "I know, you study law as an elective."

"You *do* pay attention."

"Only when it suits." Sobering, he added, "But, I don't want you involved ... I just want to know where he lives."

They slid past the supermarket and hung a left. Within a few hundred metres, Caitlin slowed as they passed a squat house with peeling paint, broken guttering, and a weed-filled garden. Beside it, a rusted shed with a personnel-access door and small window at one end, hunkered behind an apron of hard-packed gravel. Plastic drums, discarded nets and sundry rubbish hid most of the walls. Even the sparkle of raindrops in the sweep of the Mini's headlights couldn't offset the air of despondency. "Sean Hagan's place of residence and work," she said, "... besides his boat."

"Not very prosperous," Ronan offered.

"Fishing is tough," Caitlin said as she U-turned the Mini at the first intersection. "It's why Mum and Dad changed to tourism."

"Oh ... right." After a final scan of the area, Ronan added, "Let's go home."

Twenty minutes later, he was snoring into the pillow of the spare bed in Declan's flat.

40

———

MULTIPLE PROBLEMS

The previous night's rain had petered out. Remnant cloud pressed down on southern Donegal, snagging the broad shoulders of Sliabh Liag. Ronan stood at the panoramic window, hands cupping a mug of tea, gazing across the harbour at a subdued Teelin. An occasional vehicle, headlights winking in the strengthening dawn, motored lethargically along the main road, but the locals appeared reluctant to brave the day—the clock was nudging seven. Ronan didn't blame them; even when the sun rose, he doubted it would add much warmth, or light.

He turned to movement as a puffy-eyed Caitlin crutched from her bedroom. "Morning," he beamed. There was a grunted response. "I helped myself to breakfast ... hope you don't mind?"

Another grunt, and a dismissive head-shake as she headed for the couch.

"Can I make you a cuppa? Toast? Cereal?"

"Just tea ... thanks." She flopped down with a weary sigh. Fresh-groomed hair flew into immediate chaos with the sudden movement. "And don't be so damned cheerful."

Ronan hitched an eyebrow. "Didn't you sleep well?"

"Stupid dreams."

"I had mine the night before," he said, moving to the kitchenette. Making tea seemed a safer option than asking about her dreams. While waiting for it to brew, he popped a couple of Kwells and two pain-killers in preparation for the day's activities.

Caitlin knuckled her eyes, leaning back on the couch, ignoring the morning. "Saoirse and I were on *The Moods of Sliabh Liag* when this man pushed her overboard ... he didn't have any face, but I knew he was smiling." She swallowed at the memory. "I reached for her, our fingertips brushed, but then she was gone. I screamed for help, but when I looked

144

round, there was no one else on the boat. So, I threw Saoirse a life-ring ... she hung on, but when I went to pull her in, the rope dissolved in my hands ... just disappeared ...”

She paused, brow puckering. “... and she drifted out of sight with the life-ring tucked up under her arms. The last I remember was the faceless man saying, ‘You’ll never find her’ ... then I woke up.” She accepted a steaming mug. “Thanks. Weird, hey?”

“Way weirder than mine,” Ronan said, plonking himself on the other end of the couch and proceeding to describe the dual treads of his own nightmare from two nights ago. While doing so, he withheld Ylli’s name, not wanting to risk another panic attack.

Caitlin listened, eyes closed, cradling her tea, sipping blindly. When he’d finished, she said, “You have such boring dreams.”

“Caitlin ... about yesterday ...”

She groaned. “Oh ... so much happened ... my head is spinning.”

Ronan sat, watching her, wondering how best to broach the subject.

She cranked an eye open. “What part?”

There was no easy way to say it, so he ploughed straight in. “Your panic attack ...”

“Oh”—Caitlin groaned again—“that ... sorry ...”

“*I* should be apologising,” Ronan insisted, “for triggering it ... and I’m the one who slapped you.”

Her hand flew to her cheek. “You did?” She rubbed absently. “Oh, you *did* ... I remember now.”

“Sorry,” Ronan said, contrite. “But I didn’t know what else to do.”

Caitlin remained silent, staring at some point beyond the horizon.

“Can you cope with more information about that person?” Ronan baulked at saying Ylli’s name.

She nodded. “Now that I have that memory back, I don’t think it will worry me quite so much.”

Ronan related how he was taken by Vítek and Ylli at the derelict house, waking bound and gagged in the locked room in another house, and seeing the bed with the chain and manacle. While he mentioned Ylli’s sadistic streak, and clear enthusiasm for doing away with him, he thought it best not to mention the fight.

During the telling, Caitlin’s face went from healthy glow to pallid unease. Ronan wasn’t sure if it was the reference to Ylli, the memories stirred by the prison house, or the raw horror of the man's savagery. What it all meant and how it fit together eluded Ronan, and he said as much.

"Ronan, just leave it ... please." She hoisted her useless leg onto the couch, twisting toward him. "Knowing those two thugs are still about is scary enough, but now you're involved with them ... that's terrifying."

"I'm not *involved* with them." Ronan stated.

"You know what I mean," Caitlin shot back, colour returning. "I think we should go to the guards ... let them sort it out."

"We can't ... at least I can't ... I don't exist as far as the authorities are concerned. I don't have a passport or record of entry into the country ... they'll lock me up." Ronan's voice had risen; he stifled his impotence.

"I'll keep you out of it," Caitlin said.

"I appreciate that, but how will you explain how you got the information?"

Her brow creased in silence.

"I wondered about the guards when I realised Sean Hagan was in on the theft, but once I thought it through, I knew I couldn't ... not if I want to help Saoirse."

Caitlin's shoulders sagged. "What are we going to do, then?"

"You," Ronan responded, poking a forefinger at her, "are going to get ready to go to Dublin with your mother ... aren't you leaving at eight?" He gestured to the clock which had just gone seven. "And I'm going to ask Sean Hagan, very politely, for my five hundred euros."

"He ... will ... never ... give ... it ... to ... you."

"Stranger things have happened."

Caitlin threw her hands in the air. "Why do I bother."

Ronan ignored the theatrics. "Dublin ..."

"Yes, Dad." She rose and crutched toward the bedroom, halting at the door. "Seriously, what are you going to do while I'm gone?"

At that moment, her phone pinged with a text message. It was Saoirse. Ronan held his breath while Caitlin read it, first to herself—perhaps checking for sharing suitability—then aloud: "Sorry I didn't text yesterday, Dad had a tough day. Tell Paidin to keep his hedgehog calm. Can't talk now, but hope the appointments go well, S."

"Doesn't sound good about her dad," Ronan said at last. In an attempt to lighten the gloom, he added, "At least she's confirmed she's not in danger."

Caitlin studied him in silence.

"We can't do anything about Darragh," he said, "so let's concentrate on what we can do."

"But what *can* we do?"

"Find out who's controlling Saoirse, and stop it." It sounded simple, but he had no idea how.

Her scrutiny drilled into him; he ignored it, mind in overdrive. "Yesterday I wondered if Niamh and Niall were being threatened to control Saoirse, he said. "What if it's Viking?"

"But no one knows where Viking is."

"Saoirse doesn't know that ... we have to tell her." Ronan gripped her arm. "Send her a message of best wishes for her father, or whatever you'd normally do, and add something like ..." He searched for phrasing with meaning for Saoirse, but would otherwise sound harmless. "My friend from Killarney is visiting. He's always flitting about on adventures and even took Freyja's expedition to coo."

Thumbs poised over the keypad, Caitlin said, "What on earth does all that mean?"

"Ronan has taken Viking to Garret's." Ronan's tone suggested it was the only thing it *could* mean.

Caitlin's eyebrows vanished into her fringe.

"Saoirse will work it out," he said with conviction.

"How?"

"Well, I'm from Australia's Killarney; flitting sounds like flytja; she knows all about Freyja and that viking is the Norse term for expedition; and coo is—"

"Garret's dog," Caitlin interrupted, unmoving.

"She'll figure it out." Ronan hoped he was right. "Trust me."

"Okay ..." Caitlin said, thumbs leaping into action, dancing across the buttons. "Now," she said as the message sucked away, "what's the plan?"

Ronan answered with a question of his own. "Are you sure Declan won't mind if I borrow some clothes?"

"Not at all," Caitlin replied. "But what's next?"

"I'm going to collect my reward and—"

"Be serious, Ronan."

"I am," he insisted. "I'll call you with my number once I get a phone, and I'll see you in Dublin tonight."

Caitlin exhaled.

Ronan took it as reluctant resignation. "Go and get ready," he said with fake severity.

"Be careful," she murmured as she left the room.

"Always," he called after her. Setting his sights on Teelin's green phone box, he folded inward to nothing.

41

CLOSE CALL

The phone box was chilly, its side panels beaded with moisture. Ronan dropped a few of his dwindling coins into the slot and dialled Sean Hagan, revelling in the lack of discomfort, not even the tiniest ember. Six hours of sleep had worked a treat. Even so, it was a sobering realisation that his flytjing ability was limited, and had to be rationed. In addition, now the time had arrived, the bravado and certainty he'd felt when telling Caitlin how he was going to convince the man to pay up, had disappeared.

Ronan waited. The distant ring-tone burred down the line, amplifying his blossoming doubt. It stopped.

"Hello," said a gruff voice.

Rune warmth surged. "If you know what's good for you, Sean, you won't hang up," Ronan said, confidence flooding back.

After a brief pause there came a rasping breath. "What are you talking about?"

"I'm calling for my reward."

"Ha! Fat chance, mate."

"Now Sean, that wasn't our deal," Ronan said, unruffled. "You agreed to pay for information. Now, I gave you the information, so you owe me the money."

Hagan snorted. "I went out with the guards ... nothing there."

"Sean, didn't your mother tell you not to lie?" Ronan tut-tutted. "I know what you're up to, Sean"—he was bluffing—"and it really would be in your best interests to cough up."

A chair squeaked. "You're talking rubbish." Hagan's abrasive growl failed to disguise his shock.

"Let me lay it out for you, Sean," Ronan said. "Jamie, Vítek and Ylli lifted the goods from your boat on Friday night, took it to the shed behind that old house. Then, yesterday, you and Jamie loaded it all back into the van"—a sudden breath rattled down the line—"and Jamie drove it to Sligo to sell. How am I doing, Sean?" The only response was more raspy breathing.

"By the way, Sean, I have everything documented and bundled up for the guards, including photos," Ronan lied, "so you can't afford to hang up on me." The line hummed with silence. "But I'm offering you a deal," Ronan continued cheerfully. "I get the money ... you get the evidence. How's that sound?"

More jagged silence.

"Let's be sensible about this, Sean," Ronan said, "I know you got more than five hundred from your Sligo mate for all that gear. Give me the five, you keep the rest. You'll have the insurance payout on top of it ... good luck if that's your idea of an honest living."

"Interesting fairytale," Hagan grunted, finally finding his voice.

"You've got fifteen minutes to think about it," Ronan stated, unperturbed, hanging up before Hagan could respond.

Ronan stood there, unsettled by his lack of shame for deceiving the man. While he hoped Hagan would give in, Ronan had another problem: how to manage the cash handover. Whatever the strategy, he didn't want any face-to-face interaction; the less he was known, the better. Besides, he was willing to bet Hagan would bring his son, and perhaps Vítek and Ylli, to take the 'incriminating evidence' from Ronan without having to pay.

Absorbed in his problem, he slid to the floor, grateful for the phone box's old-fashioned, fully enclosed design as the morning wind probed the gaps. Wherever it was, the hand-off must be somewhere with a clear view of anyone approaching, and where Ronan could flytja in, pick up the money and leave without being seen. And he knew the perfect place. It would mean a few more jumps before heading to Dublin, but there was no stopping now; Saoirse was waiting.

Outside, a vehicle crunched to a halt on the gravel verge. Door hinges squeaked and a rough-edged voice chilled Ronan's blood. "Be quickly." It was Vítek!

Ronan tried to blank his mind, but Ylli's hard, angular features and close-set, empty eyes crowded in. The instant the door moved, Ronan drove upward, throwing his shoulder against the panelling with every bit of weight and strength. It flew open, smashing into Ylli's startled face, sending him staggering backward.

Legs pumping, Ronan shot out the opening, sprinting past the front of the vehicle, across the street, and off into a shadowed alleyway. He halted behind the corner of a garden wall, heart pounding, chest heaving. Ears straining for pursuit, body quivering from the Albanian's proximity, he touched the lump at the base of his skull. "Grandmother Freyja," he whispered, "calm me."

As if sensing his need, rune power coursed through his veins, sharpening his mind. Everything slowed, his breathing, his heartbeat, even the approaching footsteps. Deep, slow breaths. In ... out. The footsteps became creeping whispers of shoe leather. In ... out.

The air split, sucking Ronan from sight as a lean shadow stepped into the space where he'd been standing.

42

———

FAILURE

The Killybegs phone box was not as accommodating as its Teelin cousin. It was no more than a Perspex shell providing minimum shelter to the phone, less to the user. Ronan couldn't wait to get his own mobile.

The rune had set him down in the deep shadow of a building opposite. As Ronan strolled across the street, he jiggled the remaining euros in his pocket. There were enough for a few phone calls and a drink—maybe. Sean Hagan had better come good.

As he waited for the call to connect, Ronan finalised his strategy. There was no answer. After the machine regurgitated his coins, he redialled, taking extra care with the digits. This time it was engaged.

Impatience rankled him. Every few minutes he tried again; each time it was busy; each time his stomach tightened further: Hagan was up to something. And the more Ronan thought about it, the more unsure he became about the whole enterprise. But it was the only play he had. One way or the other, he must get that money, for Saoirse.

On his sixth attempt the number connected and rang. Hagan's hello was even more dour than usual; Ronan hoped it was because the man saw no option but to part with five hundred euros. "So, Sean," Ronan began cheerfully, "do we have a deal?"

A few rasping breaths later, Hagan growled, "Where do you want to meet?"

"Have the cash ready by eight. I'll call you then with instructions on where to make the swap."

Without waiting for a response, Ronan cut the connection. If he'd learnt anything from watching television cop shows, it was to always act confident—even when you weren't—and, keep your opponent off balance.

It was a dull morning in Killybegs, not many were out, and none were interested in making a phone call—they probably all had mobiles—so Ronan stayed under the Perspex dome. When he deemed fifteen minutes had passed, he dialled. Hagan answered at the second ring, perhaps eager to put it all behind him, but it didn't change his crusty tone. "Hello," he barked.

"Hello to you too, Sean."

"Cut the crap, Doyle," Hagan shot back.

Ronan complied. "Put the money in a plastic bag and go to the High-tide Pier ... you know the spot, Sean." Ronan couldn't resist the dig. "There are bushes growing up to it on the Carrick side. Be there at eight-fifteen ... drop the bag into the bushes, against the concrete, and leave."

"What about your ... stuff?" It was as though saying 'evidence' would be admitting guilt.

"Once I've checked the amount," Ronan told him, "I'll put all the evidence in the bag. After fifteen minutes, you come back and collect."

"How do I know I can trust you to do that?"

"You can't afford not to trust me, Sean. Eight-fifteen."

"It'll take me a while to get there."

"Sean, it's an easy five minutes from your house." Ronan heard surprise in the silence. "Eight-fifteen, Sean. And Sean ... come alone." Ronan hung up with a tiny thrill from the tension and subterfuge. But there was work to be done; he visualised Declan's flat.

The wall clock showed three past eight. Caitlin was gone; the wintry embrace of loneliness enveloped him. Ignoring it, he settled at the window, training the binoculars on the High-tide Pier, waiting.

A handful of cars trundled along Teelin Road; none stopped at the pier. However, one was an unwashed and dented Corolla, as expected. Even so, hairs stiffened on the back of Ronan's neck. The car U-turned and pulled in behind a clump of greenery well back from the pier, waiting.

Ronan swept the powerful glasses along the harbour. To his Australian eyes, the skirt of grass separating the waterline from the first houses of the village was impossibly green. Beyond the houses, the rising flanks of the grey mountain were more mellow, the green scattered and softened by the muted browns of heather and fern. Bringing his focus back to Teelin Road, he panned right; the Corolla jumped into his face, and further along a familiar dark van came into view. It approached the pier, slowing, pulling in at an angle, blocking the view from the house over the road, but not from across the harbour.

Sean Hagan exited the passenger side—no surprise—and walked to the edge of the concrete pier, casting furtive glances before stooping and dropping a bag into the bushes. Upon straightening, he scanned up and down the road, and climbed back into the van. Ronan couldn't make out the driver behind the windscreen's reflection, but he guessed Jamie. All the chess pieces were on the board. The Hagans retreated several hundred metres toward Carrick and pulled over.

The way they had the approaches covered told Ronan they planned to grab him when he came to make the exchange—a neat double-cross; they'd get the evidence, keep the cash, and shut him up forever. He had other plans. A tremor of anticipation crawled up his spine. With a deep breath, he emptied his mind of everything but the thicket against the pier. A pulse later, he was crouching in the foliage, the bag almost within reach.

As Ronan wormed closer, his foot dislodged a discarded beer bottle. It rolled down the bank, gaining speed, shattering against a rock. He froze, ears straining, hoping both vehicles were out of earshot. But while that thought was still forming, some primeval sense alerted him to danger, exploding adrenaline through his veins. He rolled aside as the bushes erupted into life.

Amid a bellow of triumph, a wiry body burst through the foliage, crashing toward Ronan. It was Ylli. Vítek must have let him out up the road, and he'd crept through the undergrowth to lie in wait. By the time it registered with Ronan, Ylli was swooping like a bird of prey, talons extended.

Survival overrode all thoughts of the reward. Ronan kicked at the descending body with every fibre, but the stem of a shrub deflected his foot; it found fresh air. Ylli writhed as the same bush snagged his shirt, entrapping his grappling arms. Ronan kicked again, this time sinking a foot into Ylli's midriff. The man oofed, rolling from reach, gasping. Ronan twisted the opposite way, downslope, bounding to his feet as car engines roared closer.

In a split second, the hopelessness of the situation became obvious. The concrete pier hemmed him in on one side, on the other, Ylli was bursting from entanglement, fury twisting his features, and two vehicles were charging in with reinforcements. Ronan was trapped. There was nowhere to go but down. He plunged into the icy water in a shallow dive, letting momentum carry him deeper, beyond the end of the pier. He scraped over a rock, fingers brushing something soft, yielding. He recoiled before realising it was the inter-tidal moss Caitlin had pointed out from Declan's window.

Ronan let the current drag him across coarse sand and through another bed of moss while he drifted into ró.

43

———

DISAPPROVAL

The shed beside Sean Hagan's house was quiet. Ronan crouched, shivering, among the detritus crowding the walls. There was no time for dry clothes, no time to get warm; he figured he had ten minutes at most. The more he thought about what happened back at the High-tide Pier, the more he realised how naïve he'd been: there never was any money in the plastic bag. Why would Hagan bother if he intended to grab Ronan when he came to collect? No need. Well, now the man would pay.

There was no hint of activity from the house, and Ronan doubted there was anyone at the shed; even so, he eased an eye above the windowsill, peeking through the grimy pane. Strewn paperwork and a yellowed telephone took up most of a scarred desktop, while a sweat-stained office chair canted, one of its octopus legs missing a caster, giving it a tired lean. Against the far wall, a low metal cupboard sagged under machinery spares and boxes labelled with fishing-related images. Alongside it stood a three-drawer filing cabinet that might have come from a shipwreck.

Ronan ducked, recalled the image, and was instantly standing between desk and filing cabinet, harbour water puddling round his feet on the bare concrete. Ignoring discomfort, he turned, taking in every crowded, untidy aspect of the room. Where would Hagan hide his illicit stash? If not in the heart of his enterprise, where? The house? No, Ronan was certain he was right.

A haphazard collection of maps, tide charts and photos covered the walls, most cut from magazines by the look. A pristine calendar sporting a woman draped in nothing but a fishing net, complete with orange floats, hung between the window and door. Head turned over her shoulder, she peered at Ronan through lowered lashes, vivid red lips parted, tongue caught against the upper one. Beside net-girl was a wall clock displaying 8:22.

Ronan gravitated to the desk, remembering how his stepfather kept valuables locked in a draw—Masters had hidden the key on a magnet at the back of a picture frame. Ronan didn't bother searching. Instead, he plucked a large screwdriver from the office flotsam, prising open the one locked drawer, ignoring the protest of splintering wood. Among bank statements and contracts was a passport, a couple of credit cards, and a bundle of banknotes, mainly greys, a few reds and one blue; maybe a hundred euros in all—not what he was after. 8:24.

Leaving the broken drawer gaping, he attacked the filing cabinet with the same weapon. While more resilient than the desk, the locking mechanism finally succumbed, but not without a metallic screech. Ronan crossed to the window to check the house; there was no reaction. 8:27

The top two drawers revealed nothing except Sean Hagan's illogical filing system. A frisson swept Ronan when his fingers reached the back of the bottom drawer: a black cash box nestled beneath a stack of used A4 envelopes. It was sturdy, locked and screwdriver proof, and judging by the weight, held more than banknotes. Where would Hagan keep the key? 8:28.

After a futile scrabble through the desk drawers, Ronan scanned the room, trying to think like a thief. There were no framed pictures or other ledges ... His eyes snagged on a dirt stain on the trim above the door. It was only a grey smudge, a shadow of the one near the door's handle from repeated contact by grubby fingers. He reached up, pulsing with excitement when he touched metal. 8:29.

The box was disappointing. It was full of foreign coins and notes, along with a sprinkling of rings and other jewellery. 8:30.

Hagan's stash must be in the house after all. So much for his certainty. Where was his rune when he needed it?

The rumble of approaching engines interrupted Ronan's self-doubt. Not prepared to admit defeat, he turned to the metal cupboard, ransacking the contents, but finding nothing. 8:31.

Two vehicles pulled up outside; Ronan's shoulders sagged, but he couldn't bring himself to abandon all hope. A door in the corner of the room beckoned; he assumed it led into the shed proper. Car doors slammed.

"What your next bright idea?" It was Vítek.

"It would have worked if Ylli was faster," Sean grumbled.

Ylli snorted. "Backup too slo—"

"It doesn't matter," Jamie cut in. "Let's just sit down and work out how to deal with this troublemaker."

As a key rattled in the outer door, Ronan ducked into the workshop. Only it wasn't. He was in a toilet. Behind him, Sean Hagan roared obscenities, but he barely heard them. In front of him was a cracked and stained porcelain pedestal with a wooden seat with the lid down. Two parallel water stains ran across the lid; they drew Ronan's attention to the cistern lid, also porcelain.

While aware of lumbering footsteps scrunching through the carnage he'd left in the office, Ronan whipped off the lid. As he snatched a plastic bag from the water and blanked his mind, the door burst inward. Even as he folded away, the swinging door caught the cistern lid, tearing it from his hand, smashing it against the wall, scattering shards.

It was close to eleven o'clock before Ronan left the flat. After a scalding shower and dry clothes, he sat at the table sipping tea to warm his kidneys, and counting the bag of euros. There were fourteen orange fifties; he figured it must be the Sligo payment, minus Jamie's debt, not that it mattered. All he cared about was Saoirse; he'd do whatever it took.

Despite an image of his mother's disappointment, Ronan zipped the notes into a pocket. The Hagans got the money through deceit, so why should he have any qualms using it to find Saoirse? As much as he tried to shed her disapproval, it clung.

Ronan studied the images of Parnell Street and the Mater Hospital that Caitlin had printed earlier. Even as he memorised them, the spectre of his mother's censure hovered. With shame and irritation tugging, he clasped the unearned fifties, flytjed to the Hagans' van and wedged them in the centre of the steering wheel, pressing the horn and folding away, almost in the one motion.

44

BALLOON BOY

A grey Dublin day welcomed Ronan to Parnell Street; the sky's drabness seeped down across building facades and onto the pavement. Pedestrians, bundled in pullovers and jackets, darted back and forth between bursts of traffic. Thankful the motion-sickness tablets had quelled the umrót of the long-distance flytja, Ronan stepped from his secluded set-down spot, drove hands deeper into the pockets of Declan's jacket, and crossed the street to a shop Caitlin had found on the internet.

The hole-in-the-wall phone repair place overflowed with devices in various stages of disassembly, innards spewing. A woman with narrow brown eyes and smooth skin responded to Ronan's request for a cheap second-hand phone by pulling a battered object from a waste basket and dusting it off. As he took in the crazed lens, shattered external screen, and scratched body, he wanted to ask if it worked. Instead, he said, "How much?"

The woman scrutinised him as if assessing his worth. "One-thirty."

"Make it a hundred, throw in a charger, a one-month pre-paid SIM and show it works, and you've got a deal."

She glared. He thought he'd pushed too hard, but then she smiled with resignation. Moments later, she'd inserted a SIM card, fired up the device, and dropped it in his palm. The internal screen was fine; he dialled Caitlin's number. After several rings, a hesitant 'hello?' came down the line.

"Caitlin, it's Ronan."

"Oh, hi. Is this your new number?"

"Sure is ... but, listen"—the woman's gaze bored at Ronan—"I can't talk right now ... call you back shortly ... bye."

He closed the phone, turning it in his hand, inspecting the damage. It was a wonder it still worked, but it was all he needed. The woman magicked the fifty-euro notes from his hand before he could change his mind.

"Thanks," Ronan said, dropping the charger in one pocket, the phone in another. Outside, the grey sky had given up trying to hold its sagging belly: a fine drizzle swirled.

Unable to ignore the clamour of his stomach as it transitioned from the edges of hunger to the centre of starvation, he beelined for a gaudy fast-food sign. Once settled in a corner booth with a burger, chips and hot chocolate, he plugged his battered Motorola into a convenient power point, flipped it open and dialled.

"Where are you?" were Caitlin's first words.

"Dublin."

A brief silence. "Of course you are."

"What about you?"

"We've just passed Kells," Caitlin said. "Be there in an hour."

"Good." Ronan paused, considering what to say next. "Listen, I'm on my way to the Mater." More silence. "Caitlin, are you there?"

"Yes, we've had a good trip."

It was Ronan's turn for silence. *What is she talking about? Oh ... her mother.*

"I'll let you know what I find."

"Right ... be careful of slippery paths."

Ronan admired her quick mind, another thing she had in common with Saoirse. "I won't take any risks," he said, warmed by her concern. "And, if you're trying to get me, I'll have my phone on silent, so I may not answer."

"Okay, well, you have fun. See you later."

"Bye."

While he demolished the burger and fries, Ronan's thumbs familiarised themselves with the phone, working out how to mute, turn off and on and text. It was a dinosaur. Instead of tapping a virtual keyboard to text, he had to use the number keys—there was no alternative. Sending a 'this is a test' message to Caitlin took forever and drove him nuts—he had to press the 7 key four times for each *S*.

Minutes later, hot chocolate in one hand and brand-new tourist map in the other, he pulled the jacket's hood over his head and set off northward. Ronan's decision to walk despite the light rain, was as much to save a flytja, as to give himself time to hatch a plan.

Three- and four-storey buildings huddled in an unbroken row along the street. Most were brown brick, with an occasional lighter facade to break the monotony. Cars hummed, buses lumbered, the footpath was narrow; death seemed never more than arm's length away. Sandwiched between buildings and traffic, he struggled to fill his lungs.

What the upper levels concealed remained a mystery, but the ground floors boasted pubs, cafes, specialty shops and a supermarket or two. A course of action eluded him until silver balloons bobbing in a party shop window brought him to a halt. *All Your Party Needs in One Place* was etched into the glass. With a germinating idea, he entered.

Minutes later, he exited wearing black thick-rimmed glasses and a bright blue cap over a lifelike reddish wig. Two fistfuls of bobbing, multi-coloured balloons appeared on the verge of carrying him off on an adventure.

Beyond the next corner, an enormous expanse of soaring brown brick dominated the cityscape: the hospital. Ronan found an information desk and asked for patient Darragh Kelly. They gave him a map and directions to another part of the complex, a number of interconnected buildings away, and several floors up. He dragged the balloons into the nearest elevator.

As he neared his destination, doubt started niggling. While confident Saoirse would recognise him behind the crude disguise, Ronan hoped she could contain her surprise and not give him away. For the hundredth time, his thoughts ping-ponged. Was someone with her the whole time, controlling her, preventing her from speaking freely on the phone? Or were her calls and texts being remotely monitored? The former made more sense, otherwise Saoirse would have found some other way of communicating.

Spreading warmth stilled Ronan's mental gyrations. He strode toward the nurse station, taking on a persona that sprouted outside the party shop, and had been growing ever since. *"Darragh Kelly, please?"* he asked in fluent Irish.

If the tired-eyed woman was surprised, she showed no sign. She glanced from the balloons to Ronan. "English please." She had Filipino features, an 'Amy Garcia' name tag, and a fluid, nasal accent with rolled *R*s.

Ronan repeated his request in English, with his best Irish inflexion.

Nurse Garcia hooked a dark head toward a corridor, saying, "Room twenty-seven."

Staying in character, he tapped on the door of room twenty-three, leant in and asked in Irish if they'd like a balloon. Two visitors turned their heads, with the wizened woman in the bed pointing silently at the flowers and balloons already filling the room. Ronan nodded, trying twenty-four.

A young man with his legs hidden under a tented sheet was sleeping. A nurse glanced up from a chart, smiling at the balloons. Ronan tied a green one to the foot of the bed, wished the woman well, and left.

Twenty-five held an older man festooned with tubes, lines and wires. His face was a mass of scabs and bruises, one eye swollen shut. Ronan immediately thought of Halfdan, the Norse thug he'd fought in a duel several weeks previous, but in 891. The difference was, Ronan had compassion for *this* man. He left a blue balloon.

In room twenty-six, a woman of about his mother's age was swaddled by family: a man and three teenagers. A few ragged wisps of hair clung to her otherwise bare scalp above dark-rimmed eyes gaunt with suffering. Pallid skin sagged like melting wax. Without speaking, Ronan disentangled three balloons—blood-red, snow-white and emerald-green—from his bundle, passing one to each of the teenagers. Tears welled. Ronan bowed in homage to the woman, leaving before his own flowed.

At the entrance to room twenty-seven, he paused, as much to settle his emotions as brace himself for what lay ahead. He tapped the door panel and entered.

45

CONTACT

The room was empty. Strings slid from Ronan's fingers, balloons floated upward, collecting against the ceiling, a cluster of multi-coloured tadpoles jostling at the under-surface of a pond. He'd been so certain of seeing Saoirse when he entered, he struggled to adjust.

There was a large vacant space where a bed should have been. Sentinel equipment stood waiting, screens glowing but umbilical cords disconnected. Two chairs rose from an assortment of bags emblazoned with fast food and newsagent logos. Over the back of one was a thick grey coat that didn't look like Saoirse; across the arm on another, a red one that did.

While confident they were nearby, dread clutched at Ronan. He told himself that Darragh was only away for tests, and tried to believe it. With his plan in disarray, he embraced his rune and pondered the next move.

A quick check of the corridor showed inactivity. Four long strides and his hands were in the pockets of the grey coat; there was nothing but tissues and a meal delivery docket for an address in a Glengarriff Parade. Memorising that piece of information, Ronan smoothed the coat into its pre-search position. He wanted to inhale memories from Saoirse's jacket, but the smooth glide of lift doors drifted down the corridor.

Balloons in hand, he headed for the next room along, ignoring the approaching cavalcade. But his pulse lifted when he glimpsed Saoirse's brown hair trailing the group. Beside her was a youngish woman with dark hair and a bright red slash of lipstick. Darragh's head was swathed in bandages, a few tufts of grey breaking the stark white. Two orderlies guided the bed with expert nudges, dexterous tugboats manoeuvring an ocean liner into port.

As he raised knuckles to the door of twenty-eight, Ronan shot a glance along the corridor. Saoirse's attention remained fixed on her father; the woman scrutinised Ronan. He decided to visit more patients in the ward before returning to Darragh, give them time to settle in.

Ronan only visited three more rooms. The third was beside the toilets, which gave him an idea. With his remaining five balloons on a tight leash, he dragged them into the, thankfully vacant, ladies' toilet, committing to memory the common area with its generous mirror, single basin and strange soap dispenser.

On exiting, he almost collided with Nurse Garcia. Her withering look would have shrivelled the pre-rune Ronan with embarrassment. Instead, he merely laughed with false discomfort, shook his head, and turned to the adjacent male toilet with an Irish apology for his short-sightedness. A few minutes later, he approached room twenty-seven, balloons careening in his wake.

"A balloon for your friend?" Ronan asked in Irish, as his knock faded. Even before he spoke, the dark-haired woman eyeballed him.

Saoirse jumped, eyes widening as they lifted from a magazine. *"Oh,"* she said, using the same language, *"you gave me a fright."*

Pride swelled Ronan; she was so quick.

"English!" the woman barked, glowering at Saoirse.

Ronan's muscles quivered from forced restraint. With an effort, he ignored the woman, extending the last emerald-green balloon toward Saoirse, saying, *"Does she understand Gaeilge?"*

"Not even close," Saoirse said as she took the string, their fingers brushing, lingering as long as they dared, an electric current pulsing.

"English!" The slash of red lipstick turned ugly.

Ronan caught the trace of an accent. It stirred his memory.

Bristling, Saoirse turned to the woman. "There are many people in this country who speak much better Irish than English, and there's some who refuse to speak English at all … get over it."

With his voice as neutral as possible, Ronan said, *"Don't stir her up, S—treasure."* He almost said her name; he had to be more careful.

The woman seemed mollified by Saoirse's forceful explanation, and said, "What did he say?"

"He said I shouldn't argue with my mother on his account."

"*Very smooth,*" Ronan continued, straight-faced and even-toned, "*but you're way too beautiful to be that old bag's daughter.*"

Red Lips looked from one to the other, settling a stare on Ronan as if trying to divine the meaning of his words.

Eyes sparkling, Saoirse offered a translation: "He hopes Dad gets better soon, so we can all go home."

The woman glared at Ronan. While he wanted to keep playing with Saoirse at Red-lip's expense, he sensed the latter's patience straining. It was time for phase two.

"*Can you go to the toilet in ten minutes?... by yourself?*"

She nodded. "He'll be back tomorrow with more balloons ... hopes to see us then."

Red Lips scowled.

"*Farewell, old bag,*" he said politely to the woman. He turned to Saoirse, inclining his head, saying, "*See you soon, my beautiful.*"

The heady excitement of finally finding Saoirse, and bamboozling her captor, had Ronan almost floating from the room alongside the balloons. Before long, he'd dispensed the last of them and had taken up a position beyond a corner from where he could watch the door to the ladies'.

When Red Lips followed Saoirse into the toilet, Ronan's plan disintegrated. He was still trying to formulate an alternative when the woman exited and loitered within sight of the door, a covert sentry. Plan back on track, Ronan cleared his mind and pictured the toilet common area.

46

———

REUNITED

Ronan was still stepping from the air when he was engulfed in Saoirse's dizzying embrace. Eyes glistening, her features lit. "Oh, Ronan," she cried, "I knew you'd come."

"Always," he said, returning her fierce hug, feeling as light as a helium balloon. Too soon, he eased her away. "But we don't have much time, and we need to plan. But first"—he drew her into a cubicle, dropping the lid on the pedestal, closing the door—"we'd best be prepared in case that witch comes in."

Ronan eased her onto the seat, squatted, and took both her hands in his. "How's your dad?"

"He almost died," Saoirse sobbed.

Ronan thumbed the dampness from her cheeks and knelt forward, holding her close in an awkward hug. "What happened?" he whispered.

"A lorry wiped him out when he was going to work on Monday ... put him upside down in a ditch. He suffered severe head injuries ... no airbags." Her face twisted with anguish. "The rescue chopper brought him straight here ... they had to drill a hole in his skull to reduce the pressure ..."

Saoirse buried into his shoulder, tears soaking into Declan's jacket. "The doctor said he died on the operating table ... they had to bring him back and"—a fresh wave of emotion swamped her—"he's been in an induced coma ever since." She trembled. "I'm so scared."

Ronan had no words to soothe her fear and anxiety. "What do the doctors say?" he asked gently.

"They're happy with his progress, but won't know more until he wakes up."

"I'm sure he'll be—" The entrance door clicked; they both froze.

"Where are you, girl?" It was Red Lips.

Ronan eased onto Saoirse's lap, lifting his feet to the door.

"Can't I have five damned minutes of privacy?" Saoirse retorted, anger tightening her bear hug on Ronan.

"Why are you taking so long?" Each word was precise, the *R* rolled. *European?*

"I have an upset stomach if you must know." Warming to the role, Saoirse snarled through the door, "I'll come out when I'm good and ready."

A shadow fell beneath the door. If the woman poked her nose under, their subterfuge would be exposed. He covered Saoirse's hands with his, reassuring her they were in it together, whatever the outcome. Their fingers entwined.

Curt irritation floated to them. "Five minutes."

"Well, I'm sorry," Saoirse shot back, "but my stomach can't tell the time. Wait there if you want, but I'll be here until I've got rid of this pain."

"You come straight out."

Saoirse scoffed. "What else am I going to do?"

"You heard me."

"Just leave me alone." Saoirse's appeal frayed round the edges.

Ronan gave her fingers another squeeze as the footsteps receded, the outer door hissing closed on its mechanism. But to make sure, he slid from Saoirse's lap and peered under the door. The common area was clear.

"Who is she?" Ronan straightened "And what's going on?"

"Luli is all I know," Saoirse said, proceeding to outline the events since they'd last seen each other. She had been walking out the door to catch the school bus last Monday morning, when Fionella drove up to say there had been an accident: Darragh had been airlifted to Dublin and that she, Fionella, was going that way and could take Saoirse.

"I was freaking out by then, and thought it would be the fastest way to Dublin."

"That was kind of her," Ronan ventured, not meaning a word of it, but not wanting to trouble Saoirse with his Fionella theory.

"Yeah, but I still don't trust her. Anyway, I threw clothes in a bag, and"—she made a face—"we collected Fionn from their house."

"That must've been awkward."

She grimaced. "I ignored him for three hours ... he was in the front. Fionella had a meeting at Navan, just before Dublin, so Fionn drove me the rest of the way."

"Doubly awkward."

"You *could* say that," Saoirse said sardonically. "I stayed in the back; Fionn kept trying to engage in conversation, attempted to justify his actions, but couldn't even come close to apologising." Her mouth twisted. "I told him that while I appreciated the lift, I didn't want to talk to him ... he said I would eventually, then he shut up."

Resentment swelled in Ronan's chest, but he didn't have time to dwell on the younger Egan. "Where does Chuckles fit in?" he asked.

"Chuckles?"

"Sourpuss out there," Ronan said, hooking his head toward the corridor.

Saoirse tittered. "I love your nicknames."

"Not as much as I love your laugh." He took her hands, gaze dancing over her face as he was drawn into her soft lips. All his tension and worry drained at her sweet touch; he wanted it to never end.

When they parted, Ronan thrilled at her gleaming eyes, relieved her earlier strain had softened. But it was short-lived. "Chuckles?" he repeated.

"This is where it gets really scary." Saoirse swallowed. "It was late Monday evening, Dad was still in surgery, and Luli just turns up ... I thought she was a hospital support person ... says she's arranged accommodation for me nearby ... like an idiot, I went along to see the room ...." She shuddered; Ronan pulled her close.

Once her anxiety subsided, she continued, but her voice had shrunk, its confidence drained. "It was a tiny house just up the street ... two-minute walk ... but when I followed her inside there were two men ... foreigners ... one huge ... frightened the hell out of me ..."

"It's okay," Ronan crooned into her hair, thinking of Vítek and Ylli. "Where are they now?"

"I don't know ... They said I could either do exactly what I was told, or Dad would cop worse ... almost like they were taking credit for Dad's accident, and boasting that it was only a taste of what they could do." Saoirse shook as if gripped by fever.

Ronan's outrage almost blistered his skin. His teeth clenched. "What did they want?"

"I'm still not sure, but I know what they didn't want." With a wry smile, she eased from his arms, jabbing a forefinger at his chest. "You!"

"Me?"

"Yeah … they said that if I tried to contact you, they knew where Dad was"—her breath caught—"and they knew where Mum lived."

"Which is why you sent that first message to Caitlin," he said, trying to conceal its impact.

"I'm so sorry," she whispered. "I didn't have a choice. Luli took my phone … only lets me have it to respond to messages, which she checks, or to make calls, which she listens to … and every time she reminds me what will happen if I say the wrong thing."

Ronan gripped her arms, peering into her bottomless amber orbs. "But you fooled her with your coded message."

Saoirse snorted dismissively. "It was very spur-of-the-moment."

"Which makes it even more clever."

"Pfff."

"Where are those blokes now?" Ronan wanted as much information as possible, but was conscious the woman might reappear at any instant.

"Haven't seen them since. But when they left, they said they would"—her lips quivered—"start cutting bits off Viking … if I breathed a word to anyone."

"Bastards!" spat Ronan.

"Thanks for taking him to Garret's … he'll be safe there."

He grinned. "I told Caitlin you'd work it out."

"Took me a while."

"Yeah, right."

Saoirse threw her arms round Ronan, kissing him as though seeking assurance that he was really there. "I should get back," she said at last.

"Wait, how can we communicate?"

"Come back tomorrow with more balloons," she said, pushing him away. "Now go, I need to pee."

47

———

MAKING SENSE

In an empty aisle of the balloon shop, Ronan mulled over Saoirse's words, struggling with the possibility that her father's calamity was no accident. It was more likely that Vítek and Ylli—if it was them—were inferring credit to frighten Saoirse into compliance. Regardless, there was nothing random about Luli Red Lips, or the threats. And while it might have been coincidence that the Egans were heading to Dublin on the same day, it smelt of fish.

Dragging his vacant stare from a Spider-Man costume complete with web-shooters, Ronan headed for the door. The stout woman behind the register glanced up from a magazine, did a double-take from him to the door and back again, squinting suspiciously at the wig. Brows gathering, she inflated like one of her balloons, rising from the stool as though on her way to the ceiling, puffy hands gripping the edge of the counter to prevent it.

Ronan halted, puzzled. Then he realised, and waved the receipt of his earlier purchase of wig, glasses and cap, assuring her he'd be back tomorrow for more balloons. A frown followed him onto the street.

Although it continued to drizzle, somewhere aloft, the overcast had parted, for weak sunlight sparkled off wet roofs opposite. A stream of pedestrians carried Ronan along Dorset Street toward the River Liffey until a convenient eddy in front of a sidewalk cafe allowed him to exit the flow. He flopped into a vacant seat, grateful for the awning's protection from the weeping sky, and for the fake-brick-wall barrier preventing him being swept away with the furniture by the swirling current of foot traffic. Although only an hour since his burger and fries, Ronan needed to buy something to occupy a chair, and the carrot cake and hot chocolate was too tempting.

While waiting on the order, he called Caitlin, a replay of Saoirse's account whirring through his mind.

Just when he thought she wouldn't answer, Caitlin's voice blasted in his ear. "Did you find her?"

"Well, hello to you too, Miss O'Toole," Ronan teased.

"I don't have time for fluff," she snapped. "Mum's parking the car and will be back any tick."

"Right," Ronan said, humour evaporating. "Yes, I—"

"How's Darragh?"

"He's out of intensive care ... still unconscious. But there's—"

"How's Saoirse?"

"She's fine, but there's a woman with them who's taken Saoirse's phone and money, and has threatened Darragh, Niamh and Niall ... and Viking." Ronan kept silent about Vítek and Ylli; there was no point terrifying her.

"What?" Caitlin was incredulous. "Have you rung the guards?"

"Not yet ... I want to be positive it won't make things worse."

"How can it?" Caitlin asked dubiously.

"I don't know," Ronan admitted. "I can't make sense of what the hell is going on, and I didn't want to do anything to make things worse ... wanted to talk it over with you first."

Caitlin became measured, analytical, her earlier emotion controlled. "Is Saoirse in danger?"

Ronan thought back to his conversation with Saoirse. "Not while she does as she's told." Before Caitlin could respond, he continued, "But we need to work out what we're going to do."

"When are we—" Her voice dropped. "Mum's coming."

"I'll leave my phone muted, but text me when you're free and I'll c—" The connection cut.

Caitlin had infected Ronan with her disquiet. He'd come away from his brief chat with Saoirse thinking there was plenty of time to figure out the best course of action before doing anything. Now, he wasn't sure.

With the phone open on the table beside the hot chocolate, Ronan set to work on the carrot cake as if it might be his last meal. Halfway through, the screen lit with a message from Caitlin: *Waiting for 1st apptmnt; dr always 18; prob be hr; will txt wen free*

Ronan sent back an economical *gr8* and returned to his food, but it had lost its appeal. All he could think of was Saoirse and her captor. He had to get her away as soon as possible, and without Luli Red Lips suspecting anything. But how?

Ronan dropped his fork in frustration beside the uneaten cake; inspiration had deserted him. For the umpteenth time, he checked the phone, willing Caitlin to text. To cope with his impatience, he decided to check out the address he'd found in Luli's coat pocket. The map showed Glengarriff Parade as a short street on the far side of the Mater, making it a strong contender for where Luli took Saoirse on the first day.

Guided by the map, Ronan skirted the western flank of the hospital complex, coming to a major thoroughfare that should have been North Circular Road. But who would know? In Australia, street signs were on poles at corners. But in Ireland, there might, perhaps, be one somewhere on the side of a building, maybe near a corner. He couldn't see one.

Across the thoroughfare soared a two-storey blank facade in red-brown brick, sombre castle ramparts minus crenellations and arrow-slits. According to the map, it was the ironically named Mountjoy Prison. A tremor ran through Ronan.

After the prison was a structure in the same brick, but with windows and doors, and the distinctive blue coach-light emblazoned with 'Garda' on the wall beside the entrance. High on an adjacent, and far less imposing building, was a random sign proclaiming the street to be Circular Road North—close enough. Soon after, he found Glengarriff Parade running off to the left, northward.

The target address was about a hundred metres in, but Ronan didn't notice the house number or the battered olive-green door, or the crumbling window boxes full of desiccated remnants of unrecognisable members of the plant kingdom. All he saw, parked by the front steps, was a gold Range Rover.

48

PADLOCK AND HASP

Every fibre of Ronan's body leapt to high alert. He forced his legs to keep moving, ambling past a front door solid enough to have come from the prison itself. Beside the low steps, a tiny, weed-choked garden provided a splash of life that was lost on the occupants; a blackout blind hung across the single window.

The distinctive vehicle only confirmed Ronan's suspicions, but before he could ponder further, the house door opened and out strode Egan himself, talking over his shoulder, "... grab it from the car ... won't be a sec."

Dropping his gaze and slouching, Ronan adopted the rolling gait of one who'd been too long on a horse, and hoped for the best. The vehicle's central locking system chirped as Egan barged across the path of a nondescript, bespectacled redhead with a blue cap. Ronan sauntered on. Behind him, a car door opened and closed; it was followed by a double-chirp and the weighty thunk of the building's front door.

Tension draining, he crossed the narrow street and doubled back. The houses were a single, elongated brick structure of varying shades of brown with ubiquitous slate roof tiles. It was as though each additional dwelling had been added onto the end of the previous one until there was an unbroken row of bricks, windows and doors stretching the length of Glengarriff Parade. When he was opposite the blackout blind, he checked out the inside of the parked car in front of him, a late model Renault. With it committed to memory, he knelt out of sight, pretending to tie a shoelace, and visualised the interior of Egan's vehicle.

A couple of suitcases and a canvas holdall occupied the cargo space, while the rear seat was strewn with file folders and real estate brochures. Nothing important. Ronan allowed himself a smirk before whipping his body from side to side, making the vehicle rock on its soft springs. With the car's alarm shrilling, the air sucked him away.

From the back of the Renault, Ronan watched with amusement as the house door flung wide and Egan barrelled out, thumb stabbing at a key fob. Silence returned mid-shriek. Egan glanced up and down the street, circling the car, peering through windows, opening and closing doors. With a final scrutiny of the surrounds, he hit the central locking and lumbered up the steps.

It all happened round the edges of Ronan's concentration as he focused on the slice of hallway visible through the open door. He counted to ten after the door slammed shut behind Egan, then aimed for the entryway. It was clearly unsafe, for the rune set Ronan down behind a musty sofa in a side room; clomping echoed down the hall.

The close walls made the two-seater couch seem enormous. A waist-high cupboard and a coffee table crowded round it. The walls were bare. Approaching footsteps and rumbling voices had him ducking before he could explore further.

"... and this is the lounge, such as it is," Egan said from the doorway. Ronan prepared to flee. "But then," Egan continued, "we don't buy these places for their looks ... it's all about position."

"And why this position?"

The second voice sent a wave of goose bumps down Ronan's limbs; he tried to cringe into the couch's moth-eaten upholstery. If they made a circuit of the room, they'd trip over him, but he couldn't flytja away and miss hearing something that might tell him what the hell his future stepfather—and Egan for that matter—was doing there.

"Well," Egan responded, "the Mater is the best trauma hospital in Ireland, so there will always be a premium for accommodation in this area."

"Yeah, but is it generating a good return on investment?"

"Currently fifteen-point-two percent, but the longer-term goal is to buy the whole row so we can knock them down and build a multi-storey hotel."

"That's where the money is." Greed put an eager edge on Masters' voice.

"As you can see from the prospectus, we reckon close to twenty-five percent." Egan dripped smugness, but his knowledge and business talk impressed Ronan.

"Sounds like a good investment," Masters said, leaving the room. "Tell your mother I'll be in contact."

"Will do, Bruno," Egan replied in an oily tone. "Now, I'd better get you to the airport … wouldn't want you to miss your—" The closing front door cut the rest.

Thoughts in a tangle, Ronan crouched, listening to the Range Rover burble into the distance. The meal delivery docket in Luli's pocket, combined with Saoirse's scant description, convinced him she was in this house when not at the hospital, and the snatches of overheard conversation indicated the Egans owned it. How could that be coincidence? In addition, they were courting Masters to invest in a scheme to buy more houses in the street. Accident, Egans, Luli, Vítek, Ylli, house and, now, Masters? The more Ronan teased the threads, the more certain he was that it was all the same cloth; he just couldn't work out how, or why.

A side issue tugging at his thoughts was the younger Egan's involvement; budding entrepreneur didn't sit well with the arrogant bully Ronan knew him to be. Perhaps this was what Fionella meant when she told her son back in the Raven's Roost cottage not to forget what she was doing for him. It was obvious he'd received training in real estate.

Ronan shrugged. His immediate focus was to confirm Saoirse's presence in the house. He set out on reconnaissance.

It didn't take long. The entryway merged into a hall that ran the depth of the dwelling, all rooms peeling off to the right; the left-hand wall was shared with the neighbouring dwelling. After the lounge came a compressed kitchen, small enough for a caravan. Every surface carried the debris of laziness: fast food wrappers and containers, and plates caked with festering remains of unidentified foodstuffs, many stained with equally unknown sauces and other condiments. Next was a toilet and bathroom—both grubby—then a bedroom struggling to contain a double mattress, a tangle of bedclothes and an open suitcase that appeared to have belched underclothes.

The hallway ended in a closed door with a shiny new hasp above the knob. A brass padlock secured it to the loop screwed to the jamb. It looked as much a jail as the nearby prison.

49

———

MANACLES AND CHAINS

The locked door was an obstacle. While afraid of what might be on the other side, Ronan had to be certain. Visions of the manacles and soiled bed in the prison house flooded his mind. A dark, primeval rage rose in him, swirling, blistering, intensified by the rune's influence. Part of him wanted to surrender to it, another part fought the Norse urges, clamping down on the fury and vengeful impulses. Even though the rune enhanced his skill and courage, he could not, would not, let it change who he was.

With an effort, he trained his ears toward the front of the house. No sound was good news, so he thumbed a switch on the adjacent wall. A yellow slit shot from beneath the door.

Cheek pressed against the floorboards, Ronan peered into the chink of light. A bare concrete wall, several metres beyond the door, held a rectangular tracery of hairline cracks suggesting underlying brickwork. Memorising the arrangement of lines, he allowed his mind to empty and drift into ró. A heartbeat later he was on a tiny landing where steep stairs cornered at ninety-degrees.

A single anaemic bulb hung above the upper section, its spiritless illumination swallowed by the gloom in the farthest corners of the space. But there was enough for Ronan to make out a scatter of storage boxes, pieces of furniture and assorted household items. Opposite the stairs, a space had been cleared for a narrow mattress. The turned down blanket and fluffed and centralised pillow wrenched his heart—Saoirse was exercising the only control she could, clutching a sliver of normality. Her bag, zipped tight, sat on the floor beside the mattress, and at the foot of the rudimentary bed, a plastic bucket exuded the sharp odour of stale urine. His anger ignited.

A glint near the bucket caught his eye. When he stepped closer, the anger burst into blazing outrage. Snaking out from an anchor bolt set into the concrete wall was a length of chain ending in a single manacle. Ronan stooped, snatching up the padded metal strap with a violence that frightened him. The raw hatred that consumed him during a Masters' beating was nothing compared to the current madness gripping him. The image of Saoirse lying there, shackled like a slave, was molten rage. He wouldn't let her spend another night like that.

Lost in a pulsing red mist, Ronan didn't hear the squeak of hallway floorboards; however, the rattle of the padlock jolted him from the consuming mania. With nowhere to hide, he shrank into the farthest corner, emptied his mind and visualised the musty sofa.

"Get in there, girl," Luli growled as Ronan set down in the tiny lounge room. After a brief silence, her voice turned quizzical: "I am sure I turned that light off this morning." The authority in her voice leaked into uncertainty; Ronan's fists clenched, his jaw worked.

Saoirse huffed. "You obviously didn't."

"Don't be smart with me, girl," Luli retorted. "Get in there and behave, or no dinner."

Even as Ronan twitched for vengeance, he settled. At times, it was like the rune was in a tussle with itself, driving him toward retribution while counterbalancing with calming wisdom. Regardless, they had to plan their next move with clear heads, retaliation could come later.

The lock snapped closed, he waited. When a radio began pumping out a foreign language song, he folded from the air in front of a startled Saoirse. She recovered in flash. "Fancy meeting you here," she said dryly, leaning into his arms.

"Thought you might like company," he breathed into her ear.

"Very much so," she whispered as she pulled away and rummaged in her bag. He watched in admiration as she set her own radio on a lower step, creating noise to disguise their muted conversation. It was playing something about a bloke thinking he should leave right now. "That's not me," he said when she returned.

"Better not be," she murmured against his neck.

They melted into the comfort of each other's arms; time disappeared. Ronan's phone made several muted attempts to rouse him, but they went unnoticed amid murmured reassurances and the pretence of normality. Their fantasy was broken by the radio announcing the five o'clock news. With a start, Ronan realised how much time had passed, and as much as he didn't want to, he drew Saoirse back to her predicament.

"So, what's this all about?" he asked, with a vague sweep of his arm. "And who's behind it?"

Tensing, Saoirse eased away. "I wish I knew. All I know for sure is they want you out of the picture." Her eyes narrowed. "What have you been up to?"

"Nothing you don't know about," he replied evenly, fighting the sting that she might think he caused her situation. Before Darragh's accident, he hadn't interacted with anyone in Ireland, apart from the Kellys and the Egans. A sudden crushing thought hit Ronan. Could it all be retribution for the way he'd stood up to Egan's bullying on his first visit? "Do you think Finnegan could do this?"

"Huh? No ... way above his pay grade."

Relief surged through him. "Isn't he smart enough? Or evil enough?"

She shook her head. "Too sophisticated for Finnegan."

Ronan chuckled.

"What?"

"You just called him Finnegan."

Saoirse scrunched her nose, punching him playfully. "I told you I'd end up calling him that if you didn't stop."

"He was here earlier ... with Masters."

"Fionn and ... your stepfather ... here?" Her mouth hung half open.

He nodded.

"But ... how are they involved?"

"I don't know. From what I overheard, the Egans own this house, and Finnegan was showing Masters around like a real estate agent, trying to get him to invest in buying more houses like this, something about building a hotel. And I know they didn't see this room because it was locked."

Saoirse stood shaking her head, unable, or unwilling, to process the information.

"What about Fionella?" Ronan asked.

"What do you mean?" Saoirse said, snapping out of denial.

"Could she be behind it all?"

"I don't know ... what's in it for her?"

Ronan hesitated to voice what came to mind, but nothing else made any sense. "You," he said.

50

ESCAPE PLAN

They sat on the mattress, backs propped against the cold masonry. The walls of the cellar seemed to huddle into the silence, drawing closer. The biting stench of urine hung in the stale air. "What do you mean, *me*?"

Having floated the theory with Caitlin, Ronan explored it further. "What are the odds that the person who told you about your father's accident, and drove you to Dublin, also owns the house where you're being held prisoner?"

Saoirse's gaze flitted round his face. "But what would she want me for?"

"Didn't you say she's had you married off to Finnegan for years?"

She paled. "I can't believe anyone would deliberately do that to Dad." Her features collapsed in anguish. "It's all my fault."

Ronan drew her close. "Or it might be my fault ... if I hadn't turned up, none of this would've happened. Or is it the rune's fault? Or maybe your fault for making that notebook?" He knew he'd taken his wacky logic too far when her sobbing carried above the pulsing beat of a plaintive singer appealing for understanding of what it's like to be left outside alone.

Ronan's attempt to console failed; the padlock rattled. Shrinking into the shadow of the stairs, he held his breath, silently beseeching Saoirse to look elsewhere.

Tinny music avalanched down the steps, swirling with Saoirse's radio into a cacophony of gibberish. The overhead bulb threw Saoirse's tear-stained face into sharp relief, and Ronan just wanted to hold her. The urge to flytja her away was overpowering, but he fought the impulse. They had to find a way that didn't raise suspicion. Anything that looked like an escape would invite retaliation and put lives at risk; if Ylli was involved, the threats of violence were not idle ones. Between the three of them, they had to hatch something that would appear coincidental.

"Stop feeling sorry for yourself, girl," Luli scolded.

"Why are you doing this?"

There was a thud on the landing in response, followed by the flooding aroma of greasy chips.

"Why?" Saoirse pleaded, but the only reply was the slamming door and rattling lock.

Ronan was by her side in an instant, brushing hair from her face, holding her close.

At last, she eased away, delving into her bag for tissues. While she blew her nose and dried tears, Ronan investigated the food. A burger had burst from its wrapper and smeared across the landing amid the greasy chaos of scattered chips. And lying against the wall was a bottle of water; it was the only thing Ronan salvaged.

Crouching, he offered the water, saying, "What would you like for dinner?"

"Very funny."

"I'm serious ... my shout."

Saoirse's realisation turned into a quiet tease. "I suppose you want to borrow money?"

Ronan pulled the wad of euros from his pocket, waving them under her nose.

"Who did you rob?" The flash of teeth in the murky light killed any accusation.

"I solved a crime that wasn't what it appeared," he said, relating a brief summary of the Hagans' insurance scam.

"Grand," Saoirse said when he'd finished. "You can pay me back."

The returning sparkle in her voice lifted Ronan's heart. "Of course."

"With interest."

"Of course," Ronan repeated, leaning in and kissing her softly. "How's that?" he asked when they separated.

"Mmm, my rate's higher than that."

"Good," he said. "But first, dinner. What's your fancy?"

"Surprise me."

Ronan blanked his mind and was gone.

Moments after the slit in the air sighed closed, another opened, disgorging Ronan and a large paper bag. He collapsed to the floor, clasping his head.

"Ronan!" Saoirse cried, cradling him. "What's wrong?"

"I shouldn't have done it," he moaned. "I should have known."

"Done what, Ronan ...?"

"The rune"—he panted—"... getting worse ... every time-flytja ... my head explodes ... it's on fire ..."

"Oh, you poor thing."

"I had to wait ten minutes for the food, but I didn't want you here by yourself, so I time-flytjed back to straight after I left ... shouldn't have ..."

"Well, don't next time." Saoirse began massaging his temples with her fingertips, tiny circles that eased the flames and dispersed his distress. "I'm not going anywhere," she added ironically.

"Mmm," Ronan murmured, relishing the distraction, "that's nice."

"Dad does this when I have a nasty headache."

While Saoirse rubbed, he found his Panadol in a pocket, swallowing a couple with a swig from the water bottle.

By the time he'd recovered enough to think of food, the grilled chicken and salad sandwiches were a sodden mess, having soaked up the spillage from a super-large milkshake. But the oversized cardboard pack filled with a single piece of apple slice was intact.

"I should clean up that mess," Saoirse said, gesturing toward the landing, licking the last crumb from a fingertip.

Ronan put a hand over hers. "No, leave it. Between it and the bucket, she won't be able to smell our dinner. Besides, we have more important things to do."

She gave him a puzzled look. "Do you always think four steps ahead?"

He tapped his rune and pulled out his phone. There were three text messages from Caitlin, each one more succinct and, he suspected, more irate than its predecessor:

1:36 - *Am free til 2:45, then again after 4*

1:52 - *Am still free if u r interested*

3:49 - *Where r u??*

4:37 - *You're scaring me. Text me!*

Ronan's thumbs laboured over an apology: *sorry been busy. with s now. can't call.*

Where r u? was the instant reply.

Thumbs stumbling and bumbling, he punched in: *we r locked ...*

Another message popped in, cutting off his struggle: *?? nevr mind. At your txting r8 it will take u all night to xplain.*

Ronan held up Caitlin's text, feigning offence. Saoirse grinned as she took the phone; her dancing thumbs transfixing him.

s here, this should make it faster. we r locked in a cellar ... And, for the next twenty minutes, they went back and forth until they had settled on a rescue strategy.

Saoirse was asking Caitlin about how her appointments were going when the padlock rattled. Ronan grabbed his phone, and the bag of dinner debris, and flytjed away.

51

———

SHACKLED

Ronan binned the rubbish behind the cafe where he'd bought the food, grunting with annoyance at the space-flytja's simmer. Ignoring it, he aimed for the lounge room once more.

As he folded from the air, the cellar door swung open. Luli's descending footsteps were cut off by a surprised yelp, a hefty thud, and foreign cursing. Ronan was desperate to look, but he dared not, fearful of a squeaky floor board. Instead, he imagined Luli sprawled on the landing after slipping on the food she'd thrown down earlier.

"Clean up this damned mess," she growled.

"I didn't make it," Saoirse retorted. That drew a surly response, but she carried on, defiant. "I'll clean it up if I can empty the bucket."

"Clean up and I will think about it."

"Bucket first."

Luli's tone hardened. "Go to hell, girl. Put on the bracelet."

The silence grew.

"Put it on!"

Ronan's jaw knotted, his body twitching for action.

The chain scraped and clinked on the concrete floor. After a couple of snicks and clicks, Luli climbed from the room, relocking the door. She gave the light switch a spiteful slap and huffed into the bedroom at the same time as Ronan set down in the pitch-black cellar. "Saoirse?" he breathed, swallowing the stabbing head flare.

"Ronan ..." she whimpered.

By the light of his phone, he found her slumped in misery on the mattress, back against the wall. "It's okay," he said, easing down and enfolding her.

"It's so ... humiliating." Saoirse wriggled her foot; the chain clinked.

"That witch," Ronan muttered. "Why does she have to chain you up like a dog?"

"Added security, she says." Tears glinted. "I hate you seeing me like this."

"No problem," Ronan said breezily, closing the phone, plunging the room into darkness. Luli must have gone to bed, for there was not even a chink of light beneath the door. They could have been in a coffin.

"I know you're trying to help, but you've no idea what it does when she puts that thing on."

Ronan had no words; he drew her closer.

Saoirse melted against him as if all strength had left her. "Now I know how slaves feel."

Ronan wondered if her mother's African heritage added another layer of distress. "You'll never be a slave while I live," he declared with a surge of rune certainty.

"You really are my hero," she murmured, snuggling into his neck. "But it doesn't stop me feeling helpless and ... I don't know ... dirty."

Ronan stiffened. "Did they ... have they ... you know, assaulted you?" The words floundered as dread gripped him.

Saoirse stiffened, pulling away. "You mean sexually?"

Ronan sensed her gaze and was thankful for the gloom hiding the heat rising in his cheeks. "In any way," he said amid mushrooming anger.

"Would it make a difference?" She withdrew further.

"To what?" He feared the widening gulf.

"You and me."

"Never ... not in a million years." Ronan reached across the void, finding her hands, squeezing. They remained listless in his.

"Then why did you ask?"

"So I know how much retribution to deliver," he growled without hesitation, the fiery-eyed monster stirring in his chest.

"I don't need vengeance," Saoirse said, returning his pressure. "I just need to be free of this nightmare ... I wish you could flytja me away."

"I could." Guilt chaffed him as he related the double-up flytja with Caitlin. "But we have to stick to our plan; it's the only way to protect your dad ... and your mum and Niall."

"I know." She sagged into his arms once more. "It's just that I hate this ... this ... impotence."

Ronan hugged her tight, trying to reassure. "This will be the last night, I promise, and I'll be here the whole time ... I'm not going anywhere." The words rang hollow to Ronan; he wasn't the one chained by the ankle to a concrete wall. Saoirse had endured seven nights of the indignity already. "We'll get through it together," he added, trying to imagine how she felt.

The radio in the room above clicked off, flooding silence into the cellar. And in the stillness, Ronan embraced the Norse beast within. Fionella Egan was going to pay.

52

———

WHISPERS

S aoirse and Ronan lay sharing the pillow, cheeks touching, limbs entwined. Speaking in breathy whispers, only enough to carry to each other's ears, Ronan related the gist of what had happened since he'd left her in the cottage kitchen a week earlier. She gasped at his retelling of Fionella shooting him, and was pensive during his description of his quick visit to Freyja's deserted longhouse and his father's message on the door. But his recounting of Caitlin's prickly demeanour when they first met had her amused.

"Caitlin is very black and white," Saoirse said, "but you couldn't get a better friend ... hundred percent loyal."

"Don't I know it," Ronan said, launching into an account of the trouble he had getting Caitlin to trust him, and tacking on more details of Sean Hagan's scam.

Saoirse relived the confusion, panic and dread of the accident day, and admonished herself for going with Luli to the house. "I can't believe I did that," she lamented.

"Why wouldn't you have gone with her?" Ronan asked, searching for a way to ease her self-reproach. "She gave the impression she was with the health service. How were you to know otherwise?"

"But I should have checked." Her voice had risen with her level of distress.

"Shh," Ronan soothed, stroking her hair. "You were focused on your dad."

"But I've dragged my whole family into something dangerous"—she sobbed in the darkness—"and I don't know how to get them out of it ... or even what *it* is."

A heel pounded on the bedroom floor above; it was followed by a growled rebuke about blubbering. Ronan cradled her head, drawing her helplessness and self-blame into his shoulder, whispering reassurances.

"We'll get you all out of it tomorrow," Ronan said with forced confidence. While their strategy was sound, plenty could go wrong; he wouldn't relax until it was behind them. The hardest part for him was staying removed from the whole exercise; only Saoirse and Caitlin could carry it out. Any sign of him, or other outside help, would mean Saoirse had broken her bargain. "Then," he continued, "we'll work out what it's all about and who's involved."

"How can you be so confident?" Saoirse asked.

In answer, he guided her fingers to the rune lump in his hair.

"But aren't you ever afraid?"

"All the time," he said matter-of-factly. "But not like when Masters was on the warpath." Ronan swallowed, shuddering at the name. Before he discovered his blood rune, whenever the wrath of his stepfather festered like a surly storm cloud, he would imagine a time when the man was no longer around, and there was freedom from the constant fear of his iron fists. How Ronan had longed for an end to the terror of what Masters threatened to do to Ronan's mother and brother if he ever breathed a word to anyone. "And I always found," he added, "that thinking about what life would be like without the fear, helped me to get through the fear itself ... that probably doesn't make much sense ... sorry."

"I think I know what you mean," she said, "but it's easier said than done."

"I know," Ronan admitted. Then, attempting to generate positive thoughts, he listed the things they would do once her dad was back at Raven's Roost.

"Ronan?" Saoirse ventured after he'd run out of whispers.

"Yeah?"

"I have to pee."

"Well, go pee."

"But you'll hear me."

"And then I'll have to pee and you'll hear me, so we'll be even."

She kissed his cheek again and moved off amid the sliding clink of chain. Ronan's monster stirred.

"Turn away then," she said.

He made an exaggerated squirm on the mattress as he lay staring through the pitch black toward the ceiling. "Back turned; eyes closed," he said. "Promise."

"Ah, but can you be trusted, Ronan Ryan?"

His heart lurched at her use of his full name. "Definitely not," he replied, thankful for the returning playfulness in her voice.

"Mmm," she said to the sound of tinkling.

Moments later, it was his turn to add to the bucket. "We're not drinking enough water," he said. By the phone's dim screen light, he found an old painting large enough to cover the bucket and confine the biting ammonia stench.

"Well, we'll fix that tomorrow."

"Sure will," he agreed, pulling the blankets up as she snuggled close.

"If only there was some way to rig that bucket above the door?" Ronan mused.

"Urgh ... you have an evil mind. But what a great idea."

He kissed the top of her head. "'Night."

"Goodnight," she murmured.

Saoirse's head grew heavy on his shoulder as she snuffled and soughed into a deep sleep. Ronan lay listening to her mesmeric breathing, eventually succumbing and tumbling into a cauldron of faceless men, vicious threats, and a woman with greying auburn hair and slitted reptilian eyes.

53

CRASH AND BURN

The rattling lock had Ronan bolt upright in an instant. Barely awake, he pictured the lounge room and folded from Saoirse's sleeping arms. *The phone!* He'd left the damned thing on the floor beside the mattress! Frantic for a diversion, he swiped an old china vase off the dusty sideboard. As the echoes of its shattering receded, and Luli's urgent footsteps grew loud in the hallway, Ronan aimed for the cellar.

Saoirse stirred as he folded back into the bed beside her. She smiled sleepily.

"Gotta go," he whispered, pecking her cheek, grabbing his phone and disappearing as Luli returned to the cellar door, mumbling about house spirits.

In a blink, Ronan was back among shards of porcelain. Luli's harsh voice drifted up the stairs. "You know what to do," the woman was saying. "Unlock and slide the key back to me. Good, now bring your bucket up and empty it ... the air is foul down here."

"You could have let me empty it last night," Saoirse responded sourly.

"Do as you are told, girl."

Saoirse snorted; Ronan's fists tightened.

As much as he wanted to listen further, he was pushing his luck, so with twin footfalls echoing on the steps, he jumped from the lounge room to the nearby cafe. His fourth quick flytja without even a suggestion of pain had him optimistic and energised.

After extricating himself from the refuse behind the building, he ordered a full breakfast and settled into the most concealed table position he could find. It had a rear view of pedestrians exiting Glengarriff Parade, and an oblique one across the road to the hospital entrance. While he waited and watched, he devoured sausages, bacon, fried eggs, tomato, mushrooms and a slab of soda bread; he hadn't realised how hungry he was until the aroma reached his nostrils.

Between mouthfuls, he texted Caitlin that he was in position, and asked where she was. After an age without a response, Ronan worried their plan had already derailed. He was about to text again when a reply pinged into his phone: she'd been in the shower, and was now in a taxi with her mother, heading to her first appointment.

Ronan had no expectation of picking them out of the conga-line of vehicles filing through the arrival lane at the hospital entrance. But their plan was not built on minute detail and clockwork precision, only on the assumption that Saoirse and Luli would be in the hospital when Caitlin's consultation finished.

where r u? he sent.

5 min from hosptl pinged back. *Any sign?*

not yet. tell me wen u arrive. Ronan was thoroughly disinterested in learning how to make a capital letters, and the required cumbersome button pressing—he was getting no better—overrode the desire to continue the conversation. Muttering at his lack of expertise, he sipped more tea.

The phone's ping caught him with a piece of egg-soaked bread halfway between plate and mouth. *Just pulled in,* popped onto the screen. He looked up to a column of taxis chugging through the set-down lane, disgorging singles, couples and families, but no sign of Caitlin and her mother, yet. Right when they didn't need it, familiarity coalesced in his peripheral vision, dragging his attention to the opposite footpath. Saoirse and Luli were passing.

Dropping his titbit, Ronan snatched up the phone, but his thumbs were contrary: the faster he tried to type, the slower they moved. He eventually punched *dont get out, s coming* into his phone. By the time technology sucked it up to wherever it went, and pushed it down to Caitlin's device, Saoirse and Luli had joined a gaggle of paper-reading, coffee-sipping workers waiting for the green signal to cross North Circular Road.

In a flutter, Ronan scanned the taxis, trying to identify which one was about to release the O'Tooles and scupper the rescue plan before it even got started. The only cab with no alighting passengers was parked between the pedestrian crossing and the hospital entrance. If it held Caitlin and Bridget, it couldn't be in a worse position.

The lights turned red, traffic ground to a halt, and a stream of pedestrians carried Saoirse and Luli across the street like a conveyor belt. Their adjacent arms were crooked and interlinked, companions offering mutual support. However, the black-haired woman's hand was locked on Saoirse's wrist. The monster of retribution stirred and flexed in Ronan's chest.

As he flicked his focus back to the taxi, its rear door opened to Bridget's less-than-sunny face. Saoirse and her warder were crossing the set-down lane in front of the O'Toole vehicle. Bridget climbed from the taxi. The plan had seemed so feasible last night, but now, with a fateful quirk of timing, it was about to crash and burn.

54

RESCUED

The chess pieces of their loosely cobbled strategy were about to collide. Ronan had a stop-start view of it all through the gaps between bustling vehicles on North Circular Road, and despite his agitation, there was nothing to do but watch it unravel, a slow-motion train-wreck. As he did, familiar warmth quelled his angst, bringing clarity.

No one was paying attention to his shadowed alcove, so he visualised the back door of the O'Toole's taxi, relying on the rune to set him down in the closest safe place. Half a heartbeat later, he was curled in darkness. "Just have another look, Mum, please?" came Caitlin's muffled voice.

"Your purse is not on the floor, Caitlin," Bridget shot back testily. "You must have dropped it somewhere else."

Ronan thumped the boot lid several times with the heel of his hand and filled his mind with his plate of half-eaten breakfast. He was pleasantly surprised to find himself back at the table, rather than among the bins behind the building—his secluded table had remained ignored.

Across the street, the taxi driver leapt from the car, almost colliding with Bridget as she rushed round the front of the vehicle, not more than half a dozen paces behind Saoirse and Luli. But she appeared focused on only one thing, extricating her daughter from a vehicle with someone locked in its boot. As she reached for the door handle, the boot lid popped. The driver stood, gaping with relief and puzzlement; Bridget stole a glance as she reefed Caitlin's door open, pausing, staring in disbelief at the driver. The man gestured to the empty compartment, mouthing something past an awkward smile.

Caitlin took her time climbing from the taxi, sheepishly holding up a cream purse. Bridget bristled with rekindled irritation, while in the background, the cavernous building swallowed Saoirse and Luli.

Ronan exhaled. Their plan was still alive, and Caitlin was doing her best to keep it that way. She paused to adjust her jacket, then again to scratch her scalp as she dawdled in her mother's wake. Amused by her antics, Ronan thumbed off a laborious, *gr8 work.* Soon after, she stopped, fiddling with her phone, then glancing behind, a grin creasing her face.

She idled after her mother into the stream of people funnelling through the hospital doors, like krill into the mouth of a feeding whale. A lethargic city bus full of vacant-eyed passengers trundled past, blocking Ronan's view. Through its exhaust-shrouded wake, he caught a final glimpse of Caitlin's swinging crutches as the door devoured them.

With all pieces on the chessboard, Ronan relaxed, returning to the remains of his breakfast. Caitlin's first appointment would last an hour, she'd said, so he had plenty of time. Later, he emerged from the party shop with a fresh clutch of cheerful colour jostling above. After navigating the hospital's labyrinth passageways, Ronan settled into a threadbare chair from where he had a clear view of the entrance of Darragh's ward and the bank of elevators servicing it. He waited.

Every time the elevator doors slid open, Ronan dropped his chin, hiding behind his cap visor. But each chime was a false alarm, and as they mounted, alternative scenarios began jostling for his attention. He'd narrowed it down to Caitlin not being able to convince her mother, when an elevator pinged its arrival.

Bridget looked as though she'd been talked into one more thing to fit into an already busy day. She wheeled into the ward without pause. Caitlin, on the other hand, crutched a few paces, stopped, and turned slowly, the corners of her mouth twitching with recognition. After arching an eyebrow, she turned and followed her mother. Ronan gave her a head start and dragged his balloons after her.

As he rounded the corridor to the nurse station, Bridget was saying, "... but my daughter is Saoirse's best friend."

"I'm sorry, but Mrs Kelly asked that they have no visitors for the moment." A night of rest had done little to ease the weariness etched in Nurse Amy Garcia's features, but her white blouse was fresh and crisp.

Bridget frowned. "Mrs Kelly?"

Ronan admonished himself for not anticipating that Niamh might turn up to support her daughter and ex-husband, but then he remembered, Niamh had remarried.

"The patient's wife." Garcia's tolerance was wafer-thin.

Before Bridget could voice either confusion or disbelief, Caitlin said, "Well, can we at least speak to Saoirse?"

Ronan sidled past the exchange; no one noticed the cluster of bobbing balloons.

A peek into room twenty-four showed the same young man—Ronan hoped he was recovering—in the same state of slumber, yesterday's green balloon sagging. Stealing inside, he took up a position with an unimpeded view of the nurse station, and a diagonal one over the corridor to the door of Darragh's room. For a second, he wondered whether the rune was manipulating things for him.

Garcia's heels clicked sharply across the hard floor to room twenty-seven. A drift of murmured discussion reached Ronan, then the nurse emerged, displeasure hardening her features. "Her mother says no."

While Ronan scrambled for a way round this latest difficulty, Caitlin crutched resolutely toward twenty-seven. But Garcia stepped into her path. "You must leave, now, miss."

"I'm not leaving without speaking to Saoirse." Caitlin was adamant.

"Caitlin," Bridget cautioned, reaching for her.

She shook off the hand. "Mum, no," she insisted. "Something is not right here ... Saoirse would never act like this, and neither would Aunty Niamh."

Garcia's cheeks flushed; she held up a palm. "Miss, if you don't leave, I will have to call security."

"Please do!" Caitlin shot back, swinging past the navy and white uniform.

"I'm sorry," Bridget said with an apologetic hand on the nurse's arm. "Please give me a moment ... I'm sure I can make her see sense."

Garcia radiated exasperation. "One chance."

But, as Caitlin arrived at Darragh's door, it thumped closed. Leaning toward the opaque glass panel, she said, "I didn't come looking for you, Saoirse, I promise ... I thought I saw you earlier, and when I asked at the desk, they said your dad was up here." There was no response. "Saoirse, please ..."

Beyond the door, a growled accusation preceded a harsh slap. "How could I tell anyone anything," Saoirse snapped, "you've got my damned phone."

Caitlin's face reflected determination, Bridget's uncertainty, Garcia's sudden decision. "I'm calling security," the nurse barked, striding toward her desk.

Ronan retreated into the shadows as she passed, almost missing the door to Darragh's room bursting open. A livid Luli barged out, dragging Saoirse with her, knocking Caitlin to the floor, shouldering Bridget aside.

As she teetered, Bridget grabbed at the woman's wrist, yelling, "Let her go!"

Luli windmilled her arm to break the grip.

Ronan was torn: he couldn't let Saoirse leave, but he dared not show himself. So he shrank away, determined to only intervene as a last resort. He felt like a slacker as navy and white uniforms popped from rooms at the commotion.

From where she'd fallen, Caitlin swung a crutch in a vicious arc at the back of Luli's legs. The woman released Saoirse with a sharp cry and spun on Caitlin who walloped her across the shins while Bridget clung tenaciously. Luli yelped and flung Bridget against the wall where she slid to the floor, astonishment chasing the colour from her face. Meanwhile, Saoirse had gathered an errant crutch and was now laying into Luli's back. Again and again, she hit her captor until the woman retreated, hurling curses and glaring daggers.

A red light high on the wall at the end of the corridor began blinking in time to a muted siren as the nurses gathered in a loose phalanx behind the returning Garcia. Luli's options didn't look good; she hesitated, then spat invective in all directions and ran toward the fire stairs.

Ronan allowed himself a breath. Saoirse stood shaking and ashen-faced, Luli's hand-print glowing on her cheek. As much as he desperately wanted to console her, the job was only half done; he now had to do his part. Leaving balloons bobbling against the ceiling, he cleared his mind and folded away.

55

SURVEILLANCE

Cold silence greeted Ronan when he set down amid shattered china. The solitude didn't last long: after a brief key-rattle, a breathless Luli burst in, dialling as she powered to the bedroom. While throwing belongings into the suitcase, she jabbered on the phone in a foreign language. As recognition hit, an icy blast of Siberian winter swirled through Ronan's veins. Luli was speaking the same language Ylli had used in the phone box three nights ago. It didn't matter if she was talking *to* Ylli, about him, or simply sharing the language, anything connected to that thug triggered alarm.

Connections formed in Ronan's head, like shapes emerging from fog: Vítek and Ylli; Ylli and Luli; Luli and the Egan's house. Ronan was now positive it was Vítek and Ylli who had scared Saoirse, and he was certain the Egans were involved. But for some reason, the voice of his science teacher cut through, explaining how subconscious bias can lead you to massage facts to support what you want to believe.

Ronan's reflection was cut short by Luli hustling past, bulging suitcase in one hand, phone pressed to her ear with the other. She left the door gaping in her wake, took the six steps in two bounds and turned away from the hospital. Peering after her, Ronan set his sights on the opposite side of the street.

From between two parked cars, he watched Luli's receding back. The phone returned to a pocket and she fiddled, one-handed, isolating a single key from a bunch. Within seconds, he had to flytja again, this time jumping almost abreast as she veered up the steps of a residence similar to the previous one. After a furtive glance toward the hospital, she twisted the key. The door swung open, exposing a slice of hallway; she ducked through, disappearing as the closing door cut off Ronan's scrutiny.

The recollection of Egan's boast of buying up a heap of houses to knock down and build a big, money-making hotel, had Ronan figuring this was another Egan building. While it seemed logical, and dovetailed into the narrative of the Egans' involvement and duplicity, he still wondered if it mightn't be that bias at play.

A footfall from behind made Ronan drop to a knee and fiddle with a shoelace. While the pedestrian passed without comment, he couldn't stay in such an exposed position. It was only a matter of time until he was challenged; he needed a better vantage point to watch both houses. The inside of a vehicle wasn't an option for an extended period either, and the flat-fronted residences, shallow doorways and non-existent shrubbery offered no convenient cover.

Once sure Luli was not at the window opposite, Ronan peeled off his glasses, wig and cap, stuffing them into coat pockets, then standing and walking casually back the way he'd come. The building Luli entered was seven doors down from where she'd held Saoirse—somewhere about halfway would be ideal. But, well before then, he spied a window with open curtains—perfect. He was soon in a cosy living room full of smiling photos and his own guilt.

When flytjing into a stranger's parked car the previous day, Ronan had thought nothing of it—perhaps he should have—but dropping into someone's home felt different: dirty, dishonest. Shame urged him to leave, necessity kept him there.

His swirling remorse was made worse by the friendly faces of a young couple—no hint of children—staring from numerous photos. They were most likely both at work, so Ronan guessed he might have five or six hours before he'd have to move on, but for the present, he sank into the chair's comfort to watch and wait.

It took more than an hour for the first sign of activity: two gardaí festooned with belt-pouches, shoulder-radios and hi-vis vests, striding round the corner from the nearby garda station. Caution slowed their brisk pace as they approached the unlatched door. One spoke into her radio, waited, transmitted a second time, then nodded to her partner; they eased inside, batons in hand.

Ronan would have loved to flytja across to listen to their search, but watching Luli was more important. Yet nothing stirred in that direction. Within minutes, a white van bedecked with blue lights, reflective stripes and large lettering proclaiming it to be the Garda Technical Bureau's Crime Scene Investigation Unit, swung down the narrow street, blocking it like a cork in a bottle.

The vehicle deposited several officers who were soon shrouded in disposable white coveralls complete with hoods, as well as face masks, gloves and shoe covers, all in varying shades of blue—they could have been heading into an operating theatre, or trying to survive a Covid pandemic. They were joined by a couple of plain-clothes gardaí who, similar to the original pair, arrived on foot. After a brief discussion during which the detectives pulled on matching shoe covers, the forensics officers led them into the building. The original duo strung crime scene tape and took up vantage points, feet splayed, hands clasped in front, a barrier to curious passers-by.

While he watched, Ronan shot off a quick text to Caitlin: *follwng l. hows s?* Before long, his phone lit up: *B careful. I think L was in house where Y threw me down stairs. Keep us updated. We'll be at garda station for hrs. S sends love.* The first part of the message sobered him, the last left him buoyed.

Over the next several hours, Ronan kept swinging his attention between the gardaí activity and Luli's current bolt-hole. There was no shortage of action at the former as more officers arrived, the cordon was expanded, and several media outlets tried, unsuccessfully, to breach the tape barrier to interview the detectives. The arrival of a grey-haired man with a peaked cap and uniform lapels emblazoned with red and gold insignia, caused much excitement among the cameras, but the tape held firm. Meanwhile, Luli remained like a rabbit in a burrow with a fox on the prowl.

The warm afternoon sunlight slanting through the window weighed on Ronan's eyelids; they kept sliding shut until they were too heavy to lift again. It was a fitful sleep in which a shackled Saoirse cried for help, tormenting him, but she was always just beyond his stretching fingertips, or behind a locked door he couldn't breach. Then his heart lifted to the rattle of a key.

Ronan's hopes evaporated as a strange voice cut through the dream, catapulting him into full-blown panic. The owner of the tiny flat had returned! He shrank into a corner as a man in grimy overalls—keys jangling in one hand, phone pressed to an ear with the other—walked past the open door. Ronan cursed himself, then a settling calmness cleared his mind. He recalled the sliver of hallway he'd seen earlier.

56

ANGUISH

The house was empty! Luli was gone! It didn't matter when or how, Ronan's sloppiness had cost them their best chance of solving the mystery behind everything, and ensuring Saoirse and Darragh remained safe. As much as he attempted to analyse the best way to make amends, his annoyance and sense of failure kept clouding his reasoning.

There was no clue for when Luli had left. Unlike the movies, no cigarette smouldered in an ashtray, no cup of coffee cooled on a table. When he realised he couldn't have slept for more than an hour, he knew there was a simple way to rescue the situation. While loath to do it, he saw no alternative.

As soon as Ronan visualised the living room across the way, an hour earlier, his skull threatened to disintegrate. The crushing agony ceased the instant he abandoned the attempt. He tried again, aiming for ten minutes back—more torment. Even a one-minute jump was more than he could bear.

Ronan slumped against the wall, dejected, oblivious to blue lights strobing past curtains. Heartache consumed him as he feared he may never get home again. It seemed the effects of the time-flytjas built on each other, in which case, he'd never withstand it long enough to even enter ró. And there were the strange pinging sparks with some space-flytjas. If flytjing became impossible, the only choice was to get rid of the rune and stay in Saoirse's time. Otherwise, it would whisk him to the Home Stone, and that's where he'd stay. Forever.

Anguish clutched at Ronan's lungs. Everything was spinning out of control into a dark unknown. He had five days to ensure Saoirse's safety, for when he cut out the rune, he'd be an ordinary sixteen-year-old again. And without the stone, he'd have to wait seventeen years, until after he'd left his own time, before he could go to Australia to see his mother—he'd be thirty-three! He was suffocating. Everything was falling apart. He'd failed Saoirse; he'd failed himself.

Insistent beating on the front door shattered his despair. Thump, thump, thump. "Garda! Open up!" Thump, thump, thump. "Force it!"

As the door frame shattered, Ronan set down behind the cafe, brain simmering. The departing sun spangled the top of the hospital, but below, the city was lighting up, cars, windows, billboards. He thumbed an awkward text to Caitlin: *where r u?*

Seconds later: *Been called back to hospital. No reason given. S says please come.*

Ronan's heart plummeted, the plea galvanising his thumbs. *c u in 5,* he texted back.

As he wove through the traffic, ignoring scolding toots, Ronan concocted a cover story that brought him and his mother to Dublin: she was having dinner with her old archaeology professor.

Unrestrained wailing greeted him when he entered the ward. For a shameful moment, he hoped it was coming from anywhere but room twenty-seven. As he got closer, his heart tumbled, his pace quickened. Saoirse was sprawled across her father's chest, embracing him through the sheet. A red-eyed Caitlin hugged Saoirse with one arm while balancing on a single crutch. On the near side of the bed stood a sombre priest intoning a Latin chant punctuated by repeated signs of the cross. And in the background, the array of life-support machines was mute and blank.

The scene hit Ronan in a gigantic wave: Darragh's ashen skin and slack jaw, Saoirse's shuddering sobs, Caitlin's tears, the finality of the priest's presence. Sorrow balled in his throat as he laid a cheek against the back of Saoirse's head, whispering, "I'm so sorry, Saoirse."

Renewed keening erupted as she straightened and fell against him. "Oh, Ronan," she howled into his chest, "he's gone."

Confronted by Saoirse's misery, words deserted him. Instead, he held her in silence, stroking her head, fighting against his own tears.

"It's not fair ... he was just going to work."

"I know," Ronan whispered into her hair, trying to convey comfort and reassurance through the pressure of his arms. Nothing could soothe a shattered heart, nothing but time. "I know," he repeated.

Saoirse's distress drew Ronan into her grief. "Poor Dad," she cried.

Through the swirl of his own sorrow came a sudden calmness and clarity—like the eye of a cyclone—and it surprised him. Darragh's death, coming so soon after his grandfather's, reopened the bleak gates to desolation and despair, but instead of the emotion drowning him, it washed round him. The little black pebble fused to his skin had him dry-eyed and resolute, despite Saoirse's anguish.

Bridget's entry with a bag of food triggered a fresh bout of tears and hugs, and Ronan found himself standing beside the priest who extended a friendly hand. "I'm Father McCarthy."

Ronan gripped the offered hand. "Ronan."

McCarthy raised an eyebrow. "Family?"

"Friend."

The man peered at him as if divining his thoughts. "Tis a very sad thing."

"Unnecessary." Although Ronan's gaze was on the three distraught, embracing figures before him, it hardened as he considered the possibility that it was no accident.

McCarthy sighed, repeating, "Tis a very sad thing"—he touched Ronan's arm—"when anger and pain cloud the senses."

Ronan looked down at the hand. About to give another one-word answer, he realised how churlish it would sound. "Wise words, Father. Thank you."

The priest nodded, shook Ronan's hand again, and moved to console Saoirse, Caitlin and Bridget. With a final sign of the cross over Darragh's body, and more futile words of solace, he left.

Despite a swirling desire for vengeance, Ronan knew McCarthy was right. But could he resist when next he saw Fionella Egan?

57

TEARS AND BARBS

At first, Bridget didn't question Ronan's presence. She busied herself liaising with the hospital staff and ensuring everyone had food, even though Saoirse barely picked at hers. They sat and talked, with Caitlin and Bridget avoiding the subject of Darragh, but first-hand experience told Ronan that Saoirse was thinking of nothing else.

"What's your favourite Darragh memory?" Ronan asked Bridget when there was a mini pause in the babble about weather, traffic, and the best place to stay.

Bridget paused, colour rising in her cheeks. Caitlin stiffened, and Saoirse, who was sitting across the arms of the chair, snuggled on Ronan's lap, murmured her thanks.

"It would have to be," Bridget said after consideration, "the time he drove the wrong car home from his card game."

They all chuckled, even Saoirse, but Ronan was puzzled. "Wait, how did that happen?"

"We all left the keys in our cars in those days," Bridget explained, "and there was a second red Corsa there that night." She grinned. "Darragh chose wrong."

"When did he realise?" Ronan asked.

Saoirse lifted puffy features. "When Seamus Donnelly turned up to get his car."

"What did your dad say?"

With a pale smile, Saoirse said, "He didn't miss a beat ... said, 'With all the driving you've been doing, Seamus, did you fill the tank, so?'."

Ronan squeezed her. "I wish I could've got to know him better."

"He liked you, you know," Saoirse murmured, "... said he liked your spirit."

Before Ronan could respond, a surprise walked through the door. Niamh Brosnahan was even more beautiful than in Darragh's photos, not as tall as Saoirse, nor as slim, but her hair was wavy and black as coal, and her bronze skin as smooth as a twenty-year-old, yet she had to be close to forty. Shadowing her was ten-year-old Niall, the image of Darragh, but with an even darker complexion than his mother, more like his Zambian grandmother.

"Oh, Sersh, my darling," Niamh said, enveloping her daughter. "What a tragedy."

Saoirse sobbed out her anguish. Niall pressed close, peering past his sister to the lad on whose lap she'd been sitting.

"Shh," Niamh crooned. "It'll be okay." As she consoled, she acknowledged the others, which reminded Ronan of his own mother who never forgot her manners, no matter what the situation.

"How can it, Mum?"

"I know, darling ... shh."

"Hey, Niall," Saoirse murmured between sobs. She reached out, pulling him into the huddle of family grief.

When Saoirse eased from her mother's arms to blow her nose, Niamh greeted both Caitlin and Bridget with obvious fondness. Ronan wondered whether the close friendship of the daughters led to the same in the mothers, or vice versa—not that it mattered.

"Hello, Bridget. Good to see you."

"You too, Niamh. I just wish it were better circumstances."

Saoirse took a settling breath. "Mum, this is Ronan, my boyfriend."

"Oh." Niamh recovered in an instant, stepping forward, thrusting out a warm hand. "Lovely to meet you, Ronan."

The magnetism of her dark, lustrous eyes entrapped Ronan. "You too, Mrs Brosnahan," he said, understanding Saoirse more by the minute.

"I like your manners"—her teeth flashed, white as a movie star's—"but please, call me Niamh."

"No worries," Ronan said, suddenly awkward, wondering where the rune power had gone.

Another show of teeth and Niamh resumed her conversation with Bridget as if there'd been no break. "Yes, I was floored when I got Caitlin's message ... I didn't even know there'd been an accident." The neutrality of her tone was enough accusation to trigger a quick explanation of the captivity and threats, which led to shock, horror, and another bout of consolation and quiet tears.

"Thanks for coming, Mum," Saoirse said at last.

"How could I not, my darling." Niamh embraced her daughter again.

A solemn nurse poked her head in, asking if anything was needed, telling them to take as long as they wanted. Ronan remembered how the time with Grandpa Paddy's body was way too short, any final farewell would be.

Eventually, after teary words and last touches to waxen skin, the mourners left, Saoirse hugging her mother and brother, Ronan bringing up the rear, very much an outsider. Caitlin dropped back and, with the elevator bulging, waited with him for its return.

When they finally stepped into the foyer, Saoirse and Niamh were locked in animated conversation. Bridget hovered in awkward silence while Niall shimmied on his toes across the floor tiles, avoiding the grout lines. "I would much rather you live with us," Niamh was saying.

"But Mum, that's my home ... my school ... my friends ... Caitlin."

Niamh raised an eyebrow. "And Ronan?"

"Yes, Ronan," Saoirse admitted. "But I never know where he's going to be from one day to the next."

Her mother's eyebrow remained elevated. "You're not ... you know?"

Saoirse rolled her eyes. "Having sex? Mum, no." After a pause, she added, "But I wouldn't tell you if we were."

"Saoirse, I—"

"Ah, there you are," Bridget called with relief as she sighted Ronan and Caitlin. "We're just discussing where to have dinner."

Caitlin dropped her head, pushing a disbelieving 'pfff' from the side of her mouth.

"Where am I going to sleep?" Saoirse challenged, undermining Bridget's fib. Ronan wouldn't have been surprised if her hands flew to her hips; she was never short of determination.

Niamh frowned. "Um ... Niall will have to go in with the twins"—Niall's head jerked up mid-step—"until we can build another room."

"Aw, no," Niall whined.

"Mum," Saoirse began, as though explaining algebra to a first year, "I can share Declan's flat with Caitlin, if Aunty Bridget will have me, finish high school at Carrick, then go to university."

"No, Saoirse"—Niamh held up a palm—"you should be with family at a time like this."

Saoirse's jaw tightened, her eyes flared; Ronan cringed. "Aunty Bridget *is* my family ... you left, remember?" In a swirl of brown-haired resentment, she stalked out the door.

58

SPIRIT AND COMPROMISE

Ronan found Saoirse stalking back and forth near the taxi rank, features set, cheeks glistening.

"Leave me alone!" she snapped.

The words halted Ronan quicker than a karate punch. Biting back a retort, he held out a hand. "Saoirse …"

"I said leave me alone!" She turned away.

"Fine!" Ronan said, sharper than intended. "But you can't do this on your own."

Saoirse stopped mid-stride, shoulders quaking.

Ronan's annoyance melted in the face of her anguish. "Saoirse …?" He reached for her.

"Dad's dead, Ronan," she howled, collapsing against him. "It's not fair …"

"I know."

"What am I going to do?" She trembled in his arms.

"Shh, I'm here." Ronan held her, feeling inadequate.

With her distress easing, he led her to a bench against a wall; the others, in an apprehensive knot, watched through the glass panelling. Niamh dabbed with a tissue; Bridget had an arm round her.

Saoirse sat, head on Ronan's shoulder, sniffling. "What are we going to do?"

"I can't help with that." Ronan murmured.

"I don't mean Mum, she'll come round, I mean Luli, and Fionella, and … those thugs."

"We'll think of something."

"But what?"

Ronan wanted to say something positive; instead, he made a blunt confession: "I lost Luli ... sorry ... fell asleep."

"Oh, so you're not perfect?" Saoirse jolted against him with attempted humour.

"Only on weekends," he quipped, relieved—he deserved displeasure.

"So, what do we do now?" Saoirse lifted her head, meeting his gaze. "And I don't want you time-flytjing back to pick up the trail."

"It's the obvious way t—"

"No, Ronan. It's not worth it. There must be another option, we just have to find it."

"Mmm."

"Promise me you won't."

"Okay."

"Promise."

"Don't you trust me?" Ronan said with forced indignity.

"Not with this."

"I promise not to flytja back to find Luli," he said, huffing at her lack of faith.

"Thank you." Saoirse pressed her lips to his temple. "I can't risk losing you as well."

Ronan ran a thumb across her cheek, wondering how, even in the depths of misery, she could look so beautiful. There was a balance of Niamh and Darragh in her features; he wondered which one gave her the spirit that occasionally flared. Perhaps it was Darragh, for he had once fiercely admonished Ronan. The memory amused him.

"What?" Saoirse said.

"I was just remembering your dad threatening me."

She stiffened.

Ronan laughed. "Nothing bad. Remember when he caught us holding hands on the couch?"

"Yeah ..."

"Well, when you went to make a cup of tea, about the tenth one for the day"—they both grinned—"he got in my face and warned me not to break your heart."

"What did you say?"

"Nothing. I was dumbfounded."

"What, Ronan Ryan, lost for words?" Saoirse jolted him again. "Were you worried he'd come after you?" she added.

"No," Ronan stated, cupping her cheeks, "because I'll never break your heart." He kissed her softly.

"I'm sure Mum thought the same about Dad," she murmured.

Unsure how best to respond to that, Ronan tried levity. "Wait! Are you breaking up with me?"

"Not just yet, boyo."

"Whew!"

After a silence, Saoirse said, "Dad would've done anything to protect me." The words caught in her throat. "He never lost his temper ... that I ever saw. He'd get cranky ... never furious."

"What about your mum?" Ronan was thinking of the spirit question.

Saoirse chuckled. "Boy, she could go off. Not lose control, just get worked up."

"Like you?" Ronan said, lifting her hand, twining his fingers in hers.

"What? No." Her lips twitched. "Well ... maybe a wee bit."

"I know where your beautiful smile comes from now," he said.

"Pfff."

"And the cute nose."

"Stop it." The life was back in Saoirse's voice, but it quickly fled. "It's not fair"—the tears welled afresh—"he was only forty-five."

"I know," Ronan murmured, drawing her closer.

"Why did this happen?" she sobbed.

"No idea," Ronan said, determined not to add to her current despair by voicing his suspicions—they could wait for another day. There was also the knowledge that he only had five days left to get to the bottom of everything. He wondered if Saoirse would still love him without his rune confidence. Blocking the negative thoughts, he said, "But you need to go inside and sort things out with your mum."

"Yes, boss," Saoirse said with brittle flippancy.

Ronan squeezed her shoulders. "Your mum ..."

Saoirse stood, squaring her shoulders. As if that were the signal the others were waiting on, they traipsed from the hospital.

"We're going to have dinner at a little place round the corner," Caitlin said cheerily as she approached. Hugging Saoirse, she whispered, "I think it's sorted, so just don't be too hard on your mum."

Saoirse's response was something between a grimace and gratitude.

Over dinner, the earlier mother-daughter tension dissipated, and an agreement was struck. Niamh made it clear it wasn't her preference, but she seemed relieved once it was settled. Saoirse and Caitlin would share Declan's flat, and when he came home during holidays, they'd double up in Caitlin's old room in the main house. If it didn't work out, Saoirse would move to Dublin.

The fall-back option drew a pained expression from Saoirse, but her gratitude was obvious. By the time she'd thanked Niamh and Bridget several times, there were more tears.

Niamh reached across the table to clasp her daughter's hand. "I only want what's best for you, Sersh."

Ronan wondered what drove the woman to desert her daughter and husband in the first place, but figured he'd never get an answer to that.

Saoirse nodded, pressing a soggy tissue to an eye.

"Oh, and I'm getting a new phone tomorrow," Niamh added, waggling her old one in the air, "so you can have this one."

"But it's newer than mine," Saoirse protested.

With a self-indulgent wink, Niamh said, "I thought I'd try one of those groovy little ones with the coloured screens."

This reminded Ronan that Luli most likely still had Saoirse's mobile, and with the excuse of going to the toilet, he baited a trap for Fionella. Even using every shortcut he knew, it was laborious work, and certainly no literary masterpiece: *sersh y dont u wnt 2 c me. I still love u. pleez call me. am goin bak 2 oz at end of week. love r.* As it sucked away into the ether, he wondered if it was a waste of time.

59

———

REPLAY

Three days later they were back in Declan's flat at Doonin, additional garda interviews and Darragh's funeral behind them. Saoirse's normal cheerfulness succumbed to sober reflection punctuated by periodic lapses into teary melancholy as one thing or another triggered her grief.

"How can the poor thing put it behind her if they don't find this Luli," Caitlin said when Saoirse had gone to the bathroom, "and whoever caused the accident?"

Those same issues were exercising Ronan's mind, and a wild determination to do something about it gripped him. But time was running out: it was already Friday; only two days left in Saoirse's time. If he was right about the flytja fire, the three days without any flytjing meant the next time-flytja should be torment free, the one after survivable, but then, who knew? It would be worth it if he could identify the driver or vehicle; might even lead back to Luli and Fionella.

In case he was wrong about the flytja pain, he dosed himself with Panadol and Kwells, doing it covertly to avoid resistance to his decision. After half an hour discussing why the guards weren't getting anywhere with Darragh's accident, he entered the bathroom and folded away.

Rasping branches welcomed Ronan into the bushes beside the tee-junction. There was no fire, not even a prickle. He punched the air—eleven days back and no ignition. Perhaps he wouldn't have to cut out his rune after all. While waiting for Darragh's car, he puzzled over why Freyja never mentioned any of it. Did she not know? His pondering was cut short by early-morning sunlight winking off a distant windscreen, while behind him, a powerful diesel rumbled into life. Gears crunched, the engine growled, suspension jolted over uneven ground.

By the time Darragh's faded red Corsa neared the intersection, Ronan's heart was racing, his every fibre quivering. Even though he knew the rune wouldn't let him interfere, he surrendered to instinct, surging from concealment, determined to stop Darragh before the junction. Next instant, he was further back up the field, impotence strangling his innards as a tipper truck boiled down the gravel track, filthy windscreen obscuring the driver's features.

Ronan's breath snagged in his throat, his muscles locked. The lorry roared on. When it should have been slowing, it accelerated. He watched in horror, desperate for a different outcome. There wasn't one.

Darragh, bug-eyed behind the steering wheel, had nowhere to go. The tipper's colossal steel bumper smashed into the car's midriff, sending it tumbling and crunching, upside-down in a ditch.

Ronan cried out, torn by the knowledge that Saoirse's father would never wake. Grief crushed him. He roared at the sky, impotent despite his rune, powerless to even help Darragh.

A hissing shroud of steam rose from the wreckage. The truck was roaring up the road in a black cloud of diesel smoke, Ronan's chance to do something about the injustice, disappearing with fading tail-lights. Shaking off his paralysing anguish, he locked his gaze on the rear of the lorry and drifted into ró.

There was nothing elegant about the way Ronan set down aboard the fleeing tipper. He popped from the air like a shelled pea, rolling across the steel floor, slamming into the side as the truck braked hard, swerving onto another road, sliding, spraying gravel. The rig's massive suspension was designed to compress under multi-ton loads, but with no cargo the springs were stiff and unyielding, bucking the vehicle off every imperfection in the road surface, clanging and banging the empty tip-tray against the chassis runners. Ronan wedged his back into the front corner, splayed feet holding the position, rough metal bruising his spine.

On and on they pounded, up and down hills, round corners, through groves of trees whose low-hanging branches whipped lines of grime from the paintwork. Loose joints and metal fittings rattled like a freight train; diesel fumes swirled into the slipstream of the cabin, burning the back of Ronan's throat, cloying his lungs. Only his determination to unravel the mystery of Darragh's accident kept him there.

Amid a hiss of escaping air from straining brakes, it all ceased, except for eddies of talcum-fine dust looking for somewhere to settle. Ronan hunkered low, banking that the driver had no reason to climb up to check the back. Footsteps crunched on gravel. Accompanied by bitter tobacco smoke, they circled the rig, once, twice. Ronan lost count. He had no clue where he was, but dare not raise an eye. The only thing he gleaned about his location was there were nearby trees: at least two stationary birds in elevated positions conversed in crow-like caws and mournful gargles.

As if on a signal, the birds cut off mid phrase, and Ronan's ears pulled the hum of a light vehicle from the still air. Toward the front of the truck, the footfalls ceased. The car's engine dropped to an idle as it drew closer, coasting to a gravel-crunching halt. Silence.

It didn't last long. A door slammed and the familiar voice of Vítek said, "Dammit, you might have kill him."

Ronan's skin goose-bumped even before the truck driver responded. "Boss want him frighted ... I fright him!" It was Ylli.

60

———

PANIC

Ylli's arctic presence overwhelmed the cold steel of the tipper tray. Ronan's breath died in his throat. Despite the rune's protection, the proximity of the lean Albanian rattled him. Vítek, with his daunting bulk and misshapen face, was an obvious thug, but Ylli's slim, almost girlish frame hid a cold-blooded heart that viewed torture and death as entertainment, to be enjoyed at will. And not an hour ago, he'd callously smashed his truck into an innocent motorist.

"Was just teeny tumble," Ylli told Vítek. "Not hurt mouse."

"It not look good when I pass," Vítek responded, clearly peeved. "Two ambulance ... chopper."

"Pah," Ylli scoffed. "Let's go."

"Did you wipe down?"

"Policia not have my fingerprints ..."

"But what if they get them?"

"How they get?"

Vítek loosed an exasperated sigh. "Is good your sister smarter than you."

Ylli cackled like a machine gun. "Got you ... course I wipe down."

"Deadbeat," Vitek growled, but it lacked venom.

"No understand why Luli marry you," Ylli shot back, still chortling.

More pieces of the puzzle clicked together for Ronan.

"She like handsome Polish man." Vítek said with no hint of irony.

"She need eye test—"

Shutting car doors cut the banter; they burbled away.

Ronan peered above the tray's bulwark. Perched in the top of a nearby conifer was a crow-like bird that looked as though it had bathed in ashes and could only get its head and wings clean. It turned a glassy eye on Ronan, and with a throaty gurgle, dropped from the branch, spread its wings and flapped languidly across to its mate in another tree.

Ronan's caution was misplaced; he was alone. The tipper was parked in a line with four others, equally battered and unkept, on the floor of an idle quarry. At the end of the row stood a front-end-loader with a bucket polished smooth by the abrasion of endless scoops of gravel, and big enough to go to sea in. Ronan guessed the workings had been unused for several days. Stockpiles of material carried the sheen of moisture, undisturbed puddles glinted across the ground; two recent vehicle tracks shouted their presence.

In every direction, tall pines ranged away in arrow-straight rows tangled with undergrowth. If it ever stopped raining long enough to dry out, a single match would raze the lot. Ronan immediately chided himself for reading the landscape with Australian eyes.

While he'd committed the quarry and surrounds to memory, he had no idea where it was. If he wanted to tell the guards where to find the tipper, there was no alternative but to follow the sole track out until he came to a memorable landmark or familiar signpost.

At the first tee-junction, he scrutinised the surface with a bushman's insight. The truck had come in from the right, the car after it, the latter turning left when departing. Ronan went right, loping in fluid strides, eating up the distance. Another tee-junction loomed, another scan for faint signs: the smudge of tread marks, telltale overturned stones. He went right again, following a twisting route down a steep decline, picking up a small stream and leaving the plantation trees behind.

Rugged hills kept close company on either side as he trotted on, the road pocked by muddy potholes punched out by the laden tyres of timber or gravel trucks. As the valley broadened, open fields took over, and as if underscoring the change, the unpaved section ceded to narrow bitumen. Everywhere were ditches and gutters running clear, joyfully merging into rivulets, heading for the main stream.

The further Ronan ran, the wider and more painfully green the fields became. Every animal was fat and contented, scarcely having to step outside its own shadow to fill its belly. Occasional farmhouses, dazzling white in the early morning light, sent driveways arrowing to the road. A gurgling brook running beneath a stone-buttressed bridge slowed Ronan's feet; he marvelled at the gift of frequent rain and crystal streams that never dried. Australian eyes.

Declan's cross-trainers fit Ronan well, so he upped the pace, enjoying the muscle burn of vigorous exercise. By the time sweat was flowing and his breathing laboured, he reached a ribbon of traffic on what he recognised as the 263. He figured he'd covered about seven or eight kilometres, and all he needed now was a sign post, a name. But the junction with the Killybegs road was bare, apart from a square of roofing iron nailed to a post. Hand-painted lettering advertised a ram for sale and a phone number. It had the hallmarks of a minor road that led nowhere important—unless you were a sheep breeder—but it must connect through to somewhere because Vítek and Ylli had turned in the opposite direction. They wouldn't have gone down a dead end; a fox always has a second exit.

Ronan wasn't worried, he'd bring the girls back; they'd know the name of the road. After memorising the intersection, he cleared his mind to return to Declan's flat in eleven days' time. His head erupted. He aborted the attempt amid tremors of unease. *Grandmother Freyja.* He pictured Saoirse waiting; he must go to her. Bracing himself, he aimed for the bathroom, folding away with a white-hot flare consuming his brain.

61

RECONNAISSANCE

Ronan tumbled from the air onto the bathroom floor, landing with a thump, curling into a ball, groaning. The noise brought the girls; Ronan didn't move. "Ronan," Saoirse cried, rushing to him, dropping to her knees, tears brimming. "What have you done, you eejit?"

With a skull full of glowing coals flaring to the beat of his heart, Ronan could do no more than moan and huff. Saoirse brushed hair from his face, running a thumb across his sweaty brow.

"I think he might have gone back to your dad's accident," Caitlin said, "to see where the truck went."

Saoirse's thumb stopped. "You eejit!" Her voice hardened. "You promised me you wouldn't time-flytja."

From the depths of wretchedness, Ronan wanted to say he'd only promised not to do it to pick up Luli's trail, but he couldn't muster the energy.

As though answering for him, Caitlin said, "The guards are getting nowhere."

"But I can't lose Ronan too," Saoirse sobbed.

Between them, they manoeuvred him onto the couch where she cradled his head, working magic with circulating fingertips on his temples. Ronan remained immobile, panting against the torment and rising nausea, willing the fire-breathing base-drummer to change from heavy rock to country swing.

Caitlin crutched to the kitchenette. "I'll put the kettle on."

The water went cold, was reboiled and went cold again before the thumping eased enough for Ronan to mumble through what happened, describing the narrow road from the quarry.

"I don't know where that is," Saoirse said.

"Mmm," Caitlin said, returning to the couch, "I'm not sure, but it might be Cronasilla ... Moya Dinneen's cousin lives up that way. I'll never forget going to a party there ... a fecking great timber lorry nearly ran me off the road."

"Which means there's a plantation up the valley," Ronan mused from Saoirse's lap, reluctant to break the contact, even though his brain no longer wanted to explode. "Can we check it out later?" His need for action dragged him upright. Sensing hesitation from Caitlin, Ronan added, "I'll pay for fuel." But she remained silent, apprehensive.

Saoirse leant across, dropping a hand on her friend's arm. "We won't go anywhere near him," she said.

Ronan looked from one to the other before catching on. "No, not to the quarry. We just need to go to the turnoff ... check it's the right road, then we can tell the police ... ah, guards."

"Right," Caitlin said, relief obvious.

Fifteen minutes later, having advised Bridget they were going to Killybegs, they squeezed into the Mini and beetled away from Doonin.

"Tell me about the pain from these time-flytjas?" Caitlin said as she piloted the car south along the harbour.

"Well," Ronan began, wondering if her interest was genuine, or simply quelling thoughts of the slim Albanian with the empty eyes, "the first time was when I came back here from Freyja's ... nearly blew my head apart ... made me spew." Saoirse reached back to squeeze Ronan's knee. "But then it just kept happening. At one stage, I thought it was the rune warning me I was getting close to trufla, but—"

"What's trufla again?" Caitlin cut in.

"Interference with the past," Ronan said. "The rune w—"

"But isn't anything you do in this time"—Caitlin threw a glance into the mirror—"changing the past?"

"You'd think so." Ronan frowned. "When I asked Freyja to define meddling, she said the gods decide, which I thought was a cop out."

Saoirse spun in her seat, flooding with hope. "You might be able to stop Dad's accident." It was half plea, half statement, and it hit Ronan like a gut punch.

"I tried earlier," he admitted, clasping her hand. "Sorry."

"Oh," she said, stifling a sob, reclaiming her hand, searching for a tissue.

Caitlin appeared unperturbed by Saoirse's distress. "Maybe Freyja played the god card because she didn't have a clear answer … perhaps there isn't one …"

Ronan delved into his memory. "She did say not to try changing the course of history, which makes me think it's only the important things that constitute trufla."

Caitlin's reflected gaze bored at Ronan; he wondered if she was thinking about her leg. Impotence gnawed at him.

"So what happened …"—Caitlin paused, glancing at Saoirse—"… happens … if you try to change the past?"

"The rune will heim me a short distance away."

"Heim?" Caitlin said to the mirror. "Is that a time-flytja?"

Saoirse sent a feeble smile over her shoulder at Ronan; Caitlin returned her concentration to the road.

"No," Ronan said, staring absently at stone fences puckering across the chest of a distant hillside like tribal initiation scars. "Well, similar … sometimes …"

"That's clarifying," Caitlin said wryly. Saoirse grinned.

"If it's caused by trufla or fundur," Ronan said ordering his thoughts, "a heim is a rune-activated jump to elsewhere in the same time"—he paused, thinking he might be confusing things further, but deciding to push on—"or, if it's caused by haetta, it's a long jump to the Home Stone."

"Refresh my memory on fundur and haetta," Caitlin instructed.

Saoirse's grin widened; Ronan took a breath. "Funder is encountering yourself at a previous time in your life," he said, embracing patience, "and haetta is mortal peril."

Caitlin, focus undiminished, threaded the Mini down a steep grade, between embankments and stone walls, past hedgerows, fences and verges choked with bracken. Tiny fields with their busy flocks of sheep succumbed to the industrial sheds of the outskirts of Kilcar, then a claustrophobic main street, shop fronts pressing close.

A couple of hundred metres of whitewashed buildings with colourful trims, and the town was behind them. "Right," Caitlin said, "I think I've got it: trufla, fundur and haetta are all rune activated."

"Yep."

"So," she stated, "they're all binaries … yes/no options … the rune decides."

Saoirse once said Caitlin had a very analytical brain. "Yeah," Ronan answered, unsure what she was getting at.

Caitlin rolled her eyes; Saoirse chuckled. Ronan felt like he was bottom of the class.

"A painful warning for decisions outside your control seems illogical," Caitlin stated, "so the heims should be irrelevant." Almost to herself, she continued, "So what is it about time-flytjas? Why isn't there pain with flytjas where there's no time change?"

"There is now ... not always." While Ronan thought he knew why, he wanted them to confirm it. "And it's not every time-flytja either ... when I went back to the accident earlier"—Saoirse tensed—"there was no pain, but when I returned ... oh, boy."

Caitlin's attention flicked to the mirror again. "So, is the blazing pain only with forward time-flytjas then?"

They stopped to give way at the junction with R263, easing in behind a couple of cars and a small tour bus heading for Killybegs.

"No," Ronan said. "There was no pain when I came back from Kaupang last Saturday, and none earlier today, but all other time-flytjas, forward or back, in the past week have been agony."

"Well," Caitlin said, "we need to identify what was different about those two time-fly-tjas." She turned to Saoirse. "There's pen and paper in the glove box. Can you record the date and time of all Ronan's time-flytjas?" After further thought, she added, "Actually, do space-flytjas as well. And draw up columns for direction of flytja, time difference, distance ..."

"What about pain intensity?" Saoirse asked as she drew lines on a page.

"Good idea," Caitlin said, "and one for notes, just in case Ronan thinks of something in relation to a specific flytja?"

Saoirse bent forward in concentration, hair swaying to the vehicle's motion.

"You can start with the first flytja ... last Friday," Ronan said as they neared the crash site, trying to keep Saoirse distracted. "Fifth of November, about five o'clock, seventeen years back and halfway round the world ... don't know how far that is."

"Twenty-thousand kilometres," Caitlin said without hesitation.

Ronan stared. "Who knows that?"

Saoirse's muffled snort was almost lost in hair.

The skid-marks, sundered turf and churned soil had slipped behind them when she lifted her head. Ronan met Caitlin's reflection in a brief union of mutual achievement. Three houses slid past, two with expansive emerald lawns; one with all the practical trappings of a farmhouse—barns, pens and stored fodder.

Peering between the front seats, Ronan spied the placard for the surplus ram. "This is it," he said. "On the left."

"Yep ... Cronasilla road," Caitlin said, turning onto the narrow ribbon of asphalt. At the first driveway, she executed a neat three-point turn, aiming the Mini for home.

Ronan continued listing every flytja since he'd left Australia, the pace of his words prompting Saoirse to poke the pen at him, admonishing him to slow down. Before returning to the list, she said, "Can we go via Garret's? See Viking?"

"Sure," Caitlin said, ignoring the turn to Kilcar.

"And thank you," Saoirse said, reaching back to clasp Ronan's hand, "for distracting me. I'm not ready to deal with that spot yet."

Ronan squeezed in return. "It'll be good to see the big fella," he said, "and it won't take long." He couldn't have been more wrong.

62

SAOIRSE'S SECRET

As the Mini headed northwest, Ronan kept dictating his flytjas, but at a less frenetic pace, the necessity for diversion passed. They were negotiating Carrick's main street when Ronan dropped a hand on Saoirse's shoulder, remembering something more immediate he wanted to discuss. "What's your connection to Garret?"

Saoirse sighed. "How much do you know?"

"Nothing," Ronan told her. "Caitlin said it was your story to tell. But it's obvious you ride Viking round Sliabh Liag to Garret's quite often … he knows the track really well … I wouldn't have made it otherwise."

Both girls hit him with sharp glances. "You gave me the impression the ride was uneventful," Caitlin accused.

Ronan cursed his indiscretion. "I didn't want to worry you."

"You promised me you wouldn't lie to—"

"I thought it was no more secrets," Ronan corrected, stealing a peripheral peek at Saoirse's reaction. She appeared mildly amused rather than concerned. Regardless, they deserved the full story.

"I fell asleep in the saddle and it was only Viking's knowledge of the track that got me there." It was such a bland explanation, Ronan could almost hear them wondering why he thought that would worry anyone, so he came clean. "We were caught in a flash flood and nearly washed away," he admitted. Saoirse gasped; Caitlin glared at the mirror. Ronan needed to hose it down. "But Viking's strength and long legs got us through … the rest was just miserable … wet and cold."

"No more secrets or lies all round," Saoirse said, ending the discussion with a firm tone. "Garret's my uncle," she added, whiplashing the conversation back to its original subject. "Abby was Dad's sister ... she died in an accident while driving to Malin Beg for lunch with Mum and me. I was only two, so I don't remember her, except from Dad's and Garret's stories."

"I'm sorry," Ronan said, leaning forward, touching her arm. "What happened?"

Saoirse captured his hand, but stared resolutely ahead. Ronan wondered if he'd caused tears. "She was driving the farm Land Rover ... they think she might have swerved for a sheep, lost control, went through a fence and over a cliff." She took a resigned breath and continued. "After reviewing the accident, the local council put up a guardrail along that section." Her words hardened with bitterness. "It would have saved Aunty Abby."

"And Garret never remarried?"

Saoirse shook her head. "He says living alone is his penance for allowing her to go off that day. He blames himself, but she was only going to lunch with Mum."

"He couldn't have known," Ronan said.

Saoirse squeezed his hand again. "He loves my visits ... says he sees a wee bit of Abby in me." Her voice faded.

"Have you finished that list of flytjas?" Caitlin asked, changing of topic.

Ronan sat back, returning his focus to the flytja fire. Fresh instances popped into his head, and by the time they turned off the 263 toward Malin Beg, Saoirse had recorded six time-flytjas and dozens of space-flytjas, along with their associated details.

"There's so many." She handed the sheet to Ronan. "And I can't see any pattern."

"Mmm ... not sure." He pretended to peruse the list.

"I'll have a look when we get home," Caitlin said, hugging the left-hand verge through a low-visibility corner.

They passed a neat farmhouse in wedding white, fields fanning out behind it like an emerald bridal train. Beyond, the land rose, turning brown with rank grass, merging in the distance with the foot of Sliabh Liag's cloud-shrouded mystery. Somewhere toward the base of the mountain lay Garret's farm.

Saoirse had her right arm contorted between the front seats to hold Ronan's hand, as though drawing reassurance from his touch. He absently traced the contours of tendons and veins as he wrestled with how to bring her justice and closure. Tipping off the guards about the truck's location would be easy enough, although Saoirse or Caitlin would have to do it—his accent would be a dead giveaway. Then he had a thought.

"Do I sound like a local?" he said in Irish, *"or am I butchering the language?"*

"Sounds perfect," Saoirse said as Caitlin drawled, *"Lots of blood."*

"Oh, you fibber," Saoirse chuckled. *"He sounds like he was born and raised in the bogs."*

"Never underestimate the power of the rune," Ronan pronounced.

"So," Caitlin said with affected resentment, *"it's gang-up-on-Caitlin day, is it?"*

"Only until midnight," Saoirse quipped.

Caitlin sent slitted side-eye at her best friend. *"How are you getting home?"*

"It's pathetic Gaeilge," Saoirse assured her with a straight face while squeezing Ronan's hand.

"Oi!" Ronan said, reverting to English.

"I'm not walking home," Saoirse told him by way of apology.

Ronan made an exaggerated huff. "Who needs enemies?"

"Garret's turn," Caitlin warned. A nanosecond later she swung the wheel, flicking the Mini left through ninety degrees, lining it up on the looming flank of Sliabh Liag.

"There goes breakfast," Ronan moaned.

"Do all Aussies whinge as much as you?" Caitlin asked, humour glinting in her odd-coloured eyes.

"Only with good cause," Ronan shot back.

"Stop it, you pair," Saoirse scolded. "I can't tell if you're serious or not."

"Joking," Ronan said in unison with Caitlin's, "Serious."

Their verbal jousting was cut short by Cú's deep-throated woofing as they rounded the last turn into Garret's yard.

63

———

SHOOTOUT

Garret greeted them with gruff affection that only he could manage. With Cú sauntering alongside, they went straight to the barn where Saoirse threw her arms round Viking's neck, burying her cheek in his mane. The tall grey nickered a greeting, turning his head to snuffle her back, nibbling her coat with dexterous lips. Ronan was in the stall, but giving Saoirse time to reconnect and, he suspected, continue grieving her father. Caitlin propped on her crutches, well back, evidently not into horses. Garret stood with her, while Cú kept nudging her hand with his nose, demanding attention.

"I don't think they need us," Caitlin murmured to Garret, absently fondling Cú's ears.

"Cuppa?" Garret said, not wasting words, as usual.

"Sounds grand," Caitlin replied, following him across the yard.

Cú looked from Garret to Viking and back again, whining with indecision. He settled onto his belly, dropping shaggy jowls to forepaws, lifting alternate eyebrows to Saoirse's voice or Viking's snuffles. Ronan grabbed a brush and ran long strokes along Viking's back, marvelling at the skin rippling beneath the stimulation.

In one fluid motion, Cú sprang to his feet, growl rumbling deep in his chest. Bounding from the barn, he broke into a full-throated bark. It was only then that Ronan heard the burr of a small engine. A vehicle entered the yard as he reached the door. He recoiled to the shadows—it was a nondescript Toyota Corolla of indeterminate colour, camouflaged by a layer of grime. Adrenaline surged through him.

The car was still moving when Ylli sprang from the passenger side, rushing at Cú as if to cower the dog. It had the opposite effect on the bristling wolfhound. Cú leapt at the man, sinking his teeth into a raised forearm, snarling, thrashing side-to-side, laying his weight backward. Ylli cursed, bracing himself against the onslaught. Ronan almost felt sorry for him, until a blade flashed. It plunged into the tawny body three times in rapid succession, blossoming scarlet with each strike. Cú yelped, collapsing, blood gushing.

Before Ylli could stoop to deliver the death blow, Garret roared from the house, shotgun lifting. The Albanian dived behind the car as birdshot peppered the body-work, punching holes, zinging in all directions.

Vítek rolled from the driver's seat, joining his partner on his haunches. The side window above them shattered from Garret's second shot, showering chunks of safety glass. As Garret cracked open the double-barrels to reload, Vítek pulled a pistol from a coat pocket, throwing a hand above the vehicular parapet, blindly returning fire. The weapon was toy-like in the huge fist, but there was nothing playful about its staccato pop, pop, pop, or the flying chips of stone from the house wall, or the banshee ricochets.

Ronan hesitated; he couldn't go back and change what had already happened, and he couldn't risk getting killed. Even though he would return from the Home Stone within moments, the umrót and flytja fire would have him helpless, while the girls and Garret would be at the mercy of the two armed thugs. If only Garret would get back into the house before Vítek seized on the shotgun's slow reloading time. But there was no retreat in Garret McGinley. He strode toward his trusty dog, thumbing fresh cartridges into the breech, snapping it closed.

Ronan spun to movement behind him. Saoirse's alarm was dragging her toward the doorway. Pop, pop, pop rose again as he launched himself, stifling her cry with a spread hand, sending them both sprawling deeper into the building's gloom.

Pop, pop, pop.

Holding a finger to his lips, Ronan gathered her in his arms and bullied his mind into ró despite the shotgun's roar.

Garret's kitchen had thick stone walls; Caitlin quailed in the far corner, face blending into the pale paintwork. Ronan stepped from the air, setting Saoirse down and pushing her to Caitlin in the same action. "Don't move," he growled, already turning, gathering Abby's bow and the five arrows as the shotgun blasted again.

Within a blink, he was back in the shadows of the barn door, gripped by impotence as he watched in slow motion as Vítek stood and aimed. Even as his dexterous, rune-driven hands fitted an arrow, Ronan knew he was too late. Vítek fired.

Garret had almost reached Cú when the bullet struck, jolting him. Ronan loosed the arrow. As it flew, a second bullet drove Garret to his knees. He toppled like an oak, beside his loyal dog.

Meanwhile, the arrow's pencil-point target head punched through Vítek's massive gun arm, skewering it to his chest muscle. The pistol dropped from his slack hand, his eyes following it to the ground before focusing on the fletched shaft protruding from the side of his chest and out through his arm. Vítek's incredulous stare lifted toward the arrow's origin, but Ronan was shrouded in shadow, pondering his next move. He gaped as Vítek tugged the shaft from his flesh without even a flicker of emotion. Had it been a hunting arrow with a barbed broadhead, it would have sliced a gaping wound, severing veins and arteries, and no amount of stoic tugging would have pulled it free.

Vítek tossed the arrow aside with contempt, bundled into the car with Ylli, and accelerated in a sweeping, sliding turn, speeding away. In the middle of the yard lay Garret and his faithful Cú, unmoving.

6 4

———

TRAPPED

Ronan rushed from the barn, reality slowing him as he approached the bodies. Blood oozed from two wounds in Garret's chest: one high on the right, the other to the left, closer to his stomach. Cú's shaggy coat was plastered with gore. Ronan tried to recall first aid, but every time his frenetic mind attempted to grip a memory, it shot away like a bar of wet soap.

Saoirse's scream cut through his futility. "Garret! Cú!" Feet flying, she darted from the house, throwing herself across her uncle's barrel chest. "Oh, Garret, don't die," she cried. "You can't die."

A gnarled hand inched upward to lie gently against Saoirse's damp cheek. "Not ... going ... anywhere." He drew a ragged breath, coughing a tiny spray of blood. "Cú," he rasped.

"Call an ambulance!" Ronan shouted at Caitlin in the open doorway. He raced inside, snatching up towels and Abby's pink robe from the bathroom, grabbing a sharp knife from the kitchen. Streaking outside, he cursed his inattention in first aid lessons, they'd never seemed important. By the time he reached Garret's side, all he'd come up with was 'apply pressure'. With Saoirse pushing down on wads of towel, he bound them in place with strips sliced and torn from the pink robe.

As he worked, Ronan replayed the sound of the retreating car. Its initial roar had subsided and ceased far too abruptly, but before he could work out what that meant, Caitlin reappeared. "The phone is stone dead," she called from the doorway.

Ronan's skin goose-bumped. Garret's phone was working earlier when Saoirse called to say they were coming to visit. Adding to his apprehension was the sudden silence from the attackers' vehicle—it had stopped rather than been driven beyond earshot. His uneasy scrutiny probed corners and shadows, but there was nothing to confirm his fear, only intensifying silence. "Mobile," he growled, wrapping a strip of towel round Cú's ribs. Whimpering, the dog raised an agonised eye.

"There's no service out here," Caitlin shot back.

"Shit!" Ronan spat. He gathered Cú, staggering under the weight as he lugged him inside, laying him on the kitchen floor. "Find Garret's ammunition," he ordered Caitlin.

She blanched, immobile, but sprang into action when Ronan tugged at the rug she was standing on. Years of use had thinned its pile, but the underlying weave remained strong. It was all that mattered.

Between them, he and Saoirse rolled Garret's bulk onto the unfurled mat. In the distance, a car door slammed, then another. Urgency hammered against Ronan's ribs.

With a corner of the rug and a hefty foot each, they dragged Garret across the yard. They had reached the door when a clamouring engine and gnashing gears rose above their puffing. Garret's shoulders caught on the single step. They tugged and strained, but his body wouldn't budge.

The car's furious approach thrummed off the barn.

Clunk, clomp; clunk, clomp. Caitlin appeared behind them.

The engine raged.

Casting crutches aside, Caitlin balanced, reaching down, gathering Garret's hands, straining in time with the others.

The rug surged over the threshold. Caitlin sprawled backward beside Garret, almost tripping up Ronan as he leapt forward, vaulting bodies, sprinting toward the twin bloodstains in the middle of the yard. The careworn Corolla rattled round the corner like a careening war chariot as Ronan scooped up the shotgun, bow and arrows. His momentum had carried him closer to the barn, so he kept going. It was a split-second decision that cheated death.

Ylli thrust a gun-filled hand out the passenger window. Ronan wasn't an expert, but had watched enough television to recognise the demonic chatter of a machine pistol. It must have been hidden in the car, requiring a few minutes to recover and prepare.

The pistol spewed lead and flame in an ear-splitting stammer. It arced toward Ronan but he was flying. His path across the front of the approaching vehicle reduced Ylli's field of fire with every stride. But the gunman panned the weapon as he fired, stretching his arm out, bending his wrist in front of the windscreen to bring the gun to bear.

Ronan's blurring feet seemed to slow, each pounding step punctuated by a dozen zinging projectiles, their sizzling passage melting together, each closer than the last. It was a whine he knew. He'd heard it in the millisecond before his step-father's third shot hit him between the shoulder blades, plunging him into the world of the blood rune.

A frenzied lead hornet burned past his ear; he braced for shattering impact. Instead, over squealing brakes and crunching gravel came a sharp metallic click and savage Albanian profanity.

Ronan plunged into the barn's welcoming gloom as the car skidded to a halt. Ylli rolled out the door as his thumb released the spent magazine, other hand reaching into a pocket for a replacement. The empty hit the ground with a hollow clunk; a full one snicked home.

Heaving breaths and racing adrenaline made it impossible to settle for flytja. To buy time, and to ensure Ylli's response was directed away from Viking, Ronan scurried into the opposite corner of the barn.

The gunman's soft footfalls on the hard-packed earth floor carried ominously past the blood-thump in Ronan's ears. He crouched in the darkness, Abby's bow and arrows in one hand, Garret's empty shotgun in the other. Any movement to free up a hand to take a shot would spark an instant spray of death.

"I know you in here, boy," Ylli purred. "Come out; we talk."

Tranquillity embraced Ronan like a warm breeze. "So you can shoot me?"

In response, Ylli opened fire. But Ronan was gone.

65

———

ANOTHER SECRET

The mania of Ylli's machine pistol was still reverberating through the barn when the air behind Garret's front door disgorged Ronan. He put his shoulder to the timber, slamming it home—their lives were depending on it.

No sooner had the latch dropped than bullets peppered the thick planks. They came from the rapid single shots of Vítek's weapon, irritated, small calibre popping.

Ronan leant against the stone wall beside the door, quivering with adrenaline. He swallowed, embracing the calming warmth flowing from his rune. The gunfire ceased, the sudden silence swallowed by curses and argument. Without warning the door shuddered under a fusillade of Ylli's more powerful weapon, staccato reports rolling into a solid wall of sound.

Thankful they weren't in a flimsy, weatherboard Australian house, Ronan gathered his wits, assessing the situation, wondering what the hell was going on. How did Darragh's accident, Saoirse's kidnapping, human trafficking, and Fionella Egan's real estate holdings lead to an armed assault?

In the kitchen, Saoirse stooped over her uncle, hair catching the light as it curtained round her face. Caitlin's familiar clunk-clomp approached from deeper in the house. Ronan shot across to stop her, but she'd already reached the doorway.

Ronan's movement drew a fresh volley, shattering the window, gouging chips of stone from the far wall as he passed. Flinging the bow and arrows aside, he lunged, wrapping Caitlin in a bear hug, crutches and all. Shotguns shells scattered as a half-full box tumbled from her slack hands at the impact of Ronan's tackle. He twisted as they tumbled into the kitchen, cushioning her fall with his body. "Stay here with Saoirse," he hissed.

In a low crouch, Ronan gathered a handful of the strewn ammunition, then pressed the bow and arrows at a shaken and haunted Caitlin. "Look after these."

The gunfire stopped.

"We want talk to girl," called Vítek. "We know horse here."

"Why do you want Viking?" Saoirse shouted back as she materialised beside Ronan.

"Not your business," Vítek replied. "Throw out weapons ... we not hurt you."

"It's a bit late for that ... murderers!" Saoirse screamed the final word.

Ronan pulled her in against the wall, shielding her. At the same time, the beast of outrage stirred in his chest.

"He should not shoot," Vítek responded.

In the ensuing silence, Ronan thumbed shells into the gaping double breech of the shotgun, breathing a plea to his rune to keep the girls safe. Amid his bitterness over Garret's and Cú's grievous wounds, Norse vengeance straddled the beast.

"Your boyfriend run away," Ylli taunted. "Leave you to save himself."

Easing the shotgun closed, Ronan pushed Saoirse toward the kitchen, pointing to the floor. He moved next to the shattered window, cocking both hammers as he went. In one fluid motion, he threw the stock to his shoulder, stepping into the open, firing the barrels in rapid succession. The booming echoes rolled into a crackle of return fire, but Ronan had already ducked to cover. Bullets flew through the opening, stippling the rear wall, turning the room into a deadly snow dome, full of flying lead, chips of stone and floating flakes of paint.

A lull followed, swirling with dust and the pungent reek of spent ammunition. But it scarcely registered with Ronan. He scooted into the kitchen, hugged himself tight to Garret's still form, and tried to double-up flytja to Killybegs. A heartbeat later, he was beside the phone box at the information centre, alone. Was the rune losing its power? Or was he asking too much of it? Choosing to believe the latter, he folded straight back to Garret's farm.

"I can't do it," he said, stepping from the kitchen air. "He's too heavy, but I can take both of you, one at a time."

Saoirse stared at him as if he were suggesting treason. "I'm not leaving Garret," she said, lips tight.

Caitlin's whole body was trembling but she was adamant. "Not without Saoirse."

"Right," Ronan said, cocking an ear at a sudden argument from the yard, the words indistinct, but the tone clear. He sensed the thugs' consternation: one moment he'd been cornered in the barn, the next, he was firing from inside the house. While the lull continued, he flytjed away.

From behind the Carrick post office, Ronan dialled triple nine, moving from foot to foot as it rang. When the operator finally answered, she spoke as though describing a tortoise race. Ronan shouted down the line in Irish, *"A man has been shot at Garret McGinley's farm"*—he rattled off the address—*"it's terrible ... send an ambulance ... quick!"*

Before the woman could answer, Ronan was back in amid the silence, dust and gun smoke of Garret's front room. Whatever the two assailants had argued over appeared settled, for Ylli called confidently, "Fire shotgun, you hit horse."

Through the shattered window, Viking's agitated stomping and snorting carried the truth of the statement like a billboard.

"Throw out weapons," Vítek ordered, "and come out with hands up."

"How's he doing?" Ronan asked as he stepped to the kitchen doorway, reloading, turning to watch the front window.

Saoirse looked up, strands of hair stuck to tear tracks, the rest swaying to her slow head-shake. "We have to get help," she implored.

"On the way," Ronan said, explaining how he'd flytjed to Carrick and called triple nine.

"Oh," she replied, drained.

"They'll take ages," Caitlin said, face pallid. Her anxiety was underlined by the acrid bite of smoke wafting through the wrecked window.

"The bastards are trying to smoke us out," Ronan snarled. "But if we keep everything closed up, it shouldn't draw through."

"What about the roof?" Caitlin said as a dirty grey cloud surged through the opening, rolling across the ceiling.

Ronan didn't understand. "Huh?"

"It's thatch," she said.

"Oh, shit!" he said, gazing upward.

"We'll have to surrender," Saoirse said tremulously.

Insidious tendrils seeped in round the perimeter of the front door. A tongue of flame licked through the keyhole, hungry for more fuel.

Garret's fingers twitched, his tormented gaze swivelled, settling on Ronan. "Trapdoor ... laundry cupboard," he murmured between shallow breaths. "Knife blade in gap ... in mortar above ... first course of stone"—a small cough flecked blood onto Ronan's ear as he leant close—"releases it." Garret panted several times before continuing, "Take the girls ... you'll be safe ..."

"No!" Saoirse cried, hugging herself to his bloodied torso. "I'm not leaving you."

A work-callused hand clamped on Ronan's arm. "Do it, lad ... for Saoirse ... it's too late for me and Cú." Garret's eyes were dull, anguished. "Prop me against the wall ... facing the back door ... give me the gun ... shells ..."

With immense effort, Garret touched Saoirse's cheek, but could do no more. "Go Sersh ... make your da proud ... and me ..."

Despite Ronan's theory, smoke billowed, catching in throats. "On the floor," he commanded, pulling a hacking Caitlin beneath the spreading pall.

While Saoirse hugged Garret, sobbing into his shoulder, Ronan took a butter knife to a tiny square cupboard festooned with mops, brooms and brushes. He leant in and inserted the blade into a gap in the mortar low on the back wall. With a soft click, the floor dropped away in slow motion, a pair of pressurised gas struts taking most of the weight. Had he not been expecting it, he might have fallen in.

A low-wattage bulb blinked on, throwing a weak yellow glow down a steel ladder. Ronan tossed Caitlin's crutches through the opening; they clattered onto concrete, metres below. As he extended a hand, she slapped it aside. "I'm not an invalid!"

"Then go," Ronan said, dropping the bow and arrows into the shaft before she could move. "We'll lower Garret to you ... try to break his fall."

Cheeks streaked with tears, Saoirse clung to Garret. "No," she cried as Ronan peeled her arms away.

"We'll lower him down to Caitlin," he said, gripping her wrists, trying to sound confident.

"No ..." Garret moaned, fingers reaching for the gun, "... it's too late." He coughed a cluster of bloody bubbles. "This is my ..." the words sighed into silence, his chin dropped. Saoirse howled afresh, reefing from Ronan's grip, flinging herself across Garret.

"No," she wailed.

Ronan's anger boiled against his ribcage.

Garret rallied. "... atonement," he whispered, finishing the broken sentence. "Take her ..." he added, barely audible, but an order nonetheless.

Again, Ronan eased Saoirse away. Resistant drained, she collapsed into him, allowing herself to be guided onto the ladder and pressed downward.

"Pull ... blue lever on ... cupboard wall ..." Garret rasped as Ronan settled the loaded shotgun across his lap. Somehow, he mustered the strength to grasp the weapon, lining it up on the closed door. "Go."

Ronan descended the ladder, pausing at waist level to toss a final salute to Garret. The man's eyes were clouded by pain, but they could still move; they flicked toward the back of the cupboard. The blue lever was the handle of a ball valve set in a large-diameter water pipe. Ronan pulled it down.

Water spouted from hidden sprinklers in the ceiling, creating an immediate deluge. Ronan acknowledged Garret's ingenuity with a grim nod before pulling the cupboard closed and dropping several rungs until he was past the open trapdoor. Despite the difficulty of the moment, he couldn't help but admire its engineering: thick steel reinforcing beneath wooden boards that matched the laundry floor. With a one-handed push, the secret door swung upward, aided by the gas struts.

Above, the back door of the farmhouse crashed in. Ronan slammed the trapdoor closed. The emphatic click of the rugged catch was drowned by the shotgun's roar and the manic chattering response from the machine pistol.

66

MIXED MESSAGES

R onan descended the metal rungs, thankful for the thick barrier between them and the carnage above. A distraught Saoirse's met him at the bottom.

"Garret …?" Her brimming eyes pleaded for denial.

Ronan shook his head, opening his arms, drawing her desperate wailing against his chest. He held her tight, breathing soothing words into her hair. Caitlin stared up from where she sat on the floor, her earlier terror replaced by numb disbelief.

Saoirse's grief rattled from her in wracking shudders. Ronan knew from bitter experience that nothing, not words nor gestures, could soothe the anguish of irretrievable loss. Coming so soon after her father's death, it must be almost too much to bear.

Accidents were one thing, but murder? The attack was irrational, demented. Their obsession with Viking was pointless now that Saoirse was free, but he guessed they wanted her as well. The beast in Ronan's chest growled and pawed, demanding to be unleashed.

Easing Saoirse aside, he said, "I'll be back soon." He snatched up the bow and arrows, flytjing away before she could respond.

The barn was silent, the back corner not as Ronan had left it. Light showed through a spray of holes, some as round as a bullet, some the size of a jagged fist, all between knee and shoulder high. Had Ylli's salvo caught him, he'd now be embracing the Home Stone, head spinning with umrót. Nocking an arrow, he crept to the barn door, peering from the shadows.

The farmhouse glistened in the weak sunlight. A row of previously unseen sprinklers along the centre line of the roof gushed water as if trying to sprout the thatch. Hidden sprayers up under the eaves saturated the underside, sending rivulets down the stone walls. Smoke oozed from fissures in the charred front door; on the single step, the blackened remains of piled hay smouldered and hissed as moisture penetrated its depths. The mystery of the elaborate sprinkler system and secret tunnel didn't register with Ronan; he was consumed by a bubbling fury to avenge Saoirse's uncle. He sought redress.

Vítek crouched, squinting over the Corolla at the house, one hand dwarfing the pistol. The other was hampered by his arrow wound, the arm stiff inside its bloodied sleeve. Still, he clutched Viking's halter rope without flinching, but at the very end, obviously wary of a large, unpredictable and dangerous animal. Viking appeared to be of the same mind: head high, ears toggling, nostrils dilated, pulling on the rope. Strange men, combined with blood, gunfire and acrid air, had the big horse stepping from hoof to hoof as though the ground were hot.

Ronan aimed at Vítek's heart and eased his breath away. Low overcast scudded across the last of the sky's blue; everything in the world, apart from his target, ceased to exist. A sudden chill gripped him, snapping his focus, stopping his release. An anguished cry caught in his throat. What was he doing? He'd been on the cusp of murder himself. Trembling, he crouched in the shadows, sweat erupting in a wave. The rune flared warmth; he shivered.

As Ronan battled with himself, Ylli pushed out the charred door, emerging from the artificial deluge like a harbinger of death, saturated hair plastered to his skull, water streaming from his jacket. The machine pistol hung loose in one hand, Garret's bloodied shotgun in the other. The man's sudden appearance had Viking taking a startled sidestep between Ronan and the murderers. But the horse couldn't block the men's discussion.

"He no more trouble," Ylli said, propping the shotgun against the car, "but others not there ... must have leave before I go to round back."

Vítek spat a Polish curse and keyed the transmit button of a walkie-talkie several times. Within minutes, Ronan heard a familiar low rumble, and Fionn Egan's gold Range Rover appeared, towing its matching horsebox.

"Christ," Egan breathed as he slid from the cabin, surveying the smoking house and the Corolla's bodywork peppered by birdshot. "You weren't kidding when you radioed earlier that you were having trouble. I'm pleased I waited for your signal."

"We fix," Vítek said nonchalantly.

Egan eyed the men as if it was an affront to good manners to be speaking to them. He scanned the bullet pocked walls, blackened door and streaming water before turning his full attention to Viking. "Good," he said. He looked to have slimmed and hardened in the past few days—either that, or Ronan's mind was playing tricks. "Where are the girls?" he added as he dropped the rear ramp of the horsebox, taking Viking's halter rope.

"They ... poof," Ylli said, raising his free hand, throwing the fingers wide.

Egan halted, one foot on the ramp. "Disappeared?"

"They gone," Ylli insisted. "I check all house ... they not nowhere."

"And they have boy with them," Vítek added.

"That cunning bloody gobshite!" Egan muttered, yanking the lead rope, jerking Viking's head. "He's supposed be back in Australia."

Ronan drew no satisfaction from the confirmation of a link between Luli and Egan—he'd already been certain.

"Who cares ... we have horse," Vítek said. "Just like you want."

Egan glowered, reefing the rope again. Viking sawed his head, pulling back from the ramp.

Ronan drew his bow again, this time, lining up on Egan's chest. When he reached the point of release, the chill hit him. Without easing off, he altered his aim; the chill left him. He struggled to make sense of it.

While the rune filled him with the urge for Norse retribution, its continued loyalty demanded that he remain true to himself. It was as if the magical pebble was in a tug-of-war between what it was trying to make him become, and what it insisted he remain.

Perplexed, Ronan eased the bowstring's tension, searching for an alternative way to avenge Darragh, Garret and Cú.

A few years back, he'd found an online video of an archer firing three arrows in under a second, using the so-called Saracen method. Despite diligent practice, Ronan only once managed it under two seconds, but he *was* accurate. Would two seconds be enough?

67

BREAKING POINT

Even though cloaked in the barn's gloom, Ronan felt exposed. Less than twenty metres away stood a savage killer, wound tight as a watch spring. Ylli still nursed the menacing machine pistol whose bullets punched divots in stone, holes through boards, and life from bodies. And he'd shown himself eager to use it.

The wiry Albanian scanned his surrounds as Egan tried for a third time to reef Viking into the trailer. As on each previous attempt, Viking pulled further away. Egan stomped and fumed.

"You sure dumb," Ylli sneered. "How you think horse do what you want when you treat so rough?"

"What would you know?" Egan scoffed.

"Bah! I work stalla ... um, how you say? ..." He turned to Vítek.

"Stables?"

Ylli nodded. "I work stables before you born ... treat horse good, they do what you want." Slinging his weapon's strap over his shoulder, he snatched the lead rope from Egan. With calming words and confident hands, Ylli eased Viking into the horsebox.

Egan scowled; Ylli emerged with a smirk; Vítek stood, features blank. None of it mattered, for now was as good a chance as Ronan would ever have.

As the tailgate of the trailer closed behind Viking, Ronan arranged his four arrows between the pointer and middle fingers of his right hand, with all the nocks vertical. He took a deep breath, settling his heartbeat, embracing the rune's flow. Fitting the first arrow to the string, he drew, aimed, exhaled, released. The first arrow was still in the air as he nocked the second, changed aim, released; nock, aim, release. With three arrows gone, Ronan nocked and paused, a slight stutter in the fluid grace of his artistry. Never had he shot with such speed and accuracy. But there was no time to savoured it: the machine pistol was rising. Aim, release. As he dived behind bags of feed, the air above him swarmed with death.

Ronan rolled onto his back, smiled grimly at the roof and folded away.

From the shelter of the grove of trees bracketing the entrance to the farm buildings, Ronan watched as Ylli sprayed leaden death into the barn with an impeded left arm, an arrow shish-kebabbing the muscle. The right arm hung, useless, paralysed by another shaft, this one buried in the shoulder. The earlier skewering of Vítek's right bicep was now matched on the left. With an expression that could have been disinterest, he gripped the shaft, tugging and twisting it from his flesh. Ignoring blood and pain, he palmed his gun, sweeping a careful scrutiny round as a stirring westerly spread a gossamer film of mizzle.

Egan also sported an over-sized body piercing. Like Ylli's, it was in his right shoulder; however, Egan was not moving. He'd collapsed backward, face as white as his hair, fletched shaft pointing to the clouds.

Ylli continued firing in short bursts as he, once again, searched an empty barn. A vicious kick sent Abby's discarded bow spiralling out into the yard, clonking onto the hard-packed surface. Vítek relaxed, pocketing his weapon. Ylli, arrows protruding from flesh, machine pistol drooping, launched into an undecipherable tirade.

Vítek's brief rummage in a canvas holdall in the rear of the Corolla produced a military-style first-aid kit. After spreading it on the bonnet of the car, he reefed the shafts from his companion and treated the wounds. It was only after Ylli had reciprocated that they paid any heed to Egan's inert form. Vítek walked across, placed a boot on Egan's chest, and casually drew the arrow from the shoulder, as if pulling a weed. Egan squawked, and groaned afresh. By the time they'd dressed his wound, he was coherent. "I've been shot," he moaned.

"Only little arrow," Vítek pointed out.

"Only a bloody arrow?" Egan howled. His gaze, full of burgeoning memory, flicked between them. "Wait, you were shot too ..."

"We not cry like baby," Ylli said, running out of patience, toeing the lad in the ribs. Egan yelped.

"Get up," Ylli hissed. "We go before someone come."

"I can't drive," Egan sobbed.

"Then stay ... explain to policja." Vítek spat onto the ground. "We go." He and Ylli turned to the Corolla.

"Wait!" Egan winced as he struggled upright. "I'll pay you extra to drive me."

"Double," Vítek said, face blank.

"Two thousand?" Egan made a derisive sound. "Fifteen hundred."

"Three."

"No way!"

"Drive yourself."

"Okay." Egan deflated. "Three thousand to take the horse to Mum's Ballymacfadden house, and drop me home."

Vítek nodded impassively; Ylli smirked.

"Come," Vítek said, motioning Egan into the Range Rover.

Like a good soldier depriving his enemy of ammunition, Ylli collected the discarded arrows, snapping them over the top of the door, tossing them into the car for good measure. After a brief scan of the shot-up, charred farmhouse, he climbed awkwardly behind the wheel, and followed the horse trailer from the yard. Watery taillights disappeared down the road as the misting rain turned into solid drizzle.

By the time the yard lights timed off, Ronan was satisfied the danger had passed; he jumped to the laundry where the overhead sprinklers were producing more deluge than the clouds outside. The wall where they'd propped Garret was bullet-pocked, running with water, and smeared with a dissolving bloody arc from his mighty shoulders toppling sideways to the floor. Although his rugged features were far less formidable in death, they were locked in a grim rictus, as though mocking the one who shot him. The dulled blue eyes stared sightlessly across the floorboards toward the slab of saturated grey hair that had once been his faithful wolfhound.

Ronan reached down, but caught himself before he could ease the lids closed. While it was the respectful thing to do, he'd learnt a few things from watching all those episodes of police procedurals—touch nothing; leave no evidence. The best way to honour Garret was to make sure his murderers didn't escape justice.

And the red-eyed monster of Norse retribution pawed at Ronan's conscience. Again, he fought it; the reckoning must be according to his own laws and values. Regardless, he wouldn't rest until everyone responsible was held to account.

Ronan folded from the stale tunnel air in front of Saoirse and Caitlin. They huddled on the chill concrete, against the wall, heedless of tear-streaked cheeks and dishevelled hair. Two pairs of red-rimmed eyes trained on Ronan as he crouched before them. "We have to move fast," he said. A vague plan had come together as he'd watched the assailants licking their wounds, but time was short—while he'd only called the ambulance, they would have alerted the nearest garda station.

"But ... Garret?" Saoirse's eyes were begging.

Ronan grasped her hands. "I'm sorry."

She pulled away, face collapsing as Caitlin enfolded her. Howling sobs echoed along the tunnel.

Without waiting for permission, he scooped Saoirse from Caitlin's embrace, flytjing her to the barn. In a blink, he had Caitlin there as well. Both girls were silent and withdrawn, blinking like dazzled owls when his groping fingers found the light switch.

"Listen," Ronan said, launching into what they needed to do, "they've beaten us for the moment, but—"

"Beaten us?" Saoirse's head jerked up; her voice lifted. "Beaten us?"

Ronan gaped.

"Dad's dead, Garret's dead, Cú's dead ..." Her strident words rang through the barn.

"Saoirse, I—"

But Saoirse didn't pause, her blazing eyes firing accusations like darts. "This isn't a game!"

Ronan held his hands up in surrender. "I never said it was."

Tears streaming, Saoirse's voice rose further. "Then stop treating it like one."

"I'm not!"

Bawling, Saoirse slumped into Caitlin's arms. Ronan's mouth worked silently as he teetered from the grief-stricken tirade.

68

———————

SHARP WORDS

Ronan dragged in ragged breaths, smarting as if struck. Saoirse had never gone off like that before. His heart wanted to hug her tight, his head told him to stay clear. So, he spoke directly to Caitlin who, although pale-faced and wary, didn't appear about to bite his head off. But then, she hadn't lost a father, an uncle, a beloved horse and dog, not to mention being held captive, all in one week.

"It's really important that you keep your wits about you when the guards come," Ronan began, watching Saoirse's back for a reaction. There was none, so he continued, emboldened. "They're going to ask you a million questions, and they'll go over your stories again and again, looking for inconsistencies, so just stick to the basics."

"I don't even know what they are anymore," Caitlin said, staring out the barn door at the slanting rain, absently stroking her friend's hair.

"I know," Ronan said, "but if you keep it simple, it should be fine.

"What do you mean, *simple*?" Saoirse's voice was lifeless, drained of combativeness.

Relieved yet wary, Ronan rattled on—the law must be close. "I'm going to make damned sure the guards catch up with those murderers"—he paused, trying to relax his jaw—"so your story has to align with theirs, where possible ... we don't want the guards doubting your version ... you have to live here."

"Yes, *we* do," Saoirse said, testiness returning. "You get to go back to the safety of your own time."

"I'm not going anywhere," Ronan insisted, fuming at his poor choice of words, "but if the guards find out about me, it'll make things harder."

"Right," he continued, when there was no response. "You came to see Garret ... you were inside having a cuppa an—"

243

"But they saw *you*," Caitlin said.

"The guards will believe you over them if you have a good story: when the shooting started, you tried to call for help but the phone was dead; Garret sent you out the back door ... told you to hide in the trees up behind the barn; when the Corolla left, you came back to find the front door like that." He gestured toward the charred timber. "You went in, the sprinklers were on ... you found Garret in the laundry."

Saoirse sobbed, trembling in Caitlin's embrace.

Ronan swallowed, contemplating the back of her head. Caitlin fixed him with her green eye. The story was full of holes, yet rune warmth gave him confidence. "You know what that Corolla looks like, tell the guards everything you can remember about it, but don't say anything about me or the tunnel, and don't mention Viking."

Saoirse stiffened. "Why?"

"Because I'm going to get him back now."

Saoirse spun toward the empty stall. "He's gone?"

Without thinking, Ronan reached for her hand; she snatched it away—a tiny dagger twisted in his heart. He tried to say her name, but it caught in his throat. Swallowing the blockage, he summarised what had happened while they'd been shut in the tunnel.

"Trouble follows you, doesn't it, Ronan Ryan?" Caitlin said.

Ronan scowled at her—Saoirse didn't need any stirring up at present.

"But they might kill him!" Saoirse cried.

"If they wanted to hurt him," Ronan said, "they'd have done it here instead of taking him away. No, they want him as leverage to control you again, and I'm never"—Ronan leant forward, slowing his words, pushing them out passed clenched teeth—"going to let ... that ... happen."

Saoirse didn't respond.

"What are you going to do?" Caitlin asked.

"Find Viking and take him," Ronan said.

"Then what do we do?" Saoirse said, breaking her silence. "Wait for them to snatch him again?"

Ronan flinched at her words, smothering a retort. "They won't find him this time," he vowed.

"That's what you thought last time," Saoirse shot back, folding her arms, activating a force field.

Caitlin touched Saoirse's arm, but was shaken off. "Ronan's only trying to help, Sersh."

Ronan's patience ran out. "You know what? Forget it. I'll do what I have to do, Saoirse, because I care about Viking, and I love you ..."

He whirled and stalked away.

69

HIDING EVIDENCE

Ronan only went as far as the back of the barn, annoyance driving frustrated pacing. Saoirse's testiness he could understand, but why had he fired back? Patience wasn't his strongest virtue, but without it, he might lose her. The sharp rap he gave himself on the side of the head didn't improve his mood.

As much as he tried to relax and be patient, the longer they stayed in the barn the more his tension ratcheted up. If they weren't in position when the guards arrived, their stories wouldn't correspond to the evidence. While he didn't want to push and create more tension, he peered out the door as if checking the approach road. "We should move …"

Without a word, Saoirse stalked past him, eyes front; Caitlin raised an eyebrow and followed. The yard lights popped on as they left the barn, heads bowed against the rain.

Ronan fought fresh annoyance as he watched the girls slosh across the yard and into the farmhouse. Everything was falling apart and he didn't know how to stop it. If he could keep Viking out of Egan's clutches, at least Saoirse wouldn't have to worry, and he could concentrate on bringing Fionella to justice. But if he couldn't do the latter, Saoirse would remain in danger. And how was he going to fix things between them?

Frustrated by the obstacles before him and eager for action, he bundled up Viking's saddle and bridle before hitting the switch for the interior light. Ballymacfadden was over the other side of Carrick, so it would be a while before the horse-nappers got there. As he stood in the shadows, waiting and chafing, Ronan searched in vain for the motivation behind all that had happened.

Everything started with Darragh's accident. Why had Fionella wanted him frightened? And if that was the aim of the collision, then Saoirse's captivity in the Dublin basement was all improvised, all a clever exploitation of the intended intimidation gone wrong. Saoirse's isolation was the only part of the whole thing that had any apparent purpose: keeping Ronan out of the picture.

The rain steadily increased, as if trying to outdo the night he rode Viking round the mountain. It was soon impossible to tell whether the sprinkler system was still operating. Ronan guessed not, for the girls remained inside the farmhouse, and lights came on.

Through the deepening gloom, he caught flickering on the trees bracketing the entrance road, then headlights arced across the front of the barn, sending him ducking. The car's arrival triggered the security lighting, shattering the dusk, slapping at Ronan's pupils. And as he shrank into the shadows, it threw Abby's recurve bow into sharp relief.

A white garda sedan decked in blue and yellow Battenburg checks, slushed past the melting bloodstain where Garret and Cu fell earlier, halting behind the Mini. The vehicle rocked and swayed as the occupants struggled into wet-weather gear. Ronan hardly noticed; his attention was riveted on the bow lying in the mud between the barn and the new arrivals. It would derail everything.

Two gardaí, guns in hand, stepped into the downpour, their focus on the buildings, not the ground. Sweeping their pistols in searching arcs, they approached the farmhouse door with caution. From a protected position on either side, they knocked, announcing their identity. Water streamed from their backs as they waited. They stiffened as the door opened, but relaxed in the face of a gaunt Saoirse, who must have offered acceptable answers to important questions, neither of which carried above the swirling wind and driven rain. Obviously satisfied there was no danger lurking within, the officers holstered their weapons, shook themselves off and disappeared inside.

When the fire-scarred door latched closed, Ronan returned to the problem of Abby's bow. He had to retrieve it, but not until the floodlights timed off. Even then, he couldn't just flytja out and grab it; his movement would trigger the lights. There had to be an alternative.

In the penetrating glare of the yard lights, Ronan searched for inspiration. The bow lay almost ten metres from the barn, way too far to hook with the hay rake. But the thought gave him an idea. A quick rummage produced a length of fencing wire, a pair of pliers, and a bundle of thick twine used to bind hay bales.

After fashioning a crude grappling hook from the wire, and tying on the twine, Ronan waited until the lights died, hoping the hook and string weren't big enough to trigger them again. His first cast was short, the second wide, the third better. Hand over hand, he hauled the line in, but the hook glanced off the bow. Ronan grunted with frustration, freezing as the floodlights snapped on again. A guard had stepped from the house, heading for the car. If she looked up, she'd *have* to see the bow, or the hook. The latter was halfway between the stranded weapon and the shelter of the barn. It had left twin gouges in the mud.

Eyes on the woman, Ronan backed deeper into the shadows, holding his breath, willing her to stay focused on placing her feet. She slushed to the vehicle, found what she wanted, and returned indoors. Ronan relaxed.

When the lights timed out, he tried again, snaring the string with his second cast, easing the bow toward the barn. As it dragged, it collected muddy water, smoothing out the furrows left by the grappling hook. With the current rain, there'd soon be no trace.

After sliding the bow beneath bales of hay, Ronan straightened the hook, discarding the wire in a pile of scrap. Satisfied that he'd left nothing to arouse suspicion, he collected Viking's bundled saddle and emptied his mind.

70

SPIRITED AWAY

The rear of the Range Rover was not as orderly as the last time Ronan saw it. Its plush carpet sprouted tufts of teased fibres as if it had been attacked by a weeding fork, while the air was thick with deodoriser trying to mask a background smell of wild-animal. Intriguing but irrelevant.

Despite the proximity of Vítek and his pistol, Ronan was safe enough, as long as he kept his head down. With an eye pressed to the gap between the seat-back and the door pillar, he watched their silhouettes against the headlights' reflected glow, swaying in time to the vehicle's motion. Although the rain had eased to a fitful drizzle, the wipers maintained a rhythmic accompaniment to the engine's rumble. Out the side window, the lights of Ylli's following Corolla lit up power poles strung with a single wire, or an occasional tree. A shadowed hillside rose into the gloom on the driver's side.

Ronan recognised the hallmarks of a back-country road—they must be close to Ballymacfadden. He visualised a ribbon of bitumen, almost too narrow for traffic, perhaps with a straggle of grass sprouting down the centre. Suppressing his curiosity, he stayed hunkered, ready to flee in an instant, content with his thin strip of visibility.

"I smell horse," Vítek grumbled after a lengthy silence.

Only when he tested the air, did Ronan realise how smelly Viking's sweat-stained saddle cloth was. He gripped the bundle tighter.

Egan peered toward the rear. "It'll be the remnants of that bloody hedgehog," he complained. "If I find out who put it back there, I'll have another job for you."

Vítek responded with a dry cackle. "You not find no one."

"Was it you?" Suspicion edged Egan's question.

"I not know who do it," Vítek responded, "but you not find ... you not detective."

Egan glowered at his driver. "You should remember who pays your bills, Vítek."

Air hissed from the man's crooked nose. "You might be boss's son, but boss pay bills."

"Yeah, well, I give you extra spending money," Egan shot back, "so mind your manners."

"Yes, boss boy." Vítek sniggered at his own humour.

Egan's churlish silence indicated precisely how amusing he found it.

The vehicle slowed; a building appeared ahead. "Pull round to the left," Egan said.

In the brief sweep of the headlights, Ronan got a sense of the layout. The cottage would have once been rural white with windows trimmed in red, but the walls had sullied and the trims faded. A rusted swing set stood stark and forlorn in a sea of weeds that lapped at the front door, while at the far end of the house, beside a pyramid of rotting firewood, the belly of an abandoned wheelbarrow was tipped to the heavens. Ronan gripped his bundle and aimed for the wood pile.

Hooves echoed hollowly on the horsebox ramp as they unloaded Viking. Before long, first the Corolla, then the Range Rover cast their probing lights over Ronan's concealment as they pulled back onto the lane and faded from sight, taillights blinking like watery fireflies through the mizzle. But still Ronan waited. He waited until the final fragment of engine murmur blended in the night's silence, and nocturnal animal sounds resumed. An owl's reedy call to its mate and the rasping snarl of a foraging badger assured Ronan the night held no danger. There would be no repeat encounter with a lurking Ylli. Standing, he eased the cramp from his legs and felt his way through the gloom toward sleepy equine snuffling.

Even before a fallen-down barn materialised out of the murk, Ronan began crooning, not wanting to startle poor Viking. The big grey greeted him with a low nicker from beyond a wooden pallet wired across the doorway. The sagging roof sent rivulets into a space that would cramp a Shetland pony. Ronan bristled as he stroked Viking's forehead over the makeshift door.

Getting Saoirse's horse away would be easy, but he didn't want any trail for Egan and his thugs to follow and, truth be told, he wanted to mess with their heads—more than a little.

Behind the barn he found a dozen or more discarded feed bags; he only needed four. In short time, Viking's hooves sported thick hessian boots to spread his weight and reduce the likelihood of leaving indentations.

Ronan led the saddled horse from the barn, tying him to a tree by the lane. He re-secured the pallet to give the impression it hadn't been disturbed, and dragged a fifth bag over the grass to blend in any crushed blades and bent stalks.

When he returned to his mount, he smelt trouble: Viking had pooped. *Shit! Talk about a flashing billboard.* He stood, looking down at the vague mound of rounded blobs steaming in the cool rain.

Without hesitation, he held the open bag against the pile of warm dung, pushing it in with the side of Declan's shoe. The remaining smear was already sluicing away as he slung the bag from the saddle, mounted, and rode up the lane, deeper into the backblocks.

UNCERTAINTY

Misting rain followed horse and rider up the valley. The uncertain light revealed nothing more than tree-cloaked hillsides on the right, and valley flats on the left. The tarred surface gave way to gravel that angled up a hard ridge where the trees receded, leaving them alone in open heathland, wrapped in darkness. The thought of Egan finding Viking disappeared again gave Ronan grim satisfaction.

As the night drew on, the drizzle thickened, which suited Ronan: all sign would be washed away. The downside was the increasing cold, and that the coat no longer kept the moisture out—it trickled where it shouldn't. Around midnight, a forest rose to meet them. The road turned sharp right, but the trees drew them ahead until they were embraced by dripping foliage.

Ronan found a sheltered spot beside a rivulet, where the interlaced branches of towering pines blocked most of the rain. He secured Viking to a low limb, leaving him with a reassuring word, walking from sight. Within minutes he returned with a sturdy horse blanket and rope that he'd rummaged from the Raven's Roost stables, taking great delight in leaving all lights blazing—something to exercise Egan minds.

Having rugged Viking and secured him to a long picket line from which he could reach grass, water and shelter, Ronan pictured Declan's flat and folded away. Since the shootout, he'd been so occupied and running on adrenaline, that the flare from space-flytjas could have doubled and he wouldn't have noticed. It was still only embers compared to the full-blown conflagration of a time-flytja, but the fact it was getting worse had Ronan worried.

The flat was in darkness, but across the way, the windows of the O'Toole's house were ablaze. While desperate to talk to Saoirse, even if she didn't want to talk to him, Ronan couldn't do it with others around. And given what the girls had been through, he was sure Caitlin's parents would insist they sleep in the house. So, he shot a quick text to Caitlin—*vking safe; sleep rr cottage; will call in mrning; tell s i love her*—and left.

The air inside the cottage was inky, but Ronan knew the layout by heart and was already walking as he set down, hunger driving him toward the kitchen. He didn't want any Egan intervention, so he left the lights off and crouched in front of the cupboard, rummaging through the contents as though reading braille, guessing at a packet of energy bars and a ring-pull can of fruit.

Hunkered in darkness, he tucked into his rough meal, washing down mouthfuls of nutty nutrition with swigs of ginger beer from the fridge, revelling in the sharp bite of the chilled drink. By the time he was ready for the fruit, his taste buds were fizzing with anticipation. But instead of a waft of sweetness when the seal broke, he caught the savoury aroma of what turned out to be some sort of stew. With a philosophical grunt, Ronan paddled it into his mouth with another protein bar, chasing it all down with the last of the drink.

While munching, he relived the sting of Saoirse's words. In theory she was right, he did get to go back to the safety of his own time, but he had no intention of leaving her, even if he was no longer sure of what she really wanted. Uncertainty gnawed at him.

And Caitlin had been correct: trouble did follow him. Ever since the rune's warmth first touched his skin, strife had never been far away. But he liked to think it was because the rune gave him the confidence and power to confront and overcome obstacles, rather than avoiding them.

Ronan had intended to kip in Saoirse's room and leave early, but by the end of the improvised meal, he decided there was no time to waste. Although Viking was safe, there was nothing to stop the two thugs from kidnapping Saoirse, or worse. What he needed was irrefutable proof that would get Fionella and her son arrested, along with Vítek, Ylli and Luli.

There was no other way to eradicate the threat, so Ronan let the rune's power engulf him, and lead where it chose.

72

———

FLYTJA FIRE

Ronan set down in the midst of the Corolla's untidiness. It smelt like an ashtray, while the inside of his head glowed like a cigar. The earlier rain had petered out, allowing enough moonlight past the lifting clouds for him to get a decent look at his surroundings.

The car was parked in front of a compact single-storey house in need of paint and an energetic gardener. Beside the front door, a ladder leant against the roof, while beyond the right-hand end of the building slumped a weary garden shed. It was barely large enough to hold a mower, a barrow and a handful of tools. To the left, a low wall draped by tangled shrubbery ran toward the rear.

The similarities to Fionella's Ballymacfadden investment were unmistakable: tired, unloved, secluded. Ronan suspected he was looking at yet another part of her real estate portfolio. And with no inkling of the location, he feared Vítek and Ylli might be gone by the time he worked it out and alerted the guards. He needed to act.

Without stopping to ponder the consequences, his thoughts went to disabling the vehicle: petrol and matches. He began rummaging. None of the Corolla's nooks and crannies produced matches or a cigarette lighter. He tried the glove box, and among the detritus of fuel receipts lay a moulded knife handle with a slide button on top.

Ronan chilled as his fingers closed round it, but his thumb gravitated to the button. It slid forward. Even though he knew what was coming, the instantaneous appearance of a hundred millimetres of razor-sharp steel startled him. Just as magically, it vanished when he thumbed the slide back. He worked it again. Click; click. Out; in. Ronan wondered if it was the one that had plunged into Cú's body, but guessed it was only a backup. A thug like Ylli would carry his main weapon on him at all times.

The knife provided inspiration; Ronan uncoiled into the chill pre-dawn silence.

Squatting by a wheel, he tested the blade was locked rigid, and pushed it into the sidewall of the tyre. The rubber resisted, but by gripping the handle with one hand and pushing with the heel of the other, he forced the honed steel through the thick material. Soon, all four tyres were hissing and sighing as the car settled deeper into the weeds. Ronan crouched in its shadow, scanning for any sign his sabotage had been noticed. The building remained in darkness.

Well satisfied, he retracted the blade, thrusting the weapon into a deep pocket before an overriding desire to create further mischief sent him nosing around.

The rear of the house delivered no inspiration, but it did have an uncurtained window framing a sparse kitchen. A hallway night lamp threw the cabinetry into distorted relief, the shadows of knobs and handles stretching to bloated disappearance. In a blink, Ronan was crouched in the dim light, peering about; he spied a half-used loaf of bread in a plastic bag on the counter.

Concern over creaking floorboards had him flytjing to the bread. Biting down on the renewed flare, he sat the loaf of 'soft white breakfast delight' on the electric stove ring, using his shirt tail to turn the control knob to high. The room quickly filled with the acrid stench of burning plastic, with undertones of charcoal toast. Time to leave.

From the safety of the outside gloom, Ronan watched smoke billow against the ceiling, oozing downward. Flickering shapes danced on the walls. Panic wrapped its tendrils round him: there was no response from within. Were they already overwhelmed by noxious fumes? Although they were murderers, he didn't want them incinerated, they had to face justice for what they'd done. And what if there were others, innocents, inside?

Visions of locked rooms and beds with shackles rose to haunt Ronan. Things were spiralling out of control. Why weren't the smoke alarms screaming? And why weren't they in the kitchen, putting out the fire before it took hold? Bile pushed up his throat. What had he done?

A light popped on in an adjacent room. Ylli ran into the kitchen, grimacing when he tried to throw up his arms to block the heat. He retreated, yelling. Vítek appeared, holding a shield of blankets as he barrelled toward the stove. The flickering died. Smoke surged. Vítek withdrew, hacking acrid fumes from his lungs. Ylli returned, cloth over his nose as though chloroforming himself. He darted about, opening windows and doors, flushing out the toxicity.

Relief flooded through Ronan as he jumped to the outside of the garden wall. He was still swallowing discomfort when Ylli drifted out the front door, gun held awkwardly in his left hand, his right immobilised by the thumb tucked into his belt. Ronan guessed the recent activity had stirred up his arrow wounds. *Good.*

The Albanian sidled beneath the ladder, hugging the building, eyes probing, pistol arcing across the yard, seeking a target. Ronan's skin goose-bumped. The man's sweeping gaze hesitated on the car long enough to show he'd noticed the flat tyres. Ylli continued his prowling, all sinewy grace and carnivorous focus. Ronan shivered, shrinking into the shrubbery beyond the wall, not daring to breathe.

Then came the crack of a twig, soft enough to be imagined, only a wall thickness away. The whisper of Ronan flytjing away triggered an eruption from the machine pistol. Sizzling lead blasted chips of stone, shredding foliage that had sheltered Ronan moments earlier.

He set down in the back yard, wincing at needling sparks. The hail of gunfire still echoed as he searched for a decent projectile. He found a fist-sized rock, launching it with a mighty heave at the lit panel of the rear door. Shattering glass and Vítek's guttural Polish curses drowned out the air's opening and Ronan's gasp.

Crouched against the garden shed, Ronan pushed his thumbs hard behind his ears, fingertips to his temples, pressing against the flare. What if he was wrong about the flytja fire? What if the rune was rejecting him, finding him unworthy? Dread was a leaden weight in his chest.

73

———

SHOT

While Ronan hunkered in uncertainty, Ylli darted in the front door, drawn toward the shattered glass and his colleague's cursing. An animated discussion followed, swelling in volume until it spilt into the yard, both men gesticulating and peering into the darkness. Despite the undoubted impairment of their recent wounds, they were remarkably mobile—tough enough to be Vikings.

"I find ... they die." Ylli snarled, jabbing his machine pistol at the night.

"Keep voice down," Vítek retorted. He appeared to have seniority, for Ylli shrugged and resumed scanning while his companion climbed the ladder.

Once on the roof, the blocky Pole edged upward until he teetered, one foot either side of the apex. It was only when Vítek pulled the phone from his pocket that Ronan understood. If the only way to connect with the mobile service was from a rooftop, this house was isolated and unlikely to have neighbours close enough to hear gunfire and call the guards. He'd have to flytja away and do it himself, but right now, he didn't want to miss a thing.

"Bring van now," Vítek was saying. He paused. "I don't care what time is," he hissed. "Someone here ... must go ... come now, Jemy."

With his colleague on the roof Ylli skulked, first toward the wall, then back past the shed. Ronan tossed a small block of wood in a high arc into the gloom behind the Corolla. It was still in the air when he set down beside the stone wall, head thumping. Gunfire ruptured the night, flashes of exploding propellant flaring past the corner of the building in a demented light show.

After working a couple of stones loose from the top of the wall, Ronan pitched one through an end window, sprinted to the rear of the house and hurled the other at a second pane. Before it struck, Ronan had jumped back to the garden shed, swallowing pain.

A quick glance showed Ylli disappearing past the stone wall. With gritted teeth, Ronan flytjed to the front door, pushed the ladder to the ground and ducked inside. He scooted down a bright hallway, past a grimy bathroom and a bedroom with a couple of untidy bunks against opposite walls and, stacked between them, four duffel bags stretched tight like gluttons' stomachs. The doors of the final two rooms in the dwelling both sported hasps and padlocks. Ronan's fists knotted; he imagined the cutting odour of stale urine in an open bucket. The only thing he could do about it at the moment was to work out the house's location. With that in mind, he recalled Jamie Hagan's vehicle and folded away as Ylli burst through the back door.

Dirty mattresses, blankets, food wrappers and drink cans littered the van's interior. Ronan slumped among the rubbish, moaning, each flytja worse than the previous one. But he thought of Saoirse and her obvious doubts about him, and Caitlin, who deserved to be free of the spectre of the empty-eyed Albanian. Over the flytja fire came the undeniable odour of unwashed bodies and animal fear. This was so much more than Saoirse, Caitlin and Viking. The helpless people in those locked rooms, as well as those who might follow, were all his responsibility. Ronan was the only one in a position to stop it. Resolve hardened. Regardless of the consequences, there could be no stopping.

The torment was easing by the time a courtesy light on the side of an adjacent building burst into life. It threw the van into stark relief, flooding through the windscreen, hitting Ronan full in the face. He curled beneath filthy blankets, hoping he didn't catch fleas, or something worse.

Jamie Hagan steered along the main street, past the Sliabh Liag Inn, and hung a left up the River Glen valley. Dark shapes—trees and occasional dwellings—drifted past the windows as the vehicle swayed and creaked through the night. While Ronan had never been on the road, he thought it led to Meenaneary, and a lot of other places with back-country lanes and secluded buildings. The only way to find the specific location of the padlocked doors, was to ride the bucking and pitching machine to the end.

When he wasn't concentrating on memorising the track, Ronan's mind descended into turmoil: Saoirse and his blood rune; the rune and Saoirse. Were they both rejecting him?

A cluster of houses slipped past, then an unexpected veer onto another road almost tossed Ronan across the van, but he braced his legs in time. They trundled on through a band of trees and a stretch of open country before hard braking and an abrupt turn put them on a new course. Soon after, they slowed again, negotiated a tight S-bend, followed by a sharp left where the hum of bitumen gave way to crunching gravel. After several uncomfortable minutes of bouncing and jolting, they pulled in at the house. The ladder was again propped against the roof, and an outside bulb fanned stubborn illumination across the overgrown yard to the garden shed, casting sullen shadows where it couldn't reach.

Light washed into the van as it drew up beside the deflated Corolla. Ronan shrank into a corner, concentrating on making his ears 'see' for him. The click of the driver's door catch accompanied the slide of fabric across seat vinyl. The whisper of shoes on grass grew louder, and Ylli's voice erupted through the van's thin skin. Ronan twitched.

"What took so long?" Ylli growled.

"Get stuffed," Jamie retorted, perhaps testy from his interrupted slumber.

"Careful." The word dripped threat. Jamie retreated into safe silence, perhaps regretting his shortness with the dangerous Albanian.

Footsteps receded toward the house. Ronan waited, straining for furtive sounds. The merest whisper of movement exploded into a dry squeal. Ronan flytjed away as the van's rear door flung open.

The cover of the garden shed embraced him like an old friend. The mildness of the attendant flare offered a surge of hope and optimism: maybe the blood rune wasn't giving up on him. Over at the van, a suspicious Ylli leant into the cargo space, poking at the blankets with a gun barrel—had the man used a hand, he'd have felt the warmth of Ronan's recent presence. With a final scan of the interior, Ylli moved out to stroll in a protective arc behind the vehicle, his shadow rippling across the weeds.

Ronan cursed; he had to get Ylli away from the van. His groping fingers closed on a small pebble about the size of his rune. Screwing his feet into the grass, he launched the projectile as far as he could. He put so much power into the throw he almost overbalanced, his rear foot dragging, knocking a couple of loose stones together.

Ylli whirled and accelerated toward the shed. At the same time, the airborne stone clinked to the ground, out beyond the light's extremity. Ylli's head whipped round. Ronan could sense the indecision, so he scraped his foot again. It was too much for the

Albanian; he raced at the garden shed. But Ronan was already crouched beside the van, pushing the killer's knife through rubber.

Air hissed when he removed the blade. He swore. Ylli was running. Ronan threw himself beneath the vehicle, worming behind the hissing tyre. But Ylli was smarter: he was moving in an arc to open a field of fire past the obstructing wheel. Ronan pressed the steel point to the sidewall of the other rear tyre, which appeared tougher than the first; perhaps it was because he was flat on his belly and couldn't get leverage. Bracing a foot against the far side of the chassis, he grunted and strained. The machine pistol started jabbering, creating geysers of dirt as the bullets homed in on Ronan's position. The blade sliced, burying to the hilt. Ronan was entering ró as he withdrew the knife. The insane cacophony of Ylli's gun drowned the gushing air and the sigh of Ronan's leaving.

Ronan collapsed onto the floor of Declan's flat. It wasn't the head flare that had brought him down, it was his leg, numb and unresponsive. Even as he wondered what it meant, he found himself staring at the honed steel clutched in his fist. With an involuntary tremor, he thumbed the button; the blade vanished as if it had never existed. All that remained was an innocuous hand grip; he slipped it into a pocket.

The movement sent a million nerve endings clamouring for attention. Ronan's fingers explored the area of uproar; they came away wet and sticky. He'd been shot!

His throat constricted amid visions of bleeding out on Declan's floor, then warmth surged. But it wasn't in his head, it radiated from the centre of his body. And an eerie chill chased it. "Grandmother," he breathed, seeking Freyja's calm reassurance as he fought a rising tide of dread.

A leaden hand found his mobile, thumbs stumbling over Saoirse's number. The phone seemed to burr forever. It slipped from slack fingers, clattering on the floor. A bleary voice laced with annoyance said, "Do you know what the time is? ... Ronan? ... Ronan?" Concern replaced discontent. "Hello Ronan, are you there?"

With ebbing strength, Ronan gasped, "Declan's flat ..."

"Ronan!"

Saoirse's scream was the last thing he heard before darkness engulfed him.

74

CHANCE AND PROBABLITY

Grey light oozed into the corners of Ronan's brain. A dull hum, and voices, from far away, floated past his ears, evading capture. But the velvet touch on his skin was real; he clung to it fiercely; it was familiar, comforting. As his world brightened, his left leg came alive, as if a red-hot poker had pierced his thigh. He moaned.

An angel's voice, wafting, swirled into awareness: "Ronan. Oh, Ronan ... can you hear me?" It was Saoirse, trapping his heart. He tried to reassure her; someone groaned.

"It's okay," she murmured, caressing his cheek. "You're safe. We're taking you to the doctor."

Ronan relaxed, letting his head loll into her hand, trying to close his mind to the torment. The girls had cut away the pants leg, wadded a clean hand-towel front and back—the bullet had gone right through—and strapped it firmly with a shredded skirt.

"Are you sure about this 'doctor'?" Caitlin said, voice laced with doubt.

"What choice do we have?" Saoirse replied. "The hospital will get the guards involved ... he'll be arrested and deported. Besides, Garret said O'Leary was the best, and won't breathe a word."

"*Was* the best?" Caitlin shot a quick glance from the driver's seat as she guided the Mini toward Carrick.

"He's treated a lot of gunshot wounds."

"In the army?"

"Sort of," Saoirse said.

Caitlin fired off another sideways glance. "Sort of?" When her invitation to clarify wasn't accepted, she continued, but on a tangent, "How can you be sure he won't say anything?"

Saoirse chewed her lip. "There are things about Garret I've never told you, but now that he's dead"—her voice caught—"it doesn't matter, although you can't tell anyone, not even your parents ... promise?"

Caitlin stared hard at her friend before answering. "Promise."

"Garret was an IRA quartermaster during The Troubles," Saoirse blurted out.

Through the fog of misery, Ronan recalled Grandpa Paddy telling him about the Irish Republican Army defending Catholics against Protestant discrimination in Northern Ireland, and how it spiralled into out-of-control violence on both sides. Ronan would never forget his grandfather's sadness when he'd said that 'The Troubles saw good men do bad things'.

"What?" Caitlin said, jaw sagging.

"Yeah, I know." Saoirse took a breath. "He quit after Aunty Abby was killed ... blamed himself ..."

"Why?"

After hesitating, Saoirse continued. "He'd been directed to transfer a heap of cash to another supply officer, so he packed it under the seats of Aunty Abby's Land Rover. She didn't even know about it ... knew he was IRA, but not about the money. She was to leave the vehicle with someone in Malin Beg while she had lunch ... they'd remove the money ... Aunty Abby would go home ... she never made it to lunch. They don't know what happened ... just lost control and went over the cliff."

A tear splashed onto Ronan's face, tingling into his skin. He wanted it there forever.

"I'm so sorry, Sersh," Caitlin murmured.

Saoirse sniffled; Caitlin squinted into the night, searching for a two-storey house with a tall hedge. As she eased into the drive, Ronan moaned. Saoirse squeezed his hand.

"Saoirse?" he mumbled.

"Shh. We're here." The words were as soft as the fingertips feathering his cheek.

"What's his name?" Caitlin asked, pulling herself out of the vehicle.

"O'Leary," Saoirse replied. "Press the doorbell ... tell him Garret McGinley sent us, and we have a wounded man."

As Caitlin crutched to the front door, Ronan tried again. "Saoirse?"

"Shh, Caitlin's getting the doctor."

"Saoirse?"

"Mmm."

"Viking's safe."

She smoothed the hair from his forehead. "Shh ..."

"... and Saoirse ... I love you." Ronan tried to grip her hand, but he wasn't sure anything happened; his muscles seemed disconnected.

"I love you too, Ronan," she said with a sudden sob. "And I'm sorry for ..."

Ronan tried to squeeze again, but the light faded. When it returned, he was surprised to not see the Home Stone. Instead, a shaggy grey head, gaunt face and bulbous nose with a tracery of purple veins, hovered over his leg. The man was sewing; for some reason, Ronan thought it hilarious. He tried to talk and raise his head, but Saoirse hushed him with soft hands.

"All finished," O'Leary said, snipping the last thread. He mopped an ooze of blood, stepping back, admiring his handiwork, wiping hands on a stained cloth. "The anaesthetic will wear off in a few hours, so give him these"—he passed a packet of painkillers to Saoirse—"and make sure he gets plenty of rest. These are antibiotics." He handed her a tiny foil bag. "If he doesn't want to lose his leg, he must take them four times a day until they're all gone. Bring him straight back if there's any sign of infection ... heat, redness ... or other problems, but he should be grand ... it was a clean through and through ... didn't miss the artery by much ... wouldn't be here otherwise."

No, I'd be in 891.

O'Leary never asked what happened, and wouldn't accept payment, said any friend of Garret's was a friend of his, and he didn't charge friends. When Saoirse told him about Garret's death, his face sagged. "Jesus, Mary and Joseph," he breathed, making the sign of the cross and kissing the side of his thumb. "I'm sorry for your loss ... he was a fine man."

Saoirse's hands trembled on Ronan's chest as she slid the medication into his shirt pocket. He wanted to clasp them, but the signals weren't getting through. However, the disquiet generated by O'Leary's next words registered like a struck gong.

"This lad is the image of my friend's son, God rest his soul," the doctor said. "Young Paidin fell from the Sliabh Liag cliff a few weeks back." The grey head shook. "'Twas a very sad thing." Saoirse took Ronan's hand, squeezing reassurance. O'Leary continued, "What are the odds that two lads from opposite sides of the world have the same last name and look like brothers? 'Tis amazing. Wait till I tell Paddy."

They left the man mumbling something about chance and probability, and drove off into the predawn murk.

75

———

TWO DOORS

The fresh night air was a tonic after the astringent odour of antiseptics and salves. By the time the girls had Ronan in the car, he felt half human again. The anaesthetic was bliss, pain non-existent. Attentive concern replaced Saoirse's sharp words of the previous day—Ronan guessed they were a result of the shock, grief, stress and fear. She made him take the front seat, and as he settled back, he tried to focus on the captives. While he hadn't actually sighted any prisoners at any of the houses, everything from dirty mattresses, anchored manacles and locked doors pointed to human trafficking.

"We've got to do something about the Egans and their thugs," he said.

"Speak of the devil," Caitlin muttered, as they halted to give way to an imperious black Bentley on the main street.

Ronan shot her a silent question.

"Dooley Egan," Saoirse said from the back seat.

"He's getting an early start to the work day," Caitlin observed.

"It's not him I'm worried about," Ronan said, thinking of the wife and son as he dismissed the receding vehicle. It was the car of someone who liked to look important or advertise wealth, or both. *Whatever.* "Take the next left," he added as the Bentley dragged its twin taillights along 263 toward the Detencin boot factory at Killybegs.

"Ronan, no." Saoirse grasped his seat-back, pulling herself forward. "We're not going near them ... they shot you!"

"Yes," he said, "but we can't let them get away aga—"

"*We* can't do anything," Caitlin cut in. "They have guns, remember. Besides, you're only half dressed."

Ronan looked down; he should have been embarrassed. The left leg of his pants was gone, almost to the waistband on the outside, revealing a swathe of stark white bandage, and a strip of lime-green undies. What would Declan say about his good cargo pants with its wide belt loops and deep zip pockets? Pockets? The money had been in one on the missing leg! "My money ..." he said, frantically patting the surviving pockets, only finding his phone.

Caitlin flapped a hand off the wheel as Saoirse said, "I haven't seen it."

All Ronan could think of was what it took to get it in the first place. "It was in the zip pocket you cut off."

"It'll be back at the flat, then," Caitlin said.

"Oh. Right," Ronan said, tension draining. "Don't need it now, anyway."

"You've been shot!" Saoirse thumped his seat. "We're going straight home"—her tone hardened—"and you're going to bed."

Ronan held up a hand. "Okay, I get the message, but pull over for a sec ... please?"

"We're going home," Saoirse repeated, face set.

"Just hear me out," Ronan pleaded. "It's really important." They'd turned toward Doonin before Caitlin pulled over, engine idling, headlights bouncing off the pale walls of a sprawling building.

Ronan was trying to muster his thoughts when Saoirse's hand fell on his shoulder. "I know they can't kill you," she said, "but I don't want you disappearing again." Her voice dropped to a whisper. "I need you here."

Ronan's hand found hers. "Even if they get me, I'll be straight back," he reassured her.

"But it's the thought of it I can't bear." A sob caught in her throat. "And all that umrót from the heim and return flytja ... and the flytja fire ..."

"Speaking of which," Caitlin said before Ronan could respond, "I have an explanation f—"

"In a minute," Ronan interrupted. "First, I want to tell you what happened." He began by assuring Saoirse that Viking was safe, where no one would find him, securely picketed with plenty of feed and water. He followed up with a rundown of his encounter at the isolated house, and how Jamie Hagan was stranded there as well. "We need to work out where it is so we can tell the guards ... before they vanish again." Between Saoirse's sceptical breathing at his back and Caitlin's absent stare, Ronan wasn't even sure they'd heard him.

"There won't be any danger," he added. "They won't even know we're there ... we'll only go to the turnoff, so we know where to send the guards ... and we'll come straight back."

Caitlin turned toward Saoirse, lifting an enquiring eyebrow.

"This is our chance to bring those thugs to justice ... for your dad," Ronan said, squeezing Saoirse's hand, "... and Garret." He swallowed. Having reopened the wounds of her recent losses, he was about to add to her distress, but saw no other way of convincing her. The hallway had reeked of despair, and Ronan was positive there were girls like Caitlin's friend, Lena, in those rooms. He couldn't desert them. Somewhere, loved ones were missing them, and no one else seemed to know where they were, or be able to help.

"There were two doors with hasps and locks," he said, "... like Glengarriff Parade."

Saoirse's fingers twitched in his, her tiny gasp merging onto Cailtin's long, defeated sigh as she checked mirrors, and swung the little car into a scuttling U-turn.

76

CRUTCHES

Saoirse said little on the drive up the River Glen valley. Ronan left her to whatever thoughts and fears were running through her head, contenting himself with keeping a reassuring pressure on her hand. At the same time, he relayed the details of the route he'd memorised from the cargo bay of Jamie Hagan's van. In between his instructions, Caitlin shared her theory of the flytja fire. She had to revise it when he explained the increasing effects he'd been getting with space-flytjas.

"Yes," she said, "that's plausible."

Saoirse broke her silence from the back seat. "What do you mean?"

They'd left behind dim fields studded with drifting shapes of early-grazing animals, and were traversing drier heathland, the hills to the east outlined against a lightening sky. "You didn't have any pain from the time-flytja when you hadn't done any flytjas at all for a day or so," Caitlin said. "And the space-flytjas only start hurting once you've done a lot in a short period; therefore"—her fingers tapped the steering wheel, underlining the logic—"the flytja fire, as you call it, is the cumulative effect of too many flytjas ... a warning that you're over-stressing your body."

"Makes sense," Ronan said, pleased to have his own thoughts confirmed.

Saoirse clung to his hand.

"Time-flytjas," Caitlin continued, "obviously put much more stress of a different type on your body, so the effect builds up faster, and is more severe."

"Don't I know it," Ronan said wryly.

They traversed more farmland and passed a straggle of houses, ghosts in the murk, some with windows alight with early risers. "There should be a road off to the left coming up," Ronan said, peering ahead. "Not a sharp turn, more like a veer." The headlights spangled off a cluster of reflective road signs. "This'll be it."

They diverged left, beetled up a hill and returned to heathland. "Sharp right turn soon, after the next house," Ronan said.

Caitlin made the turn. "What do you think?" she said as they accelerated down a long hill.

Ronan glanced from the approaching S-bend to Saoirse. "What do *you* think?"

"It all seems to fit."

Ronan nodded. "We're all agreed then—"

"Slow down!" Saoirse squawked.

Caitlin stabbed the brake, manoeuvring the Mini through the tight turns. At the top of the hill behind them, a large vehicle towing a horsebox lit up like an ocean liner, slowed at the junction. It turned toward them; Ronan prickled with recognition. "The driveway is a bit past the next corner," he said, "but don't stop."

"I don't even know where this road goes," Caitlin complained.

"Doesn't matter," Ronan told her. "Just keep going at this pace until over the next hill."

"Ronan," Saoirse said, peering at him. "What's going on?"

"Not sure yet"—he craned his neck to look through the rear window—"but I think that's Finnegan behind us."

"Finnegan?" the girls said in unison, as they crested the hill.

"Turn round at the first chance."

"If it's Finnegan, he'll recognise the car," Caitlin fretted.

"If it's Finnegan, he'll be turning into that house," Ronan assured her.

After a quick three-pointer, they headed back up the small rise. "Slow right down," Ronan said, "and turn your headlights off."

"But I can't see," Caitlin protested.

"It's light enough," Ronan said, "if you give your eyes time to adjust."

"But what if a car comes?" Saoirse pointed out.

"We'll see the glow of their lights before they come over the hill," Ronan said with confidence he hoped wasn't misplaced. "You'll have plenty of time to turn yours back on."

Caitlin hunched forward, squinting at the road through the beginnings of the dawn, idling the Mini up the rise.

"This'll do," Ronan said as they reached the top.

From their vantage point, the progress of the ocean liner was easy to follow. It was wending its way through and round subtle swells in the ground on the access road to the hidden house, tracking toward a smudge of forest.

"The house is somewhere in those trees," Ronan said.

After a brief silence, Saoirse and Caitlin stiffened as if attached to the same brain, but Saoirse spoke first. "They're going to move those poor girls in the horse trailer, aren't they?"

"We have to stop them," Caitlin said vehemently. "They'll be just like Lena. We can't let those bastards disappear again."

Ronan worked his jaw, easing the tension. "We won't," he said, lifting his phone into the air, peering at the service symbol. Opening the door and balancing on his good leg, he dialled triple nine. In perfect Irish, he reported multiple gunshots and women screaming at a back-country house near where he'd been camping. He gave his name as Peter O'Flannery, describing the location in great detail, urging them to come quickly. After he hung up, he perched on the edge of the seat, gathered his thoughts and began outlining what he intended to do: "I'll flytja in and—"

"Ronan, please?" Saoirse begged.

"I have to make sure they don't leave."

She gripped his shoulder. "But your leg?"

"I promise not to run round," Ronan said, forcing levity. "Besides, the anaesthetic is still going strong, and the guards will turn up before it wears off."

"Here," Caitlin said, reaching behind for the crutches, poking them at him, "take these."

"What about you?"

"I'll be grand sitting here … just bring them back."

"You can count on it … and thanks."

Saoirse clutched his arm. "Don't take any more risks."

"I won't"—he squeezed her hand—"but there's no one else to help those girls. Besides, none of us are safe round here until these blokes are in prison." He stood, testing the crutches, annoyed he lacked Caitlin's effortless mastery. "Don't go anywhere ... be back before you know it."

"Ronan ..." Saoirse cried, as if having a sudden change of heart. But he was gone.

77

PUSHING LIMITS

Ronan fell from the air among the shrubbery along the garden wall—one crutch had landed in a hole. The pleasing lack of flytja fire drew silent gratitude for the five hours since his last jump.

While he'd aimed for the garden shed, the rune had overridden him, and he soon realised why. Egan's Range Rover swung into the yard, sweeping a deluge of light over the shed, the house front and, finally, the wall. Ronan spotted Ylli patrolling at the other end of the building before he had to duck as the headlights arced across his hiding place.

No sooner had the vehicle stopped than the Albanian had the rear ramp down. Jamie Hagan, toting a stuffed duffel bag in each hand, led a procession of bewildered girls from the house, eleven in all. They carried a variety of satchels, backpacks and bulging plastic bags. None of them looked recently bathed; all had sunken, haunted eyes wreathed in confusion and despair. Ronan's fists knotted. At the tail was Vítek with the remaining two bulging duffels, one slung over each shoulder, massive hands resting on their tops. While satisfied the man's arrow wounds were causing problems, Ronan was intrigued by the four matching bags packed to the cusp of bursting. Whatever they held was valuable; they were being handled with greater care than the girls.

Desperate as Ronan was to stymie the evacuation, slashing the tyres on the Range Rover was not an option at the moment. While Ylli must be bamboozled by what had happened so far, he now knew what to expect and was squatting to one side, shining a powerful light beneath the vehicle, taking no chances. Hagan threw his bags into the Range Rover, doing the same with the two from Vítek.

Ronan needed a distraction, and flytjed inside seeking inspiration. The doors with the hasps and locks stood wide, revealing filthy mattresses interspersed with lengths of chain ending in open manacles. A single reeking bucket sat inside each door. Without thinking it through, Ronan hurled a chain against the wall, flinging a second through the open door, sending it rattling along the hallway. Another followed it before he heard Vítek's lumbering tread approaching.

Ronan returned to the bushes. Ylli was still in position, head swivelling. Egan, slouched and sullen, wounded shoulder swathed in a calico sling, hadn't left the driver's seat. Hagan's gaze darted about as he herded the last of the girls into the trailer. Vítek's curses reverberated through the building. Running on instinct, Ronan grabbed a decent stone and flytjed to the back door, hurling the projectile through the remaining intact glass panel. By the time Vítek steamrolled out the door, Ronan had crutched to the corner, slowing so the man caught sight of a disappearing heel.

Back behind the stone wall, wincing at rekindling discomfort, Ronan watched Vítek, pistol in hand, slow and approach the corner of the house with caution. Ylli split his attention between the underside of the vehicle and the front of the building; Hagan closed the ramp, locking the captives in like cattle; Egan's knuckles on the steering wheel matched his hair.

Ronan had never tried a daisy chain of quick-fire flytjas before. He swallowed. He once did a fast series with Freyja, but there had been a pause between each one. Not this time. It was pushing his limits, and it was going to hurt, but there was no option; he had to make Ylli agitated enough to abandon his post. There was no other way to get at the tyres.

Ronan picked four spots. Ylli swivelled at the air's sigh behind him, but Ronan was already gone. Ylli spun again to nothing, then he twisted to another sound. Nothing. The air deposited Ronan back near the stone wall, his brain ablaze. He couldn't stop, for Vítek must be about to round the rear corner. Abandoning stealth, Ronan stepped into the open in full view of Ylli, throwing himself backward into cover as the gun lifted. Ylli leapt into a sprint, machine pistol at the ready, but Ronan had already behind the wall, hidden in foliage, pressing his temples.

The Albanian rounded the building, eyes probing the gloom. There was movement at the far corner. He hissed in triumph as the snout of his weapon zeroed in and began spitting death. Muzzle flashes flickered from house to wall in a macabre dance. Bullets chattered in a continuous stream, punching home. Vítek recoiled, staggered, and fell, gun tumbling from slack fingers. His accomplice's magazine clicked empty. Ylli paused before striding toward his victim. After a detached perusal of his brother-in-law's bloodied form, Ylli shrugged as if he'd beaten the wrong bush trying to flush a rabbit.

Ronan seized the opportunity, picturing the space beneath the Range Rover, but his flaring head made him abort. Before he could try again, the engine rumbled into life and Egan hit the power. The vehicle surged. Amid cries of shock, the human cargo clattered to the back of the horsebox. Ylli sprinted after Egan, but the latter was not stopping for anyone; he roared off into the pre-dawn. There was no sign of Hagan who must have been aboard.

Embracing the wall's shadow, Ronan huffed against the brain flame. He was rapidly approaching his body's limit, but he couldn't sit round and let Ylli dissolve into the new day. Outrage gripped him at the prospect.

Ronan peered from cover, assessing his chances. The gunman had returned and was crouched over Vítek's body, going through pockets as though looting a stranger. While Ronan had the flick knife in his pocket, it was no use to him; his skill lay with bows and bare hands. So it was either karate or a well-thrown projectile, the heavier the better.

Now, more than ever, Ronan needed the guidance and power of his blood rune. The future and safety of many depended on him.

78

NO RETURN

Ylli rose from Vítek's body, eyes probing every shadow, seeking prey. Even with fresh arrow wounds, he moved with all the sinewy grace of a jungle cat. Ronan peered across the small space separating his hiding place from the merciless killer, wondering whether the injuries made the man more dangerous, if that were possible.

While Ronan could flytja to the Range Rover to catch up with Egan, Hagan and the captured girls, they could wait; if he let Ylli get away, the man may never face justice. Whatever his play, it must begin with neutralising that deadly machine pistol.

By the time the latest head flare eased, Ronan thought he had a way, but it hinged on two things: overriding the rune to make it set him down in the midst of danger; and coping with increasing flytja fire. The first he could do, the second had him worried. With a deep breath, he grasped a hefty stone, visualising the sequence of moves to get him from where he was to where he wanted to be. Emptying his mind, he dropped Caitlin's crutches and launched.

The air behind the man whispered at the same time as the crutches clattered beyond the wall. Ylli hesitated for an instant before diving to the side, twisting, whipping his weapon round. Despite jagged pain, Ronan swung the rock. The gun was no longer there, but Ylli's left elbow was. Bone cracked, Ylli grunted, the weapon fell to the ground. Ronan's elation was fleeting. The force of the swing had thrown weight onto his injured leg; it folded in a starburst of blazing torment. He cried out, fighting to regain balance.

Ylli, meanwhile, instead of clutching a broken limb and howling in agony, dived across Vítek's body, rolling on his shattered elbow without so much as a whimper, coming up with the dead man's pistol in his right hand.

As the weapon rose, Ronan hurled the stone, harder than he'd ever thrown a cricket ball. It thwacked into Ylli's wounded shoulder. The arm fell but Ylli kept hold of the gun. Ronan skipped on his good leg, ignoring the screaming protest from his wound, catapulting at Ylli. The weapon slipped from the man's struggling right hand as he toppled under Ronan's onslaught.

They fell in a tangle, Ylli's knee ramming into Ronan's stitches; his vision blurred. Ylli kicked maniacally, driving his heels at Ronan's head, thrashing him to the edge of oblivion.

Ronan twisted aside to escape the barrage. Chest heaving, he willed the fuzziness to clear. The hard metal of the gun gouged into his backbone. If only he could reach it, but he couldn't move. And he couldn't breathe. Clutching at his neck, he found the Albanian's thighs scissored round his throat, squeezing his life away.

"You no escape this time," Ylli growled, tightening his clinch.

Icy terror gripped Ronan. He'd failed. As impaired as Ylli was, he still had more than enough fight to overcome a sixteen-year-old with nothing more than a shiny black pebble under his skin. All of Freyja's lessons failed him; he couldn't blank his mind. His frantic fingers clawed at the wiry limbs laced round his neck. They wouldn't budge. His head felt like it was about to pop. The deranged image of a bursting balloon was replaced by the Home Stone; he'd see it soon.

But something welled from deep within, refusing to yield. Saoirse's features swam in his vision. How could he fail her? With ebbing strength, his fingers scrabbled again. They found their goal, pressed the button and swung, again and again.

Ylli crocodile rolled, obviously trying to pin Ronan's knife arm, but each stab weakened the leg pressure and gave Ronan the power for another. Salty warmth splattered over his face, but there was no stopping. The rune blazed. Nothing could stop him. Over and over and over he struck, long after the grip on his throat relaxed and air returned to his lungs.

Finally, gasping and coughing, he rolled aside, crying out when his thigh touched the ground. He lay staring, bloodied cheek pushed against the cold earth, inhaling the scent of soil and grass. The sheer barbarity of what he'd done kept him there, locked in horrified denial. But necessity overruled reluctance, he had to be certain. As the world pulled back into focus, he peered past flattened weeds and the dull gleam of gun metal, to the knife handle protruding from the middle of a gory mess. The Albanian's thigh looked to have been mauled by a shark. There was no movement.

Ronan retched but didn't feel any better. His heart cried, yet his eyes remained dry. A wretched shudder convulsed his body. Adrenaline merged with rune warmth, consuming him. He'd surrendered to the rune's Norse impulses, fighting like a warrior, a berserker, stopping at nothing. There was no going back. He had killed, and it terrified him. His fingernails ripped at the stone until his own blood mixed with that of his attacker. Eventually, he collapsed, too exhausted to care.

It was only the rumble of approaching vehicles that cut through Ronan's torpor. Gardaí! He had to go. But where? Saoirse mustn't see him like this.

The strengthening dawn caught a flash of blue and yellow checks through trees, adding urgency to his decision. Tugging the blade from the gory leg, Ronan emptied his mind.

79

SNATCH AND GRAB

The mudroom shower at the Raven's Roost cottage was ink black and freezing. Ronan's searching hand managed to find the tap and flick it on. He huddled in the corner, numbed, icy water sluicing over his sizzling head. The flow soon turned warm, then hot, but it couldn't quell the shivers that had started as flutters, jittering and twitching into life, blossoming into body-wracking tremors.

Alone and wretched, he stripped, kicked the bloodied clothes into a corner, soaping and scrubbing again and again. But nothing could remove the malignant film of violent death. And no amount of lathering could purge the slaughterhouse stink from his nostrils, the gore from his memory, or the weight from his heart. He gave up when the water ran cold.

Desperate to be dry, he hobbled across the room, fumbling in the gloom with a wet hand for the light switch. He didn't care. Perhaps he deserved to be electrocuted, or whatever other punishment fate held in store. While overpowering remorse blocked any concern about escaping light, he needn't have worried: outside, the rising sun was taking hold, drowning out any feeble man-made illumination.

The towel's fibres were as stiff as bristles on his skin as he tried to expunge the anguish, stopping only when his wounded thigh screeched in protest. With the damp towel snagged on a nearby hook, he settled his mind, aiming for Declan's flat and warm clothes. Flytja fire made him forget his damaged leg which collapsed as he set down. He fell with a cry, cursing, and wishing for Caitlin's crutches.

Despite his misery, Ronan jolted in panic: the crutches were lying behind the wall at the murder scene. The entire area would be restricted by now, cordoned off, combed for evidence. He had to get them before they were discovered, and he must get back to the girls; they'd be worried.

Nothing had gone to plan. As a result, Ronan now had to make at least two more rapid-fire flytjas. He grimaced at the thought as he pulled himself across the carpet toward Declan's wardrobe. Sitting on the floor, he struggled into jeans, a flannel shirt, solid coat, and a pair of worn runners. As he did, the knowledge that he'd crossed a line tormented him. His frenzied attack on Ylli left him wondering if he'd completely lost the moorings to his true self, whether he *had* become a Norse warrior.

A short time later, Ronan was not where he meant to be. Instead of at the wall, he was curled against the garden shed, fists pressed to his temples, cheeks working like miniature bellows. Voices ebbed and flowed past him, but the words vortexed into the bonfire in his skull, disappearing in wisps of smoke. As snippets began evading incineration long enough to register, he dragged himself forward, peering round the corner of his concealment. The place was crawling with gardaí; one was leaning over the low stone wall. No wonder his rune had set him down so far from target.

"Want me to bag these crutches, Sarge?" the fresh-faced guard enquired as he straightened.

Ronan's pulse lifted.

"Don't you touch the fecking things, Nolan," snapped a busty woman with sergeant's stripes. "Leave them for forensics ... they'll be here soon." She glanced at her watch. "Help the others, will you? There's a good lad."

Heart pounding, Ronan shrank against the iron skin of the shed. He wanted to wait, to avoid the ignition, but he had to act before more officers flooded the scene. He visualised his second target, locking it into his memory, for he wouldn't have a clear head when the time came—he may not even be able to make it. But he had to try; those bloody crutches could unravel Caitlin's life, and therefore, Saoirse's.

Biting hard on his coat collar, Ronan filled his mind with the rear of the garden wall. A flamethrower squirted through his brain as he folded away. The air spat him out beside the crutches, but he wasn't aware; he was fighting the agony, teeth clamped, lids screwed tight.

"Did you hear that?" a distant voice said.

"What?" another replied.

"I thought I heard snuffling behind the wall."

"Probably a hedgehog."

"They should be hibernating ... besides, the sun's up."

"I'll check it out."

Ronan's lids were lead weights; he forced them up. As he grabbed the metal shafts, they clanked together.

"Hey!"

Ronan tried to enter ró, but everything blurred, the fire overwhelming. "Saoirse," he mumbled, "I'm sorry."

As if in response, the rune spread a momentary calm through his tormented skull. Grasping the opportunity, he filled his mind with Caitlin's Mini. Flytja fire consumed him, the air sucking him away amid the unladylike cussing of the garda sergeant.

80

———

BIRDS OF A FEATHER

Ronan collapsed in searing agony, hands clamped to his head to stop it exploding. He curled into a ball of suffering amid tangled crutches. When he finally levered open an eye, the world was blank, he might have been in a void. He let his lids droop, seeking escape from misery. When slumber embraced him, it was filled with frenzied stabbing at an elusive target, and shackled girls, each one Saoirse's twin. A cricked neck and throbbing leg eventually woke him; he wondered if the stitches had burst. And the memory of Ylli's mutilated leg was a festering abscess in his mind. Ronan attempted to block it out by making sense of where he was.

Caitlin must have parked the Mini in Declan's garage which, clearly, was as light proof as a photographer's dark-room. He pushed the front seat forward, tried opening the door, but it scraped against something weighty yet flexible, and the movement caused a faint jingle. When his searching fingers found keys dangling from the ignition, a warning bell sounded: *Caitlin always takes the keys out.* He pushed harder. With a harsh chafe, the door opened against the resistance. Musty decay invaded the car, yet the darkness remained. Reaching out, his fingers found a stiff, coarse fabric.

A canvas tarpaulin covered the vehicle. But why? Crutches in hand, he pushed out from under the covering, finding himself in a den of dust-motes, spiders and slanting chinks of insipid light. A couple of antiquated push-bikes leant against the wall in front of the car, together with a broken garden chair and an assortment of digging, pruning and trimming tools, all rusted and cobwebbed. Either side of the canvas-draped Mini were shelves of tins, jars and plastic containers of all shapes and sizes—motor oil, garden chemicals, nuts, nails and screws. Behind the vehicle, chained and padlocked doors left enough gap for cool air and noon-day light to sneak in. He'd spent hours in pain-laced torpor, drifting in and out of sleep, reliving the morning's horror. But where was he? And where were Saoirse and Caitlin?

Disquiet gave way to alarm. Everything felt wrong, and it was his fault. It had been approaching dawn when he'd left the girls waiting in the car, yet when he'd returned to the Mini less than two hours later, it was already tarpaulin draped.

Ronan's stomach lurched. While he didn't want to think about what the locked shed and tarpaulin meant, there was no avoiding it. The vehicle wasn't intended to be found, and neither were the girls. He groaned. What had he done? In his desire to protect them, to remove the underlying danger, he'd unwittingly put them in greater peril. Or worse.

Disregarding the consequences, Ronan visualised the moment after he left them, and cleared his mind. As the thoughts drained, a fireball detonated in his skull, collapsing his legs, driving him into the dirt. He cradled his temples as wave after wave of combustion pulsed through his brain, pressuring his eyeballs.

And through the torment, came the heat of the rune itself, like a giant festering boil about to rupture, burst free, leave his body forever. He clamped both hands across the back of his head, clutching it in place. The skin was still raw from his earlier attempt to claw it out, but now he needed it to stay.

While he might still find Saoirse without it, he'd never meet his father, or get back to his mother and Ruddi if the rune abandoned him. He cried in anguish; his world was disintegrating, collapsing inward to a black hole at the centre of his being. Features contorting, he writhed against the onslaught. His stomach became a rumbling volcano, erupting over the dusty floor of the car shed. Freyja, he needed Freyja. "Grandmother," he moaned.

The pounding eased at glacial pace and he slipped into blessed oblivion. When he woke from hours of helplessness and realised he still lived, his thoughts leapt to the girls. If a time-flytja was too much for his body to cope with, he'd have to find them with space-flytjas only.

Mind whirling with possibilities, but no plan, Ronan blew dust from his nostrils, levered himself erect, and crutched to the sagging wooden doors. Through the separating crack was a sliver of rural backyard littered with disarray and abandonment. Across its centre, a single line of stark contrast: fresh washing. Past the side of the house, twin wheel tracks cut through a weedscape and a small wood, the resulting gap framing a distant hillside lit by fading afternoon light. The vague rumble of an engine drifting through the trees suggesting a nearby road.

There was no sign of the horse trailer or Range Rover. If either were here, they would surely be in the back yard, hidden from passers-by.

Regardless, the whole thing looked and smelt like another Fionella Egan investment. Ronan's heart plummeted further: the Egans must have Saoirse and Caitlin. The thought of them in shackles, or worse, inflamed a fearsome anger. Fists bunching, vengeance and violence threatened to consume him. While the rune was all that stood between the girls and an unthinkable future, Ronan feared what it might drive him to do.

He was still fighting Norse thoughts when the back door opened, disgorging two young women, neither much older than Caitlin. One carried an empty washing basket. Behind them came a slouching Jamie Hagan, leaving the door agape. Ronan's passion was replaced by sudden clarity. If Saoirse and Caitlin were in the house, as the Mini in the adjacent car shed suggested, the patch of interior wall visible through the open door offered him a way in.

Jamie leant against an abandoned fertiliser spreader cancerous with rust, gaze never leaving the girls. They pulled clothes from the line, moving in slow motion, perhaps trying to maximise their time in the open air. Their guard didn't seem to mind. The line was strung high between two trees, forcing them to stretch for each item before they bent low to place the folded article in the basket. Every move pulled dresses tight against shapely bodies.

Ronan was studying the interior wall again when he stiffened. Black hair and red lipstick filled his vision. Luli! Saoirse and Caitlin must be in there!

"Hurry up, you stupid girls," Luli sniped. Turning to the leering Jamie, she said, "Touch any of the merchandise, and the boss will have Ylli gut you like a fish." The casual delivery added to the menace.

Jamie pushed off the machine, head shaking in flimsy denial. "Don't know what you're talking about," he grumbled. "Besides, your brother isn't here."

"Then I will do it myself." Her mirthless chuckle crackled like crushed ice.

Jamie snorted, flashing a look at the labouring girls. "Watch them yourself, then," he said, lumbering into the house.

Cold eyes lingered on his back before settling on the captives. "Get inside now," she barked, standing aside to allow them past. She scanned the surrounds, pausing on the garage door. Even though she couldn't possibly see him, Ronan shrank away from the crack. Luli's predatory aura was every bit as chilling as her sibling's.

With a final glance at the car shed, she retreated, pushing the door closed.

81

SOLEMN VOW

Back propped against the inside of the garage door, Ronan searched for a next move. His leg was thumping; what he wouldn't do for O'Leary's painkillers. *Shit! ... the antibiotics.* Would he lose his leg without them? Perhaps the crutches were symbolic of his future. Shame swamped his self-pity as he thought of Caitlin. And Saoirse might not even have a future because of him. He should have listened to the girls and gone back to Declan's flat after the doctor, and dealt with the future when it arrived. But how was he to know? How was anyone to know?

He breathed deep; he was no use to anyone without a clear head, or a functioning body—he needed that medication. With alarm clouding his mind, he struggled to recall where the drugs were, but by backtracking in his memory, he realised they were in his bloodied clothes at the Raven's Roost shower. And that made his heart stutter. How could he have forgotten that incriminating evidence? It had to disappear. While loath to use up precious flytjas, he had no choice. Besides, with a bit of luck, the powerful medication might dampen future flytja fire.

The rune set Ronan down in the gloomy, windowless mudroom, his head unruffled. The light still burnt from the morning's visit; he soon found the foil bag of antibiotics in a sodden shirt pocket and swallowed one. The painkiller packet, along with the recommended dosage interval, had disintegrated in the moisture. Ronan took a guess, downing a couple.

The easy space-flytja, along with the drugs, had Ronan brimming with renewed confidence, his thoughts turned to food. But his attention snagged on the blood-stained clothes and the knife lying on the floor in steely indifference to the life it had taken. Another pain-free jump put him in the kitchen where he grabbed a large plastic bag and a can of stew. Back in the mudroom, he stuffed the damning evidence into the bag, rescuing his faithful phone in the process.

On the off chance that it might still work after hours in a water-logged pocket, he picked at it with fingernails until the battery came away and the SIM card fell out. With each part wiped dry and dropped into separate pockets, he gathered the bundle and left.

The flytja deposited Ronan in the mouth of the Sliabh Liag cave from where his father had fallen—it was the best spot he could think of. As the wind swirled up from the gunmetal Atlantic, deranging his hair and buffeting his body, he relived his father's last moments as he'd seen them from across the cliff face. "I *will* find you, Dad," he murmured, "I promise. Just as soon as I'm sure Saoirse is safe." Running a hand over the cave's rough wall, he tried to extract some essence of the man from the bleak rock.

Ronan's rune pulsed as if recognising it had returned to where it and its twin had lain buried for over a thousand years. But where was the other, the one Paidin held when he fell, the one that had heimmed him to the Home Stone before he could hit the waves below? "I *will* find you," Ronan repeated.

With a final, longing caress of the wall, he emptied the plastic bag. As well as the knife, there was a full set of clothes, including belt, socks and shoes; all must vanish, forever. After devouring the stew—it barely touched the sides—he wedged the knife into the empty can with a handful of debris from the cave floor, wondering if it was the same rubble his parents and Masters had moved to uncover the runes. After knotting the end of the single pants leg, Ronan dropped the can into the resulting pouch, following it with shoes and socks crammed with stones. By the time he'd stuffed in the underclothes, shirt and jacket, and drawn the belt tight like a drawstring, it resembled the bottom half of a grotesque, one-legged scarecrow.

Ronan had planned to swing it high into the air out over the abyss to make sure it didn't snag the cliff on the way down, but its weight, and his bullet wound, made that impossible. Instead, he sat on the floor and pushed the evidence from Ylli's death toward the edge with his good leg. With it balancing on the brink, Ronan wormed alongside until his stomach swooped. Far below in the fading dusk, laggard seabirds returned from foraging, whirling and gliding in to alight on ledge and crevice, squawking the day's news to each other, or squabbling over real estate. Their calls floated on the briny air. Ronan crossed his fingers for them.

"Sorry, Declan," he murmured, and with a gentle push, the half-scarecrow went over the edge, weighted leg sending it plummeting. Startled birds flurried from the rock face in its wake. Oblivious waves rolled and crashed against the mountain's foundations, sending spume flying, absorbing the plunging bundle without pause. There may have been a splash, even a raft of bubbles; there may have been nothing; Ronan couldn't tell. Besides, his mind was already on Saoirse.

"I'm coming," he breathed.

82

———————

UNEXPECTED RESULT

I t was dark in the laundry of the house where Luli and Jamie Hagan held their prisoners. Ronan's only discomfort was his leg. So far, so good. He eased the rubber feet of the crutches onto the floor, testing for squeaky boards before applying full weight and making a cautious hobble. Voices chafed the air, drawing his nose into a lighted central hall. To the left were two doors sporting shiny hasps and padlocks. The temptation to go there first was strong, but he had no way past those barriers—yet.

Indignation pinballed down the hallway from the far end of the house.

"Get stuffed," Jamie growled.

"You will do as you are told," Luli hissed.

"Says who?" It was Sean Hagan's surliness.

"If you have a problem with me," Luli said with naked challenge, "take it up with the boss."

"Maybe I will," Sean shot back.

Still lacking a plan on how to proceed, Ronan slipped down the hall. The first open door belonged to a toilet scented by a supposed air freshener, but which reeked of cloying indifference. Next was a bathroom with cracked tiles, stained porcelain, and a fly-specked mirror. The final two rooms faced each other across the corridor. One held two tangles of bedding and the stale odour of sweaty men; the other, obviously Luli's, smelt of feminine deodorant. Against a wall was the same regurgitating suitcase he'd seen in Glengarriff Parade. Amid his rising ire, Ronan almost missed the corner of a bulging duffel bag behind the half-open door.

A chair scraped; Ronan froze.

"I need a leak," Jamie muttered.

Ronan crabbed into Luli's room, squeezing behind the door with the duffels as clomping footsteps traversed the hallway. Pressing his eye to the gap between door and jamb, he watched Jamie trudge into the toilet. When the door shut, Ronan turned his attention to the stacked bags, the topmost level with his chin. They were the same four he'd seen going into the back of the Range Rover at the murder house. Whatever they held was valuable for the sturdy vinyl was double-stitched and the zip sliders were locked together with a twist of wire sandwiched by a lead, tamper-proof seal. It seemed Fionella didn't trust her lackeys. While interesting, there was no time for another mystery; his prime concern was freeing Saoirse and Caitlin from behind those padlocked doors. Knowing he was in no state for confrontation, Ronan searched for a clever approach; his eyes gravitated to the bags. Perhaps with the right leverage, he could convince Fionella to release the girls.

It was awkward with the crutches' forearm cuffs impeding his movement, but Ronan hefted the top bag—weighty, but not overly so. With Luli and Sean still arguing, there would never be a better time. Grasping a bag in each hand, he blanked his mind. The last thing he heard was the thunk of a crutch against the wall. *Damn!* Moments later, he was back, repeating the process, but to the sound of a chair toppling, and Luli's venomous threat: "Get out of my room, Jamie, or I will slit your gullet." Urgent footsteps from one direction mingled with a toilet's flush from the other as Ronan folded away with the remaining bags. The second time he returned, it was to the men's bedroom, wedged behind the open door, ignoring the tiny ping of flytja fire.

Luli shot into her room, spinning full circle, gaze settling on her suitcase. She then conducted a more measured scrutiny, passing over the space where the bags had been, whiplashing back to it. Dark with fury, she turned toward the toilet, opening her mouth as if to speak, evidently deciding against it. Instead, she crossed to her suitcase, diving a hand to the bottom and coming up with a small silver revolver.

Jamie came out of the toilet zipping his pants, astonishment exploding across his face when he found himself staring into the gaping maw of the revolver. "What the—"

"Where are they?" Luli spat the words at him.

He lifted his palms. "Where's what?"

"You took the duffel bags from my room." Her voice rose in accusation.

Jamie frowned. "I didn't touch the bloody things. I was in the damned toilet."

Luli's lips all but disappeared; she glared as though trying to incinerate him.

"What's going on?" Sean called down the hallway.

"Keep out of this, old man," Luli barked, pushing past Jamie into the laundry. After a string of Albanian profanities, she emerged with a clinking bag, which she threw at Jamie's feet. It landed with a metallic thud.

He stared in disbelief. "What's this for?"

"What do you think?"

"Don't be ridiculous, Luli," Jamie pleaded. "Why would I touch them?"

Luli waved the gun toward the bag. "Put them on."

Sean appeared at his son's shoulder. "Why would he take them? He's not an idiot."

"That is a matter of opinion," Luli retorted, "but the boss can sort it out. Now put them on"—she brandished the weapon again—"both of you."

"You stupid bitch!" Sean stepped forward, the revolver swung and spat.

Ronan hadn't realised his sleeve had whispered against the back of the door, but when the barrel moved past Sean, he ducked. While only a small calibre weapon, its sharp crack magnified in the hallway's confines. The bullet splintered the door panel above him, his cry as his damaged leg crumpled, merged with the gunshot's dying echoes.

83

POETIC JUSTICE

Behind the bedroom door, Ronan was twisted into a pretzel of tangled crutches and torment. His throbbing leg overrode the effort to empty his mind. The acrid bite of spent gunpowder drifted from the hallway where Sean and Jamie stood transfixed. Luli hesitated for half a beat before shouldering past them, rampaging toward the open doorway. In desperation, Ronan planted his good foot against the door, slamming it into Luli's face.

Blood gushing from her nose and mashed lip, she dropped the gun and careened across the hall, crashing into the opposite wall. Jamie seized the opportunity, diving for the weapon. With his hand closing in on the revolver, Luli recovered, pouncing onto his back, her impetus driving them both into the bedroom. As the interlocked bodies burst through the door, Ronan managed to clear his mind and set down behind Luli's door, across the hallway. Again, the flytja fire stirred.

"Get off me!" Jamie roared, attempting to raise the weapon.

Amid a confusion of raven locks and blazing eyes, Luli gnawed Jamie's ear, snarling like a wild cat, clawing at his gun hand, other arm locked round his throat.

"Aargh!" As he bawled and thrashed, his father aimed a powerful kick at Luli's ribs, but she rolled Jamie's midriff into the firing line; he oofed and sagged. Luli hung off the ear; Jamie's blood leaked, merging with her own. Sean swung another kick, but a sixth sense had Luli arching her body aside, away from Jamie's, a severed piece of cartilage clamped between her teeth. Jamie screamed, forgot the weapon and clutched at what remained of his ear. Sean's second kick cannoned off his son's ribs.

Alight with battle lust, chest heaving, Luli scooped up the revolver, panning it with both hands as she scanned the room. Sean stared, ashen-faced, immobile; Jamie clutched his ear, mesmerised by the gore dripping from her chin. "You're bloody crazy," he howled, slumping against the wall.

Luli spat gristle like a watermelon seed, but said nothing; the menacing weapon spoke silent volumes. Smearing claret across her mouth with the back of a hand, she probed the room again. "Who was in here?" When there was no answer, she pressed the cold steel into Jamie's cheek, creating a grotesque, one-sided grimace. "Someone was in here," she hissed. "Who was it?"

Jamie blanched. He tried to pull away, but the gun followed him. "What are you talking about?" he whimpered.

"There's no one," Sean said, stepping forward.

Luli thumbed the hammer to full cock; Sean froze, mid-step. Jamie's eyes became saucers. The pressure from the weapon had his chin pushing on his shoulder—he couldn't have shaken his head if life depended on it. "I only went to the toilet," he sobbed.

After lengthy consideration, Luli stepped back, flicking the barrel toward the hallway.

Sean bent to help his son who glowered at the woman as he rose. "It will heal," she sneered, "if you live long enough."

"You've got it all wrong," Jamie grumbled, pressing a handkerchief to his bloodied wound.

In response, Luli motioned with the gun toward their bedroom.

"Screw an anchor to the floor," she ordered Sean.

"You're making a mistake," the man said, not moving.

"Move," she growled.

Sean glared defiance, but his shoulders sagged when the eye of the revolver settled on his face. With obvious reluctance, he gathered the clinking bag and turned into his room.

Ronan emptied his mind, the breath of his leaving masked by the whine of a cordless drill. Ignoring the head flare, he skirted the outside of the house, past a small pane over the sink, round a corner, and beyond a picture window opposite a four-person dining table. The next rectangle of light splaying across the neglected yard was the men's bedroom. From the shadows, he watched Sean straighten from fixing a steel anchor to the floorboards. Attached to it were several lengths of chain, each ending in a gaping manacle; two soon encircled Hagan ankles.

Poetic justice.

By the sound of the opening and shutting doors and rattling locks, Luli was combing the house. When Ronan heard her at the far end of the hallway, he backtracked to between the two kitchen windows to wait. The three plates on the table were untouched; he figured she'd be back.

The scrape of a chair and the clink of cutlery were Ronan's signal. He edged a cautious eye past the frame of the sink window. Luli sat at the table, back to him. The silver revolver lay in conspicuous malevolence beside a sauce bottle, a bulging keyring and a mobile phone. Opposite, the Hagan's meals were congealing.

The tactic he'd used on her brother had worked—sort of—so Ronan thought he'd try it again, but with a slight variation. The fact there had been minimal flytja fire since taking O'Leary's drugs gave him confidence. Rehearsing the moves in his mind: the knife-hand strike to the base of the woman's neck, collecting her keys; releasing Saoirse, Caitlin and the other prisoners; chaining Luli up in their place; liberating the Mini; and, driving off to alert the guards. Easy.

Luli was halfway through a microwaved shepherd's pie when Ronan's rune began radiating. He'd never been more ready. Laying one crutch on the grass, he visualised what he must do and cleared his mind.

84

REVULSION AND FEAR

Everything went as it should until Ronan hobbled from the kitchen air behind Luli. For a simple plan, it failed spectacularly. As well as underestimating the speed of Luli's reflexes, and how much the bullet wound and resurgent flytja fire had slowed him, he hadn't given the window a thought.

If the woman had been sitting anywhere but in front of that pane of glass, it might have worked. As it was, Ronan's first movement reflected back to her. Leaning forward on his crutch, his right hand was zeroing in on her neck when she dived, fingers stretching for the gun, pie, peas and plate flying. The blow glanced her hip as the chair careened backward, ricocheting from his firmly planted crutch into his thigh, and spinning away. White-hot agony detonated through his leg. Vision blurring, he staggered.

Luli gripped the weapon as she shot across the table, momentum taking her over the other side, but not before she swivelled. The revolver barked.

Ronan lurched as pain seared his chest. His rune flared with battle lust. He drove forward into the table with a wild roar, heedless of screaming nerve ends and straining stitches, his whole being intent on driving the wooden structure through the window, taking the woman with it.

On the other side of the table, Luli's shoulder hit the floor. Panther-like, she rolled and rose, gun aiming, victory glinting in her eyes. As her finger tightened on the trigger, the table slammed into her midriff, sending her reeling and the bullet wide. The back of her head punched through the windowpane in the same instant her cat-like reflexes twisted her body to regain balance. Her neck rotated on a jagged edge of glass.

Bile rose in Ronan's throat. He averted his gaze, swallowed and flopped into a chair, staring unseeing, anywhere but the window, struggling to come to grips with the horror of what had happened. Despite the rune warmth, his body chilled, quaking. Revulsion and fear surged through him. He'd become a murderous Norse version of himself, a rune-driven assassin. If only he could talk to Freyja; instead, he sat and stared, welcoming the returning torment in his thigh. Rightful penance.

"What the hell's going on, Luli?" It was Sean Hagan. Silence. "Luli?"

While Ronan's eyelids hid the woman's contorted, ashen face, the image was already seared into his memory. And nothing could block the slaughterhouse stench. The metallic smell of blood from the regular butchering of beef on Doyle Farm had never bothered him, but now it was horrifying. Mere seconds ago, the pile of slumped flesh had been a living being, not a nice one, but a person nonetheless. He shuddered. What had he done? Clamping his eyelids tighter, he refocused. First the keys, then Saoirse and Caitlin.

"Luli?" It was Sean again. "Luli? Hello?"

With enormous effort, Ronan visualised the earlier fracas. When Luli had dived for the gun, the keys and phone had catapulted in opposite directions. Retracing their trajectories in his mind, he gathered the fallen crutch and forced himself past the overturned table, closer to the corpse. He found the mobile in the corner, pocketing it as insurance in case his wouldn't fire up.

The search for the keys drew him to the shore of the spreading crimson lake, and deeper into revulsion. Even though he was positive they were beneath the rag-doll body at the centre of the red pond, he could go no further. There must be another way through those doors. Besides, touching a single thing would leave clues for a clever detective. With that in mind, he grabbed a tea towel from the oven rail and wiped down the table's edge where he'd pushed against it.

As Ronan turned away, contemplating how to use the cordless drill to get past the locked doors, a glint against the upended table leg caught his eye. In blissful disconnection from the adjacent carnage was the jumble of keys—they must have rebounded from the wall. Their clinking as he gathered them triggered a response from Jamie Hagan. "Who's there?" he called, reefing on his chain. "We're prisoners." The chain rattled again. "Free us. Please?"

Not likely. Ronan jammed the tea towel into a back pocket.

The locked doors beckoned him, but there was only one way to get past the open door without the chained men seeing him. So, clutching the keys, he blanked his mind and visualised the far end of the hallway.

The set-down mirrored his first ever, the air disgorging him in an untidy heap. Only this time, Ronan didn't know, he was unconscious.

85

HOPE AND ANTICIPATION

Incessant burring in Ronan's pocket lifted him to the edge of awareness; kept him floating there. Muffled voices joined in the irritation, but he couldn't make out what they were saying. A familiar, resentful voice cut through the clutter, growling, "Answer your damned phone, Luli." It was Sean Hagan. *Oh, shut up!* He wanted to sleep, but it was a luxury he couldn't afford. He moved, immediately wishing he hadn't. A sharp throb ratcheted through his thigh, his ribs ignited, and a dragon's breath billowed through his brain. The burring resumed.

Ronan's surroundings began to crystallise: the chill floor against his cheek, the Hagans grumbling about chains and manacles, and softer voices murmuring confusion. Against his better judgement, he levered an eyelid up, swallowed against renewed flytja fire, and concentrated on focusing. The blur in front of his eye sharpened into a confusion of keys fanning from a nucleus of interlocked rings.

How long he'd been out to it, Ronan had no idea, but everything—Saoirse, Caitlin, the gun, the fight, the blood—came flooding back. He rolled over; wincing at torment from every direction. Energy drained, he patted pockets, found O'Leary's painkillers, dry swallowed two, almost retching as they caught in his throat.

Even though his body and rune were warning him, there could be no waiting; he had to move, had to free Saoirse. But he couldn't afford to be left helpless by another flytja.

Ronan levered upright on the single crutch, leaning against the wall until a semblance of equilibrium returned. The chatter inside the rooms ceased, as if the captives were daring to hope. One-by-one, he tested the keys, fumbling them into the first padlock. Each one he tried seemed to spawn another two on the ring; halfway through, he lost his way. With an unsteady sigh, he started again. Finally, one clicked against all the right tumblers;

the padlock fell open, the house hushed. A tingle of anticipation ran through him as he reached for the doorknob, but caution stilled his hand. Even in his hazy state, he was aware he shouldn't let those girls get a look at him, especially since they would soon be grilled by the garda. Saoirse and Caitlin would have to wait a little longer.

In the clutter of the adjacent laundry, he found a folded blue dress. Ronan recalled it swirling round Luli's legs as she'd hurried along Glengarriff Parade. Remorse rose at the memory of the woman; he smothered it, wrapping the garment round his head until only his eyes showed, Bedouin-like.

Satisfied, he returned to the unlocked door, wiping his fingerprints from all surfaces with the tea towel. With his injured leg and supporting crutch out of sight, he pushed the door open, flicking on the light. Six blinking squinting girls turned haunted, miserable faces toward him. Ronan swallowed disappointment; Saoirse and Caitlin weren't among them. His retreat triggered clamour. Shackles rattled and clanked like a sideshow-alley House of Horrors as desperate hands reached toward him. Compassion swelled, but Norse rage exploded through its centre, fighting for supremacy. Before it could prevail, the calming side of the rune settled him. He held a finger to hidden lips.

By the time Ronan found the correct key for the second door, removed the padlock and wiped down the surfaces, he was tingling with expectation. But there were only five girls where he'd hoped to find seven. Heart dropping, he pulled the door closed with the towel, sagging against the wall. He'd been so sure. Where could they be? What had he missed?

Distressed pleas erupted from the room, punctuated by an anguished wail in broken English. "Help us ... please?"

Blocking out the girls' disappointment and distress, Ronan withdrew to the laundry, leaning against the bench, floundering for a clear-eyed view of the situation, and a course of action. Fionella Egan had Saoirse and Caitlin somewhere unknown, and he was stuck here wounded and unable to flytja. His gut knotted, not with impotence, but fear. Fear that he was wrong about the flytja fire and that the rune was deserting him, fear that he'd never find Saoirse, or see his family again.

The past week replayed in Ronan's mind: Saoirse missing, Fionella's shotgun blast, the murders of Darragh, Garret, Vítek and Ylli, Luli's corpse dangling from the shattered window, the eleven captives, and Saoirse missing again, along with Caitlin. He tried to give it order, but his thoughts churned like songs shuffling after the first bar. Tremors rippled through him; sweat trickled down his back. The air was so thick with contrition and blood stench, he couldn't draw oxygen from it. He flung the outside door open, and sat on the step, head on knees, allowing the cool night air to cleanse his lungs.

Luli's phone pinged several times; Ronan silenced it.

Slowly, his brain swung into action. Over the whole week, the only people he could connect to Saoirse's captivity, Viking's theft, and now Saoirse's and Caitlin's abduction, were Vítek, Ylli, Luli, Sean and Jamie Hagan, Fionn Egan and, of course, Fionella. The only two unaccounted for were the Egans. Ronan couldn't imagine either of them sitting guard in some back-country hovel. In a rush of certainty, he knew where Saoirse and Caitlin were, and how to get there.

The weak glow from Luli's phone was enough for Ronan to find the right key, unlock the shed and wipe the relevant surfaces. As the tarpaulin chafed across the car's paintwork, he breathed a silent apology to Caitlin for the scratches. Once behind the wheel, he fired up the engine and reversed from the shed. Compared to the lumbering hippo of a four-wheel-drive he'd learnt to drive when he was ten, Caitlin's little car was a nimble gazelle. Dodging plastic containers and pieces of rusted farm equipment, he zipped round to the sink window, retrieved his second crutch, and performed a sliding U-turn that took him to the laundry door.

A clamour of imploring calls greeted Ronan's return. No matter the language, there was no mistaking the desperation in the voices of the young women. Now that he knew what he had to do, and how to do it, they weren't staying chained a minute longer. Too bad if they fled, or contaminated the crime scene.

"Hey," Jamie Hagan shouted. "Whoever you are, free us ... we can pay ... how much do you want?"

"We're victims here, too," his father added.

Ronan bit back an angry retort—Sean knew his voice. Instead, he concentrated on wiping all the keys. The clinking stoked the girls into frenzied appeals, and the Hagans into a bellowing, chain-rattling outburst.

Satisfied at last, Ronan left the keys bundled in the tea towel, stepped forward, and underarmed them into the middle of the first room.

Amid a cacophony of rattling chains, hope and anticipation, he crutched out to the Mini, collecting a weather-bleached, one-armed garden gnome on the way, and drove off.

86

THRUST AND PARRY

Ronan drove fast enough to be unremarkable, and slow enough to go unnoticed. All the practice round Doyle Farm paid off. Apart from the brief flare of opposing headlights, the darkness enveloped his youthful features, even though his concentrating frown and jutting chin made him look older.

The only hiccup was when he left the house. Ahead of him spread a narrow valley of farms, vague shapes in the gloom, except for the occasional pinpricks of lit windows. With the overcast night bamboozling his sense of direction, Ronan took a punt, turning right onto the narrow bitumen. But when he found the road trending uphill, he made a quick three-point turn, and was soon beetling down some unknown valley, heading toward the coast, out of the backblocks.

Several kilometres on, he merged onto another pencil-thin thoroughfare he recognised as the Cronasilla road. From there he swung west on 263 toward Carrick, stopping at the first bridge. While keeping an eye out for late evening traffic, he wrapped the blue dress round the garden gnome, securing it with knotted strips of torn hem. Fresh pain stopped his activity. A brief inspection of his ribs showed that, despite copious blood, Luli's bullet had only gouged a skin-deep furrow. He'd been lucky.

Moments later, the gnome arced over the parapet, taking the dress, and Ronan's DNA, to the bottom of the river.

After turning onto the deserted Teelin Road, Ronan pulled into the car park at the junction of the Glen and Owenwee rivers. Half a lifetime ago, he'd stopped there with Caitlin. Now, sitting in the glow of the Mini's dash lights, he reached for his disassembled phone, but decided to use Luli's instead—he had no idea how traceable mobiles were in 2004.

Unease gripped him when he woke it to see numerous missed calls from Vítek—could only be gardaí—and a string of texts from 'Boss', beginning with the benign, *Everything okay?* and ending with an agitated, minutes-old, *Coming now. I'd better not be wasting my time.*

Ronan swore as he pictured Fionella and her son releasing the Hagans and rounding up those poor girls before the guards arrived. Panicked thoughts churned until his rune radiated calmness. After clicking through earlier texts to get an idea of Luli's style, and recalling Caitlin's patient explanation of how to do capitals, he laboriously constructed: *Sorry, Boss. Phone was flat. Everything good.*

Keep the damned thing charged! was the immediate response.

Ronan exhaled, grateful for the foresight of taking the phone. And doubly so when he reassembled his own, for it only managed a couple of stuttering blinks before plunging into the electronic afterlife. He turned to the pilfered phone, dialling triple nine. Speaking in Irish, he asked for An Garda Síochána, reporting gunshots at a house, giving detailed directions to where Luli lay dead. After breaking the connection, he redialled, banking on a different operator, this time telling them where to find the truck that had smashed into Darragh Kelly's car, hoping they'd find clues to tie it to Fionella Egan.

After swapping out Luli's SIM card for his own, and confirming it worked, he pulled out onto Teelin Road, but stopped on the little stone bridge over the Owenwee. The separated body and battery of his faithful Motorola, plus Luli's SIM, went over the side; he drove on with visions of fork-tailed eels and three-eyed salmon.

A short time later, the Mini's headlights panned across the Egan mansion as he entered the drive. Ronan had not the faintest idea what he was going to do or say—he'd leave it to his surging rune.

"Ronan," Fionella gushed when she answered the door, "what a pleasant surprise." Her eyes swept him with a gust of winter, lingering on ribs and crutches. "My goodness," she crooned with mock concern, errant twist of auburn hair hanging past her cheek, "what *have* you been up to?"

"Sprain," Ronan said, holding her gaze.

When he didn't elaborate, Fionella stepped aside, peering past him to the car as she swept a hand toward the sitting room. "Do come in. Fionn will be most surprised ... he said you had returned to Australia."

I bet. Expressionless, Ronan said, "I didn't come to see Fionn."

"You came to see me?" she cooed, clasping her hands to her bosom like a coy schoolgirl.

Ronan studied her, unmoving, trying to penetrate the facade, but failing. "I've come to trade," he said.

"Oh, my dear boy, I lost interest in Viking ages ago ... when you made it clear that you wouldn't bring him back."

Ronan shook his head. "We both know that's not true ... Fionn stole him yesterday."

"Did he indeed?" There was not even a flicker of astonishment, concern, or any other emotion. "And now you've come to me to get him back?" Pearly teeth gleamed stark against blood-red lips.

"No, I've already taken him."

Fionella's demeanour chilled. "What a clever boy you are."

Under her reptilian gaze, Ronan felt anything but. Regardless, he tried again to unbalance her. "I've freed the girls and taken the duffel bags." It was more blurted than spoken with assurance; he didn't care.

"Is that supposed to mean something?"

Ronan shrugged. Aware that his back was to the open door, he pretended sudden interest in the same painting of a rural scene he'd employed on his last visit to the room. So much was crammed into it—horses, sheep, a couple of cows, hens and geese—the frame should have been bulging. As he turned so he could watch the door, her teeth radiated again.

Sensing he was getting nowhere, and desperate to throw her off balance, Ronan tried a different tack. "How are your Glengarriff Parade investments going?"

"Have you been talking to Fionn?"

"Not likely," Ronan shot back.

More teeth. "Of course not." After a brief pause, she continued, "Ah, the investigation. Poor Saoirse. It horrified me to think she was being held against her will in one of my houses."

"I bet."

"The gardaí have agreed it was an unfortunate coincidence." While her voice remained calm, her eyes glinted hostility.

"Just like it was an accident that Luli used your other house in the same street?"

"Who?" Fionella's acting was impressive.

"Luli ... the woman who held Saoirse captive."

"The gardaí didn't tell me her name, but it's not surprising she used two of my houses ... I own many in that street."

"And buying more?"

"As a matter of fact, I have a new Australian inves—"

"Bruno Masters." Ronan felt a small victory surge as Fionella stilled. To rub it in, he added, "When do you start your hotel?"

Fionella glared granite chips. Silence crackled through the room. At last she said, "Fionn *has* been blabbing."

Before Ronan could respond, she stalked to the doorway and bellowed into the house, "Fionn!"

87

HARMLESS ENOUGH

A heavy tread sounded in the hall; Ronan tensed, wondering if Egan might enter with a gun—too late now. With grim anticipation, he imagined the accusations and denials that were about to bounce round the room's dark leather and walnut.

"What is it, dear?" A round frame, florid face and bald dome that could only be the family patriarch, filled the doorway. "Oh," he said, puffing like an asthmatic, "I didn't know we had company." Tottering forward, he thrust a hand in Ronan's direction. "Dooley Egan," he said.

"Ronan Ryan," Ronan said, clasping the offered hand. The grip was surprisingly firm, the smile easy. 'Harmless enough' was Eoin Duffy's assessment of the man. Ronan was disappointed he wasn't facing the son.

As if reading his mind, Fionella said, "Where's Fionn?"

Dooley chuckled. "Just running a little errand for me. Why?"

His wife harrumphed. "Running off at the mouth, more like it."

"What's he done now, dear?"

"Ronan here knows far more than he should about my business dealings"—her eyes narrowed—"and it could only have come from Fionn."

Dooley raised an eyebrow at his wife then transferred it to Ronan. "Are you a friend of Fionn's?"

Ronan stifled a guffaw. "No."

"There you go, dear ... it didn't come from Fionn."

Fionella snorted. "You're so damned naïve, sometimes." She waved a hand. "Has Fionn told you about Bruno Masters?"

"Who?"

"Never mind." The woman's cold gaze turned to Ronan. "How did you find out about Masters?"

While there was a obvious lack of marital communication between the two of them, Ronan wasn't interested. "It doesn't matter," he said. "I've come to trade."

"Fascinating," Dooley puffed. "And what are you trading, young man?" The man's jolly tone held an air of disinterest, dismissal even.

"That's between your wife and me."

Dooley gestured. "Would you like a drink?" He was already moving to a side table laden with decanters, glasses, and a carbonated water dispenser. It appeared Dooley was the thirsty one.

"No ... thanks," he said, attention locked on Fionella.

As crystal clinked and liquor gurgled, Fionella must have decided it wasn't just between her and Ronan. "He said something about girls"—the dispenser sputtered—"and duffel bags."

For an instant, Fionella's grey eyes became human. Widening ever so slightly, they flicked behind Ronan. A whisper of cloth triggered an evasive reflex; he ducked, throwing up an arm, but not fast enough. Dooley's dispenser caromed off his lifting bicep, slamming above his ear.

Ronan's vision exploded into a fizzing sparkler shower. He ricocheted off a chair, crutches twisting as he fell, one catching under his wounded leg. The supernova of agony overshadowed his cheek smacking onto the floor. While desperate to slip into blissful oblivion, consciousness wouldn't release him from the torment—arm, thigh, head, ribs. Instead, he concentrated on breathing and rune strength.

Voices came through the fog, disembodied at first, then clearer.

Fionella scowled at her husband. "What the hell was that?"

Dooley stood, ashen faced, feet planted, dispenser hanging from one hand, the other withdrawing a handkerchief, dabbing his brow as he studied at Ronan. "This kid knows too much," he said, panting from exertion, or fear, or both.

"Did you have to kill him?"

"He's not dead ... only half hit him. Besides, I couldn't take the chance."

"What damned chance?"

Dooley swallowed. "He knows too much ab—"

"About what?" She stabbed the words at him.

Ronan's wits were returning, but he remained still, listening.

"My business," he wheezed, "and yours."

"Girls and duffel bags?"

Dooley nodded, jowls wobbling.

His wife's tone hardened. "What have girls and duffel bags got to do with boots?"

"Everything," Dooley gasped, flopping into an overstuffed chair that almost collapsed under the assault. "For both of us."

Fionella peered at her husband. "What have you done?"

"Why have I always *done* something?" he griped.

"Because you always do, my love." The words were devoid of affection.

"That's unfair." The man's whine banished any remaining jolliness.

"It would be if it were not true."

"Where's my drink?" Dooley said, head panning. Heaving himself from the chair's embrace, he crossed to the side table, sloshing more whiskey into his earlier mix, taking a noisy gulp.

Fionella hadn't moved, apart from planting hands on hips. "Girls and bags, Dooley?" She seemed as determined to discover what he'd done as he was to deflect.

"Who is Bruno Masters?" he shot back.

"You first."

"Oh, for God's sake, Fi"—air whistled into his lungs—"we agreed to stay out of each other's business ... I don't interfere in your real estate dealings, do I?"

"Are you sure?" Fionella's voice was as cool as her stare.

After rasping out a dismissive huff, Dooley said, "So this Masters is an Egan Estates client?"

Fionella lips thinned and tightened. "Investor ... Fionn charmed him into tipping a sizable portion of his late parent's fortune into my Glengarriff Parade venture."

Ronan couldn't imagine Egan charming anyone into or out of anything. And he wondered if the Egan Estates venture was one of those that drained Masters' inheritance.

"Good," Dooley responded with a semblance of pride. "He's been shaping up with me as well ... getting his hands dirty. Speaking of which, how did this kid find out about your Masters?" He toed Ronan's ribs, close enough to the bullet graze to trigger immediate retaliation.

Ronan grabbed Dooley's foot and heaved, stifling a cry at exploding pain. The man went over backward, landing with a thump and rattle of glasses that would have made a small earthquake proud. Even more satisfying for Ronan was Fionella's choked squawk of alarm.

Dooley lay on his broad back like a stranded codfish, limbs flapping, mouth working as he struggled for air. Fionella gave her husband no more than a cursory glance as she glided across to pour herself a drink. As he pulled himself up onto the crutches and backed into the corner by the window, Ronan marvelled at how unfazed she was. What made her immune to concern?

"Are you sure you wouldn't like a drink, Ronan?" Her words were spider silk.

"I am," Ronan said.

Fionella's shrug turned into a predatory smirk as in walked her son, cradling a shotgun.

88

———

DRUGS AND MONEY

Fionn Egan jerked to a halt, surprise leaping into his face when he saw Ronan. It flattened to disinterest at the sight of his father sprawled on the floor. The past few days had left him haggard; he looked to have lost his youth to the shadows of middle age, his snowy hair limp. The skin across his cheeks was taut, as though it had shrunk to accommodate anticipated weight loss. Dark rings cradled restive eyes flicking about for the unexpected. The shotgun was in an awkward left-hand grip; a calico sling swathed the right arm.

Ronan wondered how many shotguns the family had. "How's the shoulder, Finnegan?" he said, determined to keep the lad off balance.

Egan tensed. He thumbed back the hammers, trying to raise the weapon, wincing, settling for a glower. "It was you!" he howled, as if suddenly connecting random dots. "You shot me!" Again, he attempted to lift the gun, but with the same result. "You could have killed me!"

"If I'd wanted you dead, Finnegan, I'd have put an arrow through your eye." Ronan was conscious of not pushing him until enmity overrode restraint and misery.

Egan's lips twisted.

Fionella studied Ronan. "Very cocky, aren't you."

Ronan was riding high on rune power—couldn't even feel his wounds. He held her gaze. "Just being honest." Turning to her son, he said, "You've seen how good my karate is, Finnegan ... it's not a patch on my bow skill."

"Why do you insist on being disparaging?" Fionella enquired, with all the maternal concern of a cuckoo.

307

"What? Finnegan?" Ronan maintained a straight face. "It's how he introduced himself, and I usually stick to first impressions. Nothing has proved me wrong."

Dooley interrupted with a loud, hacking cough as though trying to dislodge a fur ball. Both mother and son glanced with indifference. *Birds of a feather.*

"What did you do to your leg, hotshot?" Egan said, returning his attention to Ronan.

"Shaving cut."

Dooley hacked again and moaned. He rolled over and pushed himself up against a chair, head swivelling in bewilderment. "What happened?"

"The floor smacked you in the back," Ronan said dryly.

Egan tried to look tough; Dooley stared; Fionella scrutinised Ronan. "Why are you so confident?" she mused.

"I've got a good hand."

"And what would that be?" Her focus never wavered.

"Only I know where the duffel bags are."

Dooley groaned.

"He's got the duffels?" Egan blurted.

"What duffels?" Fionella snapped.

While the Egans focused on each other, Ronan eased Luli's phone from his pocket, thumbed in a memorised number, and slipped it away before anyone noticed. With his previous assumptions upended, Ronan needed to confirm his latest. He waited.

A phone chirped; all eyes zeroed in on the source. A thumb pressed a button—it was Ronan's signal to end the call.

"Hello?" Dooley said, ashen faced. "Hello?" He held the phone at arm's length as if it were a live grenade.

"What is going on, Dooley?" she demanded.

Dooley appeared close to puking. "You never wanted to know my side of the business," he whined.

"Well, I do now," she shot back.

Egan peered from one parent to the other.

"It was a favour to Escardero," Dooley said, finding the floor interesting. "We just had to look after it for a few days ..."

"Look after what?" Fionella hissed. Her glare turned the room arctic.

Ronan remained motionless and silent; he didn't want to remind them of his presence.

"Drugs and money," Dooley mumbled.

"What?" Disbelief tugged at the flesh on her face.

"Drugs and money," he shouted.

Fionella ignited. "You idiot!" she screamed. "You've risked everything. You damned greedy imbecile."

"When did you ever complain about the money?" Dooley protested. "You just went and bought more houses."

"Mum ..."

"Shut up!" she screeched.

Egan flushed, but his features hardened. Ronan was already moving: one crutch, two. The shotgun lifted, its pugnacious snout seeking him. He dived. Glass shattered. The gun roared.

TWENTY MILLION

Ronan's shoulder hit shrubbery, crutches flew but the forearm clips kept them anchored. Agony detonated in his thigh, his ribs screamed, his head thumped from Dooley's blow. Egan had only fired one barrel, and he'd soon be at the window with the second one. Ronan couldn't risk another shot, so he emptied his mind.

A blissful, painless, silken slide in and out of the air put him behind the gigantic oak at the bottom of the garden. It was over an hour since he'd flytjed, and he'd taken more tablets; he wanted to pump a fist.

Egan and his mother came to the window and scanned the empty expanse of lawn. "How could he have vanished?" Fionella mused.

Her son swallowed, but said nothing. As they withdrew, Egan adopted his father's whine. "What're we going to do?"

"Shut up and let me think!"

Risking another flytja, Ronan returned to the shattered window, standing in the shadows, ears tuned to the apprehension within.

"Take that bloody gun and guard Caitlin O'Toole's damned car," she snarled.

"Caitlin's Mini?" Egan blurted out. "Dad, how did he get the car and the bags off Luli? Dad?"

"Don't know," Dooley said, quaking like a condemned man.

"Fionn, listen to me." Fionella's voice was calm authority. "He will not get far on those crutches ... he will have to circle around for the car. When he does, bring him back here ... do not shoot him. Can you do that?"

There was a mumbled response amid receding footsteps.

"Tell me everything, Dooley." It was an icy demand.

The man slumped. "I've been augmenting Detencin's profits," he said, crestfallen.

"How?"

"Bringing cheap workers into the country."

"Why?" Fionella looked ready to throttle him.

"What do you think pays for all your Egan Estates purchases?" Dooley tried to inflate himself, but coughed instead.

"I thought that was your cut of Escardero's laundered money?"

"You were spending more than I could earn and th—"

"Have you ever taken responsibility for your own actions, Dooley?" The words dripped contempt.

Ronan was almost sorry for the man.

"I had to find more money," Dooley whined, "and Escardero said our arrangement for bringing in cash could be adapted for girls ... we'd both make more."

"And how do you bring them in?"

"Does it matter?"

"Yes. It. Does." Fionella's brittle anger crackled past jagged window glass, and into the night. "If I'm going to get us out of this pickle, of *your* making," she growled, "I need to know everything."

"I have a couple of fishermen who meet a freighter in international waters to transf—"

"Who are they?"

"It doesn't ma—"

"Dooley," she hissed, "I need every little detail for ..."

"What were you going to say, dear? *Ricardo? My boyfriend?* Do you think I don't know?"

"Whether you know is immaterial. You and I have a private arrangement, and a business arrangement ... the only way we survive is to stick to both. Now, who are your fishermen?"

Dooley deflated, resistance leaving him with the leaking air. "Sean and Jamie Hagan."

"When did the girl business start?"

"About a year ago."

"And what do you do with them?"

"Hold them for a while, then pass them on to employers."

Ronan's jaw clenched, his fists bunched. They were discussing the ruptured lives of all those girls as if they were items to be traded.

"How and where?" Fionella said.

"We ... we use Egan Estates houses ..."

"How?" she barked. "They're all rented."

Dooley appeared to get a shot of confidence. "Haven't you ever wondered who Fatherson Investments is?"

"That's you?"

"Me and Fionn"—a current of smugness surfaced—"father and son."

"Fionn," she breathed.

Dooley wasn't wasting the opportunity to show off to his doubting wife. "While you've been training him in real estate, he's been steering FI to isolated houses ... and a couple in Glengarriff Parade, of course ... very convenient."

"How terribly clever of you both." Her sarcasm could have sliced leather. "There's obviously more than just you and Fionn ... how many others know about your idiocy?"

Dooley's wafer of confidence dissolved. "A Pole and his Albanian wife ... and her brother ... came in with the first lot of girls. They hold them until we can pass them on. The Hagans transport them in their van."

"Names." Fionella was now firing orders rather than questions.

"Vítek and Luli Wojszyk, Ylli Berisha."

"Good god," she said, "that's five more who know ... five more potential weak links. If the gardaí get to them, you'd better pray they don't talk."

"They ... I ..."

Fionella's features twisted. "Just as I thought."

"But ... I..."

"Shut up, Dooley!" There was a pause. "Tell me about the drugs."

"Came in with the last shipment of girls ... like I said, we just had to hold it for a few days ..."

"How much?"

There was silence.

"How much?" she rasped.

"Twen ... twenty million ... roughly ... Escardero said." Dooley's misery and defeat weighed on his shoulders and jowls.

"Why couldn't you stop at our original windfall?" Her tone was bitter, scathing. "No, you had to try your hand at embezzlement. And when I extricated you from that mess, you turned to laundering money for Escardero."

Something teased Ronan's memory, but he couldn't grasp the thread. If important, it would come again.

Dooley wheezed and coughed.

"And now you've got yourself into drugs and human trafficking ... and lost both to a young kid," she said in disbelief. "Go and make sure Fionn doesn't kill him. Go! Get out of my sight!"

90

GARDA STOOGE

Ronan remained pressed to the wall, listening to Dooley trudge toward the front door. He froze as Fionella's light footfall approached the window, accompanied by a burring ring tone.

"Darling," Fionella purred, seemingly in Ronan's ear. "Yes, I know … me too … How about next weekend? Anyway, how are you? … Oh, grand, just grand." Her sarcasm hardened the air. "Dooley, the damned gobshite. … Not harsh enough … I'm going to need your magic, my love. … What do you mean?" There was a long pause; her breathing became more and more ragged. Finally, she spoke, "Oh, feck! Feck! Feck! Feck!"

Ronan flinched.

"Just tell me what I need to do?"

It was as close to begging as Ronan could ever imagine her.

"I *am* calm, Ricardo! … Sorry … Right … Uh-huh … Thank you, my love … I'll make it up to you. Oh, what about that other matter? … Is that right? How very interesting. Thank you, again … kiss, kiss." At the phone's disconnection beep, Fionella swore with a visceral fury that threw up new words for Ronan, and he'd learnt many from Masters over the years.

Listening to the one-sided conversation had been a waste, apart from extending his vocabulary. Time to risk another encounter to finalise his transaction.

While Fionella's tirade swelled, Ronan crutched beyond the wash of light, circled wide, and approached the Mini from a different direction. He was almost at the driver's door when a gleeful sneer stopped him: "Go ahead, make my day."

Ronan halted. "You've been watching too much Clint Eastwood, Finnegan." Harry Callahan had been one of Grandpa Paddy's favourite movie characters.

Egan snorted and tried to raise the gun; it made forty-five degrees.

"All right, you win," Ronan said. "Take me to your leader."

"Smart arse," Egan growled, his features contorted by equal measures of pain, enmity and determination as he used his wounded arm to lift the barrels to Ronan's heart.

Ronan inched his hands skyward, crutches dangling. "You don't want to do that, Finnegan."

"Oh, don't I?" Egan's finger whitened on the trigger, breath coming in snatches.

Ronan cursed himself for pushing too hard and braced for impact, all in half a heartbeat.

"Don't let him rile you, son." Dooley's subdued voice came from the shadows of the porch.

With obvious reluctance, the trigger finger relaxed, the weapon drooped. And in that split second, Ronan seized the opportunity to strengthen his position. "There's a good boy," he said.

Egan cried out as he tried to reverse the momentum of the weighty gun. Ronan swung forward, planting his fit leg, stabbing one crutch into Egan's chest, knocking the barrels aside with the other. The double thunderclap of the gun's discharge smacked Ronan's eardrums, bouncing off the building's facade and rumbling off to die in the night. Snatching the weapon from the rattled lad, Ronan threw it into the Mini and locked the doors. Without a backward glance, he crutched up the steps, swung round an open-mouthed Dooley and into the house.

Fionella met him in the hall, relief chasing fury from her face, only to surrender to calculation.

"Let's talk trade," Ronan said, hobbling past her into the sitting room, uninvited.

"What an excellent idea," Fionella said, joining him. Slouching after her was Fatherson Investments, both father and son draped in reluctance, the former resigned, the latter surly. "Sit," she ordered, lips tight. "Don't speak and don't move."

Turning to Ronan, she asked in her normal silken tone, "What do you know about my house out Meenaneary way?"

"Where's Meenaneary?" Ronan said, playing dumb.

"It's where we picked up your girlfriends," Egan blurted out.

Ronan smiled to himself; his goading was paying dividends.

"I told you not to speak!" Her words slashed the air.

"But he's lying."

"Shut your stupid mouth!" Two swift paces across the room and she unwound a roundhouse open palm that lashed her son's cheek. Even as the echo died, the hand print turned beetroot. His glare bordered on hatred.

"The garda found prints and DNA there," she said in halting Irish—she must have decided that they'd shared enough information with their English-speaking Aussie meddler.

Ronan was sure they did find DNA and prints, but how could she know that? Unless ...? Feigning bewilderment, he said, "What ...?"

Fionella's gaze narrowed with appraisal. "Never mind," she shot at him in English before reverting. *"The interesting thing is that it is leased by Fatherson Investments, and"*—she glared at her husband and son—*"there are shackles anchored to the floor and hasps screwed to doors, similar to Glengarriff Parade."*

Dooley squirmed; Egan's scowl threatened to swallow his face, glowing hand print and all.

"But"—she paused for effect—*"even more interesting, there are two vehicles with slashed—"*

Her phone burred. "Ricardo," she enthused in English, scorning Dooley, "what have you got for me?" She spent the next several minutes listening, hardly saying a word beyond 'right', 'interesting' or 'uh-huh'. When she'd hung up, she resumed as if there'd been no interruption.

"One of those vehicles is registered to Sean Hagan. Guess who owns the other?"

Silence. Dooley studied the floor while Egan glowered at Ronan.

Fionella's lips curled. *"That is right, my love, Fatherson Investments."*

"I could participate if you'd use English," Ronan offered.

"I bet you could," Fionella retorted.

Wretchedness enveloped Dooley; his son was all festering resentment.

Fionella continued her bitter tirade. *"But the most surprising thing is that there was the body of an unknown man who had several Irish mobile numbers in his phone ... gardaí are still tracing them."*

With an enormous retching heave, Dooley vomited all over his shoes.

"What's that, dear?" She taunted, *"Your number is one of them?"*

Ronan fought to keep his expression neutral, but the stench clogging his nostrils was almost triggering his own stomach. In addition, his revulsion at the woman was a great knot in the base of his throat. Eoin Duffy had called her vindictive, cunning and evil. Ronan could add a few more. And she was well connected; that Ricardo was either in the garda, or knew someone who was. Either way, he was feeding her information, Ronan was certain.

"A second man was nearly dead ... lost a lot of blood ... they think he will make it."

Ronan barely heard what she said after 'dead'. An unbearable burden lifted. He hadn't killed Ylli after all.

"And just when you would have thought things could not get any worse," Fionella continued with her trademark arctic sneer, *"there is my Cronasilla house ... another body ... a woman. And two miscreants chained up, alive it seems, despite the unwanted attention of a group of foreign girls with scores to settle.*

"But that is not all"—her derision was boundless—*"the garda also found the truck that collided with Darragh Kelly."*

Dooley retched again; Egan radiated resentment.

"And in quite the surprise," she said, reverting to English, turning to Ronan, "our young Australian friend here is not even in Ireland."

Ronan tensed, fearing she must suspect his rune power, but as she continued, he relaxed.

"It appears you are in the country illegally." She purred with genuine delight.

"Or perhaps," Ronan shot back, determined to throw her off stride, "your garda stooge has looked in the wrong place."

91

EGGS AND BASKETS

The sitting room occupants were a contradictory quartet. Icy Fionella assessed Ronan as though he was not her usual prey; Ronan stood nonchalant yet coiled; Dooley slumped as if waiting for the guillotine to drop; and the son glowered at the centre of a fug of animosity.

"My garda *stooge*," Fionella said at last, "will have you arrested and deported at the drop of a hat, my friend."

"That won't happen." Ronan hoped his conviction was well founded. "Two reasons: one, there are greater powers than him involved, and two, it wouldn't be in your best interests to try it."

Her eyes narrowed. "You are very sure of yourself."

"With good cause," Ronan said, embracing the pulse of the rune.

"He's bluffing," Egan growled from the couch.

Ronan raised an eyebrow. "Am I, Finnegan?" He turned back to Fionella. "You can't afford to take that chance."

There was a brief silence as they considered Ronan's words. Dooley sat staring into space, oblivious to the vomit on his shoes and the stink he'd created.

Ronan ignored it. "We can stand round talking until the guards connect all the dots and arrive on your doorstep, if Escardero doesn't get here first."

Fionella stiffened. "How do you know about Escardero?"

"Not important." Ronan shook his head. "But I suggest we conduct our negotiations—ones that might just save your lives—sooner rather than later."

Egan snorted; his mother appraised Ronan afresh. "You are in no position to threaten," she said, indicating his crutches.

"Oh, *that* wasn't a threat." Ronan smiled grimly. "Wait till Escardero hears about his drugs and money." As the silence swelled with foreboding, Ronan pressed the advantage. "When was the last time you heard of a drug baron forgiving the loss of even twenty bucks of product or cash?"

Dooley groaned; the others were silent.

"The way I see it," Ronan continued, "your biggest concern is meeting my demands and getting Escardero's stash back"—he paused for effect—"and then you can worry about staying out of prison."

"Anything," Dooley whimpered.

"What do you want?" Fionella asked warily.

"Don't listen to him," Egan shrilled.

"Shut up!" his parents yelled in rare unity.

Fionella went straight to the point. "What do you want for the drugs and money?"

"Saoirse and Caitlin."

Fionella paused, then directed pure contempt at her husband. "This is a new high for stupidity, isn't it? And you"—she turned her ire on her son—"you I expected to be smarter. Where are they?"

Egan sulked. Dooley wiped his mouth. "Cottage," he rasped.

"Keys?" Ronan said.

"Fionn," Dooley muttered.

Ronan held out a hand.

"Get stuffed," Egan growled with increasing defiance.

Ronan touched his crutch to the lad's wounded shoulder. Egan paled, but didn't move. Ronan pushed. Egan howled, twisting away. "Only when we have the bags," he panted, holding his ground.

"You might have a point, Finnegan," Ronan said, surprised by the lad's resolve.

All three gaped at Ronan, but he was already leaving the room. They were still exchanging bewilderment and fresh accusations when he returned, rune shooting warning sparks, a duffel bag bumping awkwardly against each crutch. Fionella didn't twitch. Dooley swung his head in disbelief. "They were here all along?" he said.

Egan gawped. "They weren't in the Mini," he insisted. "I checked." Without waiting for a response, he hoisted himself from the lounge, pulled a torch from his pocket, and trotted outside, faster than Ronan had ever seen him move.

Let him search. "Tell me," Ronan said, willing the embers to cool, "why did Ylli ram Darragh?"

Dooley blanched.

Fionella frowned. "Ylli?"

Ronan eyeballed her. "You really don't know much, do you?"

Her eyes flared at him then turned full force on her hapless spouse. "Leave nothing out," she demanded past clenched teeth.

Dooley withered under her glare, cringing in defeat and fear. "He wasn't meant to kill Darragh," he mumbled, "only frighten him off."

"From what?" Fionella prompted before Ronan could.

"I only wanted Darragh to back off his demands for a pay rise. He was organising the workers to strike for more pay ... couldn't afford it ... not enough money in boots ... it was mainly from Escardero ..."

"But it was still profit." Ronan pointed out bitterly.

"It was my profit," Dooley bleated. "The bootmakers didn't have any hand in it."

Ronan struggled to look at the man. "So you had Ylli smash Darragh up?"

"No," Dooley wailed, "he was only meant to give him a big scare ... the damned Albanian went too far ..."

"Why did you kidnap Saoirse?" Merely saying the words had Ronan bristling.

"Not kidnapped," he whined, "... detained, so she couldn't talk to you."

Ronan's jaw worked, aching from the effort. "You had her chained up like a dog," he growled, stepping forward.

Dooley lifting his hands in defence. "I didn't know that," he cried. "I only told Luli to supervise her communication."

"Why?" Fionella barked.

"You know Fionn's always been sweet on her ... I thought if I could keep him"—he gestured at Ronan—"out of the picture ... it all got out of control ..."

Fionella hit her husband with icy contempt. "You idiot!"

"And Viking?" Ronan snapped.

"I wanted to use him to make Saoirse stay away from yo—"

"So you had your thugs kill Garret?" Ronan yelled.

Dooley groaned. "They were only supposed to take the horse ..." He was almost sobbing. "I just thought th—"

"You thought?" Fionella oozed disdain. "That would be a first."

"Shut up! Both of you!" Ronan was at breaking point, afraid of what he might do if he heard another word of the greed and stupidity that had caused so much tragedy. "Right," he said when he had their complete attention, "here's what we're going to do. You're going to make your son give me the keys to the cottage, and"—he paused, struggling for control—"any other locks involved. And when the girls have left, I'll take you to the remaining bags. Understand?"

Shoulders hunched, lips quivering, Dooley nodded. Fionella arched an eyebrow. "Where are they? And why weren't they all together?"

"Eggs and baskets," Ronan responded, breathing easier, more in command of both his head and the situation. "And the others are nowhere near here."

While he wanted to be done with the Egans, Ronan needed recovery time; he wasn't sure he could flytja the second pair of bags to Raven's Roost without arriving helpless. And being defenceless around this family was a distinct health hazard. The priority was to get the girls freed and home; it didn't matter if the final bag exchange took longer.

"Tell me again why I should trust you?" Fionella asked as she glided to the drinks table.

"You can't," Egan said, the glinting points of a three-pronged hay fork preceding him into the room.

The tines remained trained on Ronan's stomach as Egan eased forward. It unsettled Ronan that he'd missed the lad come through the front door. He must be tired, or the rune was napping. Either way, he was now alert; nothing like imminent skewering to focus the mind.

Fionella gave her son a searing stare. "Put that down before you hurt yourself ... and give him the keys."

Egan shook his head, continuing to advance. "Can't trust him," he said, moving to within lunging range.

Hands clasping his crutches, Ronan hummed with adrenaline and rune energy, ready to move. He assumed Egan's new-found resolve came from recognising the depth of trouble he was in, but it was a pity he didn't realise he was making matters worse: delaying was only giving the guards time to make the connections. But it made no difference to Ronan.

"You imbecile." Fionella's contempt smeared the air. "If we don't get those bags, we'll all be dead ... tell him, Dooley."

Dooley lifted his haunted gaze from the floor. "Put it down, son ... give him the keys ... we have to trust him ... it's our only option."

Egan glanced at his father; Ronan's patience expired. Swinging forward, he whipped his left crutch up under the hay fork, flinging the tip toward the ceiling. Before Egan could react, Ronan released the other crutch and brought the edge of his right hand down into the base of Egan's neck. It was a clumsy strike hampered by the crutch swinging from his forearm, but it sent the oaf to the floor in a yowling heap.

Ronan leant over, resting the foot of his crutch on Egan's arrow wound, only light pressure, but enough for a gasp and another howl of pain. "The keys, Finnegan ... all of them." There was no response; Ronan pushed harder. Egan squawked, delved into a pocket, and withdrew a jangle of keys. Ronan ripped them from the other's grip, and crutched from the house. Neither Fionella nor Dooley moved a muscle.

By the time Ronan reached the Mini, Fionella was silhouetted in the doorway, silently watching as he tossed the shotgun onto the grass and drove away.

92

FREEDOM

Ronan swung the Mini round in front of the cottage. Its lights played across the stables' facade, picking out the inconsistencies in the stonework, sending shadows stretching and shrinking. They found the mudroom and the building proper, flashing off window panes as he turned, settling on the copse of elm and privet shielding the cottage from the Egan mansion.

Without a stone, nail or roof slate being altered, the dwelling had transformed from happy home to bleak prison. So much had happened in the past few weeks that none of their lives could ever return to simplicity and innocence. Ronan wondered whether Darragh would still have been alive and Saoirse and Caitlin not imprisoned if the rune hadn't brought him here. But no, the rune had stopped him interfering in Darragh's accident, which meant it would have happened anyway. Yet what about all the other things? Would someone else have done them if he hadn't? If so, who?

Ronan was still pondering that when he twisted the key and the door clicked open. A sudden whoosh had him ducking—too late. Something clipped the side of his skull, reverberating like a struck gong. Reeling from the strike, Ronan staggered under the weight of his attacker; his wounded leg flaring in agony as it took the load. He crumpled to the floor, twisting to grapple with an octopus, arms and legs flailing him from every direction. An elbow caught his nose; a glancing blow excited his rib wound; a weight landed on his thigh. Hair fell across his face; it smelt of apples.

"Saoirse!" he yelled. The mayhem ceased. Warm breath tickled his ear; there was more on his hand. "Caitlin?"

"Ronan?" Saoirse said, "Ronan!" And she was kissing him, on his forehead, an eye, nose, chin, and finally, lips.

A body disentangled; a light blazed. Caitlin was sitting propped against the wall, outstretched fingers on the light switch. "What took you so long?" she said dryly.

"How did you get free?" Ronan asked when he and Saoirse came up for air.

"It was Caitlin's idea," Saoirse said, clambering upright, pulling Ronan up, then Caitlin. "Dooley was stupid enough to get us to shackle ourselves ... we only put the padlock through one side, and made so much fuss about his cruelty and letting us go, that he didn't check properly."

"Very clever," he said, handing the crutches to Caitlin and rubbing his head, unsure of where he hurt the most.

Saoirse's fingertips explored the rising lump; she winced. "Sorry."

"Small price," Ronan murmured, drawing her close. Looking past her to Caitlin, he darkened. "Did Finnegan hurt either of you?"

"Finnegan?" Saoirse was puzzled. "We only saw Dooley and Luli."

Caitlin held up a bruised arm. "And she was a wee bit rough."

Ronan stiffened. "When?"

"When they grabbed us," Caitlin replied.

"Tell me." Rage boiled through Ronan.

"Ronan," Saoirse said, turning his face to hers, "it's okay ... we're grand."

Breathing deep, he tried forcing tranquillity, but failed. "What happened?" he asked, jaw tight.

Caitlin waved a dismissive hand. "Not much really ... apart from Dooley proving what crap spies we are."

"He just caught us unawares," Saoirse said.

"What happened?" Ronan repeated, willing his jaw to relax.

"We were waiting where you left us," Caitlin said, "... saw the horsebox come out from that house, and turn back toward Meenaneary."

"We thought it wouldn't be long till you returned," Saoirse cut in, "but the longer you took, the more worried we got."

"And when headlights came up behind us," Caitlin added—they were like relay runners, handing the speaking baton back and forth—"we had to drive down the road a wee bit and pull into a farm gateway."

"Saoirse took over. "But the car pulled up right beside us, blocking us in."

"It was the Bentley," Caitlin said. "Dooley came to Saoirse's window, all nice and friendly, but before he said two words, that Luli appeared out of nowhere, reefed my door open and had me by the arm …"

Things clicked into place for Ronan. When they'd seen Dooley's car in Carrick earlier, he must have been going to collect Luli and take her to the house where Vítek died. Egan must have phoned his father and warned him not to go, and Dooley, already close, had improvised when he'd encountered the girls, snatching them and getting Luli to drive the Mini to the Cronasilla house. It all made sense, but how did they avoid the guards?

"I should have locked the door," Caitlin continued, "… just didn't think."

Ronan was having none of it. "It was my fault," he said, self-reproach tightening his words. "I shouldn't have let you stay."

"We weren't going to leave you," Saoirse cried, reaching for his face, fingers brushing his goose egg. He flinched; she apologised.

"I'm glad it was only that flimsy umbrella stand," he said with an exaggerated grimace, "and not a fire extinguisher."

"If I had one, I'd have used it," she retorted with good humour.

"Lucky me." Without thinking, he said, "Why didn't you leave as soon as you got free?" The answer came to him before the end of the question, but he couldn't take the words back.

"We needed Dooley's car," Caitlin piped up. "Saoirse didn't want to walk."

"She's like that," Ronan quipped.

"Bone lazy," Saoirse added.

Their brittle chuckles hung in the air as Ronan shepherded them out the door. A couple of hobbled steps without the crutches made the Egan's mansion seem in another galaxy. "Can you give me a lift to the Egan's driveway?"

"Take this," Caitlin said, thrusting a single crutch toward him. "I'm grand with one."

"Thanks," Ronan said, "but I still want a lift."

By the time Caitlin braked the car at the gap in the hedge, he'd told them about the bags he'd stashed in Garret's bunker. "I'll tell you the rest when I get back. Now go, and don't stop for anyone."

"I want to stay with you," Saoirse said, clinging from the back seat.

Ronan shook his head. "I have to finish this, and I don't want you in danger." He met Caitlin's eyes, sending her a silent plea for help.

"Come on, Sersh," Caitlin said, "we're free, let's go."

"I don't feel free," Saoirse murmured into Ronan's shoulder. "What if others come after us?" Her voice was tremulous.

"They can't," he responded gravely. "Vítek is dead ... Ylli shot him; Luli is dead ... fell through a window; Ylli is in custody ... so are the Hagans; and none of the Egans will go near either of you." While the Egans hadn't yet agreed, they would; they had no choice.

Saoirse opened her mouth, but Ronan laid a finger across her lips. They were soft and warm, electrifying. "When it's over," he said, "I'll tell you everything ... promise." Easing away, he climbed from the vehicle, embracing the tug on his heart as they drove off.

93

TERMS OF AGREEMENT

The Mini's taillights disappeared down the lane, dragging Ronan's longing with them. Every part of him throbbed; he was more tired than he could remember, and was sick of the conflict, wanting it behind him. But a deal was a deal. Not that he was worried about the Egans being on the wrong end of Escardero's wrath, they deserved it, but he had to make sure Saoirse and Caitlin were insulated. Paidin, as always, was never far from Ronan's mind, but as desperate as he was to find his father, there was no way he could leave the girls until he was certain they were safe.

As the burble of the little car melted into the night, Ronan contemplated using a precious flytja to get to the mansion. The last one had been bearable, only a warning flare, but harsh experience had shown him how quickly they escalated. Without knowing what lay ahead, and how many flytjas he might need, he chose wound pain over flytja fire. So, he limped toward the Egan edifice, each step tugging at stitches, stinging ribs, and adding misery to his aching body.

Fionella had remained on the lighted porch, a statue, apart from a breath of night air playing at the twist of auburn hanging against her cheek. She might have been fuming over misplaced trust, or awaiting the return of a prodigal son—impossible to tell. She changed not the slightest as Ronan's faltering walk carried him into the light.

"You could have left with them," she said.

Ronan stopped at the bottom of the steps; he wasn't going one centimetre further than necessary—his leg was screaming. "And have you hunting us? Or worse, Escardero? Not likely."

"You *are* a smart boy," she purred. "Would you like to work for me?"

I'd rather swallow glass. Aloud, Ronan said, "No thanks ... I've got other plans."

"Shame, I could use someone with your talents."

"I'd be concentrating on lawyers if I were you."

Fionella showed him a thin smile. "We will see."

Her lack of concern prickled Ronan. Surely her Ricardo stooge couldn't help her escape justice? He reminded himself the only thing that mattered was the safety of the two girls who had just driven off. All he wanted at the moment was for Dooley to take him to Garret's farm. He glanced past Fionella, through the open door. The hall was empty, the shotgun he'd tossed from the Mini, propped against the wall. He was thankful she didn't see the need to be using it on him again.

Indicating the weapon, Ronan said, "Is that the gun that was fired under Saoirse's bed?"

The faint flicker of surprise was so brief, it might have been imagined. "What are you talking about?" she said.

"The evidence is there," he replied, recalling the scarred floor and splintered underside of the bed, not to mention the fiery impact of the pellets. "And the Kellys don't own a gun."

"Quite the detective, aren't you?" She smirked in acknowledgement. "That was me."

The admission surprised Ronan, as did what followed.

"I heard something and thought it might have been a badger."

"A badger?" Ronan was not buying it. "Why would you think that?"

"A light was on in the cottage when there should not have been, and it was the day after someone put a hedgehog in the back of the Range Rover ... tried to dig its way out ... soiled everywhere."

"Cool prank."

She glared. "You?"

Ronan chuckled. "If only I'd thought of it." He sobered and added, "So you shot at a noise?" *Who does that?*

"Badgers are vicious when cornered ... tear you to pieces ... I was not risking that. It must have been my imagination." She paused, scrutinising him, unblinking. "What now?"

Ronan only saw one option. "I'll take your husband to the other bags, you never mention my existence, and none of you ever come near Saoirse and Caitlin, or their families ...ever."

"Or ...?"

"I've left so much evidence with my lawyer that even Ricardo won't be able to help you."

"You're bluffing ..."

The only information Ronan had was between his ears, but he held her gaze, unblinking. "You want to bet on that?"

She wavered. "Say you *are* telling the truth, where does that leave us?"

"Once you have all the bags, you pass them on the Escardero's people, or keep them for yourself ... whatever you want. My evidence stays locked up while ever you stick to your end of the bargain ... the lot of you can take your chances with the guards." Ronan shrugged. "Up to you," he added, lowering himself to the step, "but you should hurry ... before they arrive."

"They will not be here for a quite a while," Fionella said with confidence.

"Your friend, Ricardo slowing them down?"

Teeth showed through the red gash. "None of your business, young man," she said, turning into the house.

Soon after, the black Bentley purred to a halt by the steps. Ronan heaved upright and slid into its opulent embrace. As they drove off, he glanced back at mother and son standing in the lighted doorway, hoping he was seeing them for the last time.

94

COWARD'S CHOICE

Dooley Egan drove in silence, face pale, jowls quivering. The Bentley seemed to bulge beyond the sides of the road, threatening to trim hedges in passing. It murmured past dark houses, spongy suspension dipping and wallowing through imperfections in the asphalt. Ronan happily used the respite to organise his thoughts and plan how to collect the bags. By the time they glided through Carrick, he'd decided that if they went all the way to Malin Beg, he'd be well recovered for the necessary flytja to Garret's bunker. In the meantime, he'd try to get Dooley to fill in the missing pieces, starting with snippets he'd gleaned.

Only as he went to speak did the thing that had teased his mind earlier leap out at him: embezzlement!

"Why did you steal from Donal O'Mahony?" Ronan said, pretending indifference.

The man's swallow was audible, his hands tightened on the wheel. "You don't understand."

"Try me."

"I had to pay them," he said, half wheeze, half sob, "and Fi wouldn't let me touch the ... the other."

"Who?"

"I'd borrowed money from some unsavoury characters in Dublin ... repayment was due."

Ronan's earlier crumb of sympathy vanished, but his curiosity swelled. "What wouldn't Fionella let you touch?"

His voice shrank. "Money."

"Savings?"

Dooley gave a bitter, mirthless hack. "Fionella spends it before it's printed ... but she wouldn't touch the"—he appeared to catch himself, deciding on different words—"... our windfall."

Ronan's thoughts went to inheritance, or winnings from gambling or lottery.

"Only time I've seen her spooked," Dooley added, a glimmer of satisfaction emerging from his wretchedness.

Now, what would scare that woman? Ronan wondered, thinking that she had iced water instead of blood. Whatever it was—money, gold, diamonds—it was probably stolen. But illegality itself wouldn't faze her, there wasn't a single scruple under that auburn crown. The best explanation Ronan found was that the windfall came from someone like Escardero, a vengeful person who would not only want it back, but would make an example of whoever took it. Or was that simply imagination driven by too many crime shows?

The Bentley wallowed past a vague shape in the gloom, the derelict house where Jamie Hagan had hidden his father's fishing gear. Ronan didn't notice; he was distracted by little shots of charge crackling through his memory, triggering replays of his conversations with Eoin Duffy and Saoirse, examining them in light of what Fionella had said earlier, and Dooley's fresh revelations.

By the time they'd turned off the 263 toward Malin Beg, Ronan's thoughts were like a hawk circling road kill. His suspicions unsettled him. Regardless, he had to know. "When did you start at Detencin Boots?"

Dooley jolted. "Wha ... what?" His knuckles whitened.

"You heard me."

"N ... no, I was miles away."

Ronan rolled his eyes. "When did you start at Detencin?"

"N ... nineteen ninety ... w ... why?" Dooley gurgled.

"Watch the road!" Ronan yelled as the driver-side wheels ran onto the grassy verge.

Dooley dragged the Bentley back on course, and sat hunched and morose, dash lights casting Halloween shadows up his face.

"Before or after Abby McGinley's death?" Ronan relaxed his grip on the grab handle above the door as wisps of rage gathered and built like a storm cloud.

Dooley whimpered.

"Before or after?" Ronan barked.

"A ... after ..."

Was it *really* possible that the Egans had found out about the transfer and had stolen the money from an unsuspecting Abby, sending her over the cliff and making it look like an accident? Ronan wanted to dismiss it as too far-fetched, but it *would* explain Fionella being terrified of touching their 'windfall'. The IRA would have been scouring the country looking for anyone displaying recent wealth, forcing the Egans to wait until they had a successful business to conceal the money in.

Stirring anger coiled through Ronan; he took a gamble. "Why kill Abby?"

"You *know*?" Dooley moaned. "How?"

"Why?" Ronan roared, fury ballooning with the confirmation.

"We needed the money an—"

"Why did you have to kill her?"

Even in the dim glow of the dash lights, Dooley paled. He gulped, staring ahead. "The woman p—"

"Abby! Abby McGinley! Say her name!"

"Ab ... Abby," Dooley sobbed, "I'm sorry ..."

"Why?" Ronan bellowed.

"She ..."—Dooley cowered, pinned in place by Ronan's ferocity—"A ... Abby pulled my balaclava off in the struggle ... saw me ... Fi said it was the only way ... made it look like an accident ..."

The Bentley drifted within paint-thickness of a solid stone wall as they passed through the scatter of houses at Malin More. "Watch the damned road!" Once Ronan was sure his driver had refocused, he continued: "How did you know about the money ... the transfer?"

"Fi was out drinking ... in Dublin ... left me with the toddler"—bitterness deformed his features—"while she went home with some IRA fella who'd been drinking all night ... right proper mangled, he was ... blabbed about the money ... trying to impress, and ... and Fi stuck all her insulin between his toes ... his heart, they said ..."

Connections zinged round Ronan's mind. "Is that what she did to Donal O'Mahony?"

The man's hands trembled; Ronan thought he might have to grab the wheel. Eventually, Dooley nodded, all resistance gone. "She got him drunk ... off his trolley ... said it was painless ..."

Ronan pushed back in his seat, working his jaw to ease the stiffness from so much biting down on rage. They'd turned south, the dull gleam of the North Atlantic reaching toward them on the right.

Dooley wheezed. "Who are you?"

"I am justice," Ronan growled, "... for Abby ... Darragh ... Donal ... and for all those trafficked girls."

"It was only business," Dooley wailed.

Ronan remained silent, fighting Norse fury. Vengeance.

"I'm dead, aren't I?" Dooley groaned, broken, wallowing in self-pity, no hint of remorse.

Resisting an overpowering desire to throttle the man, Ronan glared contempt, seething. "No, but you'll spend the rest of your life in prison."

"Oh, God." Dooley's face lost all colour.

The night slid past; the silence grew. Ronan fought his emotions; Dooley hunched in sullen resignation.

As if coming to a decision, the man squared his jaw, jamming his foot to the floor. The massive car surged forward.

Ronan grabbed the door handle. The Bentley roared up a rise topped by a curling left-hander as the road skirted a ravine reaching inland from the adjacent cliff top. Amid billowing warmth, Ronan recognised the coward's choice. The driver tugged the wheel right. Rubber squealed as the vehicle left the asphalt, tearing through a fence, ploughing gouges through soft soil. In the instant before Ronan's mind entered r6, he wondered if it was the same spot where they'd killed Abby.

The air sucked him away as the car plunged, unchecked, into space. Dooley Egan, features contorted, scream of terror rupturing his throat, hurtled toward a watery grave.

95

FINAL DEAL

The bunker beneath Garret's farmhouse echoed cold and lonely. Sparse bulbs threw jaundiced puddles of light across walls and floor. Two black duffels sat like omens at the foot of the ladder leading into the laundry cupboard above. Although the bags contained vast misery, to interfere with them was to invite retribution from either Escardero or Fionella. All Ronan wanted was to be rid of the danger and rejoin the girls—walk away. But Dooley's suicide meant a change of plan. On the positive side, the flytja had scarcely caused a spark.

Sliding down the wall, he sat pondering the options, ignoring the concrete's chill soaking into his spine and backside. If he took the bags to Raven's Roost, the timing would be after Dooley's death, inviting suspicion. Every way he teased the problem delivered the same result. There was no option but to use a time-flytja.

Decision made, Ronan pulled himself up on the single crutch, gathering the duffels. Like a tentative swimmer testing the water, he eased his mind toward ró, gauging his body's reaction. As soon as his head flared, he retreated, panting. The exhilaration that had consumed him when he first learnt to jump through space and time, had been replaced by trepidation and reluctance to use the power. But he had no choice. Gritting his teeth, he folded into the air. Next moment he was on the upstairs floor of the derelict house, twenty minutes earlier, collapsed on the bags, puffing against the blaze in his brain. While it distracted from his leg, it couldn't do the same for what he had to do next: ring Fionella.

How would he control his revulsion, knowing she murdered Abby, Donal O'Mahony and some intoxicated, loose-lipped IRA member? How many others had she killed?

and how did she continue to get away with it? Was it only Ricardo? or others as well? Regardless, he had to repress his outrage and loathing.

With the flytja fire receding, Ronan dialled, thankful for a good recall of numbers. The purr of an untroubled engine, and the hum of tyres on asphalt, drew him to the front window. Flickering through the trees was the passing silhouette of a black Bentley, heading toward Malin Beg.

"Your damned husband has driven off and left me," he fumed into the phone as the call connected.

"Now, Ronan," Fionella chided in faux rebuke, "what have you done this time to upset poor Dooley?"

Ronan was hurting too much to admire her unshakable composure. "I was getting the bags, and he just drove off," he said, trowelling on annoyance and disbelief.

"You must have said something."

"Nothing to make him drive off," Ronan grumbled, staying in character.

"What are you up to?"

Ronan imagined her eyes slitting. "Do you think I want to be left in the middle of nowhere on one leg?" he shot back.

"Where are you?"

"Just west of Carrick ... on 263."

"Well, he will be home soon enough, then."

With fabricated irritation, Ronan said, "He went the other way, toward Malin Beg."

"The idiot! What is he doing?"

While the question wasn't meant for Ronan, he answered anyway: "No idea, but I'm not hanging round ... the bags will still be here when he gets back ... he'll just have to find them."

"You cannot simply leave."

"I can, and I am," Ronan said with finality. "Goodbye, Fionella."

"Wait! What do you mean, *find them*?"

Ronan exhaled for effect. "Never mind ... tell Dooley they're in the room to the left at the top of the stairs ... and watch out for loose boards." The warning gave him grim pleasure, not because Dooley wasn't ever returning, but because it would add discomfort to his son's imminent chore.

"What if someone finds them in the meantime?" It was the first sign of disquiet from the woman.

"Not my problem," Ronan stated. "I tried to give them to your husband."

"How can I be sure you are telling the truth?" she said, words edged with suspicion.

"Because I don't want you, or anyone else, hunting us." Ronan sensed her pondering the obvious logic of his statement.

"I will pay you to stay until Dooley comes back," she said, apparently having decided on a course of action.

Ronan wanted to hear desperation, but there was only calculation; she wanted insurance against loss, however unlikely. He supposed he'd be the same in her shoes; who'd want to be hunted by a drug lord? "A hundred euros per minute," he said without hesitation, savouring her mini gasp.

"Fifty."

Not desperate enough yet. "Hundred and ten."

"Seventy-five."

"Goodbye, Fionella."

"Wait! Okay." She caved. "One hundred, then."

Ronan pumped a fist. As Grandpa Paddy had told him when he'd paid more than he should have for a bundle of second-hand arrows he desperately wanted, you can't negotiate if you aren't prepared to walk away from the deal.

"But I'm not waiting for that moron," she continued, "... who knows how long he'll b—"

"Suits me," Ronan cut in, relishing the thought of easy money, as well as her son blundering about in the dark.

But Fionella surprised him. "I will come myself." She clearly understood the enormity of her pickle and wasn't trusting anyone. "Where are you?"

Ronan gave her directions, ending with, "Clock's ticking, Fionella. And Fionella ..."—he paused, revelling in keeping her off balance—"no money, no bags."

96

ICY FINGERS

Slumped in misery on a broken bed frame, Ronan wondered if he'd ever be pain free again. Although bearable, his head pounded, but the bullet hole in his thigh pulsed in agony, searing up his leg in waves—perhaps it was infected. And his ribs stung with every move. Torment and weariness dulled his senses.

As he waited for Fionella, he ran through the events log-jamming his life. It seemed an age since poor Garret and Cú were murdered, but it was only the previous evening. And three more people had lost their lives, with another on the verge of death, but Ronan had no sympathy for them.

Then there was bumbling Egan and his cold-eyed mother with a block of ice in the middle of her chest. While Ronan knew what Fionella had done, he had no proof, and the only person who could provide it was now fish food. And with Ricardo inside the garda, she might she get away with it. Outrage festered in Ronan at the prospect. But if he tried to mete justice to the woman after he'd recovered his strength, she and Ricardo could ensure he'd never be able to move openly in Donegal with Saoirse—ever. He and Fionella were at a stalemate, an uneasy truce where each could bring the other down.

Ronan's frustration was interrupted by gravel crackling under heavy tyres; the Range Rover rumbled to a halt behind the house. According to his phone, Fionella had taken eleven minutes. Not wanting to risk another flytja, he humped one bag down the darkened stairs and out to where she leant against the door of the idling vehicle, arms folded in studied indifference.

"How's the leg?" she said as the duffel thudded to the ground.

"Bonzer," he said ironically.

"What?"

"Grand. Where's my *waiting* money?"

"Where is the other bag?" Her eyes gleamed like steel in the dim light.

"Money first." Ronan extended a hand.

With a look that might had held respect, she reached into a pocket, pulling out two purple notes. "Here's a thousand."

"You were eleven minutes," Ronan responded flatly, in no mood for quibbling. "I want a green one too ... we had a deal."

"Are you ..." She frowned. "You *are* serious."

"Deadly."

Fionella chuckled, peeling a hundred euro note from a wad that materialised from another pocket. "Are you sure you will not come and work for me?"

Ronan paused in mock consideration. "Which part would you want me to do? Sell real estate? Run drugs? Traffic girls? Babysit your son? Murder someone?"

Her red lips were a rigid slash. "Your smart mouth will get you into trouble one day," she snarled.

"It already has," he quipped, "many times."

Unexpectedly, she broke into a cackle, devoid of humour. "Oh, I like your style, Ronan. Can I give you a lift home?"

"I'm fine ... thanks."

Fionella swivelled her head, peering into the gloom. "How ...?"

"Broomstick," Ronan said, stuffing the euros in a pocket as he returned into the house.

The stairs felt steeper and longer than last time. When he reached the top, his leg was screaming, but his head only simmered. *Small mercies.* He glanced from the window and icy tentacles slid up his spine. A shadowy figure gazed up from empty sockets, cheek bones jutting, fleshless fingers dripping blood. Movement changed the wash of car lights and shadows, and Fionella's features leapt out at him. He shivered.

Even before the sinister, foreboding illusion, Ronan had decided he wasn't going back down the stairs—too painful. Hoisting the final bag, he swung it out the window, sending it plummeting. It smacked into the ground at Fionella's feet. She didn't flinch, simply sent him a dead smile. But Ronan was gone.

97

DISBELIEF

Declan's flat was warm and welcoming. Saoirse sat on the couch, open envelope in one hand, sheaf of pages in the other. She gasped when Ronan limped from the air, clothes dusty from the derelict house, a thumbnail bloodstain on his pants leg, and a red streak across his holed shirt. Caitlin, standing at the kitchen bench with a steaming kettle in her hand, nonchalantly asked, "Cup of tea?"

"Please," he replied, slumping on the couch beside Saoirse, pressing thumbs behind his ears. While it was only a space-flytja, there was a brief warning flare; it triggered a sharp breath.

Saoirse dropped her letter. "Ronan," she cried, enveloping him.

"Hey," he murmured with contentment as he breathed her fragrance. Her closeness moderated both weariness and misery.

"Are you okay?"

"I'm grand."

"Now that," Caitlin said, placing a steaming mug on the coffee table, "sounds Irish."

"Mmm," was all Ronan said.

Saoirse nuzzled his hair, kissing his forehead, sighing. Caitlin hobbled through the silence with a second cup, then her own. She perched on the arm of the couch beside Ronan. "All sorted then?" The tautness in her tone belied the casual enquiry.

"All sorted," Ronan said from behind closed lids.

After another silence, Caitlin huffed. "Don't make me drag it out of you, boyo."

Reluctantly, Ronan opened his eyes. Pushing off Saoirse's shoulder, he took a sip of tea and started talking. Over the next hour, he related everything that had happened since the shootout at Garret's farm, including the deaths of Vítek and Luli, and when he thought he'd killed Ylli.

"Pity you didn't," Caitlin muttered.

"I agree," Saoirse added with unfettered hostility.

Clasping the cup and concentrating on the tea, Ronan chose his words carefully. "After seeing what he did to your dad, and Garret, I wanted to ... but ... when I thought I had, it was ... like ... like ... I don't know ... like doom and guilt were sucking everything good out of me ... horrible." He sipped tea, hoping it might sluice away the dark memory. "When I found out he was still alive, a huge weight lifted. Anyway, death would be a cop-out ... prison will be a much worse punishment."

"Maybe," Caitlin said doubtfully.

"You can only serve one life sentence," Saoirse said, face twisted with bitterness and unconcealed grief. Neither spoilt her aching beauty; Ronan squeezed her hand.

Desperate for a change of subject, he said, "Who's the letter from?"

Her resentment evaporated, replaced by a single tear. "Oh ... Garret left it with Aunty Bridget ... said to give it to me when he died."

Ronan didn't bother asking why it wasn't left with a solicitor—Garret must have had a reason.

"It's sad," she said, "and weird ... finding out things I never knew about family ..." She glanced at Caitlin and gave Ronan a burdened look.

"What?" he said, surveying them.

"Here." She handed him the bundle of pages. "It's better if you read it yourself."

Unease gripped Ronan; he tried to push the letter back. "Just tell me."

Another glisten appeared in the corner of Saoirse's eye as she rose and headed for the bedroom. "Read it ... please ..." Her voice caught.

Puzzled, Ronan watched her go. He turned to Caitlin, but she was leaving as well. With rising disquiet, he focused on the first page. As he read, he felt like an interloper.

Dearest Saoirse

Thank you from the bottom of my heart ... I wouldn't be writing this letter if it wasn't for you. In those darkest days after Abby's death, it was your visits with your mam that stopped me doing something foolish. You'd scurry round the house, exploring every corner and cupboard. Your mam would fuss and worry, but I'd laugh and wonder at the sweet innocence of such a beautiful bundle.

I'll never forget the day you met Cú. It wasn't long after your mam left, poor soul, and your da brought you around. I'd just got Cú, fresh off his mammy's teat, only a month old and howling and crying fit to break my heart. Well, the two of you took to each other like kindred spirits, running round the yard, rolling in the hay, lying on the rug by the fire. You and Cú became best mates that day.

Then you started riding Viking round the mountain to visit. They were my happiest hours. It was like having a wee bit of Abby back with me.

You've grown into a beautiful young woman, Saoirse (and I don't just mean the fierce good looks you got from your mam, and your da, for I always see dear Abby in you), but the person you are inside makes my heart burst with pride, as if you were my own daughter.

I want you to have the farm, such as it is (grand land but run down, mind).

Ronan paused, blinking hard; the lump in his throat threatened to choke him. Now he understood why Saoirse left the room, and why Caitlin went to be with her. His own complete lack of elation at Saoirse's inheritance told him how numb she must feel about it. Time heals all wounds, his mother always said, but that didn't make the present any easier. He returned to the letter.

You can turn it into that nature reserve you're always talking about, but there are a few things you should know about it that are not to be passed to anyone you wouldn't trust with your life. As you know, I played a small role in The Troubles, but I haven't told you about the bunker. It's where we hid guns, explosives, money, people, anything and everything (all gone now, thank goodness). It runs from the house to the barn, with another exit down by the stream. I've made a set of instructions on how to get in and out at each point, as well as some other things like the sprinkler system and the like - I'll attach it to this letter.

Sometimes in life there are problems that have no easy solutions, and we have to make decisions that are the least bad option, so I hope you can find in your heart a way to forgive what I've done and understand why.

Also, if you ever get into trouble that you'd rather not have the world know about, anything at all, don't hesitate to go to Callum O'Leary in Carrick or Padraig Ryan—

The name leapt from the page, smacking Ronan square between the eyes—he actually flinched. Images scrolled across his memory: his super-capable grandfather fixing a water pump, mending a fence, singing songs of Ireland, laughing round the table at Doyle Farm. But then there was the time he flattened Masters in the hay shed, hissing into the man's ear, "I've put better men than you on the canvas." When Ronan put it all together with

Garret McGinley's words, he came up with—*No! It couldn't be! Padraig Ryan, IRA?* Or was he assuming too much? He was too numb to think straight.

Chest tight, Ronan blinked at the compact lines of Irish. He must be mistaken. But as he re-read the sentence, he heard Grandpa Paddy's words echoing a second time that 'The Troubles saw good men do bad things'. There was no doubt in Ronan's mind that caring, gentle, wise Padraig Ryan was a good man, the best, but had he done bad things? Ronan wanted to know more about the man whose memory he worshipped, but it would have to wait for another day, another time. He dropped his gaze back to the page.

... Padraig Ryan in Killybegs. You can trust them with your life (I do), they will do you right.

You will get a letter from my solicitor, Cathleen O'Donnell, about the farm. I hope you and your da enjoy living here, and I know you'll take great care of Cú.

Thank you so much for bringing sunshine to my gloomy days. I'm ever so grateful.

Love you always, beautiful girl.

Garret.

Head swirling with questions, speculation, assumptions and possibilities, Ronan lay back, staring into space, filtering the important from the trivial, and muttering a self-rebuke. There he was, consumed by a mystery about his grandfather, while poor Saoirse, having buried her father, now had to bury a much-loved uncle. No wonder she almost bit his head off the previous day.

Ronan could only imagine the weight of loss and sorrow burdening her. He thought of his own grief for Grandpa Paddy and multiplied by two. Saoirse's heart must be crushed; she needed him now, more than ever. His issues were nothing.

98

BEYOND UNDERSTANDING

The next day found Ronan waiting in Declan's flat behind drawn blinds. Even though Caitlin's parents had insisted the girls sleep in the house, she'd convinced them it was quite safe in the locked flat, especially with two gardaí posted in the courtyard until all suspects were in custody. And, she'd promised they wouldn't go anywhere without an escort.

Both Caitlin and Saoirse had used their tag-team routine to assure Ronan it was fine for him to stay as well, despite his fear of being discovered. "Mum and Dad would never come in without my invitation," she'd told him. "Especially now that Sersh has moved in."

"They said it's our place," Saoirse added, "and our responsibility to look after it, and ourselves."

"I think it's their way of preparing us for university life," Caitlin said, "but keep the blinds closed and the door locked ... in case Conor or Eireann come poking round." She made an exaggerated eye roll.

Although it was Sunday, the girls were summoned to the garda station to clarify elements of their statements while everything was still fresh. Ronan took the opportunity to flytja to Doctor O'Leary for a check-up. After much tongue clicking at the bloodied bandage and the obvious stress to the wound, the man replaced the dressing, declaring himself satisfied with his sturdy needlework and the lack of infection. More tut-tutting accompanied the examination and cleaning of the bullet burn across his ribs.

"If you keep tempting fate," O'Leary said, "you're bound to come up short."

There was no question Ronan needed to be more careful, but he wasn't sure how to anymore. "Garret left a letter for Saoirse," he said, uncertain how to proceed, but desperately wanting to know. "It said she could trust you and Padraig Ryan with her life." Ronan studied the man. "Were you all IRA?"

O'Leary's minute hesitation as he placed a dressing over the rib wound almost escaped Ronan. "Now, what makes you think that?" O'Leary said, paying particular attention to the last piece of tape.

"Garret told Saoirse *he* was."

"Well, you shouldn't be saying things like that in front of strangers," O'Leary scolded.

"Garret said she could trust you with her life," Ronan reminded him.

O'Leary relented. "Padraig Ryan is a good man who did all he could to prevent injustice and bloodshed." His lips firmed. "That's all I'm going to say ... it's all you need to know."

Ronan was intrigued by O'Leary leaving himself out of the statement. Was it modesty, or didn't the same absolution apply? Ronan decided it wasn't important, and O'Leary sent him off with a dire warning of what would happen if the leg was not well rested.

After assuring the doctor he would comply, Ronan promptly flytjed to Viking. The greeting of low rolling nickers, at first sounded like excitement, then rebuke for taking so long. Riding in an awkward side-saddle way to avoid pressure on his thigh, Ronan took the big grey out of the forest and down the valley to the first farm that would keep him a few days for a hundred euros. At the mention of the Kelly name, payment was refused, and Ronan wondered if it was esteem or sympathy.

He returned to the flat with a surge of confidence. After an overnight break, he'd managed three flytjas in under two hours, with no sign of a flare. As he waited for the girls, he chafed, sitting, hobbling, glancing at the clock, hobbling some more. Ronan ached to have Saoirse beside him, hear her voice, inhale the sweetness of her breath. The guards were wasting precious hours; the next day was his last before having to return to his own time, or risk being heimmed to Freyja's world. *Damn the rune's nine-day rule.* But then he thought about it: suppose he could stay in Saoirse's time for two years, returning to his mother the moment after he'd left her, but looking much older. How could that be explained?

A victims-of-crime pamphlet on the coffee table kept him engaged for ten minutes. As he read about the services offered, he dwelt on what Saoirse and Caitlin had been through, and all those nameless girls. His rune surged. After his third reading of Commissioner Conroy's assurance to victims—as good as it was—the thirst for retribution was intense.

Not for the first time, he pondered the way that little pebble made him think and act, and how close he'd been to unleashing fatal arrows at Vítek and Egan back at Garret's farm. Were those chills a warning that killing from ambush was a breach of Norse honour? Or was it his conscience fighting to be heard? It seemed the rune both fed *and* starved his worst impulses. Another mystery for Freyja.

It was almost lunchtime when the girls returned, none the wiser about what the gardaí thought, or the investigation's progress. One thing Ronan knew for sure, Fionella and her surly son were in deep trouble. While she might not have known what her husband was up to, she was guilty of at least three murders, and who knew what other skulduggery. Unless her Ricardo was a miracle worker, it was only a matter of time before the noose of the investigation tightened round her. Ronan couldn't wait.

All afternoon they rehashed their missteps and looked for weaknesses in their story, holes that the detectives might identify and pick at like fingernails on a scab. As evening drew close, he broached the subject that had weighed on the afternoon. Saoirse was snuggled into him on the couch, Caitlin beside her. Ronan ran his fingers through Saoirse's hair, massaging her scalp, unsure whether he was trying to distract her or delay the inevitable. He sighed. "I have to go tomorrow morning."

Saoirse's head snapped up, her eyes wide. "No!"

Ronan put a finger to her lips. "It'll be nine days, and—"

"What's nine days?" Caitlin broke in.

"No," Saoirse cried again, "I need you here. What about Garret's funeral? I want you here, Ronan." She clasped his hands. "I need you … please."

Caitlin tried again. "What's nine days?" It was as though she didn't exist.

"But I'll be straight back," Ronan insisted. "It'll be just like I've gone for a shower … not even that."

"But what if you can't?" Saoirse sobbed.

"For pity's sake," Caitlin said, voice rising with irritation. "What's nine days?"

"What?" Saoirse and Ronan said in unison, turning as if surprised by her presence.

"Nine days?" Caitlin said, throwing hands in the air.

Saoirse, clearly unsettled, regarded Ronan. "The rune," he began, "won't let me stay more than nine days in any time apart from my own, or Freyja's."

"Your hundred-times Norse grandmother?" Caitlin smirked.

Ronan ignored the exaggeration. "Something like that."

"So, 2021 and 891 you're right, every other time, only nine days?"

"That's right." Ronan squeezed Saoirse's hand, drawing a muted response.

Concentration had put distance in Caitlin's gaze. Almost to herself, she said, "That should work."

"What?" Again, Saoirse and Ronan spoke together.

Caitlin paused before answering with a question of her own: "When was your last time-flytja?"

Ronan frowned. "Last night, when I took the last two bags to the deserted house. Why?"

"So," Caitlin said in triumph, "you have another eight days in this time ... Monday night next week."

"Yes!" Saoirse jerked upright, face glowing with elation. "Thank you," she cried, flinging her arms round Caitlin.

"It was only a few minutes," Ronan said, knowing he was pricking Saoirse's balloon. "I don't think it counts."

"Why not?" Saoirse said, excitement fading.

"If it was a time-flytja, you are in a different time." Caitlin was emphatic.

Ronan couldn't fault the logic, but he remained sceptical. "To be honest, I have no idea how it all works ... trying to figure it out gives me a headache."

"It certainly challenges reality," Caitlin admitted. "Ties my mind in knots."

Saoirse cupped Ronan's jaw, turning him toward her. "Don't you think everything about your rune is beyond understanding?"

"I suppose," he responded slowly. "But are we willing to take the risk that the nine days is reset?"

She squeezed his hand. "I am if you are."

The complete reversal of her earlier apprehension surprised Ronan. Was it wishful thinking, or blind faith in Caitlin's assessment? "And if I don't come back?"

"You will," she whispered, hugging him tight, burying her face in his neck. "I know you will."

99

FAVOURITE SWEATER

Sleep eluded Ronan that night. Even after Saoirse succumbed, and her gentle breaths whispered into the silence, his mind gnawed at the nine-day problem. If Caitlin wasn't right, he'd be heimmed to 891, and that wasn't a risk he was prepared to take. But what was the alternative?

The longer he dwelt on it, the greater his frustration became. In a hidden recess, a tiny snagged thread of recall wafted in the slipstream of memories flying past it, in and out of the vault. Ronan was sure it was important but it remained elusive.

"No, Dad ... no," Saoirse mumbled in her sleep, thrashing her head from side to side. She rolled over, flinging an arm across Ronan's face, muttering something about Vikings.

After easing her arm aside, he lay staring at a ceiling he couldn't see, replaying everything Freyja had said. She'd mentioned nothing specific about the distance or time span of a flytja, instead, using general terms like long, short and further, all of which might refer to either time or space: 'every journey invites the umrót' and 'the further the flytja, the worse the umrót'. Then there was 'a long flytja is purgatory, but a short one is no burden'.

Maybe that was it, and the purgatory Freyja referred to encompassed both the fire and the umrót. Even if it didn't, Ronan knew that going from his time to Saoirse's would be far less painful than coming all the way from Freyja's time. That being the case, the simple solution would be to flytja home, wait a few days to recover, and flytja back into bed with Saoirse—she'd never know. The problem was his leg. Although he could manage without a crutch, there was no way to hide the limp from his mother.

The solution was obvious, so he eased from the bed, dosed himself up, and slipped back in.

When he figured a half hour had passed, Ronan filled his mind with home and folded from between the sheets. He was back beside Saoirse in a beat, wrapped in a haze of torment. For an age, he lay absorbing her scent, waiting for the flames to subside and blissful slumber to flood in.

It was mid-morning when Ronan woke. He followed faint murmurings to where the girls sat on the couch, heads close.

"He has risen," Caitlin teased.

Saoirse patted a cushion. "You must have needed that," she said as he slumped down beside her.

Ronan considered keeping it to himself, but had to confess. "I went home last night ... came straight back ... had a good dose of flytja fire to sleep off."

Saoirse stiffened. "Why?"

"Need time for my wounds to heal. How can I explain them to Mum?"

"I think Sersh means, why go in the first place?" Caitlin raised an eyebrow. "I thought we had it worked out."

"I couldn't risk having to flytja back from Freyja's time ... bad enough from mine."

Amid a back and forth on the pros and cons of the decision, Ronan worked his way through a late breakfast. Then, buoyed by the reset nine-day clock, he threw himself into helping organise Garret's send-off, but from well behind the scenes.

On the Wednesday, the girls were called to the main house to hear the latest from the detectives leading the investigation. Divers had found Dooley Egan's body in his car after passers-by reported wheel tracks going over the cliff, Fionella and Fionn had been arrested but not yet charged, and detectives Hoolihan and Drisko were certain there was no further threat to the girls. The gardaí who'd been watching the flat were withdrawn.

When Saoirse and Caitlin conveyed it all to Ronan, he thumbed off a text message. Within seconds, Saoirse's phone pinged: *bak nr kbegs, lve 2 c u ??* Her honey-dipped laugh had him glowing.

"Why didn't you just tell me?"

"Cause I'm in Killybegs." He palmed his forehead. "Duh."

Saoirse gave him a playful push.

"I fancy a drive," chirped Caitlin.

"Great," Ronan said. "And can you ask your mum if I can stay until after the funeral? ... need a pretext for being here, now that the blinds can be opened and the doors unlocked."

Half an hour later, the girls left in the Mini to collect their Aussie friend from Killybegs. Ronan hunkered out of sight on the back seat, chatting all the while.

"I want to buy a wreath for Dad," Saoirse murmured as Killybegs reached out to greet them, "and lay it at the spot ... on the way home."

"He'd like that," Caitlin said as Ronan reached between the seats, grasping Saoirse's hand.

"And I'll pay for it," he said firmly.

"I suppose you want to borrow the money from me, first?" Saoirse responded, feigned outrage displacing her melancholy.

Ronan huffed. "I have my own money now, thank you."

"Which reminds me," she said, ignoring his pretend indignation, "did you ever repay me?"

"Only the interest." Ronan squeezed her fingers at the memory of those kisses.

Saoirse rubbed her chin with her other hand. "Mmm, I don't recall ..."

Ronan tugged her arm. "I thought it was an interest-only loan ... learnt about them recently."

"Well, you won't be paying yet, boyo," Caitlin cut in, "because your money is back in the flat."

"Not all of it," Ronan smirked, flaunting Fionella's payment through the gap between the front seats.

"My god!" Saoirse said, spinning toward him.

After a quick glance at the banknotes, Caitlin squinted in the mirror. "Did you keep some of the drug money?"

Ronan stilled; Saoirse squeezed. "She's joking," she assured him before turning to Caitlin. "Aren't you?"

Caitlin stared, deadpan, then snorted.

"You ratbag," Ronan said, landing a tap on her thigh, immediately contrite when she winced—it was her bad leg.

"Didn't feel a thing," she chortled in response to his apology. Ronan hit her again.

As they turned toward the waterfront, Caitlin sobered and said, "Where are we meeting you, boyo?"

"Information Centre," Ronan said, emptying his mind with a blissful absence of discomfort. Renewed confidence zinged through him as the rune set him down in a car park beside a gas tank and a couple of hatchbacks. Having discarded the crutches in recognition of his rune-accelerated healing, he limped from the air and headed toward the street. Within a dozen steps, a little beige Mini beetled into the entrance, drawing up with a cheeky toot and excited waving from the occupants.

"You pair of clowns," he whispered into Saoirse's ear after she'd leapt out and flung herself into his arms as if they hadn't seen each other for a week.

"I love you," she murmured back before pushing him to arm's length, face split by a watermelon grin. Neither of the girls' excitement appeared at all contrived.

"Ever thought of an acting career?" he said as he climbed in.

"Funny you should say that," Saoirse said.

"We're both in the school drama club," Caitlin added.

"Figures." Ronan soughed with contentment as he sank into the seat, their easy company enfolding him like a favourite sweater. He belonged with them as much as he did with his mother and Ruddi back in Australia. He hoped he never had to choose.

100

———

GREEN RIBBON

The trio lunched on fish and chips at the same waterfront bench where Ronan and Saoirse had sat only a few weeks earlier. Afterwards, they knocked a hole in Ronan's euros, buying several sets of clothes, a travel bag, toiletries, a supply of Kwells, and Darragh's wreath. And, Ronan insisted on fuelling the Mini, telling Caitlin it was the least he could do, given how much she'd done for him. While he had no idea how he was going to replenish his stash, spending the money with such heady spontaneity had him as light as a cloud.

Despite his contentment, Killybegs' importance kept intruding on Ronan's thoughts. It was his father's last known location, having flytjed there, to 1804. If Ronan was to have any chance of finding Paidin, he had to identify a landscape feature that looked as it did two hundred years ago. Aware of the likely reaction, he voiced his problem.

"No," Saoirse cried, clutching his arm.

"I have to, Saoirse." Ronan embraced her. "If there's any way I can help Dad, I have to try."

"But not now?" she said, pleading.

"Not now," he assured her.

Tears welled. "I can't bear the thought of losing you too," she murmured.

Tightening his arms, he whispered, "I'll never be more than one flytja away."

Caitlin, who'd been gazing into the distance, brow furrowed, cut into the exchange. "I think I know a place," she said, describing it to Ronan.

"Mmm, might work," he said. "But first, who's for an ice-cream?"

They left Killybegs, chocolate Cornettos in hand, car brimming with forced good humour. Caitlin took a roundabout route to the south, to a hill with an eastward view across the harbour entrance to the low bluffs of Carntullagh Head. Alongside the craggy skirts of the promontory lay a low splinter of wave-stripped rock topped by ramparts and bulwarks protecting a white tower. "Do you know when that lighthouse was built?" Ronan asked.

"Rotten Island?" Caitlin scrunched her nose. "No idea … sorry."

"Finished in 1839, according to this," Saoirse said, brandishing an information booklet from the glove box.

"That's no use, then," Ronan said, switching focus to the grass-covered sweep of Carntullagh Head. It held no time-linked constructions and his current view of it might be the only way back to Paidin. Ronan locked it into his memory.

Cornettos demolished, they headed home, winding downhill between stone walls, hedgerows, fences and verges of bracken, past sparkling white houses puffing their chests to the world, and weather-beaten stone barns content in their nondescript permanence. After passing a rock-strewn inlet, they hit a rare straight stretch, through dense woodland to the Carrick road.

Their chatter dried up as they approached the accident site where rubber smeared the asphalt like a gigantic black X.

As Saoirse hung the wreath on a brand-new fencepost set between twin gouges in the earth, she seemed lost in grief. Ronan left her to her thoughts, ready if she needed him. The memory of his own heartbreak at Grandpa Paddy's recent death was fresh. Sometimes he'd sought his mother's support or Ruddi's company; sometimes all he wanted was solitude and the comfort of memories.

Envy swelled as Ronan dwelt on the sixteen years Saoirse had with Darragh. A sudden longing filled him, an overpowering urge to go, to find his own father, whatever it took. As soon as Garret's funeral was over and some normality returned to Saoirse's life, he'd pay a lightning visit to his mother before heading to the town they'd just left, but back two hundred years—if he could. "I'm coming, Dad," he muttered to himself. "I *will* find you."

Saoirse turned, clinging to Ronan. "It's so unfair."

"I know," he soothed, stroking her hair as tears soaked into his shirt.

Caitlin tied a length of green ribbon to the top wire of the repaired fence. The breeze sent it rippling and twisting, shooting off emerald iridescence.

With a shuddering breath, Saoirse said, "Don't ever leave me, Ronan."

"How could I," he replied, throat tightening. "Even when I'm not with you, I'll only ever be one flytja away ... and I'll always, always come back."

She let out an enormous, wracking sob. "But you're going after your father."

"Yes, but not yet."

"What if something goes wrong"—Saoirse's voice lifted—"and you can't get back?"

Ronan hugged her, whispering, "I have the rune ... shh."

"But how can you be so sure? All that pain? You said yoursel—"

Ronan held a finger to her lips. "Shh ... we've been through this. What's happened to Sunday's confidence?"

Saoirse sniffed. "The closer it gets, the more scared I become."

Caitlin put a hand on Saoirse's shoulder. "We've worked out the cause of the pain," she said. "As long as Ronan allows recovery time, he'll be grand."

"My blóð rún brought me to you in the first place ... it'll bring me back." Ronan wondered at his conviction, and the strange compulsion to use the rune's Norse name. Spreading warmth explained it.

Contented and relaxed for the first time in ages, he kissed her forehead as they stood arm in arm, staring at the churned earth and oil stains beyond the fence.

Caitlin's phone interrupted their melancholy: it was her mother, urging them home. With the sun courting the horizon, they carried their memories to the Mini and left green ribbon spangling in the breeze.

GOBSHITE

The following day, beneath a funereal sky, Saoirse prevailed under the weight of another loved-one's farewell. Ronan could only admire her strength and resolve. Niamh came up from Dublin to share the bubble of grief with her daughter. As they entered the church, Ronan sensed scrutiny, and caught a gaze across the heads of mourners at the back.

The man was familiar in a nebulous way, but Ronan couldn't place him, or even be sure he'd ever seen the face before. It was like a police composite of every perfect feature, a fashion model with blonde hair so precise it might have been carved. He was there again, on the periphery, as the procession moved to the cemetery. Ronan tried to ignore him, but that proved impossible: each time he checked, the impeccable features were staring straight at him, no attempt at subterfuge. Hairs lifted on Ronan's neck.

Afterwards, standing with the O'Tooles as Saoirse and Niamh accepted well wishes from departing mourners, Ronan stooped to Caitlin's ear. "Who's that tall bloke?" he asked. "Blonde hair, dark-grey suit with all the buttons ... two o'clock."

After a stealthy glance, she replied, "No idea."

"You're a great help."

"Hang on ..." She turned to her mother, whispering.

Bridget's eyes eased right, then did a double-take. "Well," she breathed, "will you look at that, now? I believe that's Ricardo D'Alton ... he was the detective on"—she lowered her voice further, one eye on Saoirse—"Abby's case ... green at the time ... inspector now."

Cormac must have overheard, for he snorted. "They say his name used to be Richard Dalton." He derision was as thick as clotted cream. "Takes his comb to bed ... has a mirror in every room."

"Oh, Cormac," Bridget tut-tutted, eyes sparkling.

They fell silent as Inspector D'Alton glided from his position near the cemetery's stone boundary wall, headstones winking off his shoes as he approached. Ronan tensed; his rune warmed.

After a cursory nod to the O'Tooles, D'Alton said in a melodious baritone, "Ronan Ryan? A word? ... in private."

The grip on Ronan's elbow confirmed it wasn't a request. Resentment flared; Ronan swallowed it. Loath to disrupt the solemn occasion, he allowed himself to be led away. Curious stares followed them beyond the tombstones, into the deep shadow of a majestic oak.

"It would be best for you and your friends," D'Alton began, bypassing small talk, "if you tell me who you are and what you are doing in Donegal."

Still bristling, Ronan stayed silent to collect his thoughts. Being up close to the man was an experience: the pall of cologne was so thick, Ronan wondered for a bizarre moment whether an oxygen mask might drop from above his head; the man's teeth prompted sunglasses; and his irises would make a desert sky jealous. Well, Ronan hoped to cause clouds, but the name from the victims-of-crime pamphlet on Declan's coffee table eluded him. Was it Conway? Conloy? Conroy? D'Alton waited; Ronan took a punt.

"And it would be best for *you*," he mimicked, "to just forget I'm here, otherwise you'll be explaining to Commissioner Conroy why you're interested in me." Ronan held the man's gaze with all the confidence he could muster. "And if *you* don't tell him, *I* will."

D'Alton scrutinised Ronan with a mixture of scepticism and suspicion. "There is no way we would use a kid, certainly not an Aussie, for undercover work," he mused with wavering conviction. Frowning, he added, "What are you working on, and who do you report to?"

"It's not your place to be asking, Inspector." The implication hung among the oak leaves like ripe acorns. Wisps of uncertainty clouded D'Alton's restive eyes.

What the man had going with Fionella Egan, apart from a romantic liaison, Ronan had no clue, but he was in a gambling mood, and the rune's thrall. He tightened the screws. "Relax," he said, "your little side hustle is of no interest to us as long as you stay away from our work."

D'Alton's jolt screamed 'jackpot!'

Even as he marvelled at the maturity of his words and the poise of their delivery, Ronan pressed the advantage. "If we get even a whiff of you asking questions, you'll be under a microscope. Clear?"

After an extended silence in which the only sound was breeze riffling through leaves, D'Alton's blonde head bobbed with unmistakable reluctance.

"And it would be in your best interests that the Egans understand the importance of our agreement." Without waiting for a response, Ronan turned and left D'Alton asphyxiating on his own fumes.

"What was that all about?" Caitlin said when he re-joined them. Her parents leant in.

Ronan squinted back at D'Alton, ordering his thoughts. "Not sure, but he said he made a mistake ... said he thought I was the Ronan Ryan from one of his investigations." He'd tell the girls the truth later, but for now, quelling the O'Toole's curiosity was top priority. "But when he heard I was an Aussie, he apologised."

"How peculiar," Bridget murmured.

"Gobshite," Cormac muttered.

"Cormac!"

"He was none too pleased when you walked away from him, lad," Cormac said, ignoring his wife's rebuke. "What did you say?"

"Cormac!"

"I don't mind," Ronan said quickly. "I told him my mother was well-connected in Commissioner Conroy's circles, and left it at that. She isn't, of course"—he shrugged—"but he rubbed me the wrong way."

Cormac chuckled. "I like your style, lad."

IO2

─────────

RELUCTANT DEPARTURE

Five days later, Ronan, Saoirse and Caitlin were at Garret's farm. The garda had finished their forensic examination the day before the funeral, and the three of them had spent the weekend airing smoke from the building, sweeping up glass and stone chips, exploring the bunker, and reminiscing about Garret. Ronan had found enough scraps of wood to board up the shattered windows, blocking out the chilly wind and making the house secure, although much darker. It'd do until he had enough money to replace the glass. When the girls puzzled over the clean laundry, Ronan admitted it was him.

"When?" Saoirse stared at the spotless floor as if reliving the horrors it had witnessed.

"Day after the funeral," Ronan replied. "You were in the shower, and Caitlin was over at the main house." He'd flytjed to Killybegs and bought baking soda and white vinegar, scrubbing the floor until his arms ached and all signs of Garret's blood was gone.

"But why?" Saoirse said. "It would have been much easier with all three of us."

They were sitting at Garret's tiny table, sipping tea. Ronan touched her forearm. "It wasn't something you needed to be doing."

Saoirse surveyed him with moist eyes before lowering her lips to the back of his hand.

"Is that reprimand or gratitude?" Caitlin enquired.

"Reprimand," Saoirse cooed, lifting her gaze but not her lips.

Earlier, Ronan had said his thanks and farewells to the O'Tooles, and he and the girls had returned to Garret's on the pretext of dropping him back at Killybegs. Ronan took his discarded Norse clothes, changing into them as soon as they arrived—he'd need them for 1804—leaving his Irish clothes in a drawer with his phone, ready for his next visit.

The girls were waiting for him on the cracked and faded leather couch strewn with grey dog hairs. When he flopped beside Saoirse, she dropped her head onto his shoulder. "Can't you flytja home and come straight back? And stay another nine days?"

"I could," Ronan murmured, soaking up her warmth, "but you've got school ... and I have to find Dad."

"I know, but I'm scared you mightn't get back?" Her voice faltered and shrank.

"I'll just have to make sure I don't overdo it."

Saoirse studied him. "Promise?"

"I promise," Ronan said, leaning his cheek on the top of her head, breathing in her scent, revelling in her warmth.

"According to Cathleen O'Donnell," Caitlin said, glancing up from the solicitor's letter, "there's a hundred and two hectares here ... on three titles."

"Mmm," Saoirse murmured.

Caitlin rolled her eyes. "Ronan?"

"Uh-huh."

"Why do I bother?" Caitlin tossed back her head, howling at the ceiling.

Saoirse laughed. "Take a chill pill, Cait."

"I've got to do something ... you pair are no company."

"When will you come back?" Saoirse asked, reaching up to trace Ronan's jaw line.

"And there's my point!" Caitlin threw her hands in the air.

"Friday afternoon," Ronan said, struggling to suppress a grin, "if that suits?"

"I think I'll go home," Caitlin growled, pulling herself onto her crutches.

"Wait! No!" Saoirse cried. "We were only joking."

Caitlin chortled. "So was I."

Saoirse reached across to whack her friend on the arm, but Caitlin dodged and Saoirse's hand hit the crutch. "Ow!" she yowled, pretending injury.

"Are you two going to get along while I'm away?" Ronan said with affected severity.

"We get on better when you're not here," Caitlin teased.

"Well," Ronan said, standing, "I'd better be going then."

"No!" Saoirse clutched his arm. "Not yet. Can't you stay another night?"

"Then I would want to stay another, and another ..."

"Good," she said, trying to pull him back onto the couch.

Ronan resisted, turning to Caitlin instead, wrapping her in a hug. "Thanks for everything, Hedgehog."

"Any time, Sherlock ... take care."

Saoirse raised an eyebrow, looking from one to the other.

"Tell you later," Caitlin said. "Meanwhile, I'm going for a walk while you say your mushy goodbyes ... bye, Ronan ... see you on Friday."

"See you, Cait," he called as she crutched out the charred doorway.

"I'm scared," Saoirse said, rising, clutching him.

Ronan squeezed back. "Just promise me you'll be here next Friday afternoon?"

"We'll come straight from school." Her embrace intensified. "What if you can't come back?"

"If the pain doesn't behave, my next flytja will be to here ... promise."

"Okay," she murmured, lifting her lips to his, kissing him hard and long, as if it might be the last time. "Now go ... before my heart breaks."

Ronan held her face, gazing into her eyes. "I love you, Saoirse."

"I love you too," she sobbed.

With his heart wrenching, he touched his lips to hers, and folded from her arms.

103

AIRBRUSHED

Ronan's Doyle Farm bedroom was a tiny slice of his Australia. The sharp bite of eucalypts, the earthiness of dried grass, and the stale cheese undertones of dirty socks, all wrapped in tinder-dry summer air. But no apples. Already, his heart ached. And there was something he'd never noticed before, a pervading something absent from Irish air: dust.

Thankfully, the Kwells worked a treat, no umrót to speak of, only a slight wooziness as though he'd just dismounted a runaway merry-go-round.

After he'd changed and flopped into bed, he lay there, too full of thoughts to sleep. In an instant, he'd gone from the dreamy, floating euphoria of Saoirse's arms, to the hollow longing of loneliness and separation at Doyle Farm. *If love is always like this, it's a wonder the world functions.* Yet even in his doleful state, he started planning to find his father.

It had sounded so easy when Freyja had told him to 'enter ró with your only thought an image of where you wish to go'. It was so easy with places he'd already been, but Killybegs 1804? The closer it came to actually flytjing into the unknown, the more frightening it became. All he had to aim for was the view of Carntullagh Head across the harbour entrance. Everything hinged on that bluff-fringed peninsular looking the same as it did two hundred years ago. He'd soon find out.

The days passed in a blur, filled with his mother, Ruddi, school, farm chores, and trying to talk with a taciturn Fergal Gallagher. At night, in the solitude of his room, Ronan trawled the internet for information on historical Killybegs. Avoiding a quick search for Saoirse in the process proved difficult, but he prevailed. He was afraid not so much what he might find, but what he mightn't: himself. Despite his best intentions, he stumbled onto a Killybegs search result he couldn't ignore: *Killybegs Clarion: Doomed boot factory linked to murder spree gets reprieve.* He clicked the link to an article by *Roving Reporter, Aisling Byrne.*

16 June, 2008

Detencin Boots of Killybegs, which went into receivership three months ago, was thrown a lifeline when 20-year-old Glenmalin woman, Saoirse Kelly, underwrote 12 months' operating after organising the workers into a cooperative to take over ownership of the troubled company.

Miss Kelly, whose father, Darragh, was the long-term head bootmaker at Detencin until his untimely death four years ago, said she was proud to help the factory that had been such a big part of her father's life.

"Dad lived and breathed DTs, and really believed they were the best boots in all of Ireland, so it's an honour to be able to help continue that legacy and secure local jobs," she said.

'The best boots in all of Ireland' had been the catchphrase of founder, Donal O'Mahony, from when he launched Detencin Boots as a young man in 1957.

Miss Kelly repeated the widely known intention of O'Mahony to leave the company to the workers who had stood by him through the tough times.

"When Donal said he was leaving the business to his loyal workers, Dad was so excited, and full of plans to make DTs even better," she said.

But, apparently ...

Ronan scanned the rest of the story, but there was no mention of himself. With his heart in free fall, his head scrambled for reassurance. Was his absence because he was no longer in Saoirse's life in 2008, or was it because they'd been careful to maintain his anonymity? The answer wouldn't be in a news piece almost as old as him, but he continued reading.

... O'Mahony changed his mind shortly before his untimely death from heart failure, leaving his share of the company to Fionella, wife of his then accountant and business partner, Dooley Egan, who died on 13 November, 2004 when he drove off a cliff near Málain Bhig.

Subsequent investigations into a spate of contemporaneous murders in southern Donegal found Dooley Egan directly responsible for the deaths of Garret McGinley and Darragh Kelly, as well as the 1990 murder of McGinley's wife, Abby, sister of Darragh Kelly.

Egan was also found ultimately liable for the unlawful imprisonment of Saoirse Kelly, a sorry episode from which Miss Kelly appears to have emerged strong and resolute. The ordeal, along with her father's murder, was linked to Darragh's efforts to organise workers at Detencin Boots to petition for higher wages.

In addition, Egan was found to be an accessory to the murders of Polish national, Vitek Wojszyk, and his wife, Albanian national, Luli Berisha. Wojszyk, Berisha and her brother, Ylli, were found culpable for the detainment of Miss Kelly.

Ylli Berisha was serving a life sentence in Midlands Prison for the murders of Darragh Kelly and Vitek Wojszyk, when he was discovered stabbed to death in the prison shower shortly after his incarceration.

Inspector Ricardo D'Alton said it appeared to be a grisly coincidence. "While our investigations were unable to identify the person or persons responsible, there is no reason to believe this man's tragic death was anything more than a prison disagreement that escalated."

D'Alton said they were all involved in human trafficking activities. "It appears Dooley Egan was running a trafficking operation with the help of Wojszyk and the Berishas.

"We also identified two local Carrick fishermen, Sean Hagan, and his son, Jamie, who provided the critical transport link from passing ships, as well as onshore."

Father and son were each sentenced to five years and three months, while the final co-conspirator, Fionn Egan, the then 19-year-old son of Dooley, received a two-year-and-one-month sentence for his peripheral actions the court found to have been conducted in ignorance.

Ronan snorted in disbelief; there had been nothing peripheral or unknowing about it.

While the initial enquiries identified Fionella Egan as a person of interest, further investigation ruled out her knowledge or involvement.

Ronan's fist knotted on the edge of the desk as he reread the last sentence. *She* was the one who murdered Donal and Abby. How could she get away with that? Ricardo D'Alton! Even as vengeance festered in his heart, Ronan knew he could do nothing—they had a deal. Any departure from it on his part might jeopardise Saoirse and Caitlin. He wouldn't risk that.

As he brooded on the injustice, he skimmed the rest of the article.

A well-known businesswoman with extensive real estate holdings across southern Donegal and in the Dublin area, Fionella had previously expressed her shame at being duped by her husband and son, but declined a request for interview.

In an interesting footnote, Sean Hagan's wife, Mary, left the country soon after his arrest, and has been living in a luxury apartment in Estepona on Spain's Costa de Sol. The residence is owned by a Cayman Islands registered entity, DAFE Inc.

Who is DAFE? And was Dooley Egan the head of the snake? Those are questions even An Garda Síochána can't answer.

Ronan glanced back at the headline in aching disappointment. Had it focused on Detencin's reprieve, rather than those involved in the murders, there would have been much more on Saoirse, and that's what he cared about most. However, Fionella's exoneration chafed like sand between his toes. How could D'Alton have so thoroughly airbrushed her fingerprints from the Detencin takeover and Donal O'Mahony's death?

"Dooley *and* Fionella Egan," he muttered to the journalist's name at the top of the screen.

104

INTO THE UNKNOWN

By midweek, Ronan was as prepared as possible, but he resolved to wait until the weekend to allow his body a full recovery from his homeward flytja. Nervous flutters rippled through him whenever he thought about what lay ahead, excitement and anxiety in equal measures. Perhaps the apprehension was the real reason for the delayed departure. Regardless, he convinced himself he needed the rest.

In anticipation of what lay ahead, he googled historical remedies for motion sickness. While he found a few in a text called *New Collection of Tested Remedies*, there was no way he was 'drinking the urine of a young boy', and he didn't think 'hiding some earth from the kitchen hearth in one's hair' would do anything. There was another that required 'mixing ground wormwood and mint with olive oil, and rubbing it into the nostrils'. Even if he could find the ingredients, it was too complicated.

Amongst it all, he stumbled across a recipe for calming an upset stomach: some wafer-thin slices of fresh ginger, brewed like tea and sipped slowly—worth trying. Despite his best efforts, he found no hard evidence of ginger in Ireland until the 1850s. Regardless, he pilfered a root from the pantry, hoping it wouldn't be missed. It would either flytja with him, or be awaiting his return. As would the puzzle of Fergal Gallagher.

Attempts to engage the man in conversation proved futile. It was almost as if Ronan unsettled him. This perplexed Ronan, especially since Fergal hit it off with Ruddi, who followed him like a second shadow.

"Have you noticed how Fergal is really standoffish with me?" Ronan said to his mother after another unsuccessful attempt.

Maureen glanced up from the farm expenses she was entering on the computer. "He's the same with me, love," she said, graceful fingers dancing over the number pad.

"But he's fine with Ruddi." Ronan longed for such easy-going camaraderie.

"Mmhmm." Tap-tap, tap.

While Ronan knew he should leave his mother to concentrate, curiosity overrode consideration. "Why do you suppose that is, Mum?"

Maureen sighed, pushing the laptop away. Leaning forward, elbows on the desk, chin resting on interlaced fingers, she studied him, brow crinkled. It was then that Ronan realised the haggard lines of the past few years had smoothed from her features, the sheen returned to her hair—amazing what the removal of a bullying husband could do.

"Perhaps it's something to do with the trauma he suffered," she mused, emerald eyes distant.

Ronan thought of the man's raspy voice. "You mean it hurts him to talk?"

"Not necessarily."

"The burns?" The left side of Fergal's face was a Martian landscape of scar tissue, puckered and stretched by hidden forces.

Maureen pushed back in her chair. "Not just the injury, but everything associated with it ... the whole ordeal ... whatever it was."

"Have you asked him?" It would be a brief conversation, given Fergal's reluctance to use two words where one sufficed.

"He'll tell us when he's ready ... if he wants to ... up to him." She dragged the laptop closer and reached for the next pile of accounts. Ronan took the hint, going outside to shoot arrows at a hay bale, wondering what caused such horrific scarring.

Even with Fergal's dour presence, the atmosphere of the Doyle Farm homestead was light and cheery, quite the opposite of the gloom and trepidation of when Bruno Masters had been in residence.

On the Friday, Ronan came home from school to a second change: photos of his father had magically appeared. His mother had dug them up from some hidden spot beyond the reach of her late husband. There was an engagement photo at The Faulty Rudder pub in Killybegs, and one of Maureen and Paidin sitting arm-in-arm on a low rock wall in front of a gunmetal sea.

One particular shot caught and held Ronan's attention: Paidin sitting with his back against a cave wall, knees drawn up, notebook and pencil in hand, blue eyes alive with excitement as they lifted from his field notes. Ronan was sure it was the cliff cave on Sliabh

Liag. And with that certainty came the realisation it was time to go. Even though doubt plagued him, he had to try.

After dinner, he played a computer game with Ruddi, giving him a boisterous bedtime hug. His mother was sitting, one eye on a television show about a 1920s lady detective in Melbourne, the other on the instructions for a pullover sleeve sprouting from flashing knitting needles. He stooped, wrapping his arms tight.

"Whoa, Ronan"—the needles stopped mid-stitch—"what's this all about?"

Head buried in his mother's shoulder, Ronan kept squeezing. "I love you, Mum."

"Oh, my darling boy," she said, kissing the top of his head, "I love you too."

"Thanks for everything you do for me." He blinked hard, hoping she didn't notice the catch in his voice.

Maureen sniffed, patting at pockets. "And thank you for all your help, love. I couldn't do it without you, you know." She blew daintily into a robust handkerchief and dabbed a cheek. "Now off you go to bed."

With a final squeeze, Ronan said, "Night, Mum." He kissed her forehead and turned to leave.

"Night, darling." The needles resumed their rhythmic clicking. With a smile in her voice, she added, "And you can thank me by spreading the rest of that mulch on the garden in the morning."

Without turning—Ronan didn't want her to see his moist eyes—he threw an airy wave over his shoulder.

By the time Maureen retired and the house was in darkness, Ronan had changed into his Norse clothes, taken two Kwells, and secured the ginger root in his belt pouch. While the possibility that he wasn't in Saoirse's 2008 life was weighing on him, so too was the thought of Paidin waiting for rescue, somewhere. How could he do anything but choose them both? At least Saoirse was safe; until he could say the same for Paidin, he would have no peace.

Ever since Ronan's short-lived sighting of his father on the Sliabh Liag cliff, there had been a void in his chest that only Paidin could fill. Once Ronan found him, he'd return to Saoirse. The only thing making the choice bearable was the belief that his blood rune would help him make his competing worlds spin in harmony. He had to trust it.

Ronan breathed deep, embracing the rune warmth as it calmed his quaking nerves and settled his thoughts. With a brief salute to Doyle Farm, and a silent farewell to his mother and Ruddi, he emptied his mind and visualised Carntullagh Head in 1804.

Folding into a rent in the air, Ronan flytjed into the unknown.

GLOSSARY & PRONUNCIATION

The pronunciation guide in this glossary is my best attempt to help you get your tongue around the non-English names and terms in this book. I appreciate your understanding for any shortcomings.

As with The Blood Rune, for the words portrayed as Norse I have used genuine Old Norse words where possible; however, where the relevant Old Norse word was either unknown, or visually or phonetically unsuitable, Icelandic was used—Icelandic being the closest modern language to Old Norse. Without exception, the first syllable of an Old Norse word is stressed, and where there is an accent over a vowel—as in Víking—it is a long vowel sound, although not necessarily the same sound as in English.

Aisling (ash-ling) - **dream; vision** (Irish)

An Garda Síochána (an garda she-o-carna) - **The Guardian of the Peace** (Irish)

Blóð (BLOW-th) - **blood** (Old Norse)

Cú (coo) - **hound** (Irish)

Darragh (darra) - **fruitful, fertile** (Irish)

Eireann (erin) - **Ireland** (Irish)

Eoin (owen) - **young** (Irish)

Fionn (fin) - **fair-headed, white** (Irish)

Fionella (fa-nella) - **fair shoulder, white** (Irish)

Flytja (FLEE-t-ya) - **relocate** (Icelandic)

Fundur (FN-derr) - **encounter** (Icelandic)

Gaeilge (Gwal-gah) - **Irish** as in language (Irish)

Garda (GAR-dah) - **guardian** (Irish)

Gardaí (Gar-dee) - **guardians** (Irish)

Haetta (HIGH-ta) - **danger** (Icelandic)

Heim (HEY-m) - **home** (Old Norse)

Luli (loo-lee) - **flower** (Albanian)

Niall (nigh-al) - **champion, passionate** (Irish)

Niamh (nee-v) - **radiance, luster** (Irish)

Padraig (paw-rick) - **patrician, noble** (Irish)

Ró (RRO) - **tranquillity** (Icelandic)

Róisín (ro-sheen) - **little rose** (Irish)

Rún (RROO-n) - **rune** (Old Norse)

Rúnar (RROO-nar) - **runes** (Old Norse)

Saoirse (sir-sha) - **freedom, liberty** (Irish)

Sliabh Liag (Sleeve League) - **Grey Mountain** (Irish)

Trufla (TROO-f-la) - **interfere** (Icelandic)

Umrót (OOM-rote) - **turbulence** (Icelandic)

Vítek (vee-tek) - **victor** (Polish)

Wojszyk (voy-sic) - **warrior** (Polish)

Ylli (e-lee) - **star** (Albanian)

ACKNOWLEDGEMENTS

To everyone who enjoyed *The Blood Rune*, thank you for posting generous reviews and comments, and for supporting an independent author. Knowing how my characters have come to life for you continues to inspire me.

Thanks to my beautiful wife, Delia, fearless critic and sounding board. As the initial reader of my completed manuscripts, she protects the world from tedious scenes, pedestrian dialogue and ill-advised indulgences.

Much gratitude to my long-time mentor, Bruce Honeywill; early readers, Helen Avery and Naomi Scott for their valued feedback; Sorcha Walsh for her Irish lens; editorial adviser, Evelyn Quinlan; Kit Carstairs and the team at The Manuscript Appraisal Agency; and cover design wizard, Hannah Maddock.

Special thanks to my good friend, John Dalton of the singed eyebrows, for the great cover photo. I issued a challenge; he responded with one of his own. The character, Ricardo D'Alton, the antithesis of John, is the result.

To my mother, Brigid, who's daily 'have you finished that book yet?' has been an unsubtle motivator. Her focus is already on the next one ... thanks, Mum.

Finally, a taster of Book Three of the Ronan Ryan Odyssey, *The Lost Rune*, begins over the page ... enjoy!

THE LOST RUNE

The ground was cold and hard. It was moving, rocking backward and forward. Paidin's head thumped like a base drum. Foetid air filled his nostrils. Opening his eyes was going to hurt even more, so he lay there, willing his head to settle and its contents to begin working.

The memory of Rory disappearing with the townswomen came floating back. And then there was the altercation with the snooty officer. Paidin groaned. It all happened so quickly, he didn't have a chance to use his rune. At the thought of the rune, his tongue flicked in search, but only found an empty cheek. In the iron grip of panic, his tongue flailed around an empty mouth. He must have swallowed it in the scuffle. Emptying his mind, he focused on Killybegs 2004, and drifted into ró.

There was no intake of breath, no agitation, no tossing, no change to the moving ground or the foul smell—nothing. He must be dreaming. After a short break he tried again—same result.

Nerves jangling, Paidin forced himself to inhale deep and slow. It didn't work. The rune should be stuck to the inside of his cheek like a barnacle. He groaned again, forcing an eye open. It only increased his anxiety. He was in a small cell, three walls of cross-grating and the fourth of solid timber, sloping in at the bottom. Above him, an open hatch with similar grating let in weak yellow light. To his left, another cell—empty. On the opposite side, a sly gaze came though the grating. Paidin sat up, hand to his head to prevent it falling off. The scrutiny never left him. They belonged to a bedraggled, whiskered individual who looked and smelt like he and bathing were not acquainted.

"Feelin' poorly, cove?" the man asked, flashing an assortment of rotting teeth and festering gums.

When Paidin didn't respond, he continued, "They was none too gentle wiff ya when they frows ya in 'ere. Risdon was right royal peeved wiff ya."

"Who's Risdon?" Paidin asked reluctantly, pulling a rough blanket round his shoulders. He just wanted to be left alone.

"'is royal 'ighness, Lieutenant James Risdon … him wot runs the pressers."

"Oh." Paidin pictured the arrogant officer with the mousy hair and a missing hat.

"Ya got 'im right stirred up, ya did. Wot ya do to 'im?"

"Stopped him starving a family." Paidin sighed, realising he wasn't about to get the peace he craved.

The man thought about that for a while before appearing to make sense of it. "Missin' sumfin?" he asked in response to Paidin pressing his cheeks like a doctor checking for swollen glands.

Ignoring the question, Paidin asked his own: "Where am I?"

The man chuckled, devoid of humour. "His Majesty's ship, *Camilla* … at the pleasure of Captain Brydges Watkinson Taylor." The man thrust his hand through the grate, saying, "Jimmy Smiff."

Paidin shook the man's hand. "Paidin Ryan," he said.

"Well, Paidin Ryan, ya gave Risdon the right royal case of the gripes, ya did."

"How's that?"

"Well, when they frows ya in 'ere, 'e squeezes ya mouff open an sez, 'Thems uncommon good teef for a Irish farm boy', then he sticks 'is finger in ya mouff and sez, 'Wot's this then?' an 'olds up this little shiny black fing."

Panic tightened around Paidin's chest like the coils of a starving python. Head spinning, the edges of his vision fading, he heaved a breath in spite of the constriction.

"Ya orright, cove?"

Heart thumping against his ribs, Paidin dragged a hand across his face. He was imprisoned on a Royal Navy warship with the rune gone, stolen by Risdon. He would never see his beloved Maureen again. Paidin's heart was tearing apart. He wanted to scream his agony. He did nothing.

Jimmy Smith, anxious to finish his story, didn't wait for an answer. "'e slips the pebble inta 'is pocket an sez, 'Who are ya, farm boy?'" He shook his head. "An' I'm the only one who sees and 'ears it all."

Paidin wasn't listening. Slumped against the hull of the ship, unable to order his thoughts, all he could think of was Maureen. They were going to get married, but then he fell off the Sliabh Liag cliff. Why didn't he leave Rory to his own fate? And why didn't the rune heim him? Couldn't it tell that it would be stolen? How strong were its powers anyway?

A sob choked in the sudden constriction of his throat. Dropping to the floor, he curled into a ball, wishing for death.

[Scan the QR code on the back cover to be notified of the release date of *The Lost Rune.*]

www.ingramcontent.com/pod-product-compliance
Lightning Source LLC
Chambersburg PA
CBHW030507120726
47904CB00005B/1376